LOW DOWN DIRTY VOTE

VOLUME 3: THE COLOR OF MY VOTE

ANSHRITHA   ERIC BEETNER   STEPHEN BUEHLER
PATRICIA E. CANTERBURY   SARAH M. CHEN
DAVID CORBETT   JACKIE ROSS FLAUM
KATHARINA GERLACH   BARB GOFFMAN
DAVID HAGERTY   JAMES MCCRONE   ANN PARKER
CAMILLE MINICHINO   THOMAS PLUCK
MIGUEL ALFONSO RAMOS   EMBER RANDALL
TRAVIS RICHARDSON   FAYE SNOWDEN   MISTY SOL
DJ TYRER   GABRIEL VALJAN   BEV VINCENT

Edited by
MYSTI BERRY

Berry Content Corporation

PO Box 320612

San Francisco, CA 94132

We are one, maybe two, elections from losing our democracy for a generation or more. That is why we must fight every single day to expand the right to vote and protect free and fair elections.

MARC ELIAS, DEMOCRACY DOCKET

CONTENTS

INTRODUCTION

MYSTI BERRY

When the title LOW DOWN DIRTY VOTE burst into my head unbidden back in 2017, I never thought we'd need to still be doing this: collecting stories from writers and publishing them to raise money to defend voting rights. But here it is, Volume 3 and the fight is as fierce and necessary as ever.

As you read these stories, whether cozy or noir, comic or deadly serious, you'll notice a change from the previous anthologies: this year, everybody is fed up. Angry. Frustrated. Boiling up from these emotions, an implicit theme emerged: biting the hand that feeds you. It must be from the zeitgeist: a feeling that voting rights suppression should have been prevented by the people we elected to represent us. Since the opposite is happening, we the people are preparing to... what, exactly?

What do we do when the color of our vote matters still, 150 years after the American North won our Civil War? When we're so close to a tipping point from democracy to autocracy? What comes after "we're mad as hell and we're not going to take it anymore?"

If you are an author, you write about it. You testify.

This collection contains testimony set in the past, present, and future. You'll find award-winning crime writers and writers published here for the first time. Cozy mysteries, suspenseful character studies, historical crime, and humorous stories all address the question of what happens when you have to be a member of a particular club to have a voice in your own fate. I'm especially grateful to authors David Hagerty, Camille Minichino, Ann Parker, and Travis Richardson, each of whom has delivered wonderful stories in all three volumes.

This year's collection contains more stories that are blended with speculative fiction. As the submissions came in, I began to wonder if my beloved crime fiction was morphing, much the way film noir morphed into science fiction, juvenile crime, and police procedural in the 1950s. Or maybe this crisis point in history is making us all wonder, with everything at stake, what comes next?

This year's anthology donates 100% of the sales to Democracy Docket, a group of lawyers headed by Marc Elias who are fighting every day for voting rights in America. They brought 61 suits and won 60 of them relating to the 2020 election, and continue to successfully fight gerrymandering and voter suppression bills in every state that indulges in them. By the time this book is published, we'll have sent them an advance on sales of $10,000, and our thanks for fighting for democracy.

I hope you enjoy these stories as much as I have. See you at the ballot box!

AN INCIDENT AT THE CULTURAL FRONTIER

DAVID CORBETT

PLACING the necessary signage outside Second Baptist Church—maximum number of persons allowed in the polling place, physical distancing required, face coverings mandatory—I took note of the sleepy line of early voters, all of them properly masked, standing six feet apart, huddled inside coats and scarves against the autumn chill, hoping to cast their ballots before heading off to work. The queue snaked down the lamplit sidewalk—half hour before daybreak, a crisp November morning. The fog smelled mentholated from the towering eucalyptus trees up and down the block, masking the lingering fetor of smoke from the late summer wildfires.

It wasn't till I'd started back up the church steps that the trouble appeared.

A small convoy of long-bed pickups, headlights piercing the thready haze, proceeded slowly up the street and pulled to a stop directly across from where I stood. Each bore a giant flag unfurled at the back: the Stars and Stripes, both colonial and contemporary versions, the Gadsden flag ("Don't Tread on Me"), and the Three Per Center Flag.

The pickups sat there for a moment, engines throbbing at idle. Then, one by one, the doors swung open.

A squad of hard-eyed men appeared, fourteen in all, kitted out in makeshift battle-rattle: jump boots, boonie hats, corps caps, and a strange array of camouflage, from hunting fatigues to military-issue BDUs. They wore draping neck-gaiter masks, black in color, covering not just the mouth and nose but the throat, chin, jawline, and neck, like bandits in a John Wayne movie.

A handful of the men looked hard and fit enough to be actual vets. One was crabbed and gray—if he'd ever served, it was back in my time. Two seemed no more than overgrown boys: blubbery, jittery. No doubt needlessly mean.

The chiseled, the grizzled, and the pissed—an uncharitable assessment, and I was chiding myself for that when I noticed the plastic zip ties dangling from several belt loops, their visibility of doubtful inadvertence. And more than one of the men had a rucksack strapped to his back—no telling as yet what lay hidden inside, but previous incidents around the country involving similar characters provided a clue: bear spray, tasers, collapsible batons, "walking sticks" carrying a 950,000 volt charge. And, of course, other weapons, more lethal, more cowardly.

Carvela Buselle came up beside me in the church's porchlight. Statuesque in height, thin as a baton, her short-cut natural flecked with gray, she wore an ankle-length skirt and a white embroidered blouse beneath her thick, wool overcoat, its lapel bedecked with an official pin—our inspector, the person in charge of the polling station.

Looking across the street with a stare that could cut glass, she said, "Silly me." That crisp, no-nonsense diction, even muffled by her mask. A lifelong educator. "Hoping all the scare-talk was overblown."

"That's so often the problem with hope," I replied.

Just a little earlier, we'd quietly shared what we'd heard on the news while driving here. In Houston, two hours ahead of us, "roaming inspectors" had shown up at the polls, not just hostile but armed.

They'd carried out a mock beheading, a bit of populist agitprop, street theater to demonstrate what would happen if "they" gained control. Churches closed, bibles confiscated, Christianity banned. Socialism. Sharia law.

Similar incidents were reported in St. Louis, Milwaukee, Detroit, Philadelphia, and Miami, men and women both, some armed, others just loud, hell-bent not on observation of the proceedings but disruption.

Here the risks differed—open carry being forbidden in California, concealed carry permits have become laughably easy to obtain, especially from our own county sheriff, who makes no secret of his views on the matter.

First came the protests in the wake of several officer-involved shootings down-county—by which I mean here, Rio Mirada, an exurban No Man's Land lodged midway between the glimmering towers of San Francisco and the tony vineyards of Napa, an outpost along the cultural frontier between the liberal coast and the conservative inlands, the city a mere forty percent Caucasian, the rest Black, Latino, Asian, Filipino, Pacific Islander, and so on. The protests here were loud, angry, but largely peaceful, while the rest of the county proudly, defiantly backed the Blue.

Then came the pandemic's latest wave, with the predictable resurgence of delivery requests into rough neighborhoods. Sure, the drivers carried no cash, everything paid by credit card up-front, but some had been held at gunpoint while whatever they were delivering —groceries, housewares, carry-out—got off-loaded into another car that promptly sped off.

So a show of good cause required little more than belief in a dangerous world—too many bad people have guns, meaning good people need more guns and need them at all times.

Fender-benders became armed standoffs. Barfights turned to slaughter.

As for a show of good character to earn your permit, no felonies on record met the new threshold, as long as you met the unspoken qualification. You didn't even need to know someone or someone else who knew someone. You just had to look the part.

Then there were the permits granted in the hinterlands, where anti-immigrant, anti-minority, anti-government fervor ran hot. Get your permit there, it was good throughout the state. And everybody from those quarters knew where the real trouble was. And who was to blame.

So the fact only zip ties were visible meant little, same with the as yet unknown contents of the rucksacks. Every masked man standing over there glaring at us could be armed. We'd be fools to assume otherwise.

Meanwhile, from within the small, dark house beyond the masked platoon, a large dog—pit bull perhaps, maybe a Rottweiler—began barking fiercely, menacingly.

Nikki Barno came up on Carvela and me from behind. One of our greeters—thirtysomething, alto in the Second Baptist choir, star athlete in track through college, now owner of a cupcake bakery named *Delish Delights*—she wore a pink, down vest over a violet turtleneck, her long microbraids swept back into a ponytail.

"The fuck is this?"

"Girl, don't start," Carvela said. "That's all they want, a fight. And blame us for kicking it off."

"All due respect, you know well as me—"

"Ain't blind, ain't stupid, all right?" Carvela folded her arms tightly across her narrow frame. "Whatever trouble this is, let's not escalate it."

Nikki pointed down the sidewalk. "Christ almighty—people already scared off."

Over half the early voters had stepped out of the queue, returning the way they'd come. Cars pulling into the parking lot promptly turned right back around.

"Seems to me we ain't the escalators," she said.

One last man exited the foremost pickup before the caravan pulled away. Unlike the others, he wore gray slacks, a powder blue sport coat, dress shirt, and no tie. His mask bore the letters "USA." After a brief inspection of his dragoons, he crossed the street, shoulders back, head high, with the stride of a man convinced of his innate authority—anytime, anywhere.

Mounting the half-dozen concrete steps to the landing where Carvela, Nikki, and I stood waiting, he scanned each of our faces with vacant affability, as though wondering which of us to patronize, and which merely to ignore. Boot-button eyes, aptly brown—if he wasn't ex-military or law enforcement, those peepers had missed their calling. Sandy hair parted so impeccably on the left I half-imagined him adding the final touches with a knife. And yet there was also a calm about him, a self-possession that augured well, at least for the moment. He hadn't come ginned up and ready to blow. Then again, maybe he just believed he'd already carried the day.

"I'm here to observe the election on behalf of Americans Demanding Election Security."

Carvela stiffened almost imperceptibly, which she disguised with a blinding smile. "I received no prior notice of—"

"Not required. Prior notice, I mean. The guiding statute makes no mention of it."

"I'm aware of the statute. This ain't, as they say, my first rodeo."

"Ma'am—"

"I've worked elections in this precinct for over thirty years. I don't remember seeing you before. Not to mention those, I dunno, *men*," a desultory flick of her hand, "over there."

Nikki made a coughing sound, strangling a laugh. Carvela shot her a fierce side-eye.

"We don't need to be from this precinct," he said, "to observe the voting."

"Just for sake of discussion," Nikki replied, "how come you all aren't *observing* the vote in your own precinct?"

A smile of calculated warmth, betrayed by the eyes. "People are concerned about the integrity of the vote. We're here to address that concern."

"No fooling. Well I'd say folks in this here precinct are gonna be pretty goddamn concerned about the integrity of the vote now. Pack of cracker thugs standing right over there, scare everybody off."

"There's no need for insults."

"Oh, kiss my Black ass."

Miss Carvela held out a cautioning hand, but he'd already taken out his phone, thumbing in *an observation.*

"Those men," he said, finishing up his note, "are standing beyond the 100-foot perimeter dictated by statute. And they're not electioneering, as defined in the relevant regulations. So there's no legitimate objection to be made—"

Carvela cut him off. "Are they armed?"

"Why ask me?"

"Let's not be coy, Mister—"

"Paxton. John Paxton."

He did not extend his hand. Wisely so. No one would have taken it, just as we doubted that was his real name.

"My point," he added, "is that you should ask them."

"No, sir, the *point* is that they're intimidating voters."

"Do you have proof of that?"

"Just saw them run off with my own eyes."

"Maybe those people were late for work. Maybe they intend to come back later."

"Oh, listen to him," Nikki murmured. "Slick as a crawdad's ass."

Out came the phone again. Another *observation.* Wisely, Nikki turned and headed inside. Paxton slipped his phone back inside his pocket.

"I'm going in now, look over the layout. See if it conforms to best practices."

Carvela pulled her own phone, digging it out of her overcoat pocket. "I'm calling the county voting registrar. Have them contact the police."

"I'm doing nothing illegal."

"It's in my sole discretion whether you are impeding the proper functioning of this polling place. Understand? I'm the one who decides, not you."

"Go ahead." Again, that contrived smile. He eased past us. "Notify the county, call the police. Be my guest."

Carvela made the calls but we both knew nothing would come of it. The registrar's office had suffered massive turnover given the increasing threats of violence, with the net result being a host of new staff members from up-county, all beholden to the same delusion of mass fraud and extensive irregularities down here. Only their incomprehension of the process and suspicion of the people who didn't look like them exceeded their zeal. Regardless, any help we might seek from the county office would come late, if ever, its inner workings consumed with self-generated bedlam.

Even worse—not surprisingly, given Paxton's smug certainty—the police dispatcher made it clear that no squad cars could respond in any way for several hours.

"They've had bomb threats at three other polling places." Carvela looked ashen as she thumbed off, and dropped her phone back into its pocket. "Another got set on fire early this morning. There's fistfights damn near everywhere, gunshots across town."

"They're not even worried the sabotage is so obvious."

She smiled bravely. "I'm gonna need you to do me a favor. You got the ballot scanner and the bins all set up already, am I right?"

"Before I came out to help with the signs, yeah."

"I'm gonna pull Calista off greeter duty. Nikki can handle it alone, especially now with the line dwindled down. Calista can cover for you on the scanner."

"Meaning you want me to—"

"Tag along with our . . . visitor. I don't want him pestering anyone, getting into business he has no right to. Do that for me?"

Paxton was glaring through the plexiglass divider, one more health-and-safety precaution, as Lupesina Matafeo finalized her setup of the poll pad and ticket printer.

"She's going to create a test ticket to make sure the printer is working," I said, "then a summary report showing the number of voters processed so far is zero."

"I'll want to see that."

"Once she has it, sure. I can't let you stand behind her. Meanwhile, if you want to look at the paper roster for the voters registered in this precinct, I can get that for you." I glanced at my watch. "Just couple minutes, we'll start letting voters in, the ones not scared off."

"That's on them if so," he said, "not us."

"The first voter will inspect the ballot boxes, auxiliary bin, ticket bag, and provisional bag to affirm they're all empty."

"What if they're not?"

"They will be. They are. You can check them yourself if you want."

"You bet I do." He ambled from spot to spot, peering into the various receptacles.

"If anyone just wants to drop off their mail-in ballot, they can do it in the yellow bag there at the door. That, too, is empty right now if you'd like to check."

I resisted the temptation to tell him that individual voter fraud is as rare as counterfeiting coins, and for the same reason—what's the payoff? And only the willfully ignorant or innately hostile believe there aren't numerous, effective countermeasures in place.

Instead, I told him, "You can use your cell phone to text or make notes, but no pictures. If you want to place a call, I'm going to ask that you step outside so you don't interfere with anyone casting their ballot."

He studied my name tag: Michael Kanaga. "That African? The name, I mean."

He apparently thought I'd changed my surname out of some unfathomable solidarity.

"It's Swiss. My father's people were Mennonites. My mother's were Irish, more or less, within the confines of American mutt-hood."

"Why are you here?"

"Excuse me?"

"Why are you working this polling place?"

"This is my precinct. Live just a few blocks away. Have for over thirty years."

Judging from his eyes, he considered this, too, unfathomable.

"I suppose I could've moved when my wife passed, but why? This is my home. I teach at Marshall High. Carvela, our inspector, who you met—she's the principal. We're old pals."

His bafflement had moved on to a kind of amused boredom. "Mennonite. They're like, what, Amish?"

"The Amish prefer to retreat from the world. Mennonites not so much."

He gestured to his chin, as though to suggest flowing whiskers. "What about the beard?"

"Not required. Though pacifism is."

The bored eyes hardened.

"I was a conscientious objector in the Vietnam War. Did my alternative service teaching English to Vietnamese high school students in Tam Ky, middle of a war zone. Funny thing, our little bungalow was the only place that housed Americans the Viet Cong didn't attack."

"Because they knew you were communists, like them."

"The early Christians were communists—Acts 4, Verses 32 to 35, look it up. No, the reason they never attacked us was because we were unarmed. Just like everyone working at this polling station."

"We're not here to attack anybody. Unless provoked."

"Glad to hear it. I mentioned my mother's people being Irish. She was a big fan of Daniel O'Connell. The Liberator. Had a profound influence on both Gandhi and Dr. Martin Luther King. 'The altar of liberty totters when it is cemented only with blood.'"

If eyes could groan. "Yeah? Easter Rebellion, 1916. That wasn't bloody? Five hundred dead."

"More than half civilians."

"The point—Ireland gained its freedom." He leaned in closer. "Think you're the only one who knows his history?"

"Actually, Ireland didn't gain full independence for another thirty—"

"The problem with your kind," he was aiming a finger at my chest now, "you think we're all stupid. Well wake up, buttercup. It's a brand new day. And your peacenik bullshit won't change a goddamn thing. Cowardice isn't a virtue, no matter how pretty you talk it up."

Beneath my mask, I smiled. *Your kind.* And his? So easy to provoke. So easy to scare and shame.

"So, you taught gooks in Nam," he said, "now whatever-the-hell down here. Ever think of teaching American kids—or is that beneath you?"

I was now the one who'd grown bored. Glancing up at the clock, I said, "Look at that. Seven on the dot."

I found Carvela, and tapped my watch. She nodded, marched to the entrance, and in that rafter-rattling voice I have grown to love over the years, capable of cutting through even the most raucous teenage din, she called out into the neighborhood, "This polling place is now officially open!"

She gestured for the first voter to enter—elderly woman, size of a child, wobbling forward with the aid of a cane—and guided her to the various receptacles and asked her to ensure they were indeed empty, then led her over to the roster clerk to check her in. Paxton watched all this as though expecting snakes to emerge from beneath the old girl's coat.

"Her name's Hermione Maxwell," I told him. "Moved here from Alabama with her parents and younger brother during the Second World War, like a lot of Black families in town. The shipyard needed workers. Lives over on McNaughton, has for over thirty years. You can confirm that on the paper roster if you want. Registered to vote in '66, right after the Voting Rights Act passed."

"No one checked her ID."

"Not required in California. But you know that."

He turned away, went over to collect the voter roster and validate what I'd said, or pretend to.

I drifted back toward the entrance, checked to see how many other voters were waiting—a mere half dozen now—and noticed Nikki furtively texting on her phone. When she realized I was standing behind her she lowered the screen, so I couldn't see.

Only then did I realize the dog, the one inside the house across the street, had stopped barking.

A half hour passed, a mere trickle of voters, mostly older, inured to intimidation. One, Marta Ramirez, got followed after casting her ballot, chased down by one of the goons across the street once she hit the 100-foot boundary.

Carvela gave me the nod, I hurried down to intervene.

"There a problem?"

It was one of the chubby, young ones. Eyes like bloodshot moons above his black mask. Acne scars at his temples. One hand rested on the tangle of zip ties at his waist.

"She needs to show her papers."

I stepped between him and her. "Papers—you get that from a movie?"

"Prove she's a citizen."

Marta, wearing nurse's blues beneath her down jacket, clutched the shoulder strap of her purse like she was preparing to unshoulder the thing and swing it at him. Her dark eyes bulged in her angular face, her long hair pulled back in a ponytail. I'd taught her son Rodrigo before he dropped out to join the Air Force.

"She's legally registered to vote, we confirmed it, she cast her ballot, now leave her alone."

"We need to see she's legit."

"You need nothing of the kind." Gently, I took Marta's arm. "I'll walk you to your car."

We eased away in silence side by side, me wondering how many more times this sort of thing would be necessary, trying not to picture how much worse it could get.

The young man shouted at my back. "We're taking this down, what you just did."

Please do, I thought. I could feel Marta trembling beside me. Under her breath she exploded in a torrent of whispered Spanish, muffled by her mask. The only two words I felt sure of were puto and chingamadre.

Another caravan appeared midmorning—not pickups this time. Two Beemers, two Mercedes sedans, a Cadillac Fleetwood, and a tricked-out vintage Impala, the windows tinted, front suspension jacked, spinner rims on the wheels. From the dark interiors, throbbing bass lines rattled the chrome and glass.

Word had spread: outsiders at the polls. Invaders. And now, if I wasn't mistaken, here came the Southside Blackstone Killas, responding to the call.

Carvela rushed past me, murmuring, "Oh hell no."

I followed her down the steps and into the street as she flagged down the lead car. The men across the street began reaching inside their vests or jackets, pulling off their backpacks, tensing, twitchy, while behind us, atop the church steps, Paxton had his phone out again, getting video. Though I couldn't see them, I imagined the far-side windows on the idling vehicles sliding down, like gun ports on a line of frigates.

No wonder the dog had stopped barking. Its owner, tipped off, had dragged it away from the front of the house.

These newcomers, didn't they see they were playing right into the hands of Paxton and his crew? A fight, maybe gunfire, turn the polling place into a crime scene—what better way to suppress the vote?

Carvela bent at the waist as the lead car's driver-side window slid down. I couldn't make out the man behind the wheel, nor what she said to him or him to her given the thundering bass, but shortly the door behind him opened slowly.

A tall, reedy young man in a black suit emerged, white shirt buttoned to the collar, dreadlocks spilling from beneath a skinny-brim trilby, shades concealing his eyes. He ambled confidently around the front of the lead car and up the sidewalk toward the line of camo-clad men—a slight gesture of his hand to part them, make way—then eased past, climbed the porch steps, and knocked gently on the door.

A thousand eternities passed before the door eased open. First came the dog, at the end of a chain. Not a pit, not a Rott: a Presa Canario—even more formidable, tall, barrel-bodied—seeming all the more immense given the diminutive size of the figure at the opposite end of the leash. The man was birdlike, ancient, and not even his fur-collared overcoat and pearl-gray Homburg could disguise his fragility. The younger man towered over him, a gentle hand resting on the older man's shoulder.

The dog—its breed notorious for loyalty to owner, and suspicion of strangers—bristled at the sight of the men blocking its master's path. Even from across the street, I could hear its growl. Its brindle coat rippled from the tension in its musculature.

"I suggest," the younger man bellowed, "that you trespassers step the fuck off and allow my granddad to pass. He intends to cast his vote today. And y'all ain't got a say in that, understand?"

Paxton, by now, had crossed the street, still recording the scene with his phone. He signaled to his men to back away. The young man and his grandfather, led by the statuesque dog, crossed the street and slowly climbed the church steps. The young man took the leash and gestured his grandfather inside.

Carvela, having followed along, now stepped forward. "Hey now, Geno, been *way* too long." She hooked her arm in his and guided him to the roster clerk to check him in.

I stood on the porch beside the young man, considered petting the dog, and thought better of it. "Thank you for helping your grandfather."

He waved that off, pointed across the street. "Who's Scorsese?"

Paxton was going car to car, pointing his cell phone camera into every window.

"He the leader of these jackasses?"

"So it seems." I was preparing myself to say more, trying to find the words, when he turned to me. Between us, the massive dog sat perfectly still, ears pricked.

"We didn't come to stir up shit. They did, am I right? But we sure as hell ain't backing down, neither."

"All we want," I said, "is for people to show up, not be scared, vote."

"Outside my control."

"Is it, though?"

He waved his hand toward the line of cars. "This thing here? It ain't the end. Just wait."

"For what?"

Granddad Geno reemerged from inside the polling place, collected his dog, and returned the way he'd come, with that same slow pace, his tall slim grandson protectively at his side.

For the next hour, clear to midmorning, the standoff between

Paxton's men and the Southside Blackstone Killas continued to charge the atmosphere—the threat of one stupid move, one wrong word, one gunshot hovering in the air like a match an inch away from its fuse. All the while, the thundering bass from each of the cars pounded away like war drums.

Just wait.

A little past eleven o'clock—we'd not checked in a voter in over two hours—a school bus pulled into the church's parking lot.

Reinforcements? Paxton's men apparently thought so. They closed ranks, murmuring man to man, never letting their eyes stray long from the open windows of the cars lined up before them, even as they tried to steal the occasional glance at whatever this was now entering the picture.

A figure draped in a long, black robe emerged from the yellow bus. Not a judge—the collar was purple and gold. A choir robe. The woman wearing it, short and round, with square eyeglasses, and a copper-colored wig—Natralia McDonald, choirmaster, Second Baptist Church, another former student—signaled to those still waiting to come out, and one by one the other choristers emerged, men and women, young and old.

Judging from the reaction of Paxton's men, unmistakable even from across the street, they found this development bewildering. And no less frightening than the gang members.

The thumping music faded away as the choir ambled up the sidewalk toward the church entrance, and took up position on the stairs. Natralia raised one hand while the other hand lifted a pitch pipe to her lips. The choristers snapped to attention. A single reedy note from the pitch pipe identified the root of the coming chord, and the leader brought down her hand in one swift motion.

When Israel was in Egypt's Land,
  Let my people go,

Oppressed so hard they could not stand,
   Let my people go.

Go down, Moses, way down in Egypt's land,
   Tell old Pharoah: let my people go.

Before continuing with the next verse, the entire choir began to mark time with handclaps, doubling on the downbeat—*tap, tap-tap, tap, tap-tap*—and they swayed to the rhythm.

The Lord told Moses what to do,
   Let my people go,
   To lead all of God's children through,
   Let my people go.

As Israel stood by the waterside,
   Let my people go,
   At God's command it did divide,
   Let my people go.

Carvela and Nikki came up beside me in the doorway. Tears winnowed down the younger woman's cheeks as she joined in—I realized now who she'd been secretly texting when I'd come up behind her earlier—and even no-nonsense Carvela's eyes glistened as she leaned close and whispered, "I have been advised we should expect a better turnout from here on."

Maybe so, I thought, but Paxton and his men as yet made no sign of decamping, and the line of Southside vehicles hadn't budged.

When they had reached the other shore,
  Let my people go,
  They let the song of triumph SOAR!
  Let my people go.

Lord, help us all from bondage flee,
  Let my people go,
  And let us all in Christ be free,
  Let my people go.

We did indeed enjoy an uptick in voters from noon on, unfazed, or at least undeterred by the standoff outside the polling station. The continuing presence of the choir no doubt helped. To hear those voices ringing out through the neighborhood hour after hour, refusing to be silenced, refusing to let hatred triumph over hope—maybe we were all unwise to believe it, but the tension in the air seemed to diminish from a growl to a whisper.

The after-work rush was especially encouraging, at least in contrast to what had come before, and we had a line down the block as the polls closed. I took up position at the end of the queue, to advise any latecomers the polls had closed, and Paxton once or twice wandered up to make sure I didn't sneak a straggler into line.

Carvela and I, and the other volunteers, closed up the poll, sealed the ballot boxes, printed out the day's tallies, disappointing as they were—a mere sixty percent of the expected turnout. Hopefully at least some of the difference would be made up by mail-in ballots, but we were already getting word that the up-county contingent in the registrar's office was challenging all VBMs from down here, and doing so on the most blatantly spurious grounds.

As we worked, Paxton hovered over and around, asking ridiculous questions, and getting reasonable answers that he promptly dismissed. By then, though, his zeal seemed spent. Well before we locked up, he'd drifted away, along with his men. Shortly thereafter the Southside Blackstone Killas drove off. If there were any subsequent dustups between the two camps, I was not witness to them.

After bidding one another goodnight and thank you and job well done, we all headed off home. As always, my living room greeted me with its warmth and silence and memories. Using the same kettle and teapot my wife had loved, I made myself my usual evening brew of hibiscus, jasmine, and rosehips. I'm not a drinker, few Mennonites are, but my Irish side felt tempted.

I sat alone in the dim light of the crane-neck lamp beside my armchair, waiting for the phone to make one of its annoying little sounds. It came a little after eleven—a text, from a number I didn't recognize:

That's right. We know who you are.
    We know where to find you. Keep
    that in mind during the days to come.

Only rarely have I ever felt grateful that Edie passed away—she died too young, too hard—but better I deal with this alone. While I considered investing in some plywood, board up my windows, at least the ones facing the street, the phone came to life again—a different annoying sound this time, an incoming call.

"How you doing, old man?"

Carvela. Checking in.

"Interesting you should ask."

"You just get the same message I did?"

"Read it to me." She did. The same. Word for word. So predictable, that lack of imagination. "They likely got our numbers from their allies in the county office."

"Spies you mean. Addresses too, no doubt. You watching the news?"

"Can't quite bring myself just yet."

A long pause. "We're in a world of trouble, Michael."

I wanted to say, "This too shall pass," or, "We shall not merely endure, we shall prevail," but what does history tell us if not that, when the law fails, it's men with money, and men with guns, who make the rules.

"It's not just here, Michael, it's everywhere. We dodged a goddamn bullet today given what I'm seeing. Not just the violence. State legislatures all across the country already saying they won't accept the urban vote counts. Suspicious irregularities, massive fraud, blah blah blah." A ragged sigh, while in the background her cat, no doubt perched in her lap, purred greedily. "You know me, I don't scare easy, but Christ Almighty . . . "

Her voice trailed away, and we sat there for a while in our separate silences.

"I appreciate all you did today, Michael."

If only it were enough. "See you tomorrow bright and early?"

"What do we tell the kids—about what this is, what it means?"

"The truth." I took a sip of tea. It had grown cold. And bitter. "They'll call us out if we don't. Kids don't fool easy, as you well know."

Another silence, longer this time. "Blood's gonna run in the streets."

"And we'll do everything in our power to stop that. Like before. Like always."

Cowardice isn't a virtue. Tell Pharoah.

THE OBSESSION OF ABEL TANGIER

FAYE SNOWDEN

WILLA TANGIER BURIED her fourth husband a week before the local school board would decide the fate of the Black history curriculum in Caddo Parish schools. During the graveside service, her cousin Ethel complained that the weather was a goddam Louisiana cliché: the sun yellow as piss in a washed-out gray sky, the humidity boiling until the air was thick like molasses.

"You'd think he'd shut up so we can get out of this heat," Ethel said of the good Reverend Thurston, who was probably thinking that Abel Tangier was owed more than a hasty goodbye.

"If you're so miserable, maybe you should just hop in there with him," Willa said.

"Maybe I should," Ethel answered. "At least it'd be cooler."

Willa didn't pay her any mind. Ethel was the woman you called when you needed help washing your dead. She nursed the sick, and provided the down-and-out a bed and a hot meal when needed. Ethel was the kind of woman who'd sit at the bedside of your dying mother while you ran out to buy tampons, or anything else you might need to get on with the business of living. Only her mouth was unkind. It was the place she carried her bitterness. No, Willa didn't mind Ethel's words. It was Big Buddy, their fellow school board member, and the tiebreaking vote on what kind of history Byrd's Landing schools would teach that did her in.

~

Willa hadn't seen Big Buddy at the church or graveside services, but here he was now at the repast. He blew through her front door with his gleaming bald head and big personality, shaking hands with everyone he knew. His laughter quieted when he spied her and Ethel across the room. He became somber, shaking more hands, and chuckling respectfully as he made his way to them.

When he reached them he pressed Willa's hand, as if they weren't at the tail end of a pandemic, and said, "Feels like old times with the three of us together."

By old times he meant how they used to play when they were kids. He was just Buddy then. They ran Byrd's Landing streets from dawn to dusk, earning the nickname "the fearsome threesome." In high school Buddy joined the football team. That's when he became Big Buddy and went his own way.

"Abel was a wonderful history teacher in our schools for so many years," Big Buddy was now saying to Willa. "He helped a lot of kids. I hope that brings you some comfort."

"What would bring her comfort is a mask covering your big, cast-iron-skillet face," Ethel said.

He laughed, patted Ethel's bony shoulder, and squeezed hard.

"No matter what happens, you're going to still be Ethel, ain't you?" he said. "PhD or no. Retired principal or no. Still loud and ignorant as the day is long."

Ethel jerked away.

Willa watched the anger move across Ethel's face with greedy eyes. Willa wore her own kindness like a heavy cloak, rarely daring to take it off. She was known for not having a mean bone in her body. People said she was the kindest person they've ever met. Since Abel's death the label had started to wear thin. It was beginning to smother her.

"I may be all that, ignorant, whatever you say," Ethel said. "But at least I'm not a killer."

Buddy drew up to his full seven-foot height and stepped closer to Ethel. Ethel, who had wrangled high school students for twenty years at Liberty High, didn't take one step back. If not nose-to-nose she stood toe-to-toe with Big Buddy.

"What did you say?" he challenged.

"What, money make you deaf? Abel was on the phone with you when he stroked out. It's your fault he's dead."

"The man was obsessed," Buddy said. "He was pushing himself too hard."

Yes, obsessed, Willa agreed silently. Abel had gotten his blood up about May 13, 1985, the day Mayor Wilson Goode bombed a Black neighborhood in West Philly, or, as Abel put it, bombed his own people. What bothered Abel most was that he hadn't known that Goode dropped a satchel of C4 from a helicopter on the MOVE compound, an organization that Goode and the police hated. That decision killed eleven people, almost half of them children. Sixty homes burned to the ground.

Ethel was drunk, and meaner than ever, the night Abel was going on and on about it. She teased him, and asked for another margarita before saying, "Hurts your ego, don't it? You should know *all* the things, right? A history teacher in Byrd's Landing, Louisiana? Even something that happened on the other side of the country almost thirty-five years ago."

"The police in the United States bombed its own citizens in 1985. They burned children *alive*. Yes, *I* should have known this. *We* all should have known this!"

After that night Abel covered the walls of his study with the evidence—one group picture of MOVE members in their signature dreadlocks, with slight smiles that said *we want nothing from you, not*

your technology, not your meat, and maybe not even your Black solidarity.
Another photograph, just after the bomb dropped—flames of yellow,
gold, and red backlighting the narrow row homes like a sunset. And yet
another image of a naked boy of about thirteen in the back of a police car.
Willa swore she could see smoke rising like mist from his burned skin.
And more and more pictures of cruisers, police in riot gear, residents
pointing, crying, and what looked like acres and acres of rubble.

"He got himself all worked up," Big Buddy said, pulling Willa
back to the moment. "You not going to put that on me."

"Obsessed or not, he was trying to do right. What are you doing?
Siding with the MAGA hats so they'll hire your sorry ass security
company to protect their shit. "

"He was trying to turn me into a sheep."

Willa thought that Ethel had gone too far. People were staring.
They were at her husband's repast, for Lord's sake. And Willa
couldn't believe that Big Buddy, the boy she had grown up with, the
man she had known all of her life, the man Abel had known, would
vote to wash away sins committed against his own people. There was
still a chance he'd vote the right way. She couldn't let Ethel ruin that.

"Abel's dying wasn't Buddy's fault," Willa said. "He had high
blood pressure, didn't take his pills on the regular."

She placed a hand on Big Buddy's forearm, and felt it relax under
her touch. "Thank you for coming," she said in her best pleasant
voice. "I'm sure all this emotion will be put to rest after the vote.
Maybe we could all get dinner and talk about the old times."

Ethel started bringing a loaded Smith & Wesson .45 to every school
board meeting after the death threats started. She'd put it in her purse
before she left home, and slip it into the place for her personal
belongings at her spot on the dais. No telling when she would need to
defend herself against those crazies, she told Willa.

The Friday following Abel's funeral, Willa sat in the big leather chair next to Ethel, who pointed under her desk, and said, "Just like the video on YouTube told me to do it, safety's off. Red, you're dead." She grinned at Willa. "In case you need it."

"Be serious, I can't see myself shooting anybody."

Ethel gave her a "suit-yourself" look and gazed at the crowd on the floor. Just like the last few board meetings, this one was full to bursting. All the extra folding chairs that had been brought in had asses in them. People who couldn't find empty seats lined the walls, some of them in MAGA hats and rigid with outrage, others leaning against the wall with their arms folded. A broken air conditioner added to the tension, the room was so hot that Willa felt like she was in a stew. Three ancient ceiling fans clunked overhead, doing nothing but add more noise to the strident voices below.

Someone went to the podium and yelled into the microphone, "Ethel Anderson, you Nazi lover!"

The board chair, an elderly woman in a tan suit and a brunette wig pounded a gavel while shouting, "Order, order, order!"

"That's a new one," Ethel said dryly.

Willa squinted, sat up, and leaned closer to her microphone.

"Aren't you Lana Rayburn's son? I taught your mama in tenth grade. How she doing?" she said, hoping to shame him.

The man waited a beat before saying, "She's fine. Getting along real good. But we ain't talking about my mama now, we talking about what y'all wanting to do to our kids."

"We don't want to do anything to your kids except give them a good education," Ethel said. "What we don't want to do is raise a pack of idiots with heads full of cotton."

"Now, come on, Willa," Big Buddy said. "Ain't no cause for that kind of talk. We discussing this in an objective fashion."

"Ain't nothing objective about what we discussing here," Ethel said. "Especially when we talking about whitewashing history."

"Why you always got to bring race into it?" Big Buddy asked.

"And why don't you ever?" Ethel said. "As dark as you are, I'm sure you never got a pass from being Black."

"Can you please restore some order to this meeting?" Big Buddy shouted at the Chair, who was now shaking. "Even though we a small town, we don't have to behave like a backwater."

Willa watched them, not knowing what to say. Her mind had started running like a river in one direction since she buried Abel. All she kept thinking about was May 13, 1985. The helicopter overhead, the bomb dropping. And everybody seeming to forget it ever happened.

". . . on the other side of the country about a bunch of criminals," Big Buddy was saying. "Why we need to wallow in all that? It ain't got nothing to do with us."

"Because it's history," Ethel said. "The kids should know about it. Just like they should know about Tulsa and Houston and Chicago. And these fools want to shut it all down."

Willa wasn't paying attention to Big Buddy or Ethel. She kept thinking about all that fire that Goode let rage on. No water on that fire for hours.

"What's that, Willa?" Ethel asked.

Willa gave her a confused look. "What?"

"Sounds like you finally got something to say," Ethel said. "We listening."

"I didn't say anything."

"Yes, you did," Big Buddy said. "You said to let it burn."

Next thing Willa knew she was in her bright kitchen with a cup of chamomile tea in front of her. Another thing that had been happening since Abel died, grief ate holes into her realities. She'd be one place and not know how she'd got there, say something, and have to reach way back in her mind to find out what she meant. The only thing that felt real to her were the flames burning her alive.

"Looks like you got plenty of casseroles left. Probably need to throw them out, but one more day of eating on them won't kill you," Ethel said as she wiped down the counter.

Willa didn't answer, just gripped the warm cup and brought the tea up to her nose so she could breathe in its fragrance. She hadn't thought about food in days.

Ethel stopped wiping and came and sat at the table across from Willa.

"You're worrying the shit out of me, girl. Maybe we should check you for Alzheimer."

"I don't have Alzheimer."

"Then what's wrong with you? You were weird tonight."

"I just can't seem to get out of my dreams," Willa answered. "I keep seeing snatches in my mind, smelling that fire. It's like I was there."

"You mean that MOVE thing that had Abel in an uproar?"

"Looks like it has the entire town in an uproar. If Abel hadn't proposed that we have a May 13, 1985 day of remembrance in Byrd's Landing, we wouldn't be having these conversations."

Ethel scoffed. "We'd be having these conversations no matter what. This has been going on all over the country. Stupidity is contagious."

"But I have nightmares about it. I feel like I'm being burned alive in my dreams."

Ethel narrowed her eyes. "Where you been sleeping lately, Willa."

"In my bed, my room. Where do you think I've been sleeping?"

"I've told you that you should spend some time at my house," Willa said. "But you stubborn."

"I don't want you worrying about me, Ethel."

"That's the problem. You don't want nobody worrying about nothing. You want to fix things for everybody else, but won't do anything for yourself."

"Don't fuss. Please don't fuss," Willa said.

"And you don't speak up when people do wrong because you

worried about their feelings. Been like that all your life."

"What do you mean?"

"Big Buddy. That man's a jackal and you still talk to him with sugar in your voice."

"He's our friend. We grew up with him, remember?"

"Well, he doesn't think like us, no matter how many times we went roller skating together. What kind of man tries to erase the history of his own people?"

"You're too hard on him. He's a human being. He'll come around."

When Ethel left Willa made her way to Abel's study. She slept there because it smelled like him. There was a lingering fragrance of his woody cologne, and the lemon drop candies he favored. She slept there with the memories of the bombing all around her—the flames, and faces of those who suffered. She laid herself down on his worn leather couch so she could soak up the memories of him, and hold onto the last thing he cared deeply about. But all she got were faint scents that would soon be gone, and the horrors of May 13, 1985 settling deep into her bones.

The next school board meeting was just like the last one. Ethel slipped the .45 in the desk at her seat on the dais. Willa sat next to her before looking past her to Buddy, who sat where the dais had started to curve. He waved at her, gave her a wink, and a big, wide-toothed smile. *He's looking at me*, she thought. *That means we have his vote.* With his tiebreaking vote, they could put this strife behind them and get on with the business of educating children. And she could get on with the business of grieving.

"You still think he's going to do the right thing?" Ethel whispered to her.

"Don't, Ethel."

The Chair, her wig slightly askew, gaveled the meeting to order.

Reverend Thurston led the hall in prayer. Willa glanced around while most heads were bowed to see Ethel leaning back in her chair with her arms folded across her chest. At least the crowd was quiet, though, and patient a good long time while the reverend prayed for something even God may not be able to give them. Peace.

It wasn't the boy who had called Ethel a Nazi lover at the podium during the public comment period, but there were plenty of others using words like "lies" and "shaming." Some spoke in favor of letting the teachers teach, but they were quickly booed down. When Old Man Millet stood up, the audience and board members groaned. Ethel covered her face with her hands. Willa thought she heard a *Lord help us* behind her shut fingers. Old Man Millet owned three acres of sugarcane on the outskirts of town. He didn't pass the ninth grade, but prided himself on finding out things for himself and wasting a lot of your time telling you about it.

"Come on," Big Buddy said amid the groans. "Y'all had your chance to speak, so let Mr. Millet have his."

And Mr. Millet was definitely going to have his chance. He hitched up his pants before laying some papers on the podium. He cleared his throat and wiped his nose with a red handkerchief before stuffing it back into his shirt pocket. When he reached for his reading glasses, someone said, "Come on, Old Man Millet. We ain't got all night."

The Chair slapped the gavel on the dais. Millet licked his thumb before turning to the papers.

"Now it seems to me that all this talk started when Abel Tangier wanted to have a day of remembrance down at the school for them MOVE people."

"That's not all we're talking about here, Old Man Millet," Ethel said. "We're talking about teaching our kids Black history in the schools."

Big Buddy sent her a warning look. "Be respectful," he said. "In this room, it's Mr. Millet."

"He wasn't Mr. Millet when your ass was stealing his cane to chew on."

Actually all three of them used to steal Old Man Millet's sugar-cane to chew on. But neither Willa or Buddy corrected her.

"It's all right," Millet said. "Don't confront me none what you call me. But these MOVE folk y'all won't to defend up in here today, I just gotta say something."

"We aren't defending anybody, *Mr.* Millet," Ethel said.

"So you say, but what I'm saying is how all this foolish talk started. Abel Tangier, God rest his tired soul, wanted to have this MOVE day. And when kids' parents found out about it they rightfully put a stop to it."

"Let him speak," Buddy said before Ethel could interrupt him again.

Millet bounced on his heels and said, "I want to discuss why we making so much noise and causing so much community hate about these kinds of people."

"What kinds of people?" someone from the crowd spoke up.

Millet ignored them.

"Now these MOVE folk wasn't like any of the Black folk in this town. They didn't eat no meat, take care of their children, or love Jesus. Why, I read that they children were so hungry they ate outta the garbage. That and they parents spewed curse words and filth, saying mother-trucking this and mother-trucking that from a bullhorn that they had stuck up on top of the roof. That's what the bomb was aiming for. Drove the neighbors to distraction hearing all them filthy things."

"They used the bullhorn so they could raise awareness about the other MOVE members in jail for things they hadn't done," Willa said, surprised at the annoyance in her voice.

Millet kept talking as if he hadn't heard. "It was they own Black neighbors what complained."

"The neighbors didn't ask Wilson Goode to drop a bomb on their neighborhood, Mr. Millet," Ethel said.

"Them police must have had good reason," Millet answered.

"Because they killed a cop," Big Buddy said. "They murdered a cop before moving to Osage Street."

Willa looked at him in surprise.

"I can read, too," Big Buddy said.

"See, that's a good reason, right?" Millet said, motioning to the board with a wrinkled hand. "Them's bad people."

"Let me ask you something, Mr. Millet," Ethel said, leaning over the dais. "How would you like the sheriff's department to burn you out of your house because your neighbor, not you, but your neighbor, was thought to have killed somebody."

"I'm just saying we shouldn't be tearing our town apart over them."

He sat down then, amid pats on the back and "amen, brother."

Willa, her voice in a whisper, said, "They set the place on fire and said let it burn, Mr. Millet. When members of MOVE tried to escape, they drove them back into the flames with gunshots. They killed children. Burned down an entire neighborhood. Doesn't that count for anything?"

"Willa," Big Buddy said.

She looked over at him and tried to catch his eye. But he turned away.

"Doesn't it, Buddy?" she asked.

He bowed his head and pretended to shuffle papers around.

"We ready for a vote?" Big Buddy asked the chair, his voice brisk. "Any more public comment?"

"Motherfucker," Ethel said under her breath.

Willa knew then that they had lost Big Buddy. Without his vote, there would be no talk of May 13, 1985, or any Black history curriculum in the schools that hadn't been sanitized beyond all meaning and belief. This man wasn't the boy she and Willa had ran with during their younger years, played red light, green light from sunup to sundown on the streets of Byrd's Landing.

It barely registered that Ethel was standing, leaning over Willa, and jabbing her finger at Buddy, calling him a sellout. No, this man didn't resemble the boy who defended them on the playground, and who, in turn, was defended by them, especially by Ethel who knew how to play crazy to scare off a bully. *Red Rover, Red Rover*, Willa thought. *Send Buddy right over*. Except the Buddy they knew was gone.

The entire room was up in arms. Chairs fell over. A couple of young boys were climbing over the front two rows to get to the school board members on the dais. Old Man Millet yelled, "Hey, hey, hey!" The two off-duty cops who were supposed to be keeping things under control hadn't moved from their spots. The only threatening thing they did against the crowd was to take their billy clubs out.

Over it all Willa heard Ethel shrieking at Big Buddy, who was telling her to get ahold of herself. It was then the room exploded with a single gunshot. Silence, for the space of a single breath, and then chaos. People rushed for the door, or flattened their bodies against the floor.

Willa couldn't believe it. She knew the gun was dangerous, but didn't believe that Ethel had it in her to hurt anybody. Big Buddy clutched his chest while blood poured through his fingers. His eyes rolled back into his head.

Willa's own hands were stinging. Why were they stinging?

And then she felt Ethel's sweaty hands on her own, prying something from her, saying, "Come on, come on, Willa, put it down, give it to me." Ethel pressed Willa back into her seat. She bent down to smooth her hair.

It was the gentleness in Ethel's touch that helped Willa understand that she had stepped through another hole in reality. Ethel didn't shoot Big Buddy. It was her, Willa. She had snatched the gun when Ethel was arguing with Big Buddy and shot him. The woman who didn't have a mean bone in her body. She dropped her face into her hands and sobbed once.

"Hey, now don't you worry," Ethel said. "We're going to get through this. Not your fault. Besides, couldn't have happened to a better asshole."

PICK A COLOR

ERIC BEETNER

"OKAY, LET'S TAKE ANOTHER VOTE."

Raise your hand. Raise your hand you shriveled up old hag.

I see four hands up, including mine. Then there's Mrs. McCaffrey, arms crossed with her dried apple face, her sour lemon lips, and her black olive eyes. There is a collective groan from the board members and the room of residents who came to this meeting.

I let out a big sigh that doesn't even begin to express my frustration. "It's not that big of a deal, Mrs. McCaffrey. It's the color of the pool house and gym walls, we're not deciding to go to war or anything."

"I don't want blue."

She's got to be north of eighty years old, but she still sounds like a spoiled preschooler. It's been three weeks, three board meetings, three rounds of voting on colors, and she is the only holdout.

My patience is gone.

"Why not? Blue is literally everyone's favorite color!"

"It's not mine."

Her arms are locked across her chest like she is in a straightjacket. *Oh, I wish.*

The number of residents this time is triple the usual attendance.

Word has gotten out about her intransigence and Marjorie McCaffrey is a bit of a legend around the building. The longest continuous resident here and one with zero friends or allies among the other owners, who are on average fifty years younger than her.

I see several residents in attendance with their cell phones out and ready to go at a moment's notice in case this turns ugly. If I lose it or somebody starts screaming at her there will be a half dozen YouTube videos online in an hour.

I try like hell to keep it together.

"That's the third vote on the third color."

"They're all blue."

Calming Sea, actually. I pick up the color swatch thing, the one that looks like a bookmark with four different shades on it. The one I scooped up a dozen of at the paint store so everyone would know exactly what color we were planning on repainting the pool room, the locker and changing area, and the gym. The color we have to get unanimous board approval for.

"I don't think I've ever even seen you use the pool or the gym, Marjorie. You wouldn't ever have to look at the color."

"That's not the point. The vote has to be unanimous." Mrs. McCaffrey lifts her hands and raises her shoulders as if to tell me it is all far beyond her control. "I don't make the rules," she says.

That's it.

"Yes, you do! The charter was written twenty-seven years ago, when you were on the very first board of this complex so, yeah, you are the only one here who literally wrote the rules, goddamn it!"

I slam my hand down on the table and it slaps so loud several people jump. I see cell phones raised and thumbs poised over record buttons, waiting.

I shouldn't have done that. I hate that she gets to me like this. But there it is, the smug smile. The knowing look when she knows I'm beat, and for no other reason than she doesn't want me to get my way as board president. A position I was elected to by the other residents. A position I beat her out for, and she's been bitter ever since.

"Okay, look." I try to calm myself. "Maybe we should adjourn for this evening and we can come back to the paint issue at the next meeting, okay?"

The other board members grumble for a second and I rap my knuckles on the table to signal adjournment. Several of the residents stare daggers at Mrs. McCaffrey as she slowly rises and makes her way out of the room without a word to anyone. But I stare bullets. Poisoned-tipped flaming arrows. Nuclear warheads.

"God, I need a drink," I mutter to what I think is only myself, but from behind me I hear:

"Oh, me too."

I didn't know my neighbor, Karen, was there. We're friends, or friendly anyway. I don't think she knows I have such a huge crush on her, but she might also assume that every guy she's ever met has a crush on her and I don't know if she'd be wrong.

She's got supermodel good looks and a female wrestler body. She also has a boyfriend.

Nico joins us at the bar. He's tall, muscular, and looks like an extra in a Scorsese movie just waiting to get called to set. He's got an indistinct Eastern Seaboard accent that sounds like everything he says to you is trying to sell you stolen TVs or fake timeshares in Tampa. He wears a gold ring on his pinky and chews gum all the time. And yet, you kinda can't help but like the guy.

He's charming in the way the best con men have to be. And he's good to Karen. He's not a misogynist asshole. He treats her right and he knows how lucky he is to have her. Fucking Nico.

Three drinks in, two whiskey shots and an imported beer, and I'm saying things out loud I shouldn't.

"I hate her. I fucking hate her."

"We all hate her," Karen says. "She's a wicked witch."

"It's a goddamn paint color," I say. "Just shut up and let us pick."

Nico nurses a Jack and Coke slowly, making it last, and making me look like more of a lush. "Sounds like a real bitch."

"That's being kind."

"Some people," he says, like it's the most basic truth in the world, and maybe it is.

"I wish she'd just die already." I hear it after the words are out of my mouth. Plus, I see Karen's face and I know I overstepped. "I didn't mean that. I'm just mad."

Karen looks like she is stifling a laugh.

"And drunk," I say.

"I don't think you're the first to say that," Karen says.

"Still, I shouldn't say that about another board member."

"Why not?" Nico says. He chews his gum a few times for emphasis. Never takes it out of his mouth, even when he's drinking. "Some people should die."

"No, I'm just . . . God, I'm as bad as her. It's just friggin' paint color."

"People have died for less."

A second beer is set down in front of me. I don't even remember ordering it.

"I gotta . . . " I aim my thumb at the restrooms and walk there in a less-than-straight line. The board meeting went over the allotted time and I'm realizing now I never ate dinner.

Standing at the urinal I close my eyes and exhale, waiting for the flow to start. When it comes it is a giant relief.

"I could fix this for you."

My eyes pop open like I'm waking from a bad dream. Nico is there next to me, but I don't think he's peeing.

"What?"

"This old lady. Sounds like trouble. I could take care of it for you."

"What do you mean?"

"Look, Karen likes you. Says you're a good neighbor. A solid guy. You don't hit on her or nothing. I like doing favors for good people." He spits his gum into the urinal. "Besides, I don't like bitchy old ladies. I grew up around two old aunts and two grandmas that weren't exactly the baking cookies types, y'know? Real See-You-Next-Tuesdays."

He winks at me and I realize I can't pee anymore.

I'm uncomfortable and buzzed and I just want this to be over. "You'd be my hero," I say, and then laugh it off. I don't know what else to do but make it a joke. I flush and Nico is patting me on the back before I even zip up.

"I like that. I always wanted to be a hero."

"My Superman."

"Can I be Batman instead?"

"Whatever you want." I make my way to the sink with his hand on my shoulder. "Just get rid of Mrs. McCaffrey and you can be whoever you want."

I gotta get out of this bathroom, get his hand off my shoulder.

When I get back to our table, I tip the new bottle of beer to my lips, drink half in one gulp and say, "I gotta go."

I have a plan. Next meeting I'm going to propose that we vote to put the color choice to a building-wide vote. We'll put up paint samples in the lobby and have each resident weigh in. If we vote on that plan, and to usurp the rule that only the board gets to decide in a unanimous vote, we can end this and have a color that a majority has picked and it would be harder for anyone to get annoyed about.

She'll find a way, I'm sure.

I draft an email to send to my fellow non-Marjorie board members to see how it goes over. If I have a united front it will be easier to bulldoze over her. Not simple, but maybe easier.

Running her over with a bulldozer is a thought that hangs around in my head for a few moments until I have to snap myself out of my reverie.

I step out into the hall, turn, and lock my door. Karen is outside her door. I jolt at seeing her unexpectedly. I'm about to make small talk when I see the stricken look on her face.

"What's wrong?"

"Mrs. McCaffrey is dead."

I drop my keys. I almost ask if she was run over by a steamroller, and if she was I would go out and buy a lottery ticket or maybe open up a psychic shop.

"She is?"

Karen nods.

I'm curious, but don't want to seem morbid, but I really want to know how she died. Heart attack? Failed liver? Died on the toilet? (Oh please, oh please.) She was in her eighties so any number of causes of death would make sense.

"Fell off her balcony," Karen says, as if she could hear the questions in my head. Maybe she should open the psychic shop.

"She what?"

"Or she jumped."

"When?"

"Late last night or this morning. Carl found her in the courtyard when he was walking Sprinkles."

"Jesus."

"Yeah."

We stand in silence for a moment, but my legs want to move. They want to carry me to the courtyard to see for myself.

"Awful," I say to put a button on it. "Well, I have to go to work."

"Yeah, yeah. You go. See you."

I walk away a little too fast and go down the elevator to the courtyard where I find strings of yellow police tape like party streamers celebrating her death. A small crowd of residents are gathered, whispering their theories about what happened. Being board president, everyone knows me, even if I don't know them by name.

"Hi, Michael," says the woman from 5C whose name I think might be Gina, but I'm not confident enough to say it.

"Oh my God. I just heard."

"I think she jumped," says Ashley from 3F, and this sets off a full-voice continuation of whatever argument they were having before, with Ashley taking the suicide vote and Maybe Gina choosing the accident angle.

"She had no reason to kill herself."

"You don't know her well enough to say that. None of us did."

"Why would she care about what color the pool locker room was going to be if she was planning to kill herself?"

"Maybe she didn't plan it. Maybe it was a spur-of-the-moment thing. Overcome with melancholy of her lost youth?"

"Oh, come on, Ash. A little dramatic, don't you think?"

"Ok, if she fell, why isn't the railing broken or any of her plants upset?"

Maybe Gina has no answer for that one. I back away, watching the yellow tape wave in the wind. I wish I could have seen the body. Did she go splat? Did she fall face first? Did she land in the azaleas?

Karen walks over, her face pinched with worry like she actually cared about Marjorie.

She stands next to me and we listen to Ashley and Maybe Gina argue back and forth for a little while. They both make good points, neither of which are going to bring the old crone back to life.

"Her husband killed himself, you know."

I turn to Karen. "I didn't know that."

"Yeah. Like twenty-five years ago or something. Shot himself."

"So she was living here then. He did it here?"

"Yeah, I guess so."

"Oh, God. I wonder if she stayed in the same unit. Can you imagine?"

Karen's shoulders do a little shudder. "Living another twenty years in the same apartment your husband shot himself in? No, I can't."

"Still . . . " I stop myself from finishing the thought. Karen looks truly upset and I don't want to say anything hurtful.

"What?"

"Never mind."

"No. Still what?"

"Well, I just . . . I mean . . . " Screw it. She was on my side last night. "I mean, can you really blame him? Being married to her. Yikes."

Karen turns away from me and looks over at the scene, at the two police officers looking bored and talking about something else. "Yeah. I guess so. Maybe it all caught up with her, those years of guilt for driving him to it. Or maybe she was nice back then. Maybe she turned the way she was after he did it."

I hadn't thought of that. Marjorie as a pleasant person. I can't see it.

"Yeah, maybe."

~

All day at work I make plans in my head for all the things we're going to do now that Marjorie won't be there to block us. Paint the damn pool room blue. Get that speed bump in the parking lot. Lift the restrictions on hanging signage (like my Green Bay Packers flag).

Before I know it I'm home and the place looks a little brighter. The yellow tape is still there, but one end has come loose and it waves in a light breeze and I swear I've never seen a prettier shade of yellow. Almost makes me want to paint the pool room that same police tape color.

Almost.

I go out on my balcony to water the plants. I'm on the third floor, same as Marjorie. As I empty the can into the hanging pots and boxes of perennials, I gaze out over the edge and imagine her climbing over the side and flinging herself down. I wonder if she finally realized what a hateful, miserable person she was. As hard as she made it on all of us, can you imagine being trapped inside that rotten meat bag of a body for all those years?

"Big news, huh?"

I spill some water on my shoes. I look up and there is Nico standing on Karen's balcony, a protein smoothie in a cup and a sly smile on his face.

"The old lady," he clarifies.

"Yeah." I decide against any fake sympathy.

"Solves a lot of your problems, huh?"

"Well, we can paint the pool area now."

"Yeah. All fixed up."

He raises his protein shake like he's toasting me. It's the gesture, the grin, the smugness in the way he leans against the balcony railing like he knows no matter how big he is he won't break it, and how in the hell could Mrs. McCaffrey have done so weighing a third as much as him.

The pieces all fall into place. Yeah, I'm dumb and slow on the uptake, so what?

The conversation in the men's room plays in my ears. He looks so proud of himself.

"Holy shit." I set down the watering can and go closer to the edge of my balcony. They're only about three feet apart so I can whisper-shout to him and try not to be heard by anyone else across the courtyard. "What did you do?"

"What do you mean?" He drips with sarcasm and that grin goes from shit-eating to huge piles of manure-eating. This sick, crazy bastard.

"Problem solved, huh?" he says. "It's what neighbors do."

"You don't even live here."

"Not yet. Karen and I are pretty serious, thanks for asking."

"Jesus Christ . . . did you . . . ?"

"I heard she jumped."

There's a knock at the door. He raises his cup to me again and I want to slap it out of his hand.

I go inside and open the door to a cop. I choke on my own spit. He's in a suit, but with his badge hanging from the breast pocket.

"Hi there. Detective Diaz. Mind if I ask you a few questions about the suicide? I assume you heard?"

"Yeah. I mean, yes, I heard. And yes, you can. Ask me."

I sound like the world's guiltiest man.

"Did you know Mrs. McCaffrey?" He has a small notebook out. Other stuff is written in it. He's clearly been going door-to-door.

"I did, yes."

"Know her well?"

"Well enough."

"Ever have a fight with her?"

That one stops me. I can feel my pause, my hesitation that tells him everything he needs to know about my involvement. I try to speak again as fast as my tongue will let me and I end up blurting out, "Some times, yes, we all did, I guess, maybe. She . . . the board. And stuff like paint and things, you know."

He nods patiently and writes in his book. "And you're the board president, yeah?"

He knows who I am. I only realize now he didn't ask my name. He already knew.

"Yeah. Uh-huh."

"And last night things got a little tense?"

I force a laugh that sounds . . . forced. "I mean, no more than usual. You know how it is when you try to pick a paint color."

He doesn't acknowledge that he knows how it is in the slightest.

"Do you know any reason why she would take her own life?"

"Her husband died," I say, way too fast. "Years ago. She was sad about it. Depressed. Never the same, really."

"So you knew her before?"

"Well, no, but . . . you live with people for years like we did and you get to know them."

I don't think he bought my fake all-in-it-together bullshit, but he folds his notebook and thanks me, then walks away down the hall.

Nico is still out on the balcony, but the protein shake has been replaced by a stick of gum in his mouth.

"How'd that go?" he asks.

"I can't believe you did that. They know it wasn't a suicide. They're going to find out it was you."

"No, they won't."

I've never said a sentence in my life with as much confidence as he said that.

"How do you know?"

"I know."

Had I already made myself an accomplice by lying to the police, or not telling him what I knew? Do I have an obligation to tell them this psycho took an offhanded remark at a urinal and went and killed my neighbor?

"I can't lie for you, y'know."

The smile vanishes from his face. "I did you a favor."

"I didn't ask you to . . . " I stop myself from saying anything out loud. For all I know the cop is listening at the door. "I didn't ask you to do that."

"And yet things can look one way and be another way, can't they? Like if cops come sniffing around they could find direct evidence that leads straight to you, Mike."

If anything he might have said that with even more confidence than knowing he wouldn't get caught.

"You're gonna frame me?"

"I got no reason to." He stares at me and I have to look away. "Do I, Mike?"

"No, no. No. I just . . . it's a lot, y'know?"

"Yeah. I know. And now *you* know."

He's got experience in this. I can see it. This isn't his first time.

Do I tell Karen who she's dating? Does she know already?

No. Shut up, keep my head down. Let it all blow over. He's not going to get caught. If he doesn't caught, I don't get caught. Nobody ever needs to know the truth.

∾

No way I can think of cooking tonight. I'm not much of a cook on any night, I eat most of my meals out. Bachelor life, I guess. Karen runs to catch the elevator ride down with me. She is dressed in workout clothes on her way down to the gym. The gym that's going to be painted Calming Sea Blue very soon. Of course, by then I might be staring at the gray walls of a prison cell.

"Oh, hey," I say.

"Hi," she says.

Normally talk flows easily between us. You could call it flirting, and not only from my end, I think. But tonight I have nothing. The words caught in my throat all want to scream that her boyfriend killed Marjorie McCaffrey. He's a killer and he's done it before. Maybe if she knows the truth she'll dump him and we can be together. That's a big leap, I know, but my mind goes there anyway.

But how do I even start that sentence? How do you tell someone their boyfriend is a killer?

I don't have to worry about it because the elevator reaches the ground floor and she gets out with a quick goodbye and I'm so flustered I walk to the laundry room instead of the garage.

Two days go by and nothing. No police banging down my door. No word from Nico. No ghost of Mrs. McCaffrey haunting my apartment.

I'm headed out for dinner again when I bump into Detective Diaz in the lobby.

I can practically hear the cell doors closing on me.

"Got a minute?" he asks.

"Sure."

"I'm just asking around, doing some follow-ups about Mrs. McCaffrey."

"Sure. Yeah. Whatever you need."

My only solace is that I have the real killer in my back pocket. Whatever punishment might be headed my way, I can probably cut a deal by giving up Nico. Who knows what kind of stuff they'll find when they run his fingerprints. What kind of *stiffs* they'll find.

"Is there anything else you can tell me about her? Did you ever see her have interactions with other tenants?"

"Not really. She kept to herself pretty much. She didn't have many people here her own age."

"So I gathered. Were you aware she was wealthy?"

"No. I didn't know much about her personal life." That's the truth. But, wealthy? How wealthy?

"Last time we talked you said when you live next to people you get to know them."

It takes me a moment to catch my breath. "Did I?" I scrunch up my face like I'm trying to remember if I said it or not, but he's got a frigging notebook with my words written in it. "I mean, some people you know better than others I guess."

"You never saw her interact with her children?"

"I didn't even know she had any."

He writes more in his book. "Ok. Well, thanks again."

As he walks away I call after him. "So do you think it was suicide or not?"

Diaz stops and turns around. "Coroner said she died from the trauma of the fall. No indication of a struggle. Her door was locked. Nothing taken. If it's anything but suicide, there's no evidence of it."

Damn, Nico is good.

"Should I ask you the same question?"

He turned it on me. I didn't expect that. I can feel myself sweat. Now's my chance. I can turn in Nico, or at least give him my suspicions. They can crack this case and who knows how many others?

But Nico seemed pretty sure he wouldn't get caught even if the cops knew more. He seemed to be pointing the finger at me. I can hear his gum chewing in my ear and I know it's too risky. Anyone who could get into her apartment and stage a fake suicide like that knew what he was doing and could pin something on me if he wanted to.

"You're the pros," I say. "I'll go with whatever you say."

Diaz nods at me once, not entirely convinced, and walks away. I go back to my apartment, no longer hungry.

~

"Y'know," Nico says. He's cornered me in the hall as I was about to go inside. "You'll be needing someone to fill that extra board position."

"Yeah. I guess so."

"What about Karen?"

Jesus, did he kill Marjorie to get his girlfriend a seat on a stupid building board? No, he killed her because I said how great it would be if she was dead.

"Yeah, I think she'd be great." It's true, and not the first time I'd thought of it.

"Great. Thanks for that. When's the next meeting?"

Man, this guy just jumps to conclusions.

"Well, we'd have to vote on it. The remaining members."

"I know you'll take care of it." He smiles and I can see the wad of gum. Then he winks at me. I fumble for my keys and go inside.

~

The next board meeting comes up fast. We voted already and approved Karen to fill Marjorie's position until the next election. It's been two weeks since I heard from Detective Diaz. Marjorie's apartment has been painted, the HVAC upgraded, carpets torn out, appliances replaced, and new tenants move in next month.

I rap my knuckle on the table to call the meeting to order and I get right into it.

"First item is the paint color for the pool locker room and gym area. All in favor of Calming Sea say aye."

Around the room it goes one, two, three, four "aye's" and then Karen. She sits up straight in her seat and says, "I want pink."

My jaw falls open and my eye finds Nico in the gathered crowd of tenants. His foot is up on the seat in front of him, his jaw is working overtime on his gob of Double Mint. He gives me a thumbs up *and* a wink.

I turn to Karen and I swear to God she's chewing gum.

RIVIERA RED

SARAH M. CHEN

JANICE FIDGETED IN HER CHAIR. The tiny broadcast studio she and her husband sat in was making her anxious. Or maybe it was the pressure of the radio show. Joel instructed her on everything she needed to say and they practiced enough times, but still.

"We've got to look like a united front," Joel had reminded her. "As president of the secession committee, image matters. Otherwise, people won't take the referendum seriously and they won't go to the polls. We need every single South Riviera Beach resident to vote."

South Bay Scotty, their radio talk show host, sat in a T-shirt and shorts like he'd just returned from the beach, which he probably had. The aging surfer with his scraggly hair and signature wraparound shades perched on top of his head was in stark contrast to her perfectly put-together husband in his designer suit.

"Residents of the South Riviera community are tired of carrying the load for everyone else in Riviera Beach," Joel laid out his usual spiel. "We pay more taxes than North Riviera, yet we get less out of it. Crime has gone way up and what we need is a new police department and new city leaders. We have to start fresh. A new city for a more promising tomorrow."

That was the South Riviera Beach secession campaign slogan

that Evelyn, Janice's mother-in-law, came up with. She had it printed on red baseball caps, red T-shirts, and red stickers with the logo she designed herself. Evelyn owned a marketing firm, the same one Joel worked for, so, of course, all the advertising and PR fell on her shoulders. Something she insisted upon, the control freak that she was.

"What about the impending court case?" South Bay Scotty asked. "Any chance the referendum will be declared invalid?"

"Not a chance," Joel said. "It's totally legal and the judge will see the case is a waste of time."

As soon as the California state legislature approved the referendum last year, the city leaders of Riviera Beach sued, saying it violated the Voting Rights Act of 1965 and the equal protection clause of the Fourteenth Amendment. The hearing for an injunction of the referendum was scheduled for next Friday, four days before Election Day.

Janice readied to say her plug. Her husband just had to say "Protect our small businesses. We need our specialty stores and boutique hotels to flourish. Businesses like the Janice Lawrence Gallery on Riviera Street."

She had to remind herself not to sound rehearsed.

Need a gift for that special someone in your life? Come to the Janice Lawrence Gallery for one-of-a-kind pieces. Peruse a curated selection of photographs, homemade candles, and jewelry. All lovingly made by South Bay artists.

Joel thought Janice's photography was a cute little hobby, but Evelyn had stunned everyone by loaning Janice the money to open the business. A gesture that in hindsight should've given her pause, yet Janice couldn't resist the idea of having her own space for her pier photos.

Later, she realized her mother-in-law just wanted to show off "her gallery" to her snobbish friends. Which wasn't really that shocking. Janice knew the manipulative nature of Evelyn. Plus it wasn't like Janice was that exceptional of a photographer where she deserved her own gallery. What she did excel at was spotting talent in others. Which led to the first of many confrontations with her mother-in-law.

"This is for *our* photographs, dear," the elderly woman had said when she raised her eyebrows at the ceramics, glassware, and other pieces on display. "Why sell other artists' pieces?"

Janice flinched at the "our photographs" but ignored it.

"I want this to be a space for *all* local artists," Janice had said. "A South Bay collective."

Janice knew how hard it was for artists to get their work out there, which was why she reached out to the community. Her first art salon at the gallery was so popular it was now a monthly event. Evelyn had no concept of struggle or making ends meet. She ran a multi-million-dollar marketing and design company that her father passed down, which Joel would inevitably inherit. Janice, on the other hand, was raised by a single, immigrant mother from China. Struggling was what she'd done her entire life until she'd married Joel.

"Vote yes for the City of South Riviera Beach. For a more promising tomorrow," Joel said, breaking her from her thoughts.

Janice scooted to the edge of her seat, poised to speak into the microphone. This was her moment.

"Vote yes to protect small businesses like the Janice Lawrence—" Joel continued.

"Hey, your wife here can rally all the Asian votes, right, dude?" South Bay Scotty interrupted. "There's a pretty big Asian population on the border. Just tell them how to vote. Those that are actual citizens of course." The radio shock jock put his hands in front of him, like he was praying, and bowed his head. "Ah, yes, veddy, veddy good," he said in a mocking Asian accent. "Me no speak English, but want to be American. Me so proud to be American."

Janice gasped. Was this asshole trying to be funny? He was a shock jock and said controversial things all the time, but for God's sake, she was sitting right in front of him. She turned to her husband but he seemed just as shocked as she was. It took a lot to render Joel speechless, but South Bay Scotty had succeeded.

"Hey, I'm kidding," South Bay Scotty continued. "I know Asians don't vote." He erupted in a loud guffaw.

Janice opened her mouth but nothing came out.

Joel must've felt her struggling and leaned into the microphone. A nervous laugh escaped him. "All joking aside, we need everyone to vote." He looked at her expectantly. To continue as if nothing had happened.

She swallowed down her hurt. It *was* just a joke, right? She smiled at her husband weakly, and he motioned for her to say her spiel. She cleared her throat but the shock jock cut her off.

"You heard him, folks," South Bay Scotty said. "Go out and vote to save our neighborhood. This is South Bay Scotty, and I'll catch you all on the down low. Rock on, dudes and dudettes." He pressed a button and yanked his headphones off. "That went pretty good, I think."

Joel flung off his headphones and slammed them on the desk.

"Hey, man, be careful with that," South Bay Scotty said. "What's your damage, dude?"

Joel stood up, scooting his chair into the wall. "You didn't let me finish. I had a whole part about the stores people would lose if they don't vote. How am I supposed to scare the bougie soccer moms into voting?"

"I had dead air, waddya think I'm gonna do?" He pointed to Janice. "Wait for her to wake up?"

Janice winced. "I was going to plug my gallery." She sounded like a petulant child.

"You snooze, you lose, sweetheart."

South Bay Scotty didn't even have the courtesy to look at her.

Joel's jaw tightened and he beckoned for Janice to follow him out. She stood up. Anger and humiliation surged through her. Screw being a good sport, it was an upsetting joke and she wanted to tell the shock jock off.

But the guy was talking to the show's producer. Laughing about something. Probably her.

She turned around and slunk out of the studio, more angry with herself than the shock jock.

~

"Forget about him," Joel said as they pulled out of the station parking lot. "You gotta let it roll right off you, honey."

"I know." How could she explain how much her own husband's dismissiveness at the joke hurt too? Maybe even more.

"That's what he does. He's a shock jock."

"I know," she repeated, irritated. Maybe she *was* overreacting. She was always too sensitive. She needed to laugh it off, like her husband said.

"We need to focus on the important things," he said. "The campaign."

She sighed. Her feelings, her pride, were all secondary to the stupid secession campaign.

"And tomorrow's show," he continued.

Ugh. The *South Bay Sunrise* morning talk show. Her stomach churned. Sure she got to plug her gallery to thousands of viewers but the idea of being on live television terrified her. She hated being in the spotlight like that. Plus, after today, her confidence had taken a nose dive.

"I—I don't know if I can do the show," she said slowly. She didn't dare look at him. Stared at her hands in her lap.

"That's fine," he said lightly. "I can do it alone."

Janice exhaled, relief flooding through her. They drove in silence until Joel perked up.

"Hey, I've got an idea. I bet Mother would love for you to speak at the breakfast fundraiser." He smiled at Janice. "You can do that instead."

Janice swallowed, her heart sinking. She wanted to do the fundraiser even less than *South Bay Sunrise*. Evelyn would drag her up to the podium and make her talk about all the horrible things that would happen to the downtown businesses, like her gallery, if secession didn't pass. There'd be vacant storefronts. Cheap discount shops and check-cashing places everywhere.

It was bad enough Joel and Evelyn made her hang those secession signs on her storefront. Even after she explicitly told them her place was a sanctuary, free from politics. Many of her customers were northerners, not to mention Tasha, her young part-timer.

It was a whole different thing, though, to stand in front of a crowd and scare them with rhetoric that she wasn't a hundred percent sure was accurate.

"I have a morning meeting with some clients," she lied.

"Reschedule it."

"I don't know . . . "

"You'll be fine," Joel said, oblivious to why she didn't want to do it. Thinking she was just nervous about speaking in front of people. "I think that's even better than you coming onto the show with me. It's the home stretch, honey," he said. "These are the most important weeks of the campaign."

Janice said nothing. She couldn't wait until the election was over. So she wouldn't have to pretend she cared anymore. Hopefully the secession would pass—it *had* to or else Joel would be in a miserable mood—and they could go back to life as normal.

"Should I call her?" Joel looked at her.

Janice hesitated, too afraid to voice her objections. "Okay."

He nodded. "Good. Mother will be pleased." He reached over and patted her leg.

Janice stared down at his hand. Anxiety churned through her.

The next morning, Janice knew she wouldn't be able to go through with the fundraiser. She'd barely slept, she was so anxious about it. She decided to make up something about an early delivery that she needed to be there for since Tasha had called in sick. The Tasha-calling-in-sick part was actually true. Her assistant left a voicemail message late last night. Come to think of it, it was her third absence in less than a month.

Sorry, Mrs. Lawrence, but I can't make it in tomorrow. Something has come up and I can't get out of it.

If Janice didn't have anxiety about calling Evelyn, she would've called Tasha back and given her a warning. She really didn't want to fire the college student, but these absences were becoming a problem.

Joel was in such a rush to get to *South Bay Sunrise* that he merely nodded when Janice told him she'd have to back out of the fundraiser.

Now she had to notify Evelyn.

"I'm sorry, Evelyn, but I'm unable to make the fundraiser this morning," Janice said when her mother-in-law answered with a brisk "Good morning." "Tasha called in sick and I have to open early for an important delivery."

Silence on the other end. She could hear Evelyn's breathing.

"I—I'm very sorry," Janice said, pacing in the kitchen.

"I see." Evelyn's voice was clipped. "Very well. That's disappointing, my dear, especially at the last minute," she said. "I'll have to scramble to find another speaker. I have no idea where I'll find someone as suitable as you."

Janice didn't dare remind her that she wasn't even supposed to be scheduled at the fundraiser in the first place. And what she meant by suitable, Janice had no idea.

"I'm sure you'll manage." Janice mumbled another apology before hanging up.

Emily, her teenage daughter, breezed by, grabbing a juice from the fridge. "You're wearing that to the fundraiser?" She eyed Janice's jeans and T-shirt. "Evelyn won't like that." She lifted her nose in the air. "You look so pedestrian." Her voice haughty.

Evelyn refused to let Emily call her "Grandma" and insisted on Emily using her first name.

"I'm not going."

Emily raised her eyebrows. "Good for you, Mom. How'd Her Royal Highness take it?"

Janice swallowed. "Fine."

Emily rolled her eyes. "Yeah, right. Evelyn does not take rejection 'fine.'" She used air quotes before taking a swig from the juice. "Don't let her bully you. Like that awful dude yesterday. What was his name? Scooter?"

Janice made a face. "South Bay Scotty."

Her daughter pointed at her with the juice bottle, "Yeah, him." Something between pity and frustration in her eyes. "That show was totally cringe, Mom. What a racist asshole."

"That may be so, but you know your father," Janice said, ignoring her daughter's cursing. "When I screwed up yesterday by not saying my spiel—"

"You didn't screw anything up, Mom," Emily interrupted. She grabbed a granola bar from the pantry and stuffed it in her backpack. "Don't let him do that to you."

"Do what?"

"Gaslight you like that."

Janice stared. "Where'd you learn that word?"

Emily stopped to give Janice a kiss on the cheek before heading out of the kitchen. "You need to do what you believe in, Mom. Not worry about Dad, or Evelyn, or the campaign."

Janice blinked at her daughter. Emily was applying to colleges to study journalism. She volunteered with so many organizations, Janice couldn't keep track.

My girl is all grown up. A lump formed in Janice's throat.

"Gawd, Mom, stop it."

"Stop what?"

"You've got that look on your face."

"What look?"

"That 'my baby is all grown up' look."

"I do not."

"You do." Emily came around and hugged her. "Love you, Mom. Gotta run and meet Keyanna at the shelter."

Janice's heart caught in her throat. "Be careful. If your father finds out you're volunteering at the homeless shelter, he won't be happy."

Emily rolled her eyes. "Whatever. I'm not scared of Dad." She gave Janice a look. "And you shouldn't be either."

Janice bristled. "I'm not scared."

"Mm-hm. Don't wait for me for dinner. Keyanna and I'll grab something by the pier later."

When her daughter left, Janice felt the emptiness of the room. This was how it was going to be when she was off to college. A quiet void sucking everything up like a giant black hole. The realization depressed her. Normally her shop filled that void, but lately it had felt suffocating. It was no longer the sanctuary she envisioned.

Janice was about to close up for her lunch break when the bell at the front signaled a customer. She hurried from her back office to find Joel standing by the register. His posture stiff.

"Hi, honey," Janice said, approaching him cautiously. "How was *South Bay Sunrise?*" She'd wanted to watch it before she saw him but figured that wouldn't be until tonight.

He looked around. "Where are the secession signs?"

Janice swallowed. She'd moved them to the back of the shop a week ago, hoping to appease the customers who had stopped coming in. "It was difficult for window shoppers to see inside," she said lamely. The same excuse she told an irritated Evelyn. "I . . . I'm sorry, I can go get—"

Joel waved his hand. "Doesn't matter. There's something you need to see." He thrust his phone at her.

Janice leaned over to see a blurry YouTube video. She peered at it, trying to figure out what she was looking at.

It was a crowd of people talking and laughing. The focus sharpened and she recognized the mayor of Riviera Beach, Mayor Massey, in the middle of the crowd. He walked slowly toward the camera and entered a store. Janice recognized her gallery.

"Joel Lawrence, head of the secession committee, says the mayor is soft on crime and wants to defund the police," a female voice said.

Something familiar about the voice but Janice couldn't place it.

Janice watched herself walk up to Mayor Massey and greet him with a handshake. They chatted briefly, but you couldn't hear what was said.

Janice glanced up from the video at Joel. Raised her eyebrows. He nodded.

"Just wait."

Nervous about what could possibly be on the video, Janice resumed watching. She and the mayor chatted. Then he bent his head down toward her like he was whispering something. A few seconds later, the mayor threw his head back and laughed. Janice smiled up at him, her face shiny with admiration.

"So why is Lawrence's wife cozying up to the mayor?" the voice-over continued, "Why should we bother voting to secede when the committee president's own wife can't put Mayor Massey's feet to the fire?" The image froze on Janice's upturned smiling face.

"What the hell, Janice?" Joel yanked his phone away from her and shoved it in his pocket. "Why didn't you tell me about this?" The hurt was obvious in his accusation.

"I didn't even know this video existed," Janice sputtered. "Who posted it?"

Joel frowned. "That's the thing. I have no idea. The user is Truth Teller but there isn't any other identifying info. No other videos or posts either. Just this one." He sighed. "Where'd this come from?"

Janice shook her head. "It's from Small Business Saturday. There was a big sidewalk sale downtown. The mayor came into everyone's store and chatted with them."

"Why does it look like you two are all lovey-dovey?"

Janice grimaced. It *did* look that way. She recalled what the mayor had said to her. "He said I should join him at the city's beach yoga sessions since it was my pier photos that inspired him to host them there."

Joel's penetrating glare made her nervous.

"I said he was being too kind or something like that. And that he surely didn't want me there with my pathetic attempt at turning myself into a human pretzel." She laughed. "You know how terrible I am at yoga."

Joel looked dubious.

"C'mon, honey. I can't be rude to the mayor. How would that look? I sold a lot that day. It's just doing business, okay?" She sounded defensive, which upset her even more. She didn't deserve to be in the hot seat like this. "This person, whoever they are, obviously turned it into something that it's not. I have no idea why."

Joel's sharp eyes bore into her. She stared right back at him, struggling not to cry, or beg him to forgive her. But why should she? She did nothing wrong.

Finally he nodded. "Okay." A deep breath. "Obviously *someone* wants to rattle us. Any idea who?"

"Barb Coffman?" Janice thought of the president of the Keep Riviera Beach Together committee. A soft-spoken retired librarian in her eighties. It didn't seem like something she'd do but, with the election right around the corner, maybe she had no choice but to resort to desperate tactics.

"Was she at your store that day?"

Janice shrugged. "I don't recall seeing her but that doesn't mean she wasn't there." She frowned. "It's not really her style though. I don't even think she knows how to make cell phone videos."

Joel snorted. "Yeah, I was thinking the same thing."

Janice tried to think of people who wanted to make them look bad.

"How about your customers? Or the artists you work with?" Joel asked. "Maybe the secession signs pissed them off."

That thought had entered Janice's head. All the artists she collaborated with were northerners. Surely the secession signs she hung were offensive to them. But she couldn't imagine one of them posting something like this. "I don't think so."

"We can still spin this to our advantage," Joel said. "Say it's been heavily edited. The other side is resorting to desperate measures." He paused. "If we have to, you can claim the mayor sexually harassed you and you didn't want to say anything because you didn't want to embarrass his family."

Janice widened her eyes. "I will *not* say that, Joel. Come on." This was something she had to put her foot down on. "That's going way too far."

He pursed his mouth. "Yeah, maybe you're right."

She stared at him. "Geez, Joel." She didn't realize how dirty he'd play.

"I said alright."

Janice exhaled slowly.

"But we've got to remain a united front," Joel said. "There can't be any question about where you stand. Especially now that we're in the home stretch. You'll attend rallies with me. Luncheons. Hand out flyers to your customers." He shook his phone at her. "We have to prove this video wrong."

Janice was quiet. Remaining on the sidelines was no longer an option. She had to join her husband. Put herself in the spotlight.

"Janice?" He stared at her.

"Of course."

After he left, the video haunted Janice the rest of the day. She finally pulled it up on her phone to watch it again and see if she could spot anything that would indicate who posted it.

There was the crowd of shoppers. The mayor walking toward the camera.

Janice recalled there were very few people inside her gallery that day. Most of the action took place outside where she'd set up tables filled with art pieces and her photographs. It was a sidewalk sale and the street had been cordoned off to encourage pedestrians. There was no reason to go inside unless you had to use the restroom.

Whoever shot this video did it from inside her gallery. And there was only one other person who was inside as much as her that day.

Tasha.

The next day, Janice was just about to head to work when her cell pinged.

A text from Tasha.

Gimme a call before you come in.

She stared at the text. Why would Tasha need to talk to her before she went there? Unless she figured Janice saw the video and wanted to explain herself?

Janice decided to ignore her text. She needed to talk to her in person.

On her way to the garage, Joel came downstairs, heading to work, and handed her a stack of flyers with the slogan "A more promising tomorrow" in bold red.

"Here," he said. "Remember, we're not mentioning the video unless someone brings it up. Then immediately shoot them down. Say it's been taken out of context and heavily edited."

"Got it."

"I think we quashed any doubts with what we put out yesterday," he said, looking pleased.

They'd slapped together a quick video and posted it to their social media. One with Joel and Janice, side by side in front of her gallery, reminding everyone to vote to secede if they wanted to attract high-end businesses downtown. For a more promising tomorrow. She hated involving her gallery in these PR stunts but it was too late now. Her sanctuary space was now fully in the pro-secession camp. And so was she.

"I hope so," Janice said.

Joel pecked her on the cheek before grabbing the thermos of coffee she'd prepared for him as he headed to the garage. Janice allowed him to leave first, then she backed out and drove to work. Her impending conversation with Tasha ran through her head.

No more being the pushover, the nice and understanding boss. It was time to put her foot down and take action. She'd stood on the sidelines long enough.

When she arrived at Riviera Street, the main street that cut through the heart of downtown, traffic came to a standstill. What was going on?

Janice turned down an alley and parked in her spot in the rear. She made her way inside, passing her tiny office in the back. Muffled voices could be heard up ahead.

Just as she turned a corner to enter the large main space of the gallery, she heard Tasha yell, "Mrs. Lawrence, stay where you are."

Janice froze. "What? Why?"

She remained shrouded in the shadows in the narrow hallway but could make out a small crowd outside the front display window. Tasha behind the sales counter on the far side of the shop.

"What's going on?"

Tasha glanced back at her. "I told you to call me first." She sounded irritated but there was something else. Fear. "They're here for you. Don't let them see you." She waved for Janice to stay back, but it was too late. The crowd spotted her. Shouts outside.

Janice shrank back. "Who are they?"

She strained to decipher what they were saying while creeping forward, ignoring Tasha's frantic gesture to remain where she was. The sea of red shirts and hats with the secessionist logo outside sent a chill through her.

"The secessionists. They've been here since I opened." Tasha emerged from behind the counter and made her way to the back toward Janice. "They're demanding to speak to you."

Obviously they saw the video. The room started to close in on

Janice. She felt like she was going to pass out and put one hand on the wall to steady herself.

"Kathy Tisdale is with them," Tasha continued. "She keeps yelling that you're a spy." Concern clouded the young woman's features.

Janice's stomach dropped. Kathy Tisdale was terrifying. One of those aggressive zealots who didn't listen to reason or facts. From her vantage point, Janice could make out the ringleader, with the frizzy brown hair, right in front of the doors. Carrying a "Janice Lawrence is a traitor" sign. Others carried signs as well.

NORTHERNER SPY

SECESSION SELLOUT

Tasha guided a dazed Janice to her office, away from the angry crowd, and sat her down. She wondered if she should call the police but immediately dismissed that idea. She was on the same side as them. Supposedly.

The chanting seemed to get louder.

"Traitor!"

"Sellout!"

Fists pounded on the doors. The windows rattled.

"Are the doors locked?" Janice whispered, as if the crowd outside could hear her.

Tasha nodded. "They were here looking for you when I arrived this morning so I didn't even open yet."

That meant the mob had been here chanting for over an hour. She prayed they wouldn't start throwing rocks or try to break the glass. Luckily she had an alarm so, if they did, the police would arrive immediately. Or so she hoped.

"Why are they here?" Tasha asked. "What did you do?"

Janice stiffened. Remembered why she was in this predicament in the first place. "What did I do?" She stood up, the chair slamming into the wall. "This is because of you."

Tasha looked taken aback. "Because of me?"

"You released that video. Said all those horrible things about me and the mayor. Why didn't you just come to me if working for me was so awful?" She huffed. "I didn't even know how you felt about all this. You never told me where you stood."

Tasha shook her head. "I have no idea what you're talking about. What video?"

Frustrated, Janice pulled out her phone and thrust it at her part-timer. "Here." She played the video. Studied Tasha's bewildered face as she bent over Janice's desk to view the phone. Her brow furrowed.

"Why should we bother voting to secede when the committee president's own wife can't put Mayor Massey's feet to the fire?"

That voice. It definitely wasn't Tasha. She must've had someone else narrate.

"I know it was you," Janice said. "It's the same video as the one from Small Business Saturday that you posted to our account."

Tasha looked confused. "It's the video I posted to our Twitter account, but I didn't post *that*." She pointed to the phone. "Someone doctored it up. They stole my video and added that other stuff."

Was that kind of thing even possible? Janice had no idea. She never posted a video on social media before.

"I can't believe you think I would do that to you," Tasha said, hurt flashing in her eyes. "Do you even know me?" She shook her head. "Don't answer that. It's obvious you don't. You know why? Because you don't even ask."

"Is it about the campaign?" Janice asked. "If my stance bothered you, you should've said something."

Tasha stared at her. "You're the boss, Mrs. Lawrence. It's not my place to say something."

Janice blinked. She knew Tasha was right.

"Besides I didn't know what your stance was," Tasha continued. "For months, you refused to discuss the campaign. Saying it was divisive. Then, next thing I know, you're hanging secession signs everywhere. I mean, I figured you'd be with your husband on it, but I still had hope you'd be sympathetic to the other side. How seceding would literally bankrupt all the northerners left behind who still had to pay off the city debt. People like me."

Janice swallowed. Didn't really think of it like that. "Why didn't you just quit then?"

Tasha pursed her mouth. "You think I can quit my job just like that? Like I don't have bills to pay, or responsibilities? I don't have a benefactor like you."

That stung. "You should still come to talk to me," Janice said, "instead of calling in sick or slacking off." As soon as she said it, she regretted it. Tasha worked hard even if she had been sullen the past few months.

And deep down, she knew Tasha didn't post that video. It wasn't in her character.

Tasha blinked back tears. "I had to get another job, okay? My mom's sick and I have to take care of her. I didn't want to tell you because I figured you'd use that as an excuse to fire me. I thought I could juggle both."

Janice felt awful. "I wouldn't have fired you."

Tasha shook her head. "Maybe you wouldn't, but Her Royal Highness would."

"It's my call," Janice said.

"Is it?"

They stared at each other. The chanting outside now muted in the background. Was the crowd dispersing? Janice hoped so.

"You'll never be one of them," Tasha said suddenly. "As soon as you're not useful, they'll turn on you."

Janice thought of what South Bay Scotty said about her securing the Asian vote. How Joel laughed it off and told her it was just a joke.

Tasha turned and headed out of the office.

"Where are you going?" Janice asked, fear seizing her at the prospect of being alone.

"There's a march downtown to city hall. For the Keep Riviera Beach Together campaign." She paused in the doorway. "You wanna come with me?"

Everything in Janice told her to leave with Tasha. But Joel would kill her.

"Good luck, Mrs. Lawrence." Tasha was gone.

Janice heard the back door open, then slam shut. Now she was alone. No point sticking around like a sitting duck.

She grabbed her purse and hurried out of her office, sneaking out the back. Made sure to lock the door. She was grateful they didn't think to ambush her in the back alley.

"There she is."

"Trying to sneak away."

Janice turned to see the mob of red shirts, led by Kathy Tisdale, coming toward her from the end of the alley. There were men and women of all ages, including a few burly guys who looked strong enough to knock her out with one meaty fist. Her heart hammering, she scanned the area for Tasha but there was no sign of her. Janice ran to her car, her head ducked down. Her breath shallow. Shouts from behind.

"Get back here, Janice! You've got some explaining to do!"

"Traitor!"

"Where do you think you're going, bitch?"

Janice jumped into her car, and turned the ignition with shaking hands. She reversed out of her spot, fishtailing as she went.

Wham!

She slammed into a dumpster, her whole body reverberating with the crash.

"Shit."

Janice threw the car into drive and stomped on the gas pedal. She cranked the wheel hard to the right, away from the fast-approaching mob. A thud to the back of her sedan. Another thud. Were they hitting her car? She didn't stop to find out.

Speeding down the alley, she turned left onto a side road that would take her to Riviera Street. A sawhorse blocked her path and she slammed on her brakes.

"What the hell?" She swiveled around to see the crowd behind her, rapidly closing the distance to her car. They looked bloodthirsty. Especially Kathy Tisdale. Panic gripped her. She was just about to plow right through the sawhorse when a stream of people marched past her down Riviera Street. They carried signs "Keep Riviera Beach Together." The chanting rang loud and clear.

"We all belong, Riviera strong. We all belong, Riviera strong."

The march Tasha mentioned. This was probably why there was so much traffic earlier. The entire street was blocked off. She spotted a couple police cruisers parked kitty-corner from her but nobody inside. They must be stationed elsewhere for the march, maybe at city hall, further down the block.

She couldn't plow through the crowd. But she couldn't remain there either. Panicked, she threw the car in reverse and backed up so fast her rear end struck a light pole.

Bam!

Pounding on her car. Screams of "Get out traitor." Something struck her windshield, and a crack spiderwebbed the glass. Janice screamed. The car rocked side to side.

The mob had arrived. She'd never been so terrified in her life.

The locks. She frantically pounded the button to ensure the locks were engaged. Her passenger window shattered. Glass covered the seat. A hand reached in. Janice shrank back. Another hand. Reaching and grasping for her. She spotted Kathy Tisdale coming at her with her sign. She swung it above her head, striking the hood of her car.

Deafening noise above. Like a herd of cattle dancing on her roof. Her car lurched to one side, then the other.

Janice hit the gas and the bodies fell away. She didn't want to run anyone over but dear God, she had to get out of there.

People yelled.

"Don't let her get away!"

"Watch out!"

Cruuuunch!

She plowed into another car that seemed to come out of nowhere.

Probably the side street she had been trying to turn into. A young couple appeared shaken inside. She prayed they were okay.

Desperate, she reversed as fast as she could, but her driver's side window shattered. Janice screamed. The door opened and she tumbled out onto the asphalt. Hands grabbed her arms. Her legs. Fists hit her. Shoes kicked her. In the stomach. Her ribs. Her legs. Again and again.

She tried to cover her head with her arms, but someone whacked her. Pain radiated all over her skull. Tears blurred her vision. She prayed someone would tell her family where she was if she was left for dead out there.

Then strong hands gripped her. Shouts.

"Leave her alone. Get away from her."

"Mom! Are you okay?"

Emily?

Janice coughed. Something was in the air. Something that made it hard to breathe. Her eyes stung. Everything stung. She gagged.

Someone pulled her along from underneath her armpits. Dragged her until she was lifted up and hoisted into the back seat of a car. A door slammed. Janice groaned and turned onto her side into a fetal position. She couldn't see. Everything hurt.

"Mom, are you okay? We're taking you to the ER."

Emily. She sounded a million miles away. Sirens in the distance.

The car lurched and she closed her eyes. Everything faded away.

When Janice stirred, the first thing she thought of was water. She needed a drink. Her mouth was parched. The smell of disinfectant hit her. The beeping of a machine. Her eyes fluttered open. She was in a darkened hospital room.

She struggled to lift her head and spotted Joel and Emily asleep in the corner, slumped against the wall. As if she sensed Janice was awake, Emily opened her eyes.

"Mom!"

Emily flew to her side and grasped her hand. Janice smiled up at her weakly.

"Hi, honey." Her voice raspy. Like death.

"How are you, Mom?"

"Eh." She coughed.

Joel had woken up by this time. He appeared beside Emily.

"Omigod, honey, you're awake. How you feeling?"

She coughed again. "Water."

"Nurse!" Joel yelled, while Emily thrust a flimsy paper cup of water at her.

She gulped it down, water dribbling down the sides of her mouth and chin.

A nurse hurried to her side, and checked her vitals.

"How long have I been here?" Janice asked. Her head felt like it weighed a thousand tons.

"Just a little over thirty-six hours," the nurse said.

"What happened?"

"You suffered from a concussion. Four broken ribs. You had some internal bleeding but you'll be fine. You're very lucky, Mrs. Lawrence, that your daughter found you when she did."

"Thank Tasha," Emily said. "She's the one who pepper-sprayed everyone and rushed us to the ER."

At the mention of Tasha, Janice felt a hollowness in her chest. She'd accused Tasha of stabbing her in the back, yet the girl saved her. Exhausted, Janice leaned back in bed and closed her eyes.

"You just missed her," Joel said. "She stopped by to see how you were doing."

As Janice drifted off, she thought she heard Emily say something about Tasha's mother being on the fourth floor. How she had cancer and Tasha was at the hospital every day to be by her side.

"Let her rest," the nurse said as Janice succumbed to sleep, the drugs, and the guilt.

"Morning, dudes and dudettes! It's four days 'til Election Day. South Bay Scotty here with today's surf report. Live from Riviera Beach under sunny skies. Current air temperature seventy-two. Water's sixty-five. Surf out of the southwest as Malibu checks in. Got a couple chest-high sets. Fair to good. While the South Bay, it's not really catching the south. Two to three foot. Poor to fair here.

"And now for some local political news that I think folks might be interested in. A judge ruled that the secession referendum's valid. Our election will be happening. So, Joel, my man, you were right.

"*But hang on.* We've got a gnarly little twist, dudes and dudettes. Because if South Riviera Beach becomes a new town, it's still gotta pay its share of Riviera Beach's debt. Even if it becomes its own city. Something about the loan was approved years ago based on the assumption the two communities were one city. That's a whole lotta mumbo jumbo—too much for me this early in the morning—but what it boils down to, folks, is money. What's the point of splitting off if you're still on the hook for the other's mistakes?

"Hey, but what do I know? I'm just a simple dude looking for the perfect wave. Cowabunga, surf's up, and that's it for the beach report."

Janice said goodbye to the last guest, thanking them for coming, and locking the door behind them. She threw discarded plastic wine glasses that littered the gallery into a trash bag as she made her way to the back. Joel sat, slumped in front of the big screen TV they'd rented for Election Day, surrounded by the red secession posters. She set the trash bag down and put her arm around him. He flinched, then relaxed when he realized it was her.

"I think it's time to close up and head home," Janice said.

Joel nodded. He sighed, deflated. "It wasn't even close."

Janice rubbed his back. Knew nothing she said would comfort him.

"I didn't think we'd win," he said. "Not after that bullshit ruling about the debt obligation. But dammit, I thought we'd at least get thirty, maybe forty percent of the vote."

The vote to secede lost by a huge margin. Not even ten percent of the vote. South Bay Scotty was right. It was all about money. Nobody wanted to bother forming a new city if they were still indebted to the old one.

She was sad for Joel, but relieved the campaign was over. Now they could go back to normal. Although what "normal" meant was unclear. The divide between the secessionists and loyalists was even greater. Mayor Massey now had the difficult task of uniting the community and moving forward. The extremists, the Kathy Tisdales, remained emboldened as they waited for the next opportunity to wreak havoc and ignore reason. She'd pled guilty to assault and battery but avoided jail time, much to Janice's outrage. Janice planned to file a civil suit against her. She and her attorney were busy trying to track down the others in the mob who had joined in, but nobody was talking. The police were investigating but without a video there wasn't much they could do.

The terror she felt from that day haunted her. She woke up every night, drenched in sweat from the nightmares. The bruises and swelling had finally gone down, but she suffered from excruciating migraines.

It wasn't over. Not by a long shot.

Evelyn emerged from the bathroom. Her nose wrinkled in disgust. "People are pigs." She pointed behind her. "Janice, honey, you'll want to clean in there."

Janice glared at her mother-in-law, but Evelyn didn't notice.

"Don't look so sad. We did our best, dear," Evelyn said to Joel. "We'll try again when the city debt is paid off."

Joel shook his head. "I'm done. It's time to move forward." He sounded resigned.

Janice was grateful for Joel's attitude. "Yes, let's put this behind us."

Evelyn scoffed. "And what does that look like? More crumbling roads and cheap discount stores?" She shook her head. "I'm surprised, Joel. You've gone soft."

Joel glowered at her. "It's called waking up, Mother. Facing the music."

Evelyn tsked. "Stop acting so self-righteous. It's not a good look on you." She fixated suddenly on Janice. "If you'd been on board from the beginning, we could've stood a chance."

Janice was taken aback. "Me?"

"You have your hand in so many groups, Janice. The artsy-fartsy types. The bougie soccer moms. The Asians. If you'd done your part, campaigned hard, and played dirty, we wouldn't be here right now."

Janice gaped at her.

"Mother, that's not fair," Joel said.

"You didn't take advantage of your situation here," Evelyn said, ignoring him. "Remember, this gallery wouldn't even exist without my help. My money."

Rage filled Janice. She felt herself flush. "That may be so, but I'm the one who built the local art community into what it is now. One from *both* sides." It struck her in that moment that that was what really mattered to her. Not the stupid gallery.

Evelyn waved her hand. "Oh, please. Enough with the kumbaya bullshit. You were nothing before you married Joel. A poor immigrant with a useless community college degree in art history."

"Mother, this is not the time—" Joel began.

But Evelyn cut him off. "We made you and we can easily unmake you." She laughed. "People believe anything. Look how easy it was with the video."

Janice blinked at her as what she said sunk in. "You mean the video of me and the mayor? Accusing me of being a spy?"

Joel stared at his mother. "*You* did that?" His face was stricken with realization.

She shrugged. "She wasn't using her platform. What was I supposed to do? I figured it would light a fire under both of you. And it worked."

"I almost got killed," Janice yelled. "You sicced Kathy Tisdale on me. That woman is delusional."

Evelyn glared. "I did nothing of the sort. Is it my responsibility what that woman does?" She sniffed. "Besides, for all we know, she was upset about Emily marching with the libs and commies, and they were calling *her* the traitor. Which she is by the way."

Janice stared at Evelyn, stunned.

Evelyn plowed on. "She volunteers at the homeless shelter too, did you know that? My God, that girl has no shame."

"That's it." Janice slammed her hand down on the counter, making Evelyn and Joel jump. "Don't you dare drag Emily into this. She has more integrity in her pinkie finger than you would ever have in your entire Botoxed, liposuctioned body."

Evelyn gasped.

"I'm proud of Emily for standing up for what she believes in. A lesson I could learn." She gathered her purse and headed to the back. "I'm going home."

She didn't bother to see if Joel was following her. She didn't care.

"Wait, am I locking up?" Joel called out.

"Ask Evelyn. It's *her* gallery," Janice said.

As she passed the secession signs papering the wall she reached out and tore them off. One by one. Ripped them into little pieces with a fury she'd kept buried for years. She scattered the shreds of poster paper across the floor on her way out the door, like a trail of red confetti. Which was fitting considering Janice was in a surprisingly celebratory mood. She was free from the gallery. Her future may be unknown but, from now on, she would be the one in control.

It was a more promising tomorrow, indeed.

C.O.D.

GABRIEL VALJAN

HE APPEARED BEFORE THEM, a man to fear, a man in black. When he walked, one heard a soft sound, a clink, though there were no spurs and no horse. The crowd parted before him because death clung to him. He saw the sheriff and the sheriff saw him. The lawman Dempsey knew the stranger's name.

Midas Utter.

The rest gathered there, all employees of the great Anaconda Cooper Mining Company, didn't know Utter as Utter: they referred to him as Preacher because he'd mix his speech with words from the Bible. Midas Utter was neither a man of the cloth nor a man of peace. His holster displayed two Remington revolvers, one on each hip. Preloaded cylinders studded his belt.

His car rested on the side of the road behind him. The make and model of the vehicle was recognizable from ads in *Life* magazine. Mr. Henry Ford had discontinued the use of brass in the headlights that year because the price of the metal was on the rise, and the alloy of copper and zinc was destined for producing ammunition for the war in Europe. Even before the US committed to the conflict, Anaconda, the government, and Mr. Ford were selling munitions to both sides.

Utter's arrival that early in the morning in August suggested that he'd traveled overnight, as if he had raced the pale rider himself to the awful scene. When Utter had exited his Model T, before anyone became aware of his presence, the townsmen were in the throes of that time-honored tradition of having their picture taken around the deceased. The General Store in town would profit from the spectacle: a photograph of when a man's feet had not touched the earth. A man's life cost the two cents it took to mail the postcard.

The men stepped back as Midas Utter moved forward. He looked up at the spectacle.

Above him hung the battered and bruised body of a Wobbly, a labor organizer, a man who agitated employers wherever he traveled, from golden California to Middle America to his final destination, here in Big Sky Country. The victim had pamphleteered and roused the rabble, on matters of equality, fairness, and patience. He'd never suggested insurrection, but he implied Judgment was inevitable.

And there he swayed in a dry summer breeze. The violence visited upon his legs suggested that he'd been dragged. His face and body had endured a ferocious beating, and then there was the final insult of the trestle, and the hangman's rope.

"He was a troublemaker," someone in the crowd said to Utter.

Sheriff Dempsey hushed the voice. "I'll handle this. I'm the law here."

"*And Ye have done all this wickedness: yet turn not aside from your work,*" Midas said.

The corpse twisted to reveal a message pinned to his nightshirt. It read: *Others take notice, first and last warning, 3-7-77.*

"Preacher?" a miner asked. "Are those numbers from the Good Book?"

"No."

"A riddle then?"

"These are words of prophecy, a tongue of fire. These numbers signify death."

The miner squinted. "A prophecy?"

Utter answered. "Three feet wide, seven feet deep, 77 inches long."

Dempsey asked Utter, "And how is that death?"

"Measurements for the gravedigger. Take the man down, Sheriff."

A burly man stepped forward. "Hold on there, Mister." The man held a Kodak Brownie in his hand. He was new to town, and slower than a beaver out of water in understanding how things worked. "Say what you will, but I intend to take more photographs."

"Even in death, you will not let this man rest in peace?"

A fellow elbowed the photographer. Others in the crowd understood what the lens man did not. When Utter said "this man," he may have meant himself.

Utter looked at the small box in the man's hand. "I met George Eastman once. An intelligent man, a wise man. He said, 'Embrace light. Admire it. Love it. But above all, know light.' I'd suggest you turn away from darkness and see the light."

"And if I don't? A man has a right to make a living, don't he?" The man searched around for support and found none. "Consider this matter historical then," he looked to Dempsey, "as evidence, ain't that right, Sheriff?"

There was silence until Midas Utter spoke again.

"One-seventeen film allows six exposures. How many have you taken?"

"Four. Why?"

Utter reached into his pocket and unclipped his billfold, and peeled off a crisp twenty. "This note equals two weeks' pay. I'd suggest you take it and surrender the camera to Sheriff Dempsey."

Utter inserted it into the man's shirt pocket.

"I didn't say I'd accept your money."

Dempsey extended his hand. "Hand me the damn camera, Reilly." He tilted his head, eyes on Utter. "Do as the man says."

"And if I don't?"

Midas Utter stepped away and faced the field on the side of the road. He sniffed the air and his eyes narrowed. In a flash, he drew and fired one of his Remingtons. The shot hit the dirt and kicked up a prairie rattlesnake, decapitated it, and threw the serpent's carcass several yards from where it had nested.

Utter holstered his weapon, approached Reilly, and stared into the man's eyes. "And so *the serpent deceiveth the world, until he was thrown down to the earth with all his angels.*"

Reilly handed the Brownie over to Sheriff Dempsey.

Utter said to the sheriff, "I'll see you soon."

The sheriff sat down at his desk later, fortified against the evening hours with a cup of coffee that he had prepared before Midas Utter walked into his office. Dempsey had heard the man before he saw him, the one–two sibilant sound of silver heels against the hardwood floor.

Midas noticed the brand of coffee and said, "Good to the last drop."

"Wouldn't know it, would I, since you interrupted the pleasure."

"Utter interrupted," Midas said with a smile. "Euphony."

"You're not a man I'd associate with the peaceful or the pleasant."

"Ah, an example of alliteration. Well, you're wrong, Sheriff. *When the evil spirit from God was upon Saul, that David took a harp, and played with his hand: so Saul was refreshed.* I am here to help you resolve this foul affair."

"Here to refresh me, are you? I think I'd rather enjoy this coffee here." Dempsey lifted his cup and toasted Midas Utter, and then sipped some of his dark brew.

Midas pointed to the canister. "Few people know Teddy Roosevelt coined the coffee company's slogan, in Nashville, 1907, and in the former home of Andrew Jackson."

"Thank you for that needless tidbit."

"Needless?" Midas's cold eyes stared. "Everything is necessary and needful, Sheriff Dempsey, given proper context and perspective."

"Afraid you're wasting your time. Perhaps, another quote from the Bible, something useful?"

"Useful?" Utter asked. "How about the Bard?"

"If you think it necessary."

"*Our rash faults make trivial price of serious things we have, Not knowing them until we know their grave.* We are all before the grave, some closer to it than others."

His mug banged against the wood. "What do you want, Mr. Utter?"

"As Mr. Gradgrind said in Mr. Dickens's splendid novel, *Nothing but facts, facts, facts.* Tell me what you know, and don't preface your history that this was a death foretold because the victim was a union man, an anarchist, and a member of the Industrial Workers of the World. The world outside of this town, no matter how well paid the newspapermen are, will find it hard to believe that a man, blind in one eye, and who walked with a crutch, was a threat. An orator of power, yes, but he was no William Jennings Bryan. What I want from you, Sheriff, are facts, facts, and more facts."

Dempsey conveyed what he'd learned about the deceased's last hours. The man had rented a room at a local boarding house. The landlady reported that three men had barged into her home in the middle of the night. Fearful, she confronted the men in the stairwell, where she noticed that they were all wearing masks. She believed them to be armed. They demanded to know the man's room, and began to creep up the stairs, a promise of violence upon her if she didn't cooperate. She provided the room number to the man who had demanded it of her.

"Did she recognize this man's voice?"

"No."

"Despite these masks, did she recognize the size and shape of any of these men?"

"Afraid not."

Sheriff Dempsey continued. The cadre had roused the victim from his bed. They seized his person and directed him out of the house, in his underwear, into a waiting car. The lady remarked later that she had heard a car idling, but had forgotten this fact because of the commotion the intruders had created.

"She heard a car," Midas said, his fingers touching his lips in thought. "Did she see it?"

"Yes. She peered through the curtains in a window at the end of the hall."

"Recognize the car?"

"Ford Model T."

"No, I meant, did she recognize to whom the car belonged?"

Dempsey looked up from his notes. "No. Ford Model T, black as they all are."

"And where were you while all this was happening that evening?"

"In the saloon."

"On a Wednesday evening?" Utter asked.

"The bar is across the street. There were witnesses."

"And what else did she witness from her window?"

"The car drove a short distance and stopped. The men tied him to the rear bumper and dragged him down Main Street. You can imagine the rest."

"A granite surface would explain the scrapes and abrasions. Down the town's most traveled street, and nobody saw or heard anything?"

"Nothing."

"Blindness," Utter said. "*He that hateth his brother is in darkness, and walketh in darkness, and knoweth not whither he goeth, because that darkness hath blinded his eyes.*"

"It's all I've got until the doctor is done with the body. Unless you have any other questions, I suggest you wait." The sheriff returned to his coffee.

"One last question. What can you tell me about Reilly the photographer?"

"Why?"

"In my experience, the man with the camera is often numbered among the perpetrators. He remains on the scene to document the deed. Proximity provides convenience and a demonstration of pride."

"Reilly is new to town and, while that could make him a man of mystery, I doubt that he was party to the lynching. The only fact," and the sheriff emphasized the word "fact", "is that we have an unreliable witness, a woman."

"I see."

"See what?"

"The mystery of lawlessness is already at work."

"Good day to you, Mr. Utter."

Utter visited the town doctor. He found the man in the antechamber to the morgue, at his vanity. The physician took to heart the great Doctor Semmelweis's advice. He washed his hands with chlorinated lime after an autopsy. The Hungarian physician's wisdom had come at the expense of the death of a friend, after countless deaths of women in labor. Cadaveric fever, he'd conjectured, could be averted with hand hygiene.

These days Dr. Hoffmann tended to the ills and injuries sustained in the mines. He was a catchall man of the healing arts, animal and human. He helped cure the diseases that came with every season and he stood at the bedside of his brethren from cradle to grave. He saw Midas in his mirror.

"I'm surprised you cast a reflection, Midas."

"I'm not that far gone yet, Carl."

"Assume you're here about the lynching?"

"I am."

"Is it because you knew the man from Ludlow?"

The lynched man had been one of many Wobblies in Colorado that fateful spring of '14. He'd survived the confrontation between strikers and the Colorado Fuel and Iron Company's militia, formed at the behest of part-owner John D. Rockefeller, Jr., and the National Guard troops, ordered by President Wilson.

"I had heard the man might've been at Ludlow," Utter said.

"Were you?"

"I had no part in the massacre. No, I was not in Ludlow."

When IWW men and leaders of the strike had approached the tent to negotiate terms, Rockefeller ordered guardsmen to mow them down with machine guns. The body in the doctor's morgue had avoided the ditch and dirt, only to earn the rope and a crude gallows.

"Is there more to the man's death than the obvious?"

Hoffmann dried his hands and draped the hand towel on a small rack. He invited Utter to take a seat, asked if he wanted a drink. They'd opposed each other once, but he was civilized, a doctor, and not a barbarian. Midas Utter chose to stand.

"Your unionist sustained injuries and he'd been beaten to a pulp."

"Figured as much," Utter said. "Anything else?"

"Tortured."

"How so?"

The doctor didn't consult any notes. "Cigarette burns to the soles of his feet."

Utter nodded. "Hadn't thought to look there, though he was bare-foot. Anything else?"

"His attackers rifled his pockets."

Utter squinted. "What pockets, the man was in his nightdress?"

"That might be the case, but his IWW Membership Card was crumped and jammed into his mouth."

Utter considered the floorboards. Nice, treated pine. Maintained. He tapped a foot.

"Hanging him wasn't what killed him, Midas."

"Suffocated on the card?"

The doctor shook his head.

"The rope didn't break his neck," Utter said and shook his head. "He strangled slowly."

"Correct."

"How long?"

"Twenty minutes."

"While they watched," Utter said.

"Not that this matters, but the man suffered from chronic pain."

"The missing eye and his bum leg?"

"No, older wounds. Fractures that'd never been set. Splintered ribs. It's a miracle the man was walking around. There's another curious matter."

"Curious how? Utter asked.

"Ligature scar around his neck. Someone had tried to hang him before."

Utter weighed this revelation and said, "Though he walked through the valley of the shadow of death, he feared no evil."

Midas Utter thanked the doctor, wished him well.

Hoffmann asked him a question. "Why, Midas?"

"Why what?"

"Is it atonement, some penance for all those years we worked for Carnegie and Frick?"

Midas looked around the office. "Was becoming a doctor your way of making amends?"

"Touché," Hoffmann said. "You know those two are still alive."

"With any luck, and God willing, they'll jump into the grave together."

"I'd spend a handsome sum to have Henry Frick on my table."

"Alive, I presume," Midas smiled. "Good day, Carl."

Midas Utter walked the town, curious to have a conversation with the lady owner of the boarding house. The unexpected mention of the names Carnegie and Frick, and the comment about redemption, had surprised Midas.

They were younger than Frick, in their early fifties, whereas their boss, the King of Steel himself, was three decades their senior. Midas and Carl had acted as demons to Henry Clay Frick's devil. It was Clay, and not Jay Gould, who said that he "could hire one half of the working class to kill the other half."

As for reparations for a misspent life, Midas watched Andrew Carnegie seed libraries, the way grannies doted on their gardens. Frick, however, on the cusp of his seventh decade to hell, concealed his wealth—and encouraged his friends to do likewise. Anything to not pay the tax man. He hid his money in the façades to buildings of charities and philanthropies.

Carl left first. Midas Utter parted soon thereafter. As limestone was the catalyst in the king's steel plants, the Homestead Strike provided the crucible. Twenty-five years later, Midas had never forgotten how Carnegie and Frick crushed the vote to strike for better wages. They'd hired Pinkertons, thugs, locked the gate, and set immigrants against each other, until shots were fired, dynamite was thrown, and the field bled red: until martial law was declared.

Though they'd left, it didn't get better.

The Haymarket Affair in Chicago had occurred before their Battle of Homestead in Pennsylvania, then there was that textile strike in Lawrence, Massachusetts and, most recently, the Ludlow Massacre in Colorado. Out of all of them, the only time workers triumphed with the vote against the captains of industry was in New England. Bread and Roses.

Midas remembered Lawrence as a hollow victory. The Haymarket Four had been hanged, and Joe Hill had been executed, shot against a prison wall.

Big Money couldn't count the bills and change fast enough, now that there was a war on, now that President Wilson had appointed George Creel as the head of the Committee on Public Information. Creel worked the loom of propaganda, and he stoked the fire, a hatred for all things German. Libraries were ransacked and books burned. It was only a matter of time, Midas thought, before they'd come for Dr. Carl Hoffmann.

Now was the time for war, a time to harvest and to count cash, a time for winners and losers, a time for the rich to become richer and the poor poorer, a time for money to be made. Caesar had taught Divide et Impera to centuries of kings and queens, and the robber barons had mastered the art of Divide and Conquer. Now, union leadership imitated them. At every turn, unions attacked each other, while a corporation like Anaconda Cooper slithered its way through the grass into Chile and Mexico, and the workers, whom a lynched man had tried to help, starved.

Frick had been right. 'You were either at the table or on the menu.'

Weathered from years of worry and drink, hers was not the face of a woman who'd grown into satisfaction with her life now that the sunset was on the horizon. The decades had etched into her countenance lines of bitterness, regret, and sadness. Midas Utter found in her eyes the nervous twitch of the trapped animal, and in her hands, the knit-one purl-one of fingers with a threadbare handkerchief.

"There's nothing I can tell you that I haven't told Sheriff Dempsey already."

"I understand, ma'am, but I'm not here to ask you what you saw that night."

"You're not?"

"No, ma'am. What interests me are the man's belongings. What did he leave behind in his room?"

"Not much. He carried simple, as he lived his life. Nothing but the clothes on his back; but mind you, the man was no hobo. Dignified and decent he was," she explained. "I showed the sheriff them clothes, and he thought nothing of 'em. Why would he? There was a pair of pants, shirt and vest, socks, and shoes."

"Was there a billfold?" Midas asked. "The man paid for his stay, correct?"

"Indeed, and I shewed the sheriff the wallet, too. There was money inside of it. Anything else, Mr. Utter?"

"Any personal effects, something practical or sentimental—spectacles or a wedding ring?"

Midas recalled the dead man's hands. His killers hadn't bothered to tie his hands together. There was no band on his finger and no need for optics when he possessed one eye.

"Now that I think of it, Mr. Utter, he had on him a timepiece."

"A timepiece?"

"One of 'em pocket watches a man might keep in his vest, except his lacked a chain. I remember it now because he'd taken it out and verified the time while I wrote his particulars in the ledger. He was a polite man, Mr. Utter, and this part I recall as clear as day. He laughed when he'd checked his sidewinder."

"Laughed while he checked the time?"

"It was broken," she said. "You said 'sentimental' and it was to him."

"How can you be certain?"

"The watch belonged to his father, a doctor, and it was the only legacy he had from the man. He said it reminded him of his father and brother."

"His brother?"

"They worked in the mines in California together. His name was Walter." The woman's face lit up. "The back of the watch bore his father and brother's initials, which were the same: WL."

"You've done well. I'm grateful."

"I wish I'd told the sheriff about the timepiece because, of all the things left behind, the watch ain't one of 'em. I hope that I've been of use to you, Mr. Utter."

Midas Utter reached out, lowered his head and kissed the back of her hand. He paraphrased a verse from Psalms. "Your words are a lamp to my feet and a light to my path."

She accompanied him to the door. She said that she'd tell the sheriff what she'd forgotten, and Midas agreed that she should tell Dempsey about the missing watch. Midas didn't spend time reviewing what she'd seen from the window, but he did ask her if there were many Fords in town. She joked that even though Mr. Ford had bragged about lowering the cost of his contraption with each passing year, and he had delivered on that promise, few people in town could afford the $500 to own a Model T. She told Midas that she could count on one hand those who possessed the vehicle, and there was even one man in town who owned two Fords.

"Two Tin Lizzies?" Midas said. "He must be a wealthy man."

"He's an Anaconda man, a manager. Anyhow, one of his cars ain't even black."

"What color was it?"

"Red as the fire brigade. Never knew there was such a thing."

Midas explained to the old woman that the first models of Fords came in bright red, brown, green, dark blue, maroon, and gray."

"You know automobiles, Mr. Utter?"

"It came with the job. About that man's address."

She gave it to him and asked, "You worked for Henry Ford?"

"Ford Service Department. You could say I helped speed up production."

The afternoon was hot and drowsy with the scent of fresh-cut grass. The first sign of conspicuous wealth was that the house was on a hill, alone, and away from the other residences. A high wooden fence was another indication, important for what it contained inside and excluded outside.

Midas walked up a paved driveway, after he pushed the gate inward. He ignored the house and focused his attention on the garage, the open door, and the view inside. There were two Model T Fords. The red Touring Car, and the man tinkering with it, interested him.

Midas didn't care about the owner's more recent model because he was certain that it had been the car that'd dragged the activist to his appointment with death: in fact, he was convinced that he'd find proof that a rope or a chain had been lashed to the rear bumper.

No, he was interested in the red car. An earlier version of his own car.

The car was crimson as a cardinal; Henry Ford had produced less than ten thousand of them. The vehicle cost almost $900 to the customer, and the process at Ford's River Rouge factory to make one was intense and expensive, this before Ford perfected his assembly line. Midas would bet all the money in his billfold that this one had a lever rather than a floor pedal for reverse. The man working on the car had his back to Midas.

"A fine machine you have there."

The man said, "Why thank you," and his face dropped when he had turned around.

"I couldn't help but admire it. I was walking by."

"You do know you're on private property?"

"Point taken." Midas placed his hands on his belt buckle. If the weather had been colder, he would've parted his jacket, but the man in front of him understood the message.

"People don't walk around armed like that these days. This isn't the Wild West."

"But it is the west, nonetheless. Never can be too careful."

"Do you really need all them cylinders? Last time I heard of them being used was during the War Between the States."

"War is a state of existence. Haven't you heard?"

"I won't argue with a man with two revolvers." He wiped a wrench down with a rag.

"I do have one question for you, though."

A car jerked to a stop behind Midas. He heard Sheriff Dempsey's voice behind him. "Afternoon," the sheriff said. He said softly to Midas, "I didn't expect to find you here."

"And why am I not surprised that you are here?"

"What's that supposed to mean?"

The car owner approached. "Ain't you the fellow asking questions about the incident south of town? You said that you had a question for me. I have one for you."

"Ask your question?"

"Who do you work for?"

"Not for Anaconda."

The man contemplated the wrench in his hand. "I hope it isn't for IWW."

"No, not them. I know how folks like you, and others in these parts, feel about Wobblies. I read the day's headline after the fact. 'Good work: Let them continue to hang every IWW in the state.'"

"People don't like socialists, and they don't like someone who questions our place in the world, and why we're in the war in Europe."

"So I heard," Midas said.

"Heard in the wind," the man said, "a bunch of drunks killed the man, but it's hard to prosecute a rumor when there are no witnesses. I've also heard told that you're fond of scripture. I don't suppose you have any wisdom on this matter?"

"He that justifieth the wicked and he that condemneth the just, both alike are an abomination."

The man smiled. His fingers gripped the wrench. "You had a question for me?"

Sheriff Dempsey interrupted. "I think we ought to leave."

"What did you want to ask me, Mr. Utter?"

"What time is it?"

The question perplexed the man and it showed in his face and his grip. He switched the wrench from one hand to the other and reached into his pocket. His hand surfaced with a pocket watch, the back of it visible. Midas saw the engraving. The man turned the timepiece over and his finger sprung the cover. "I'm sorry but it seems my watch has stopped telling time." He held it to his ear. "I ought to get it repaired."

"I'm sorry, too," Midas said and walked away.

Sheriff Dempsey joined him.

The next morning Sheriff Dempsey sought out Midas Utter. He planned to tell Midas that he'd overstayed his welcome in town. The car was gone, as was Midas Utter.

Dempsey returned to his office and, while he was hanging his hat, a postman walked in. Dempsey saw the small box in the man's hand.

He told the mailman, "Just leave it on my desk."

"I can't." He raised the box for the sheriff to see it. "It's C.O.D."

"What the hell is C.O.D?"

"A new postal service. C.O.D. Cash On Delivery. You have to pay for it."

"Everything comes at a cost these days," Dempsey said. "How much?"

The carrier named the price and Dempsey handed him change.

Dempsey worked loose the envelope taped to the box. His name and address, not handwritten but typed. No address for the sender. Dempsey pierced the side with a letter opener and extracted the piece of paper. He unfolded it and read the typewritten message.

Woe unto them that call evil good, and good evil; that put darkness for light, and light for darkness.

He opened the box and found, on top of a square of cotton, a pocket watch. He opened the cover and saw time arrested. He closed the cover and turned it over, and read the initials WL.

A deputy rushed in said it was an emergency. There had been an accident, on the road into town. Three men dead, all with Anaconda.

The sheriff's first thought was 3-7-77.

THREATS AND BRIBES

JACKIE ROSS FLAUM

BLOOD SMEARS, trampled voter registration forms, and scattered #2 yellow pencils crisscrossed the cement courtyard in front of Harvey's Department Store in Ashbury, Kentucky.

Sally Warner stared wide-eyed and sick to her stomach. A former public defender, Sally had seen violent crime scenes. This certainly looked like one.

The pencils Dennis Howard sold, the forms he handed out, his . mangled, metal lawn chair near the store's Halloween display, and blood on the pavement—maybe his—screamed violence to her.

Clutching her sack of coffee and an apple muffin in one hand, Sally stood frozen to the spot where the young blind veteran usually sat. She always brought breakfast to Dennis before starting work as a clerk at Harvey's.

W-what in God's name? Who would want to hurt a blind man?

Behind her, Ashbury's only city bus wheezed to a stop and the noise made her glance around. The first thing she saw was campaign poster for mayoral candidate Mary Lou Kitchens plastered on the bus's side.

Her bewilderment turned to rage. She may not understand the why, but she was pretty darn sure of the who.

Whatever happened to Dennis started weeks ago on the morning Sally discovered voter intimidation in her hometown.

～

On that fateful morning, Sally had just locked her apartment door when she noticed her landlady coming down the hall. She lit out for the stairs.

"Sally! Stop," called Mary Lou, owner of Paradise Apartments.

Sally sped up. She huffed and puffed down two flights to the lobby.

Chiding herself for being out of shape for someone only thirty-two, Sally admitted to a puny character too. She should stand up to Mary Lou. But honestly, today she couldn't take another shrill demand for her vote.

Of course, she could escape Mary Lou by moving back to the Nance family home on Ashland Avenue permanently. Not like she hadn't run home before. Her father had hammered at her about politics and practicing law again, while her mother had nagged her to cook.

She'd rather outrun her landlady.

Sally raced across the building's lobby like a scalded dog and hit the street with Mary Lou closing ground fast. After half a block she glanced back to see Mary Lou leaning against the front door of the building and clinging to the gold necklace around her thick neck.

"I-want-to-talk-to-you, Sally!" she called.

"Got to get to work!" Sally wished she had on running shoes instead of the black pumps she wore as a clerk in women's wear. She should start a diet. Tomorrow. Today she needed a muffin.

Since Mary Lou had dropped her pursuit, Sally slowed to enjoy the walk, although these days the number of empty storefronts didn't bring much pleasure. She longed for the time when stores were full and merchants set out pumpkins, scarecrows, and cornstalks for fall decorations.

The city streets used to teem with people shopping or going to work. Drivers jockeyed for a place to park, and mouth-watering smells drifted from open restaurant doors. As a child her Grandpa Nance brought her downtown to the family law offices, and as a teen she ran her father's errands. Every shop and store owner knew her.

Looking toward Harvey's, all she saw today was Dennis under the store's courtyard awning. The man, who looked to be in his late thirties, placed his tray table and lawn chair where folks gathered to wait for the bus, have lunch, or read. He gave away voter registration forms, but he sold pencils from a cigar box on his tray table. The three-for-a-dollar pencils made him a businessman and not a beggar— an important distinction for city code enforcers.

"Whoa," a distinctive bass voice boomed. "What time does that guy get there? He's all set up . . . looks like he's been there for hours."

From a side street Sally's co-worker James Madison fell into step beside her and gave her a friendly nudge.

"Before the first bus, I imagine," Sally said.

"I heard Mary Lou yelling at you when I walked by your building. She after your vote?" James said. "Ya know, she campaigns day and night for her father's seat. She seems to think it should be hers, like his apartment buildings."

Mary Lou's father, the silver-haired, fork-tongued mayor, had died of a heart attack six months ago. Downtown merchants assumed someone had jumped the mayor and driven a stake through the blood-sucker's heart. He'd promised a downtown rebirth for years but delivered only outlying malls.

"You can't dodge Mary Lou forever," James ran a hand through his thick, black hair.

"It's not much longer until the election. Six weeks, maybe? I can avoid her until then," Sally said. "I can't imagine why she thinks my support is important."

"Because everyone else in town loves you."

Sally snorted.

Unlike many aging high school football stars, including her ex-husband, James had kept his manly physique. He ran Harvey's men's department and dressed well. Women shopped at Harvey's in droves, lured by James's sex appeal or dreaming some of it would rub off on clothes they bought their husbands.

"Breakfast is right this way—bacon, eggs, biscuits. Or muffins." James batted his eyelashes at her, took her arm, and steered her down the street.

He was such a shameless flirt. Even Mary Lou fawned over him.

"Let's go to the West's Shop," Sally suggested.

"Well, it is apple muffin Monday," James quipped.

A nasty remark formed but she bit it back. James may be arrogant and his humor a tad sharp, but he was harmless. Besides, he was right.

"I've become predictable," she admitted.

"You gotta change your habits if you wanna keep ahead of Mary Lou."

Sally snarled. "I'm really tired of her hounding and threatening me."

"Threatening?" he asked as they crossed Main Street.

"She corners me and says, 'You'd better support me' in her own endearing way. Makes me think she's going to steal my school pencil box again."

"Come on, she's not all bad."

True. Mary Lou had helped her move into her apartment and never said a word about why Sally was back in town. She'd been a caring neighbor for one of their childhood friends with cancer and even led the church youth group.

Still, Sally couldn't muster any guilt for not supporting Mary Lou.

"She and her father invested in malls and let downtown go to pot," Sally said.

"Well, she ain't her daddy. For one thing, she pays better for your vote," James said as he waved at someone in a passing car. "Gave my neighbor thirty dollars."

"She gave someone money to vote for her! Said it plain . . . and out loud?"

"The color of voting is green around here," he said.

"Seriously!"

"Honey, I love it when your blue eyes catch fire." James held the coffee shop door open for her, and the smell of bacon wafted out. "Not only said it out loud, said she'd look in his face on Election Day and know if he earned his money. See, now your eyes are bugging out of your head."

"Did she bribe you too?"

James held a finger to her lips. "I wanna know, how could you grow up in Kentucky and not know about vote-buying?"

"Besides being illegal, it's stupid. How could Mary Lou—or anyone—know if the person they bribed actually went through with it?" Sally asked.

"She said she'd blame Brian personally if she lost," James confided.

"Are you telling me it's on the honor system?"

His laughter turned the heads of several women in the shop.

"Not always. My uncle lives in Clay County. Once he agreed to vote for a particular candidate for twenty dollars. A voting official peeked at his ballot and when he saw my uncle voted right, the guy gave him a ticket. My uncle took the ticket to campaign headquarters and got paid." James kept walking to a back booth.

Sally added naïve to her list of negative personal qualities.

"But why?"

"Oh, Sally, look around. Not everybody's a Nance. Most folks are uneducated and poor. They scrape to find a dollar." James waved to someone ahead. "This mayoral election could have a big turn out, what with Bush and Kerry running for president. That favors Mary Lou's opponent, John Robinson."

"John's doing a great job as interim mayor. He's already got a hotel looking at moving into downtown." Sally took the seat facing the back of the café. "I love John. We were in the high school band together."

The waitress handed them menus and held up a coffee pot.

Sally inhaled the scent of fresh coffee and nodded, "Yes, please. And an apple muffin."

"Same." James winced and shielded his face as the bell over the front door announced another diner customer. "It's Mary Lou."

Sally slid down in her seat, prompting James to chuckle.

"Boy, she scares you. People are gonna think Mary Lou's invincible if a Nance fears her." James shrugged. "Come on, she's not here. I was kiddin'."

Sally threw a wrapped pat of butter at him.

"I'm not scared of Mary Lou, I'm sick of her whole family. Her father wouldn't help Collin's Electrical Supply and people lost their jobs when it closed. Mary Lou's pushed me around since we were kids. Funny how those old feelings linger after you grow up."

"Maybe she'll lose," James suggested.

"She could win! She owns all the apartments in town," Sally said. "If the tenants vote for her that's a chunk of people. Imagine what those voters could mean in a close election."

They fell silent as their muffins arrived.

"Well, that explains why she's going door-to-door in each building." James blew across his coffee, then said, "And why she wants the Nance family behind her."

Sally scoffed, "They never listen to me."

"Hey, either give in to Mary Lou or be braver."

Sally signaled the waitress. "Coffee and an apple muffin to go, please."

"For you or the blind guy?" James polished off his muffin and licked his fingers. His nails looked clipped and trimmed as though he'd had a recent manicure—something Sally needed in the worst way. The realization that she'd let herself go while James worked on his appearance flew all over her.

"The 'blind guy' is Dennis Howard, a former army sergeant, who lives in the Veteran's Home across the river in Ohio. His wife and child died in the same car accident that cost him his sight," she snapped. "You should know him."

"Why?" James seemed truly puzzled. "You see his shoes? Weejuns. A piece of history."

"You go on," Sally said. "I'll wait for the takeout."

"Okay. Hey, cheer up. I think pudgy blonde cowards are sexy." James laid money on the table.

James's remark sizzled through her. Coward? Pudgy? She usually accepted James's needling as an entertaining distraction, but today it cut to the bone.

Not long ago Harvey's courtyard planters had sprouted flowers, and snappy-looking, white, wrought iron tables with green umbrellas had dotted the courtyard. The drug store on the opposite corner had a soda fountain counter right up until it closed two years ago.

Sally shook her head as she walked toward work and wished she could wave a magic wand over downtown. Over her own life.

"Good morning. Is that fresh coffee I smell?" Dennis turned toward Sally, though he never homed in on her location.

She'd stopped being surprised that he could tell who approached. Her footsteps or perfume must be distinctive. She held her paper bag out for him to see then felt stupid.

"And an apple muffin, Dennis. How are you this morning?"

His hand reached in the air in front of him several inches from the bag. She gently placed it against his hand.

"Thanks." One hand wandered across the tray table looking for something. "Mr. Madison walked by earlier. Don't you usually come in together?"

"I stayed until your breakfast came," she said.

"Quarrel?"

"I—I got up on the wrong side of the bed," she said.

"You don't need to take the blame if he was a jerk." Dennis unwrapped the muffin then asked the same question he asked everyone, "Whatta you think about the election?"

"I wish it was over." She resisted the urge to unbutton his red plaid shirt and button it correctly.

"That's all folks is talking about at the bus stop. Lots of folks on the bus today. Two of them took registration forms. Those forms usually gets folks to talking politics."

"Is that why you come here every morning—to register voters?"

"Na, I like talking to people about politics. Better than sittin' in my room all day," he said. "Folks around here say Mary Lou Kitchens has the inside track."

"She's a cheater!" Sally blurted out.

"Do tell," Dennis leaned forward slightly.

"She's offered money to people to vote for her," Sally fumed.

Dennis inclined his head. His long, sandy-colored hair, what she could see of it under a Cincinnati Reds baseball cap, curled around the edges of his hat. Drops of dried blood dotted his chin where he'd nicked himself shaving.

"I heard something about that. An old man with a bad cough told someone he 'weren't proud of it,' but she watched him vote absentee ballot for her—and he didn't much like it." Dennis polished off a big bite of muffin.

"Isn't that illegal?"

Dennis chortled, "Who's gonna turn her in?"

"And turn her in to whom?" Sally scoffed. "Her cousin is the police chief!"

"Problem of a small town—kin everywhere. How about the FB and I in Louisville?"

Sally laughed. "Like the FBI would listen to me."

"Well—"

She couldn't stand it any longer. "Your shirt is buttoned wrong. Let me show you."

Dennis chuckled as she took his hand then put his finger on the wrong buttons. His head swayed in a rhymical motion she'd noticed in other blind people, but he fixed the shirt.

"I mean, the FBI never listened to my father," she continued. "Besides, I don't have proof."

"You could be a witness when she bribes someone o-o-r call a meeting and see what people say. Maybe get a few to talk," Dennis suggested.

"No."

"Yeah, I get it." Dennis heaved a sigh. "Nobody volunteers. Kinda like the army."

Sally bristled. "Why do you care?"

"Don't." He eased back into his metal lawn chair. "My cousin takes me back to the Veteran's Home every night, no matter how this cookie crumbles."

"Somebody's got to do something."

"Politicians been doing dirt since the Lord made kings." Dennis rubbed his eyes under his dark glasses. "Ain't yours to fix, is it?"

Still, Dennis's words poked like a burr under her saddle all day. Sometime between selling a dress to her high school English teacher and helping a friend select a birthday gift, Sally decided she would ask around about Mary Lou.

Dennis had given her a clue about where to start—an old man who coughed a lot talked about the election. Must be a dozen men like that, but she only knew one who always used the same phrase about pride.

~

Sally's next-door neighbor, Thomas Prillaman, coughed, glanced at her sideways, and fiddled with his cane. The two of them sat in Sally's kitchen munching fresh chocolate chip cookies and enjoying the aroma of melted chocolate.

"Why would I tell the FBI that Mary Lou threatened to toss me out of my apartment if I didn't vote for her? She didn't say that," he said.

"What did she say then?" Sally pushed the plate of cookies across her kitchen table to him.

"You look like your Grandpa Nance right then—questionin' everything," Mr. Prillaman said. "Handled my case when the C&O Railroad tried to steal my land. Won too."

Thomas Prillaman had been a family friend for decades. Her grandfather had often talked about what guts it took for Thomas to sue a big company like the C&O.

"What did Mary Lou say?"

"Okay, okay, lemme recollect. She said, 'Thomas, I might renovate the building if I lose the election. You'd have to find a new place to live until the work was done. Then I'll be raising the rent. If I was the mayor, I'd be too busy for such things.' Somethin' like that."

"What! She redid this building two years ago!" Sally pointed to her kitchen sink with its new arching faucet and blue tile backsplash. The pale-yellow walls in her apartment had just lost that fresh-paint smell.

"She watched me when I marked my absentee ballot for her and sealed it," Thomas said.

Sally's jaw dropped.

"Don't look so surprised." Thomas reached for another cookie. "Her daddy did the same kindly thing."

"How could you let her do that!"

Thomas shrugged. "I ain't proud of it, but it don't matter in the long haul."

"If I write this story down, would you sign that it was true?" That was the lawyer in her. Sally heard herself, but didn't believe she was doing it. Why didn't she drop it like she did her law practice after the divorce? Like she'd dropped everything and run home.

Thomas must have had the same thought. "Whatta you want do a fool thing like that, Sally? Jest let it be. She could lose anyway."

The answer rippled through her like fire. "It isn't right."

The old man guffawed.

A knock made them jump. Sally rose and approached the door like it might burst into flames any minute.

"Who—who is it?"

"Oh, honey, it's me. Dolly from down the hall."

Sally sagged against the door and massaged her forehead. How was she going to unmask Mary Lou if a knock on her door nearly made her vomit in fear? Wait, when had this gone from asking questions to toppling Mary Lou's bid for mayor? Sally wiped her hands on her apron and opened the door to discover a woman in her twenties holding a smoking baking dish.

"Oh, hey, Mr. Prillaman," Dolly stared at Sally. "What's wrong? You look like I scared you out of a year's growth?"

"Oh, it's—"

"Mary Lou, isn't it? Like Jess across the hall." Dolly shut the door closed with her back foot. "That poor man won't answer his door for love nor money."

Sally glanced at the dish Dolly held between two potholders. "Is this a burnt offering to the Lord?"

"Not on purpose," Dolly said. "Can you help? My boyfriend's coming for dinner."

Mr. Prillaman rose as the women came into the kitchen and peered into the burned dish. "That ain't edible."

Tears pooled in Dolly's eyes.

"Well . . . let's see what we can come up with." Sally opened her refrigerator. "Hm-m. Mr. Prillaman, would you like to slice onions for Dolly's new dinner while I cut up some celery?"

"Nope. But write that story I told ya. I'll sign." He nodded to the women and hobbled out.

"What was that about?" Dolly asked.

"Oh, the election."

Dolly set the dish on the stove and dabbed her eyes. "Like I told Mary Lou—I don't vote. She and the plumber were in my apartment when I got home from work."

"Wish she'd fix my singing toilet," Sally muttered.

"Honey, it's the cheap washers in those potty handles. Anyway, the fella fixed it and left, then Mary Lou got awful pushy . . . and generous."

Early the next morning before work Sally knocked on Jess Christopher's door. She checked the hall and assured him she was alone. He let her in and chained the door behind her.

"Sally, I-I got yur money . . ."

She had known Jess since grade school. He graduated from Ashbury High a few years ahead of her, fell into alcoholism at college, recovered, and had a good job. But his job disappeared when the electrical supply company folded.

"I don't care about that, Jess."

"Come on in and set a spell before you go off to work," he said.

"Why is it dark in here?" she muttered as they walked through the living room to the kitchen.

"How's your dad?" Jess asked.

"Dad's good and ornery. You got a line on a new job?"

Jess motioned her to have a seat at the kitchen table and smiled, showing the gap between his two front teeth that made his s's whistle. "I gotta job in Louisville."

"I knew you'd catch on somewhere," Sally said. "Think you'll leave before the election?"

"If there's a God," Jess said.

A loud series of bam-bams on the front door made Jess's eyes go big. A woman called his name. He put on finger across his lips, "Sh-h-h."

"You behind in the rent?" Sally whispered when it seemed the visitor had left.

"No, thanks to you. Let's make that square." Jess moved to one of the mismatched cannisters on his kitchen counter. He opened it and took out some bills, which he handed to Sally.

"Mary Lou getting to you?" Sally folded the bills into her pants pocket without counting them.

"Told her last week I wasn't gonna vote at all," Jess said.

"Just to get her to leave you alone?" Sally asked.

Jess handed her a cup of coffee across the kitchen table, and sighed, "Ya know, it's a pure sin. I won't answer the door or turn on the living room lights for fear she'll show up."

"Do you want to vote?"

He shrugged. "Yeah—and I'd vote for John Robinson. As it stands, even if I'm in town I wouldn't go to the polls!"

"So, Mary Lou is keeping you from voting?"

"Her, her husband, and that woman who campaigns with her. They knock on the doors around here day in and day out. Makes me crazy. Haven't they come by to see you?" Jess took a swig of coffee, and the face he made showed how much he wished it were something else.

Energized and recharged by her discoveries, Sally remembered why she loved preparing for cases and interviewing witnesses. Why, she might even renew her subscription to *Lawyer Monthly*.

In two weeks, she had four signed statements from people saying Mary Lou had threatened or bribed them to vote for her. Other people hinted Mary Lou had offered them money but refused to say more.

Their stories floored Sally. She had no idea such corruption was going on under her nose—or that people would be so willing to talk about it.

Maybe . . . maybe she should resume the practice of law. Maybe start small with a few defense cases. She wondered what James would say about that idea.

As Sally left her bedroom for work on the Friday, she walked by the written statements she'd piled on her dresser next to her perfumes and felt proud for the first time since she moved home. When she thought about it, her husband's assault on her self-confidence no longer stung as it had.

Once she got those witness statement pages into FBI hands, she'd have accomplished something important for the first time in too long a time.

She was smiling as she flung open her apartment door. Mary Lou stood there poised to knock. Sally gasped.

"Hi there, sweetie! You've been busy. I've been trying to get ahold of you to get you to vote for me—and your mother, father, aunts and uncles too," Mary Lou said. "Election's Tuesday!"

"Mary Lou, I . . ." Dread drenched Sally. Did Mary Lou know what she'd been doing?

"You plan to vote, don'tcha?"

"Yes, but—" Sally began.

"Well, vote for me. You got a big family. Lots of votes. We don't see eye-to-eye on downtown, but I'm gonna increase the school budget and repair our sewer system."

"I-I'll think about it." That was the same answer she'd given when they were voting on Homecoming Queen. Which Mary Lou won.

"Let me know what you think, quick. I need to make plans," Mary Lou's tone sounded dark, and her lip curled on one side.

Sally froze.

Suddenly Mary Lou grinned and threw her arms open wide. "I'm wantin' to include you in my victory party! You know what they say, those who aren't for you are against you."

"I can't b-be late for work." Sally felt Mary Lou's eyes follow her as she locked her door and scurried down the stairs to the street.

At the coffee shop James dismissed her set-to with Mary Lou.

"Oh, you took all that wrong," he said. "I heard she's givin' $200 to the football team at homecoming tonight."

Sally forgot about returning to law practice.

"Besides," James continued, "why would she make trouble for you?"

"I've been asking about voter intimidation," Sally whispered.

James's eyes grew large. A man in the next booth cackled and slapped the tabletop at something his companion said. Sally flinched then told James what she'd done.

"She can't hurt me," she finished.

"Not that she'd want to, but maybe she hurts someone you care about?" James suggested.

Sally shrugged. "I don't have kids or a boyfriend, so . . ."

"Then forget it." James began prattling about the new mall movie theater. He acted like he'd never seen the splendor of the old downtown Paramount Theater, or cared that Mary Lou owned the mall theater.

"James, I've got to get Dennis's breakfast," she said at last.

"I'll wait with ya," he smiled.

If James dismissed how much Mary Lou's visit upset her, Dennis noticed something wrong right away. When Sally handed over his coffee and muffin, his head jerked.

"Your hands are cold. You okay? Or is my shirt buttoned wrong again?" One finger rubbed his blue-striped shirt front.

"You look fine," Sally said.

"Mary Lou?"

"Yeah, she came to see me this morning. I-I folded."

Dennis tilted his head. "Tell me."

When she finished, he said, "You know the difference between a defeat and a strategic retreat?"

She pursed her lips before she realized he couldn't see her disdain. Just as well.

"In the army," he continued, "a strategic retreat means you regroup and fight another day. Have a pencil."

He was right. She still had the weapons she needed to win this fight.

"Would you like to have dinner at my place tonight?" She asked suddenly. "I-I could drive you across the river to the Veteran's Home afterwards."

Dennis beamed. "That'd be real nice."

"I'll see you later. We'll walk to my place together and I'll fry chicken," she said.

After work she helped Dennis pack his things, then took his arm and turned him in the direction of the apartment. He held onto her forearm and used a white cane to guide his steps.

"I-I take my cues from you," he explained as they entered the apartment. "Kinda like dancin', only the girl leads. Nice place. Bright and cheery."

She stared. "How would you know?"

"Oh, ah, I-I can see flashes of light. A-and you seemed happier when we stepped inside. Geez, I shoulda brought a hostess gift—I was raised better," he stammered. "Uh, where's the washroom?"

"Down this little hall. First door on the right." She guided him to the hall. "If you get to the bedroom, you've gone too far."

His tapping cane made muffled noises on the carpet. Sally went into the kitchen, tied on her apron, and began pulling out the pots and pans.

After a few minutes she wondered what happened to Dennis. They collided as he came out of her bedroom. With a gasp, he grabbed her arms to stop her from falling.

"I-I got lost. Sorry." He spoke to the wall over her head, but didn't let go.

Suddenly she realized the pounding came from the front door, not her chest.

"Sally! Sally Warner!" Mary Lou bellowed.

Sally inhaled deeply as she went to the front door and cracked it open.

"How dare you go 'round telling people I'm bribin' voters and threatening voters!" Mary Lou stiff-armed the door.

"What-t?"

"Your father tried that horse manure with my daddy. Well, I'm gonna sue you for slander a-and libel!"

"Truth is a perfect defense." Where had that come from? Sally felt sick.

"What?" Mary Lou blinked.

"Plus, you haven't been harmed—yet. You'd have to show the court how you got hurt to win a lawsuit."

"Hello? Do we have company, Sally?" Dennis strode out of the hallway. He'd washed his face, wet his hair to comb it over, and was busy tucking in his shirt.

Mary Lou stared. "Oh-h. A boyfriend."

"He's—" Sally began.

Mary Lou's chuckle sounded almost demonic. Her slamming the apartment door vibrated the walls.

"U-h-h, what just happened?" Dennis asked.

Sally slumped on a nearby chair.

"Remember I mentioned Mary Lou's election cheating?" she said. "Well, somehow, she found out I'd talked to some of her victims. I'm cooked."

"Cooked? Nothing's cooked. I don't even smell somethin' frying," Dennis observed. He held out his hand. "If you tend to the chicken, I'll peel potatoes. Lead me to the sink, hand me potatoes and a peeler. Then tell me about her voter intimidation."

After taking Dennis back to the Veterans' Home, Sally fought the Friday night high school football traffic to get back to her apartment. Didn't seem that long ago she was in the student cheering section for that game. She didn't think of it until then, but what was Dennis doing in her bedroom instead of the bathroom? Was he really lost?

She turned on the bedside light and checked the contents of her jewelry box and the statements, which were on the nightstand by the novel she was reading. Everything looked fine. Foolish. She really was getting too distrustful of folks. Still, it was time for the professionals to take over. She would tell the FBI first thing Monday.

When she did call on Monday, it took a long time to connect to an FBI agent instead of a secretary. Then the man barely listened before he brushed her off.

~

Staring at what was probably Dennis's blood on the sidewalk two hours later, Sally wished the idiot at the FBI office was standing beside her.

A tan sedan braked at the curb to allow Mary Lou and two campaign workers to climb out. They set up a card table in the courtyard, decorated it with red, white, and blue balloons, then set out MARY LOU FOR MAYOR keychains.

"Nice place to meet and greet," Mary Lou observed as she unfurled an American flag to stick in a stand.

"Where's Dennis?" Sally demanded.

"Your boyfriend didn't have a business license," Mary Lou smirked.

"He's not my boy—what?" Sally's fingers grew numb.

"Put up a fight when the police removed him." Mary Lou rearranged a few keychains on her table.

"A blind man?"

"He's cute. Right, Sally?"

Mary Lou's campaign workers snickered and laughed. The city bus screeched to a stop, and the candidate rushed over to greet the passengers.

Heart in her throat, Sally hurried into the store and went directly to the employee breakroom. Fury raced through her and incinerated any cobwebs of fear and doubt.

Using the telephone on the counter, she dialed the city hospital. No Dennis, so she called the Veteran's Home.

"Who?" said a woman who answered the phone. "I'm new, but I don't see a Dennis Howard on our list of residents."

Sally described him.

"I know for sure we don't have any blind residents here. Is he in a Veteran's Home somewhere else? Hello?"

Sally stared at the telephone receiver in disbelief. When she finally glanced around, her eyes landed on a voter registration form that someone had wadded up and thrown in the trash. Suddenly, she remembered she hadn't left those witness statements on her night-stand near the novel. She'd left them on her dresser next to the perfume.

Had Mary Lou come into her apartment and seen them?

Rattled, she started to men's wear to brainstorm with James when she remembered something else. James was the only person she'd told about her voter intimidation investigation before Friday.

Sally took her betrayals deep into women's wear and retreated into the mindless rote of re-hanging clothes from the dressing rooms and unpacking boxes of new merchandise. By late afternoon she was hungry, cranky, and determined to find answers.

"I didn't bring a hostess gift the other night, but I have one now," said a voice behind her.

"Dennis!"

He wore a butterfly bandage across his right temple and both lips were swollen.

"Good God! What happened? No, wait—who are you?" she said.

He removed his dark glasses to reveal a shiner. "I'm not blind, or a pencil salesman."

"Really." The word dripped sarcasm.

"My father was blind, though." He reached into his gray sports coat and removed a wallet. "I'm an FBI Special Agent investigating allegations of voter intimidation."

"You should fire the idiotic FBI agent who answered my call this morning."

Dennis's grin was maddening.

"Sally, we had an operation underway and he couldn't say anything to you. FBI agents have spent the weekend talking to victims of voter intimidation. Knowing others have already come forward opened the floodgates. Walk with me."

He took her arm, and she was too startled to object.

"Did Mary Lou's policeman cousin do that to your face?" Sally asked.

Dennis shrugged. "Not personally."

"Okay then, how did you know about this voter intimidation in the first place?"

"A tip," Dennis said. "Speaking of that, I, uh, appreciate your tipping us off to people who would testify. I must have talked to a hundred people since I got to town—and nothing."

The light bulb came on in her head. "A tip? Is that what we're calling snooping in my bedroom?"

"Now that was an accident, a fortunate one. I try to keep my eyes closed when I'm acting blind, so I missed the bathroom door. I literally fell against the witness statements on your dresser," Dennis said. "When I realized what they were, I took them to the nightstand where the light was better and ran out of time to put them back."

"Uh-huh."

"God's truth." Dennis held up two fingers as though reciting the Boy Scout pledge. "Until then I didn't know you were investigating voter intimidation too. That took courage. Then you told me all about it over a delicious dinner. I-I was honored."

"You used me!" She tried to shake off his arm.

"Wait a minute," Dennis guided her into the elevator. "Didn't you call the FBI to report what you'd learned? Where's the foul?"

Okay, he had a point. Sally still fumed.

When they reached the main floor two men joined them, and all four exited the store. Once on the sidewalk Dennis pulled Sally to the side.

In the courtyard Mary Lou and one campaign worker had buttonholed a hapless voter. A chilly breeze danced with the American flag as the other campaign worker tried to keep papers from flying off the table. Mary Lou never saw the FBI agents until they arrested her in front of God and everybody. The campaign workers gaped, and the voter fled. Mary Lou shrieked for a lawyer while the agents stuffed her into a waiting car.

It happened so fast. Sally watched in wonder.

Dennis cleared his throat. "Thank you for dinner, Sally. And, well, everything else."

Sally grinned. Over Dennis's shoulder she noticed the empty drug store cattycorner from Harvey's. Nice storefront, nice wide space with shelving. Perfect for a law office.

CITY MOURNS SLAIN POL, CHICAGO STYLE

DAVID HAGERTY

City Mourns Slain Pol, Chicago Style
March 5, 1963
by Mark Rica
Chicago Daily News columnist

EVERYONE TURNED out for the funeral. They overflowed the Galilee Missionary Baptist Church on Chicago's far West Side, thousands of them spilling into the streets, including politicians, businessmen, police, and family. Each silently pondered the same question: "Who killed Ben Lewis?"

Compared to a generation ago, when bootleggers and gangsters controlled this city, it's uncommon for an alderman to die violently now, and many people still looked shocked. I shared their surprise, so I watched the proceedings from the rear of the sanctuary, where I could see all the mourners and listen closely to their tributes.

Leading them up the aisle came the pallbearers, including the five remaining Negro aldermen on the city council. Lewis was the best known of them, a rising political player in a city ruled by the Boys from Bridgeport. The Irish machine has controlled all the Cook County democrats for decades, but few as firmly as The Silent Six, who always voted as they were told, knowing this is the way things work in the City that Works.

Following them came Lewis's only child, Joan, a school teacher, and his widow, Ella. They filed past the open casket for a final look at the nearly departed, then around the dozens of bouquets that filled the pulpit. Compared to the rest, they looked composed, even resigned, as though they already understood his unexplained death.

As the pews filled, accompanied by organ music and the competing perfumes of flowers, I watched the other celebrants, who fidgeted against the stony chill of the sanctuary, for evidence or insight.

First to the dais came Ald. Reginald Coates, who recalled that Lewis's family had moved up from Georgia when he was little, part of the Great Migration that brought so many Negroes to this city. As a young man, Lewis worked hard to support his own wife and child, taking jobs as an elevator operator, city housing inspector, and CTA bus driver. He prided himself on being a loyal father, husband, and party member.

Officer Shea O'Malley, who guarded the rear door from the thousands left outside, shook his head as Coates completed this eulogy. The beat cop stood out among the mourners, with his blue dress uniform, red hair, and freckled face. I could see why they'd chosen him as bouncer—he could intimidate with just a look. Since he patrolled the ward, I asked what he knew about the deceased.

"Dat guy was a pathological skirt chaser," said O'Malley, in the charming brogue of this city.

"You know this for a fact?" I said, with deliberate naiveté.

"He had a different broad for every night of da week," said O'Malley, swaying on his flat feet. "Even made a play for 'Shakey Tom' Anderson's wife. What kind of guy goes after a hoodlum's girl?"

"You think that's who killed him?" I said.

"Most likely," said the cop. "Some mug probably found out and took umbrage."

I could imagine the alderman as a lady's man. He radiated style and charm, quick with a joke and a proposition. He trailed cigarette smoke like an aphrodisiac. Still, as I watched his widow, who looked dignified dressed in a black fur coat and black fur Cossack hat against the foggy chill of winter, I wondered what she knew of his reputation.

Next to testify was Sal Goldsworth, a longtime precinct captain in the 24th and holdout from the days when whites dominated the ward. Goldsworth paid tribute to Lewis's entrepreneurial activities. After serving in the army during World War II, he returned to his hometown to start a real estate and insurance business. These became profitable enterprises in their own right and, as is often the case in city politics, grew in proportion with Lewis's political influence. Wise constituents knew the way to approach an alderman was through his accountant.

The mourners nodded silently at this tribute to the American dream, which was represented by two banners on the stage, the stars and bars of the US flag, and its close imitator, the City of Chicago's, which held equal influence in the eyes of most locals.

Nearby, though, I noticed another local businessman frown at the comment, so I eased through the crowd to his side. I knew him as JoJo, owner of a local rental office that had leased apartments in Lawndale for thirty-seven years. Although he too had risen to prosperity, paint speckled his forearms and scars dotted his knuckles. He nodded as I nudged his elbow, already aware of my presence.

"You did business with him?" I asked.

JoJo nodded again.

"Profitable?"

He glanced to my reporter's notebook, so I pocketed it in my sport coat.

"He owed money to everyone in the area," said JoJo.

"For?"

"Unpaid insurance premiums, overdo rents."

I shook my head at the scandal of it—a politician not paying his debts!—and asked why people would continue transacting with such a rapscallion.

"Clout," he said, invoking the local term for influence. "If you wanted to play in this ward, you had to play with him."

"You think that could have motivated somebody to shoot him?"

JoJo took in the huge turnout for the funeral and shrugged.

The Rev. J.D. Strong rose next to the lectern, attired in the flowing black robes of his profession. With a booming voice that rose to the balconies, he quoted Timothy II, "I have fought a good fight, I have finished the course, I have kept the faith."

The reverend might have invoked the many mementos at the office where Lewis was found dead, all testifying to his industry: a shovel, said to be from his first job with the WPA, and an autographed photo of President John F. Kennedy, who the city's machine helped to get elected. He also might have extolled Lewis's charitable work with the local youth, including those who joined other political factions, youth groups such as the Egyptian Cobras and the Viceroys.

Instead, he compared Lewis to John the Baptist. "Even the righteous can get killed," explained the reverend.

The audience members all nodded in solidarity, their black clothing unifying them.

But standing at the back, I saw a figure who did not nod nor smile, a tall, well-built, white man in a charcoal-gray suit. Based on his outfit and demeanor, I pegged him as a witness from our federal government, specifically its investigative branch, the college athlete type favored by J. Edgar Hoover, so I moved in close enough to smell the starch on his collar.

"What's the FBI's interest in this?" I said.

He stared straight ahead as though he hadn't heard me, but he spoke to the question. "We take an interest in any suspicious deaths."

"What's suspicious about a politician getting killed in the city of Chicago," I said. "Not so long ago, it happened all the time." One local newspaper dubbed Lewis's death "Return of the Rubout."

The G-man straightened at this prod and shot his shirt cuffs but did not reply.

"You mean the method of his demise . . ." I said. The alderman was found in his office handcuffed, face down on the floor, a cigarette clutched between his fingers, and three bullets in the back of his head. "You think it was a hit?"

Again the FBI man bristled at the rough language of our city. "We're investigating a variety of explanations."

"Including the Outfit?" I said.

Almost imperceptibly, he shrugged.

"Why would the mob care about an alderman from a ward of poor Negros?" I asked innocently. In fact, the 24th had the highest unemployment rate (officially) and the highest percentage of people on relief in the city.

"His lifestyle exceeded his salary," said the FBI man, modestly.

I glanced toward the open casket, where Lewis lay in a fine wool two-button. His tall, slim figure often appeared about town in $200 suits, driving a Buick Wildcat sport coupe. He dined at fine restaurants and golfed at private clubs. He liked being called "Big Cat" and the "Duke of Dixieland." All on an alderman's $8,000 annual allowance.

"You're suggesting the deceased was involved in something illegal?"

Again, the FBI man stiffened. "The policy racket is well established in this ward, and presumed to be managed by Mr. Giancana."

I nodded at this revelation, which was no secret on the West Side, even to the patrolmen empowered to stop it. Momo Salvatore "Sam" Giancana has run Chicago's Outfit and all its operations for half a dozen years, including the policy racket, better known as the numbers lottery, which generated large profits for his organization and payoffs to the police.

Lewis could not have remained ignorant to it after being raised and schooled in the "Bloody" 20th Ward, which has been controlled by the city's crime syndicate since the days of Al Capone. That the alderman might have become unwittingly involved in such activities should have shocked no one, but only the FBI man dared to invoke it at his requiem.

Before I could ask for clarification, the star of the show mounted the stage, none other than the boss himself, Richard J. Daley. Although he was not listed on the program, the mayor would not have missed such an occasion. He frequented funerals of the great and small, paying final tribute to friends and foes alike. I wondered which camp Lewis occupied.

Despite being short and jowly, with a glowering visage, and an inelegant grasp on the English language, the mayor inspires great loyalty from voters and aldermen. He well understands Machiavelli's maxim "it is better to be feared than loved," and has adapted it to include corruption, election fraud, and patronage.

The mayor himself had contributed to Lewis's rapid rise in the West Side political structure, where he became the 24th ward's first Black precinct captain, its first Black alderman, and finally its first Black committeeman. To those unfamiliar with the ways of city hall, this last is most significant, because it gave Lewis not only a seat at the table, but also a plate to serve up the feast of patronage jobs and favors that sate voters.

Daley concluded that the alderman "gave everything he had" to the people of the 24th—the highest praise that could be heaped upon a mere cog in his machine.

A few patrons in the crowd nodded at the tribute, but most sat still and silent, as the boss preferred from his supplicants.

Nearby I saw another local, a barber from the ward who'd kept Lewis's hair short and neat. However, when I asked him about the mayor's tribute, he replied "Shh!" in a hiss loud enough to chide the whole crowd. Since his shop usually acted as the newsstand of the neighborhood, I asked again for a polite quote I could put in the paper. "We don't talk about that," he said nervously.

"Why?" I said.

But he walked away as quickly as his clacking heels would carry him while the other mourners eyed me with fear, despite a dozen police officers patrolling the aisles.

After such various recollections, my notebook overflowed with quotes, almost too many to occupy a single article. What I thought would be a simple obituary was turning into an autopsy. As explanation for a violent death, I had the cops saying a jealous husband did it, the FBI hinting at mob connections, his business partners alleging fraud, and his friends too afraid to talk. At the same time, I'd heard tributes to him as a dutiful father, husband, and businessman.

I waited until the bearers had removed the body, the final notes of "I've Done My Work" had sounded, and the congregants had adjourned to the dank chill of the street. As they prepared to follow him one last time, I drifted toward Lewis's personal assistant.

Like his boss, Gene Dobbs cut a dashing figure in a slim-cut black suit, crisp white shirt, and a large gold watch. A thin mustache dressed his lip, and his gray hair clung close to his scalp. He'd worked in Chicago politics since Lewis wore short pants, and thus could interpret the subtext better than anyone.

"I've heard a lot of speculation about why someone would kill an alderman," I said. "What have you heard?"

The other man shook his head and looked over the crowd, which included an honor guard of 125 police and firemen from the city. "He tried to rise too far too fast," Dobbs said.

"Meaning?"

Dobbs cupped his hands against the damp to light a cigarette, invoking the tobacco earthiness of the Old South. "Back when Ben first moved here, Jews ran this neighborhood," Dobbs said. "His was one of the first Negro families to settle here, and not a welcome addition. He used to say 'I learned to run before I could walk.'

"By the time he joined the party, whites were already fleeing to the suburbs, but they kept a hand in the ward. Didn't matter that eighty percent of the voters were Blacks. Lewis may have held the office, but the Donkey Club held the power."

"Plantation politics," I said.

"An objectionable term for it, but yes."

"Surely he knew how things worked," I said. "All aldermen do as they're told, or they don't do at all."

"Ben had bigger ambitions," Dobbs said, and nodded vaguely to the east.

I looked up the street, which displayed boarded-up store fronts and cars missing their hubcaps. I thought he meant such blight until I recalled that US Rep. Thomas O'Brien, age eighty-three, was nearing the end of his final term on this earth. "Lewis wanted to run for Congress?" I said.

Dobbs nodded solemnly. "He told me, 'I'm counting my chits.' "

The only other Black man from the state of Illinois to rise so high was Bill Dawson, a party loyalist who worked quietly for change. Compared to him, Lewis appeared not just flashy but defiant. And Lewis hated Dawson. "So you think his death was . . ."

"A message," Dobbs said. "A warning not to forget your slave roots."

"He rarely spoke out against the party."

Dobbs nodded. "He wanted a share of the power. He was appointing our people as precinct captains and demanding more patronage jobs for them from city hall. Some folks called him cocky and braggadocious. They wanted to control him, but he wouldn't be controlled."

"The machine has more subtle ways to control its partisans."

"Nothing subtle about killing a man two days after he's reelected," Dobbs said.

I imagined Lewis in his final hour, receiving a late-night visit at his office on Roosevelt Boulevard, named after another loyal Democrat, F.D.R. I imagined him smoking his final cigarette with his killers —who he undoubtedly knew—as drunks passed below, trailing the scent of beer and the call of insatiable thirst. I wondered what he thought as the assassins applied the handcuffs and asked him to lie face down on the floor. Did he know what awaited him? Did he worry about staining his good suit? Did he wonder which sin had brought him to this fate? Or did he believe that, like so many times before, he could escape with charm? Did he believe, as they placed a pillow overtop his head, that at age fifty-three, his ambition had caught up to him?

"The police are looking for a jealous husband . . . " I said to Dobbs.

"So they don't have to investigate the real killers."

Unconventionally, they had let reporters photograph the body only hours after his death, almost as though they wanted witnesses to document the crime scene.

"You don't think his business associates were to blame?" I said.

"Many people want you to believe it so," he said, and glanced toward the FBI man.

"He was known to associate with gangsters and racketeers."

Dobbs watched the crowd as though expecting to find J. Edgar Hoover eavesdropping. "They may have had a hand," he said. "They may have. But not without the go ahead from the organization that truly runs this town."

"Meaning the machine?"

He nodded solemnly.

"You think they'd kill one of their own?"

He turned toward me with grim resolve. "That is the essence of an assassination."

I thanked him for his input, none of which I dared to repeat in such company, and merged with the other mourners as they flowed through the streets in a flood of grief. Among them I saw several other reporters also seeking explanations. Although we rarely shared notes, I moved next to one from the *Chicago Champion*, the voice of the city's underclass, which helped convince many of the race to move up from the South.

"You think we'll ever know who did it?" I asked him.

He merely shook his head. "Nobody wants that story told."

Epilogue: Ben Lewis was the last politician murdered in Chicago. His killing remains unsolved.

JOEY CUCUZZA LOSES HIS ELECTION

THOMAS PLUCK

JOEY CUCUZZA DIDN'T WANT to shoot the guy, but he didn't get a vote on it.

They were parked in a remote section of Newark's Weequahic park, between the jogging paths and the cemetery. Nowhere to run. The shot from his Baby Beretta would crackle off the autumn-painted trees, and some dog walker would find the body once it got ripe.

If someone had seen him beckon the young man out of the massage parlor and into his electric blue Alfa Romeo sedan, they wouldn't talk. Not in that neighborhood. Not if they liked their families on this side of the grave.

As the partner of a mob captain, Joey walked a fine line. It gave him great privilege and power, but also caged him in ways a citizen could never conceive. Such as having to ice a dumb masseur who'd given a happy ending to the capo of the juiciest slice of northern New Jersey, so he couldn't flap his gums that the boss—a high school foot-ball hero gone to seed, a real swinging dick, a man's man—was not only bisexual, but a power bottom.

The young guy barely said a word. Joey wasn't sure he spoke English. But you could rat in any language.

Joey had said no to the handy offered by his own masseuse. He'd chosen the chestiest of the women to keep his appetite from distracting him, because he never got a rubdown without a few tokes off the pinch-hitter pipe that he kept in the car. But Aldo Quattrocchi, the best-earning capo of the Mastino crime family, and his partner of eight years, was not one to restrict his appetites.

So the massage therapist was fertilizer. He just didn't know it yet.

From the look on his face, it looked like he thought Joey wanted a taste of what Aldo got.

Joey could see why Aldo had gone weak in the balls over the guy. He was built like a young Bruce Lee. Ripped, athletic. Joey was no slouch himself, for fifty-five. He hit the gym every day, unlike Aldo, who preferred to hit Hobby's delicatessen for a pastrami, Jimmy Buff's for an Italian hot dog, or Fiore's for a chicken parm with fresh mozzarella. A big Italian bear.

That was Joey's type. The massage therapist was as far from that as possible. Petite, nearly twinkish—and guessing—mostly hairless. But he could probably outrun him, so the best way to kill him was while he was occupied. With his pants down, or his mouth full. So he couldn't scream.

Joey walked him to a shady spot in the trees away from the road, and tried not to think about it.

Aldo had needed the release of a good massage and fucking because of the election coming up. After that sfachim Chris Christie, who had screwed over the mob's offshore online poker empire by legalizing gambling, the leadership had taken extreme care in vetting future candidates at all levels. The mayor of Newark was usually a lock. Whatever party won, they had to play ball, unless they wanted a garbage strike or the snowplows to start breaking down during a blizzard. Even if they went out and shoveled their neighbor's steps like Cory Booker had.

"He's one of us," Aldo had said about him. "You should be happy. You care about that shit."

By "one of us," Aldo meant that he thought Booker was gay, because he wasn't married, got pedicures, and had a stereotypical mannerism. But Joey had the better gaydar, and had hit on enough big, sweet hotties like Booker only to find out they were just nebbishes who wanted a girl who was just like mom, and would stay single until they found her.

By "that shit," Aldo meant that Joey followed politics beyond who they had to bribe to keep their slice of protection, prostitution, and smuggling through the port. It gave Joey agita, but he followed the news.

He hadn't for the longest time, having become cynical after seeing how cheaply many politicians could be bought. But after his niece Nicky got interested in his old computer and the records she found in his Ma's attic, they started hanging out, and she never stopped with climate change this, voting rights that, and white privilege vaffanculo!

For a while, he humored her. Then he played devil's advocate, to see if she would quit. But she never did. She quoted sources, scrolling on her phone. Busting his balls like a kickboxer with a Ramones haircut and a goth wardrobe. Half the time she dressed like Lady Gaga, and the other half like Johnny Ramone. Sometimes both at the same time.

Joey got that. He'd known he was gay after the first time he woke up from a wet dream. But in the clubs, he'd played around with his identity, after dealing coke to Club Kids and drag queens alike. And it wasn't the drugs that made him do it. It was the freedom he'd never had growing up. His father didn't kick him out, but he beat the shit out of him, to toughen him up for "the life he chose," as his old man called it.

Now Joey presented the sharkskin-suited persona of a rangy light-heavyweight, a pantomime he'd come to enjoy. When a ruthless mob fixer wears a hot-pink shirt under his jacket, even the crassest homophobes don't say shit. Not when his street name is "the Big Cucuzza."

Cucuzza is a pale green squash the size and shape of a baseball bat, comical in nature, where Joey was nothing but.

On the street, Joey Cucuzza was said to be hung as long as the eight-inch Sicilian stiletto he carried. And was also said to keep a rusty, iron sash weight from an old style windowsill to break bones and crack skulls when diplomacy didn't work on a hardhead, a cappadose.

Neither were true—he was above average in size, and the sash weight was merely a prop. He left the physical work to the gorillas on their payroll. From experience, Joey found that personal violence was like any other drug: it left you with bills to pay. Some psychological, some at the dry cleaners.

Or maybe his niece was making him soft. He had to keep his phone silent now, because of her. He caught up on her texts, with the phone under the table.

She was a vegetarian, and he nearly found himself arguing with Aldo about ordering the osso bucco at their outside table at Regina Margherita. But some things were sacred.

But there was nothing sacred, or arguable, about who would be a better mayor of Newark for the Mastino crime family in the next election. Brick City was as hard as the bricks from which it got its nickname, and brooked little idealism. But the two candidates had polarized people.

Including him and Aldo.

The incumbent mayor was a progressive firebrand who wanted to continue the police reforms that had brought peace to the city, and improvements like the lead water pipe replacements that had been completed three times as fast as predicted.

But the police reforms had come at a cost. They hurt their business.

Because the police weren't busy stopping cars in the poorer neighborhoods to fill quotas, shaking down kids for "furtive movements," and chasing homeless sleepers from under bridges near the train station, they now had time to keep an eye on the port, where their interest was not wanted.

The port operated day and night, and a lot of money was made by workers who took double shifts, often with the assistance of pharmaceuticals. As dock boss, Aldo was paid for every hour that anyone was working at the shipping terminal. And Joey, as hiring manager, kept the shifts spread out so overtime was made, and Aldo was paid OT for twenty-four hours a day.

But when your employees got pulled over for driving sleepy, because their man couldn't deliver speed and nose candy, it had a domino effect. And it was hitting him and Aldo in the pocket book. Their traditional revenue streams of protection, prostitution, and pharmaceuticals all required kick-up to the bosses, and could often fluctuate, with collection. The port paycheck was all gravy, and this was the first time in Joey's memory that they'd taken a hit.

"Raimondo Torres is better for the union," Aldo said, eating a tender piece of veal. "Which means he's better for us."

"In the short run," Joey said, poking at his mushroom risotto. "In the long run, he'll feed us to the rats, and smile while he does it."

Torres was a former cop running on a hard-on-crime ticket. Not that crime was bad, but with crumbling infrastructure, a paucity of jobs outside the gig economy, and rising rents, people were angry, and wanted someone to blame. Torres took advantage of that, pushing the "family values" line that appealed to the older, church-going constituents, but he only valued a certain type of family.

He'd made his name as a coach, collecting a school salary along with his cop pension, and going after trans kids on the opposing teams. Right-wing news made him a mainstay, and after he resigned rather than coach a trans kid at his own school, the usual suspects made a hero out of him.

Torres was running as a Republican, so the union couldn't openly support him without raising the ire of the Essex County machine. But there were other ways to get him elected.

"You tell the crew, no overtime if the eggplant gets reelected. They'll spread the word. The leadership might support him, but the working man don't."

Joey saw something on his phone screen that made him clutch his spoon like it was the stiletto in his suit jacket pocket.

"Calm down, babe," Aldo said. "It's business. You like going to Capri, don't you? Sometimes we gotta eat shit."

Joey nodded, without a word. Aldo always voted green, and that didn't mean Green Party.

"I'm pragmatic, and you vote with your heart," Aldo said.

Joey thought he was the pragmatic one. You could always make money, long term. Short term gains that cost you to fight hard-fought battles again weren't worth it.

"Don't go behind my back on this. Didn't I take care of those two citrullos at the coin show? That wasn't free. They were paying customers."

They had also been Nazis. Joey knew that he'd have to pay for that, sometime. This was that time.

Joey drove down Route 21 fast, and the Ramones on the stereo made fun of Reagan. After the original Ramones all died, he'd read that Johnny, the guitarist, was a hard-line conservative who stole the singer's girlfriend and thus inspired Joey Ramone to write "The KKK Took My Baby Away." He wondered how they held it together, with dueling songs like "Bonzo Goes to Bitburg" and "Too Tough to Die."

People might say the same about why he and Aldo were together.

Joey might eat shit for the job—the job had done him well—but he'd be damned if his niece was going to eat it, when he could do something about it.

He's Here was all that she'd texted, and that was enough.

Nicky wasn't trans, she'd said, but that didn't stop the other kids from teasing her, and the kids who were. And the rise of Raimondo Torres had made things a lot worse for them all.

Nicky's school was one of the best in the city, the same one Joey had gone to. There was a police cruiser in the parking lot, and a couple of black SUVs with "Vote Torres" signage. He left the stiletto and Beretta in the car.

The school administrator told him that candidate Torres was speaking to the children in the auditorium. "Your niece, uh . . . caused a disturbance. We let her take study hall instead. I can have the school officer take you to her."

"Thank you, I'll find her."

He found Nicky in the quad, hugging her knees under a tree.

He sat down next to her. The grass would stain his suit, but that dry cleaning bill he could handle.

"What did my little hell-raiser do?" He gave her an admonishing glance, but his eyes showed pride.

"We booed him. And when the principal had us taken out, I yelled that Torres was an ignorant bigot who was only brave enough to attack little kids."

"Can't argue with that."

She stared straight ahead. "They chant his name at us, now. They know the teachers won't do anything, in case he's elected."

No threat Joey made to them could top what Torres could do as mayor. The local teacher's union supported the incumbent, but the last thing they wanted was attention from Torres and his supporters putting them in the news.

But the parents of the bullies, they could be leaned on. They had jobs, businesses, and homes in his territory.

"There's got to be a ringleader. Let me help."

"Help how?"

"I could talk to them."

"Like you did to that guy on the phone?"

She'd been in the car when he'd straightened someone out, and he'd had to explain how his job was essentially acting as a referee and diplomat, so people with anger management issues didn't kill each other, or get themselves killed for being a cappadose. Sometimes that meant listening to them vent until they accepted reality, other times it meant playing middleman between two hardheads so they made *him* the bad guy instead of each other—as a made guy, he was untouchable, so killing him was out of the question—and sometimes, well, it meant brandishing the Big Cucuzza.

Not literally swinging the iron sash weight that he kept in the trunk of the Alfa, but making them think about what it would do to their fingers and toes.

But more often, it was swinging the figurative Cucuzza: not even voicing the threat, but letting your target think about what a connected guy could do to their business, career, or family life if he applied the appropriate amount of pressure.

Like your garbage not being picked up for a couple of weeks. A minor annoyance at first, until it started to stink. And the health inspector came around. Or a truck parked in front of your driveway or loading dock, and mysteriously, the police and towing were busy when you called. Or that delivery you were expecting? The truck broke down. And then it was stolen. What bad luck. They'd heard the nightmares, and didn't want them happening to them.

"Not exactly like that. But sometimes people need to know there are consequences for their actions."

She rocked back and forth, her Chuck Taylors digging in the dirt. She was more Ramone today. "I don't want you doing that for me."

"Why, you getting too old for your uncle to help you out?"

"No, Uncle Joey." She rolled her eyes. "Because it's wrong."

"And what this stronzo Torres does is right? Don't give me that 'they go low, we go high' bullshit. In a fight, they go low, and you go high? They hit you right where it hurts."

She shook her head, as if to rattle out the crap he'd dumped in her ears. "Just don't do it, okay? Promise."

"All right, I promise. But these little shits lay a hand on you, all bets are off. Their parents are gonna fall down some stairs."

"They know better than that. The bullies know their way around zero tolerance." She rested the back of her head on his knee, and looked up through the branches. "Remember what I said about wanting comfort, not advice? This is one of those times."

He sat quietly and let her talk until the bell rang for next period.

"You gonna be all right?"

"Will you come to Nonna's on Sunday and play Demon Attack?"

"Only if you let her put bracciole in the sauce this time."

She hugged him hard, and he kissed the top of her head.

After she hit the doors, he double timed it to the parking lot, against the flow of teenage salmon getting to class. He was a head taller than most of them, but he felt vulnerable, like he had when he was their age. He felt relieved when he made it to the parking lot. But he had guessed right. The cruiser and SUVs were still there. They would wait until the next class started to escort Torres out to his truck.

He lit a cigarette from a rose-gold case, and waited.

He hadn't promised Nickie that he wouldn't talk to Torres himself.

He fiddled with his phone. He'd been using the thing a lot more since Nicky got him remembering how he'd used to program his Atari. They had all the old games on the phone now. And a lot of other things.

Joey had become a stickler of the no-phones rule at meetings now, which made him the bad guy to silverback capos who liked their Facebook and Candy Crush.

Torres strutted out with his entourage, which included a YouTuber shouldering a Steadicam rig with an iPhone bobbing at the end, which Torres gesticulated at while ranting about teachers indoctrinating children. His police escort looked starstruck.

When Torres was finished jabbering, Joey pocketed his phone and flicked his cigarette under the police cruiser.

"Mister Torres, a word?"

The officer moved to block him before Torres waved him off.

"I'm a representative of the stevedore's union." Joey showed his Waterfront card. Everyone who worked on the port had one.

"I thought you guys always went Democrat."

"We like your stance on crime. A word in private, if I may? My superiors would like to talk, but like you said, it would be inexpedient to do so publicly." Joey flashed his shark smile.

Recognition bloomed. "I got a minute for Joe Cucuzza."

The officer frisked him, to earn his OT.

Torres led him to a hill by the library. Behind it, a red brick church peeked through the trees. "I went to school here, class of '89. This is where we settled our differences."

"I was four years ahead of you. Church Hill. That's how we called you out."

"Church Hill," Torres said. "I haven't thought about that in years. But you didn't come here to talk about that, did you, Guido?"

Ah. So that's how it was gonna be.

"No, Do-Re-Mi, I did not." Joey used Torres's nickname on the force, because his hand was always open for dough.

Torres bared smoker's teeth. "If you think I'm dumb enough to take an envelope from a goombah on the campaign trail, you're wasting your time. You guys made your bed with the county machine. Why should I even talk to you?"

Joey let him dig himself a hole. The fool didn't even consider that he had the stevedore vote locked. Zero street sense. The smart beat cops learned that the Italian crews were pro-police because the cops hassled their competition. "And yet, here we are. The dark money from the Koch brothers dry up?"

Nicky had told him where Torres got his financing.

"What, you think anyone cares about that? They're afraid of freaks like you in their schools, maricon." Torres winked, like Joey's orientation was secret knowledge.

It wasn't, but Aldo's was.

"Why you think I'm staying visible? I ain't going off alone with you. Nice try, fag."

"Don't flatter yourself. The management wanted me to talk some sense into you, to ask that you not break the peace. It's bad for business. And we know you took money then, and you'll take money now."

"Well, you tell them, in their language, vaffanculo." Torres made the Italian salute. His crew couldn't hear what they were saying, but they saw the gesture and cheered. "But you'd like that, wouldn't you? Up the ass. I got the police union, the Port Authority, and the churches. Crawl back home and tell your bosses I don't need the guinea vote. You better get used to kissing my ass, because I'm gonna be mayor of this shithole."

Torres walked back to his crew, making a face for the camera.

Joey slunk back to his car, to make them think they'd won.

The massage therapist didn't run, and Joey was glad for that. But when they found a nice shady spot for afternoon delight, or a murder, he didn't drop to his knees, either.

"I know who you are," he said, turning slowly. The young man's accent was gone. "You have nothing to worry about from me."

Joey cocked the Beretta in his pocket. He'd hate to ruin a set of bespoke trousers. He drew it out. "On your knees."

The guy thought about running. Joey was glad when he didn't. The guy sank to his knees easily. Joey backed up, out of lunging range. "So, who am I?"

"You're the Big Cucuzza."

"And?"

"I'm Kyle."

"Kyle, in the car you acted like you were fresh off the boat."

"I know. But your, uh, boss? He assumed I couldn't speak English, and I played along. He liked it better that way."

Yeah, Aldo would.

"It's unfortunate that you know who he is, Kyle. Do you understand?"

"What was I supposed to do? He handed me a bankroll thicker than what you're rumored to be packing in those Italian wool trousers. I've got student loans. Why else would I be working a side hustle at a sex parlor?"

Kyle had been squeezed. Like the poor bastards that Nicky didn't want her uncle squeezing. You couldn't say no, and when you said yes, it was just as bad. Damned either way.

"Go back a bit. Why don't I have anything to worry about?"

"Duh?" Kyle sighed like Joey was stupider than a box of cocks. Like Nicky had begun to do. Young people. He nearly shot him in old-man exasperation.

"Kid, you're not helping yourself here."

"Because you're gay? I mean, you're like a street hero. Everyone knows which way the Cucuzza swings. It would be like me ratting out John Waters."

Point for Kyle, for knowing who John Waters was.

"I appreciate your respect, but there are people who will do things to you, much worse than I can do with this," he wagged the Baby Beretta, keeping the barrel aimed at Kyle's torso. "They'll make you betray us. You won't want to, right before you die, but you will. Trust me, I've seen it."

They had a plastic shredder at the port. Hanging above that, hoping they'd get to go home with their remaining stumps, even the toughest would say anything.

"Well, shit. How am I supposed to get out of this, Mister C?"

Joey's finger tightened on the trigger. Crack crack crack. Two more in the head. Then toss the gun in the lake, dry clean the suit, hit the gym and the shower, and pop a few pills so Kyle didn't haunt him in his sleep. Tomorrow there'd be another problem to deal with, and Kyle would be forgotten, until the next massage.

But Nicky's words dug at him. Wrong. What was wrong, in this world? She always said every choice mattered. He couldn't leave the life, but he had choices.

"You been to California, Kyle?"

"I told you I have student loans. I'm lucky if I get to Brooklyn."

Provincetown was closer, but he and Aldo went there when they were supposed to be deep-sea fishing. If Aldo saw the guy waiting tables, there'd be hell to pay. San Francisco, though. Aldo would never go back there, after he stepped in human shit on the sidewalk and threw out a pair of eight-hundred-dollar loafers.

"You wanna live in San Fran a while? Few years, maybe?"

"Fuck yes, Mister C."

"Give me your license."

Kyle rolled his eyes. He took out a stack of cards and bills held together with a rubber band, and tossed an expired Rutgers student ID card at Joey's feet.

His name really was Kyle. Joey pocketed the ID, and the gun.

"Get up. Unless you're feeling curious about my street name."

Kyle blushed.

Back in the car, Joey gave him the glove-box money he kept for fixing problems. It would hurt to replace. But it would go a long way, even in SF.

"The Castro, Kyle. I mean, it's cliché, but it's our place. No question. You'll live in Oakland, probably. With roommates. But you'll have a hell of a better time living there. Maybe you'll find a sugar daddy to pay off those loans. If Aldo was single, he sure would." He kneaded the back of Kyle's neck. Maybe he nudged him down, but Joey preferred to think what came next was born of gratitude.

Back outside the massage parlor, he took a photo of Kyle's ID with his phone. "You come back to visit home, I'll know."

Kyle kissed him on the cheek. "Why would I come back here? That scumbag Torres is gonna be mayor." He ran back inside.

Joey thumbed his phone from the tinted-window solitude of his Alfa Romeo. He played back the sound clip of Torres that he'd recorded.

Aldo hated the slur "guinea" most of all. If he still wanted to vote green after hearing that, Joey would play it to all the Italians on the docks. They'd go with their hearts, not their green.

The real gem was Torres calling their home town of Newark a shithole. The city was tough, but it had its pride. And Torres lived in the suburbs. Joey didn't know where to upload the clip for the best results, but Nicky would.

He hit send.

Fuck Capri.

VIOLENT CHOICES

KATHARINA GERLACH

MILAN SHIFTED UNEASILY in the chair with the curved back, although it was the softest one he'd ever sat on. The reason he was there without his superior's knowledge made it impossible to sit still. He had to see the prime minister. He was the only one who could stop the folly his comrades in arms were planning—not that he liked Archduke Franz Ferdinand, but this was going too far.

Still, he hated being the one who had to report. If only his superior, Rade Malobabić, was in his place. After all, Rade was the Serbian Military Intelligence's chief undercover operative, but Milan knew he could order his tombstone if Rade learned about him being here.

The splendor of the Serbian prime minister's antechamber made him feel uncomfortable. Wooden panels covered the walls, expensive paintings with golden frames and busts of famous Serbs seemed to dull the light that streamed through the window. He'd seen all this before whenever he and Rade had been here for one of their infrequent reports. But today the busts seemed to stare at him accusingly, implying that whatever was coming was his fault.

How Milan longed to be free of his duty, but every detail of the room made it clear that he'd never be able to shake the shackles he forged himself. How he wished he'd never enlisted thirty years back, but in 1884 he'd been a young hothead ready to serve his land whatever the cost. He'd changed since then.

"Sir, Prime Minister Pašić is now free." The servant held the door open, and Milan got up, pulling his hat deeper over his face. If his comrades in arms of the Black Hand figured out that he was a government spy, he was a dead man. More than that, his death would be extremely painful. Since only the leaders of the Black Hand knew exactly who belonged to the secret organization, he had to be careful.

For the unlikely chance that the servant was a member, he lowered his head and walked past him, obscuring as much of his face as possible. Only when the servant had closed the door behind him did he take off his hat and look up.

He knew the massive writing desk that dominated the room filled with overflowing bookshelves well, but the man behind it had become a stranger the moment he'd been elected prime minister. He was more now than the comrade in arms he'd been when they were younger and fighting against the erstwhile Serbian king.

"Milan." The prime minister nodded but didn't get up to greet him. "Why did you come? I expected a written report by you or Malobabić."

"Malobabić is getting out of hand, Nikola. He's enjoying the things the Black Hand is planning. He even organized bombs. Six bombs!" To this day he hadn't been able to shake the memory of the boy who bled to death in his arms during an assassination attempt a couple of years ago. He'd only participated to rise in the ranks of the Black Hand, and that event changed him. He'd sworn to himself to make sure no innocent would ever be hurt again if he could help it, so he forged ahead with his request.

"You must intervene before it's too late," he said.

"Rade Malobabić has just made his way to the top of the Black Hand. His information is far too valuable. I can't order him out yet." The prime minister rubbed his beard.

"He probably wouldn't obey anyway." Milan's shoulders sagged.

He slumped in the chair facing the prime minister's desk. "Still, we can't let him go through with his current plan."

"Should I know about it?" Nikola asked.

Milan and the prime minister went way back, but hardly anyone knew anything about their connection, which was just as it was meant to be. The Black Hand was far too dangerous an organization. They might get it in their heads to not only kill Milan as a government spy but also Nikola Pašić, one of the few levelheaded politicians trying to ease political tensions between the Serbs and the Austro–Hungarian monarchy.

Milan shivered when he remembered the reactions of his so-called friends when Austria annexed Bosnia. "The Black Hand plans the assassination of the Emperor's heir. They've found three youngsters, full of zest and ready to die for what they believe is right. Rade is delighted, and he ordered me to train them."

"And you did, I presume." Nikola kept his tone carefully neutral.

"If I hadn't, I'd not be sitting here." The two men were silent for a while.

"What do you expect me to do, Milan." Nikola got up and began to pace. "I told the Austrian ambassador that it's not a good idea to end the maneuver on the national anniversary of the biggest battle against the Ottoman Empire, 525 years ago, but he wouldn't listen.

"And when a friend of mine in Vienna managed to get an Austrian official to mention the possibility of an attack to the archduke, Franz Ferdinand said that he wouldn't be placed under a glass dome. He knows his family always faces death and is prepared to trust God. If the archduke himself refuses to listen to common sense there's fairly little I can do."

Milan sighed. "You need to tell him exactly what's going on. In the last few days, they've established a second cell with three people plus a go-between, seven people in total. Although the second cell won't be involved directly, they're there to distract the populace long enough for the true assassins to do their deed."

"I can't reveal that much, and you know exactly why." Nikola pushed his receding hairline back, a gesture so familiar to Milan he wanted to cry. Why on God's green earth had he agreed to infiltrate the secret network of the Black Hand as a spy if what he found out wasn't helping to prevent an assassination attempt that endangered innocent Serbs?

"It can't be that bad." But Milan knew it was. If Nikola reported all the facts to an Austrian official, his fellow Serbs would consider him a traitor, which meant certain death—and Nikola had family. And if he kept his knowledge to himself, allowing the Black Hand's plan to unfold, they were surely facing a war.

"Can't you simply arrest the leaders of the Black Hand for treason?" Milan slipped forward on his chair. "Rade was supposed to hand in a list with their names. I know he wrote it up last night."

"It would have been an elegant solution, but he hasn't done that yet." Nikola was still watching the park and river behind the government building. Well kept lawns and sculpted trees in a soothing green along the banks did nothing to ease the tension in the room.

Milan sighed. "Can you at least arrange my withdrawal from the service?" With his hope shattered, all he could do was leave. Travel to places where he didn't have to witness the result of the plans he'd been forced to assist.

Nikola shook his head. "I'm sorry but I need you to keep an eye on Rade."

Milan felt his shoulders sag. "Isn't there a way to alert Austrian authorities it in a roundabout way?"

"I'll see what I can do. Our ambassador will be meeting the Austrian minister of finance soon. And Biliński is known as a level-headed fellow." Nikola folded his hands behind his back and stared out of the window at the river Miljacka. It sparkled in the sun, throwing highlights at the three-story houses on the other bank of the waterfront. His voice sounded wistful. "It's so deceptively peaceful. I wish we lived in better times."

So do I, Milan thought. Since he could achieve nothing by staying, he got up and left. His old friend never turned.

≈

Normally Jovan Jovanović loved his job as ambassador, even though he was rarely welcome in Vienna. The pay was exceptional, his residency was luxurious, and Vienna was nearly as beautiful as Sarajevo, his favorite town on earth.

The sun was a little too warm, but a breeze from the Danube eased any bodily discomfort he might have had. Still, his heart was heavy. The letter he carried in his breast pocket, hand-delivered to him personally this morning, burdened him and made it impossible to enjoy the short drive with his private coach to the ministry of finances. How could Prime Minister Pašić expect him to breach a subject so delicate without knowing at least a few details. It was exasperating.

However, the minister had made it clear that the information had to reach the Austrian government. As much as Jovan despised the archduke, he feared for his homeland. Sure, their men, especially the young, were all good fighters and would do their best to protect his beloved homeland, but the Serbian army was small compared to the combined Austro–Hungarian forces. They only had a chance if the tsar helped. With Russia's support, Slavia's brave young men could defeat the empire's army. But the tsar faced his own problems, so Jovan wasn't sure he'd keep his promise.

With a knot in his belly, he climbed the stairs to the ministry and walked along the corridors toward the minister's office. If only the Heir Apparent had agreed to meet him personally. He didn't like to rely on an intermediary. At least Biliński was levelheaded. Maybe it was possible to convince him to talk Franz Ferdinand out of the visit. It was Serbia's only chance.

As always, the reception was friendly and jovial. Biliński was one of the few politicians who made Jovan feel welcome. For a while they talked about the usual financial affairs, but after their second cup of coffee, they relaxed into small talk.

With his heart beating like a steam engine, Jovan approached the subject. "Surely you are aware that the day you set for the end of your summer maneuver falls on a national holiday in Serbia?" He tried hard to make it sound like a question, not an accusation.

"Naturally." Biliński smiled and offered him a cigar. "Archduke Ferdinand's visit will emphasize the normalization of the strained relationship between our countries."

"Some people might see it that way." Jovan swallowed. His throat felt parched. "I just fear that many more will take it as an affront. Some of the young men are rather rash, these days."

"Aren't they everywhere? They are so filled with storm and stress." The minister puffed a smoke curl. "We are well aware of potential dangers and will ensure the safety of the Heir Apparent."

"Sir, I do not suggest something shouted in words, but rather fired from a barrel." Jovan wondered if he had gone too far. This was pretty much the whole information Prime Minister Pašić had given him. It had to be enough to set the Austrians on high alert.

But Biliński laughed. "Let's hope it won't come to that."

"Won't you warn his Highness?" Jovan's thoughts raced. If a direct warning didn't help, what else could he say?

"Why should I? Unless we learn details about a specific threat . . . " Biliński shrugged.

Jovan's hands grew cold. He forced a smile and changed the subject. He'd done his best. If he pressed the matter, the Austrians might assume the Serbs knew more, and that just wouldn't do. At the moment they could truthfully insist they had known nothing specific should Franz Ferdinand be hurt. Until then, Jovan would burn the letter from his breast pocket and return to being the polite Serb ambassador he'd always been.

Milan leaned against a tree at the rim of a forest outside of Sarajevo. It wasn't as beautiful here as it had been in Topčider Park in Belgrade where he had secretly trained the combatants, but the setting sun sparkled on the city's wet roofs, and the soil smelled musky from the rain. It reminded him of his childhood home.

How can it be so wonderful here, when we're planning an assassination that will demand more than the life of the intended target? By the end of tomorrow, at least three young Bosnian lives will be forfeit, and who knows how many bystanders will suffer. Once more the face of the dying boy surfaced in his memory. He pushed it aside, his trembling hand wandering to the bag with the 'material' on his belt.

There was absolutely nothing he could do. If only he had the list of names Rade should have handed in. With it, he might at least get his own skin out of this mess in one piece.

"Are you sure they've learned to shoot well enough?" He asked Rade Malobabić. "Čabrinović hasn't managed to hit the target very often."

The Serb shrugged. "He'll get one of the bombs. An idiot can work those."

"I still think it's a waste to have three young men go to their certain deaths." Milan folded his arms in front of his chest. "Two of them could have been used on other targets. That way we'd have maximal exposure."

"If this goes as planned, we'll get more exposure than you can ever imagine, my friend," Rade grinned, showing yellowed teeth.

He always reminded Milan of a pike. Before he could answer, three dark shapes appeared in the distance, walking toward them. The forest was far enough from the city, and they'd chosen a hidden cluster of trees that wasn't even frequented by the local populace, so the three could only be the young men they awaited.

He shivered as he contemplated their deaths. This whole operation was a mess right from the start. If they'd settled on a trained marksman with a long-range gun, who could take out the Austrian heir with a single shot from a distance, Milan would have been the first to volunteer. But the fact that they were going to use bombs set him on edge. Forcing his face into a neutral mask, he watched the young men approach. Soon he recognized their faces.

Still, Rade requested the password when they were close enough to be heard. A lanky boy, Milan knew to be nineteen, rattled down the required response.

"Welcome, friends." Rade smiled again, but Milan noticed how cold his eyes were. "We will now determine who will get what kind of weapon. My friend, Milan, here will examine your shooting skills and then I'll distribute the weapons."

The next half hour, Milan was too busy determining if the inexperienced youngsters could handle a handgun without killing themselves to think about a way to stop the assassination attempt. At the end, it was fairly clear that Gavrilo Princip was the most decent shot of the three. Milan handed him the best of the handguns. "You'll have to get as close as possible," he said. "These guns aren't precision instruments. They've been designed to create as much havoc as possible at short range."

"I'm prepared to die." Eagerness flashed in Gavrilo's eyes. "No guard will stop me, no girl will sway me from my chosen path."

Milan squirmed inside. The child hadn't learned to value life yet, and now it was too late for that. If only the prime minister had acted when asked. Now, Milan had to force himself to play his role well. After all, he wasn't prepared to die yet. "Make sure you're only aiming at the designated target."

"The archduke will accompany me in death."

Gavrilo looked to a tiny bottle with a transparent liquid in it that Rade showed him and the others.

"This is cyanide. Death will be fast." When the three took one bottle each, Rade's smile became even more predatory, as if he was looking forward to the end of the youngsters.

Milan thought the man had always been too obsessed with death, but kept silent.

"We will take it without hesitation."

The three young men put their hands on their chests. To Milan they looked like schoolboys eager to please a teacher. What a waste.

Rade took the bag Milan had brought and handed him the newspaper that had been wrapped around the bottles. "Double check the archduke's travel plans. They should be on page three. It's fortunate for us that they broadcast the route. It'll make things so much easier."

He handed out the guns, and six old military bombs, while Milan read their target's travel plans out loud.

When he was done, Rade wiped his hands on his jacket and announced, "We'll meet with team two near Delicatessen Schiller at eight tomorrow morning. That's on the banks of the Miljacka. The Heir Apparent will arrive at the train station of the tobacco factory by nine thirty, which will give us enough time to find suitable places." Another grin. "If you can't get away easily, use the cyanide. We cannot allow anyone to get caught."

The boys nodded silently. Patting each other's shoulders, they said their farewells and left.

"Did you know the archduke's wife is coming along?" Milan frowned at the headline of yesterday's newspaper. "The Duchess might get in the way."

Rade shook his head. "Remember how she's always kept out of official representation? The Emperor doesn't consider her noble enough for his Heir Apparent. He even forbade her husband's siblings to attend the wedding."

"The news says she'll be traveling with her husband." Milan folded the paper and shoved it into the now empty bag. "We're not waging war on women. Maybe we should call the boys back."

"And lose our best chance? I don't think so." Rade looked furious. "Ferdinand won't endanger the mother of his children. She'll be safely tucked into a car with her maid or one of the dignitaries."

"If you say so." Milan withdrew. It didn't do to make Rade suspicious. After all he needed to visit him in his hideout to see if he could discover the list of names his superior had made. Hopefully Rade hadn't burned it. Milan vowed to himself that he'd see the prime minister one more time, whether he found the names or not. Maybe Nikola could at least increase security in a way that'd make it impossible for the young men to get close enough to the procession.

~

Nedeljko Čabrinović's heart thundered, threatening to burst out of his chest with pride. Finally he was able to do something for his native country. His fingers stroked the rough surface of the bomb he was hiding under the coat he'd hung over his arm.

It was a warm day, so no one wondered about him wearing the coat like that. It had seemed less conspicuous to him than a bag, but his arm grew weary already. Hopefully the convoy would come soon. He longed to be the one to end Austria's tyranny.

He scanned the crowd on the other side of the river, but his comrade was nowhere to be seen. He smiled. After all, being invisible until the last moment was the whole point.

Cheering erupted in the distance, carried along by the wind that always prevailed near the river. Nedeljko wiped his free hand on his trouser leg. Not much longer. He forced himself to breathe slowly while he strained to see the convoy.

The first automobile was approaching the Ćumurija bridge, and he could see that all cars had their convertible tops down. How fortunate for him. If he could lob his bomb into the car's foot space, no one would be able to get it out in time.

There were six cars. Now he only needed to find out which was used by the Heir Apparent.

Suddenly his fingers grew cold. A policeman walked past the onlookers, eyeing everyone with a frown. Nedeljko checked the coat on his arm once more. No, the bomb wasn't visible. Still, sweat broke out under his arms. He tried to smile when the policeman's gaze found him. The frown deepened. *Oh dear, I need to do something or he'll get suspicious.* Nedeljko's thoughts raced. What could he do? Then, he remembered the saying, attack is the best form of defense.

"Please, officer, could you tell me which car his Majesty will be traveling in?" He tried to look as innocent as possible. "I promised my mother to describe every detail to her this afternoon, so I'd like to look at him as long as possible."

The policeman chuckled, and his face relaxed. "In that case you'd want to focus on the second car, lad."

"Thank you, sir." Nedeljko watched him walk on. A wave of relief washed through him, and his knees grew weak. He leaned against the pole of a lantern next to him, turned, and watched the convoy's approach.

The cars were going slowly. Too many people crowded the sidewalks. Nedeljko's gaze clung to the second vehicle. He dismissed the driver and copilot as well as the man sitting with his back to him as unimportant. His field of vision shrunk until it held nothing but the round face of the Heir Apparent.

The man's mustache with the twirled ends jiggled as he talked to a woman at his side, but she wasn't important either.

For a second, Nedeljko wondered why his comrade at the other end of the bridge hadn't started shooting yet, but he pushed the thought aside. Maybe he hadn't been able to figure out which car to shoot at.

Nedeljko considered himself lucky. He nudged the bomb against the lamppost. The safety ripped off and the timer began to tick. He'd set it at a few seconds. With practiced ease, he hurled the small bomb toward the approaching car.

To his horror, the driver must have noticed the projectile. He accelerated. The car jerked forward.

Franz Ferdinand lifted his arm, as if to protect the woman beside him. Well, that wouldn't help him against the bomb.

Nedeljko dropped his coat, pulled the small flask from his trouser pocket, swallowed the cyanide without hesitation, and jumped over the bridge's balustrade. Before he hit the water, the bomb went off.

Panicked screams erupted above him, then the cool water embraced him. Unfortunately his feet hit the river bottom immediately. There wasn't enough water in the river to carry him away as he had planned.

He moaned, noticing a couple of men hurrying down the bank.

His stomach twisted with gut wrenching pain. *No*, he thought trying desperately to keep the poison down. *No, no, no!*

He vomited, and vomited, and vomited. When strong hands grabbed him and blows rained down on him, his consciousness drifted off.

~

Some time before, Milan had paced impatiently on the train's platform near the tobacco station. He was furious that the prime minister had refused to receive him last night. Now all he could do was to warn the Heir Apparent directly—if he was able to get close enough, he still had a chance. He swore under his breath. Never in his life had he expected to be forced to save the life of an enemy.

The train arrived in a cloud of smoke and steam, spitting out so many people that Milan was pressed against a wall. Before he could work his way through the crowd, the archduke and his wife had been welcomed and swept away by some officials. Milan swore some more, drawing irritated looks. He didn't care.

As fast as he could, he ran to his pushbike, sat on it, and pedaled. The convoy would travel slowly along the river's bank. He might just have enough time to stop the assassins. It would blow his cover for sure, but he couldn't allow this to go on. Too many innocents would suffer. Also Serbia wasn't strong enough to win a war against Austria–Hungary, not even if the tsar sent weapons as he'd promised.

He pedaled harder. A headwind dried the sweat on his forehead. Soon he saw the crowds on the banks. Avoiding the roads close to the river, he made it to the Ćumurija bridge where the first assassin was stationed. Dropping the bike carelessly, he hurried toward the bridge, when a shadow stepped from the doorway of a building.

Rade pointed a pistol at his chest, which stopped Milan in his tracks.

"Guess what?" Rade said. "Last night, Ilić, remember the go-between, told me he'd seen you enter the prime minister's private house right after you left my place. Imagine my surprise. I worried you got this," he patted the pocket of his jacket and grinned wolfishly, "but you didn't find it, did you? Traitor."

Milan knew what was coming. The Black Hand never accepted excuses. If someone was suspected of treason there was only one way they dealt with it. And Rade loved this kind of punishment, as was evident by his gloating face. Milan didn't bother explaining. He attacked, ignoring the bullet from the pistol. Fortunately it missed. Rade should have waited until he got closer. The missed shot gave him the chance he needed. His fist connected with Rade's jaw, sending the man sprawling. Milan grabbed the gun, bent down to pull the list he'd so desperately searched for from Rade's breast pocket, retrieved the small bag with powder and bullets, and ran on. The bridge wasn't far. If he shot one of the boys, sad as it would be, the police would react and whisk off the archduke and his wife.

He ran like he'd never run before. His chest hurt with every breath he took. Already he could see the sparkling of the river through the gap between the houses. A crowd of cheering people blocked his way, but he pushed through nonetheless. Where were the boys? He looked around frantically, pushing past complaining citizens, gun at the ready but hidden under his vest. It wouldn't do to start a panic. There! Nedeljko! He surged forward when the young man's throwing motion told him all he needed to know. Too late!

Panting heavily, he stopped and watched the small, black object. His whole body turned to ice. He stared open-mouthed at the bomb flying through the air at a snail's pace. It hit Archduke Ferdinand's raised arm, bounced, and rolled over the folded convertible top.

"Down!" Milan shouted, but the crowd's cheering drowned out his voice.

BOOM!

The detonation turned the merry crowd into a mass of panic-stricken individuals, all trying to get out of the way as fast as possible. Milan noticed policemen dragging an unconscious Nedeljko from the river, protecting him from furious civilians.

Tears rolled down Milan's face as he surveyed the carnage the bomb had caused. The third car of the convoy lay twisted and broken on its side, people inside were crying and wailing. All around him, wounded men and women stirred. At least fifteen innocent bystanders had been injured. He cursed.

When one of the policemen glanced his way, he turned and shuffled away as if he had been taken by the same surprise as everyone else. *Thank God*, he thought, *the duchess is safe.*

Without raising suspicion he reached the place where he had left his bicycle, and found that it, as well as Rade Malobabić, were gone.

Franz Ferdinand was furious. How could someone dare to throw a bomb at them? He still felt the sore spot on his arm where it had hit him.

The minute they arrived at the town hall, he stormed up the stairs to the mayor and interrupted his carefully planned speech. "Mr. Mayor, I came here on a visit, and I am greeted with bombs. It is outrageous."

He meant to go on, but Sophie tugged at his sleeve. He bent down to her, listening intently as she whispered.

"Darling, remember you're the Emperor's heir. What will people think if you let quick anger rule you?"

She was right. Ferdinand breathed deeply, straightened, and allowed the mayor to continue with his speech. He even managed to give his own speech, although he had to wait for the rest of the convoy to arrive to do so. Only then did he insist on visiting the wounded members of the convoy in the hospital.

"We would seem heartless if we kept to the planned schedule without regard for those who suffered," he said.

Naturally his request was met with disapproval by those responsible for his safety, but in the end, he got his way. The Bosnian governor suggested a different route to the hospital to avoid the crowds and any potentially lingering assassin, and soon they were on their way.

Franz Ferdinand squeezed his wife's hand, knowing they were doing the right thing.

Gavrilo Princip stared into a cup of coffee he'd ordered in the nearest coffeehouse to avoid capture. His fingers clenched around the cyanide bottle. Should he? He looked around for pursuers, discovered none, and forced himself to relax his fingers. Maybe no one knew yet that he was involved. He might still be able to get away to regroup for another try. He was still young, there would be plenty of opportunities to help his country.

Not far from him, the window of Delicatessen Schiller reflected the sun. Glancing at his watch, Gavrilo realized that barely an hour had passed since his friend had thrown the bomb, been captured, and nearly been lynched by an angry mob.

He wondered if that wouldn't have been preferable to being captured by the police. *The idiot should have taken the cyanide,* he thought. Two ambulances drove past, but Gavrilo didn't waste a thought at the injured inside. He pulled out his purse to pay, when a black car stopped in the middle of the road.

"Turn back to the quay," the front-seat passenger said, and pointed.

Gavrilo's eyes widened as he recognized the passengers in the backseat. The tyrant and his wife! Was this to be his lucky day after all?

Suddenly, his heart pounded so loud it drowned out the street's noises, the honking of the car as pedestrians hindered its turning, and the wailing of ambulances in the distance.

He got up, pulled the gun from the front pocket of his best suit and the bottle with cyanide from his trouser pocket, and stepped into the road as close to the car as he could.

All he saw was the tyrant with his impressive mustache with the twirled ends. His moment of glory had come. Why then were his lips so dry?

He swallowed and pointed his gun at the Heir Apparent. The archduke's dark eyes widened as he realized what was going to happen.

Gavrilo pulled the trigger. The backlash of the gun made him stagger.

Blood appeared on the archduke's throat.

Drat. He'd aimed for the heart.

He pulled the trigger again.

The duchess screamed and clutched her belly.

"Sopherl, Sopherl!" The archduke's voice rattled. "Don't die! Live for our children!"

Gavrilo froze, and his throat went dry. He hadn't meant to shoot the duchess. He took a step back.

The car accelerated and sped away. Everything had happened so fast no one realized what he'd done until an enraged voice screamed, "He's murdered the archduke!"

Angry people turned toward him. Before anyone could grab him, though, he downed the cyanide. All of a sudden, everything ceased to be important. He'd done what he'd come to do. His country would be proud of him. He didn't resist when hard hands grabbed him.

And then, vomiting cramps shook his body, making it impossible to raise his gun to his temple.

In the evening, Milan found Rade on the banks of the river Miljacka, in the poorest part of the town. Not that he really wanted to see his ex-superior, but the prime minister had considered this the only way to get the Black Hand off Milan's back. Rade was burning papers in a metal bin.

When he noticed Milan, he sneered. "All your meddling came to nothing. The tyrant is dead." He reached for the gun in his coat on the ground.

"Keep your hands where I can see them." Milan pointed his own gun at his superior's head, and Rade froze. "Yes, the tyrant is dead. As is his wife. And Serbia will now face a war that'll be damned hard to win if the tsar doesn't sent the promised troops." Milan's blood boiled and the finger on the trigger twitched. "Our men are arrested on flimsy claims. Most of them are facing death. I should shoot you like the rabid dog you are."

"No one can connect the Serbian government with the assassination." Rade beamed, a mad glint in his eyes, and pointed at the fire. "Why, do you think, I'm burning these. Now, hand me the list you stole, and we'll both get out of this with no one the wiser. I'm still your superior."

"You make me sick, Rade." But Milan hadn't come to execute his opponent. That would be the duty of others if the court decided to hang or shoot him.

"Why are you here then?" Rade pulled a cigar from his vest pocket. He lighted it, waiting for Milan's answer.

Milan smiled and felt like a wolf grinning at its prey. "As much as I dislike it, the police are coming for you. They're not far behind me."

"You're warning me?" Rade's eyebrows rose. "Despite our disagreement?"

"Well, you know my name and whereabouts. If they catch you, I'll be hanging too." Milan put a finger to his lips. "Did you hear that?"

The thumping rhythm of marching boots rang through the evening.

"Shit." Rade kicked the metal bin. It toppled into the river. Burning flakes of paper floated and landed on the waves but most of the fire was extinguished by the water.

"Rade Malobabić and Milan Ciganović, you are arrested for murder and treason." The voice came from the top of the bank, where it was too dark to see.

Milan fired a shot, knowing full well that there would be no one he could accidentally hurt. Nikola had arranged the apparent arrest too well.

Shots were fired from the bank, but all of them missed the two men that were now huddling behind some bins and a little driftwood. Sand fountained around them.

Milan's hands shook, although he knew that the men shooting at them had been ordered to miss. What if one of them didn't obey the command?

"To the river," he whispered to Rade. "It's too dark for them to see us there."

Rade nodded, sent a couple of shots to the top of the bank and ran. Milan followed him. More shots sent sand fountains into the air.

"Aaaargh," Milan screamed and bit down hard on the small bladder of pig's blood he'd hidden in his cheek. He moved forward, pretending to stumble, and collapsed at the water's rim.

Rade turned for a second. His eyes widened when he noticed the blood. He turned and ran as Milan turned his eyes until the white showed and closed them. He could hear Rade splash in the water. Without a doubt he wouldn't be coming back to rescue Milan, regardless the fact they'd been comrades in arms for so many years.

The men on the bank kept shooting a while longer, then they swarmed down the bank, grabbed his arms and legs, and carried him off. He only opened his eyes after they'd dumped him in the rear of a delivery coach. Making sure no one could see him from the outside, he sat up and turned to the only other occupant.

"All went well, Nikola."

"I hope he'll inform the Black Hand of your death." The prime minister handed him a towel, a clean shirt, and a dry coat. "As far as the Serbian Military Intelligence is concerned, you've never existed."

"Good. The list is in the secret compartment under my bed." Milan slipped out of his wet clothes and began to dry himself. "I'll leave the country for a while. France is said to be wonderful at this time of the year."

"I don't know." The prime minister's voice sounded worried. "With alliances the way they are, and a war more or less unavoidable, you might not find it as relaxing as you think."

"It'll be over in a blink and then I can come home." Milan smiled. "Or I'll go to the Americas. No war has ever pulled America into it."

Neither of the two could know how wrong those words were.

GREEN IS GOOD

STEPHEN BUEHLER

IT DOESN'T HAPPEN OFTEN, hell, maybe every five years, but four con men sat around a table in a greasy diner telling tales about the grifting life.

"I walked away $25,000 richer," Skinny Lester said.

"That's not much," Hands Howard said. "I've made more than that running a three-card-monte over a weekend."

Skinny was peeved. "$25,000 may not seem like a big score, but it's the right amount to take from a wealthy mark, I'll tell you. It's not high enough to break their bank and not enough so they feel they need to report it. If social media finds out he'll be branded as a loser. It's better to keep his mouth shut and write off the loss."

"I rarely work on a long con," said Hands. "I don't have the patience to hustle the same client day after day. I like to meet my mark and take their money all in one sitting. How 'bout you, Devon? You know a lot of people in our line of work." After speaking, Hands shoveled a big hunk of flapjack in his small mouth.

Devon did know. His uncle and cousin worked the con along with his father, Nick Townson, a short-con artist and legend among grifters. Never been caught. Devon had just completed a big score, but decided to tell the story of a friend who pulled off a successful con but didn't make any money.

"Okay," Devon said. "You guys know Rick Rogers, right?"

One nod and two shrugs.

"He ran a long game that I would never have the balls to pull off. He was at the end, ready to take the mark's money. He needed one more convincer. Some big business tycoon named Jonathan Smyth."

"Those contacts lenses are amazing," said Jonathan Smyth, standing behind his massive desk. He looked excited, like he saw a genie appear from a magic lamp. Except this wasn't magic, it was science. But not really.

"Go ahead, ask me another one," Rick Rogers said, planted in front of that giant desk.

The old businessman thought for a moment. "Okay. What's the speed of light?"

Rick's eyes danced back and forth several times. "299,792 kilometers per second through the vacuum of empty space. In the US, we'd say, 186,282 miles per second." Rick smiled, proud of himself. But not really.

To check for accuracy, Smyth hit a few keystrokes on his keyboard. "Right as rain." He leaned back into his chair. "Have a pair of magic lenses for me? I want to try."

"Even if I had another set of Oculus Detectors, it takes a week of training to learn how to use them properly," Rick said. "When you do, you can access the internet, pay for purchases, and even watch movies like you had a computer screen in front of you by moving your eyes like they're a mouse. Click it with a blink. These contact lenses are about to revolutionize the tech industry. To think you thought about investing in pharmaceuticals. This," Rick pointed to his eyes, "is the future."

Of course, Jonathan Smyth didn't know that Rick wasn't getting information from the Oculus Detectors. The con man had an assistant in the next room whispering answers through Rick's virtually undetectable micro earpiece.

"I've always wanted to invest in the future," said Smyth. "I'd give you more than $200,000 if you'd allow it." He smugly placed a briefcase on the desk. "Go ahead, check it out."

"No, that's okay, I believe it's all here," Rick said, lifting the briefcase up.

Smyth put his hand on top of Rick's. "Please, I insist."

That's the moment Rick sensed something wasn't right. Immediately, he shifted on his feet, ready to run.

"I'll show you," the businessman said, breaking Rick's tight hold on the handle. The old man's wrinkled fingers pushed the latches outward, and the lid popped open.

The other thing to pop open was the office door as four men in plain dark suits poured in. One of them pushed a woman in her twenties with her hands cuffed behind her back. Carrie, Rick's new associate, the one with the microphone to his earpiece. She searched Rick's face. Was this part of the plan? Rick usually had a backup plan.

Rick shook his head. He was pissed. He had ignored telltale signs, like how Jonathan Smyth seemed too eager to buy into Rick's scheme, and the fact that the mark didn't try to barter for a bigger cut. Rick had never been caught perpetrating a con.

One lawman pulled out an FBI badge. Held it in front of Rick's eyes for three seconds before shoving it back into his breast pocket. This guy's suit needed pressing and Rick thought he saw a mustard stain on the collar.

"I'm Special Agent Haskell," he said, his breath tinged with something sweet, like orange juice. He motioned with his chin. "Get everyone out of this room, except for Mr. Rogers. We're going to have some one-on-one time."

Rick studied the man's face. Haskell didn't smile, he didn't grin, he didn't grimace. Even with all that, Rick knew this guy was nervous. About what?

Before going through the door, Smyth stopped. "I hope they throw the book at you," he spat at Rick. "You think you can fool me? You're the idiot. The money these days is in drugs not some sci-fi invention you tried to peddle to me."

"Out," Haskell yelled.

With Smyth out the door, the FBI agent sat in the throne Jonathan Smyth called his desk chair.

"You're good at what you do, aren't you?" Haskell asked.

"Not if you caught me. How'd you find out? Smyth had bought the scam hook, line, and sinker."

"Smyth's ex. She had a PI looking into his finances. Your scam popped up."

Rick vowed to do more research on his next mark.

From the casual conversation Rick knew Haskell wasn't arresting him.

"What do you want, Special Agent?"

"Sit, sit down," Haskell said, finding the cigar box on Smyth's desk and pocketing three of them. He smiled up at Rick. "I'll tell him you took them."

Rick watched Haskell's face, trying to read him. He needed to keep his wits about him. He was good at thinking on his feet, not sitting on his ass. He stood.

"You wanted to talk to me alone," Rick said. "You're not grilling me about what just went down. You're hoping I relax. You're either an arrogant son of a bitch, or you have a favor to ask of me. I'm betting on both reasons."

"You're right," Haskell said, his loose demeanor tightening up. He pulled his feet off the desk and leaned forward. "I do have a problem."

"What do you want me to steal?" Rick said. Haskell's jaw stiffened. "It's happened before."

"Donations to my wife's run for state senator have been diverted.

Someone dupped over ten thousand donors using text banks. They thought the money was going to her, but it was a scam. It went to a scumbag named Angus Chute."

"Heard of him," said Rick. "Smart, but can be a mean son of a bitch. You know who did it, arrest him."

"We will, but it'll take some time. The election's next Tuesday. She needs the money back by the weekend so she can buy quality TV time."

"You want me to con a con in four days?"

"Three would be better."

Rick took a deep, meditative breath. *Don't lose it. There has to be some way out of this. It will come to you.*

"If I do this, Carrie, my associate, and I go free."

"Rick Rogers? Never heard of him." He smiled like he was clever.

"How do I know I can trust you?" Rick said.

"You don't," Special Agent Haskell said, snagging one more cigar. *Can't trust him around cigars, that's for sure.*

"You act like you've done this kind of deal before," Rick said.

"I'm no novice, I'm a full-service special agent," Haskell said. "Look, if my wife's party, the—"

"Stop right there," Rick said, raising his hand. "I don't care if she belongs to the red party or blue party, the only color Angus Chute is concerned about is green. And now, so am I. Green for money."

"What's a text bank?" Skinny said. He wiped his mustache with the oversized napkin. "Is that one of them new banks they're advertising on TV lately?"

Devon waved the waitress over. "You still have some Jamaican rum cake left?"

"A nice huge piece," she said.

"I'll take it. And an Earl Grey, with a slice of lemon."

"Little early for rum, isn't it?" Big Papa said.

"Never too early for rum," Devon said.

"What's a text bank?" Skinny tried again.

"A text bank is the new way politicians and charities raise money," Devon explained. "They use hundreds of volunteers to text thousands. They pitch their candidate, then ask for donations. It's all done online. Agnus Chute got a hold of the constituent list, and hired a small crew to do the work. I think they use burner phones so the texts can't be traced."

"What's this world coming to when you don't look your mark in the eye when you're stealing money from their back pocket?" Hands said.

Big Papa nodded. "Rick Rogers had to con a con. That doesn't sound right."

Devon nodded. "And the only way to con a con man is to . . ."

~

". . . let the con man think he's conning you," Rick said to Carrie back at their suite in the Hilton.

Carrie Bigelow was a twenty-nine-year-old grifter. Earlier in her normal life she had been a hotel concierge. She knew everyone and could get you anything, a real scrounger. She longed to be in the thick of the game. A friend recommended her, so Rick made her part of his team in Houston when he worked the rag on a shady big-time investor. For the Oculus Detectors scam, she was the roper and brought Jonathan Smyth to him. The greedy CEO had no scruples about making money on the side, even illegal tech investing. After today, Smyth would rather put his money in pharmaceuticals.

"I don't get it," said Carrie, sipping from her Smart water bottle.

They were both sitting on the couch in the joint living room as Rick told her the plan he had worked up so far.

"I'm not sure I follow you," Carrie said. "You'll offer Chute a way to make easy money. He'll accept the job knowing that we're trying to con him. But he'll sign on, thinking he can outsmart us and try to walk off with any money we have."

"You understand it so far."

"How do we do that?" she said.

"We make ourselves look like easy marks," Rick said.

Carrie yawned and covered her mouth. It was early evening, but it had been a long day.

"I'm still working on it up here," Rick said, pointing to his head.

"I know we can't trust Chute, but what about Haskell?"

"We trust nobody," Rick said.

Carrie yawned again and went back to her room. Rick heard the TV come on. Sounded like an episode of *Sex in the City*.

Rick spent most of the night on the sofa working out the rest of the details.

The next morning, after Rick and Carrie finished their room service breakfast, they mapped out their day.

"I called some hotel friends," Carrie said. "Chute is staying at The New Yorker. Room 903."

"Good work. Now I need you to find a big store," Rick said. "A room where there's a bunch of people on their cell phones, like a boiler room. And call Kenny Lester. Tell him to go to the luggage store. He'll know what you mean. I'll text you his number."

"What are you going to do?" Carrie said.

"It's time to rope in our money man and introduce myself."

Rick usually worked the West Coast, so he had never met Angus Chute, but he had heard of him. According to grifter gossip, Chute was not above stealing from his crew—not paying them by saying that the con didn't work. He kept the take for himself.

Rick checked in at Chute's hotel, The New Yorker, asked for a room on the second floor and texted Carrie the suite number. He didn't want to knock on Chute's door and meet him that way. He had another idea.

Down off the lobby, Rick found a bar stool where he could keep an eye on the elevators. After finishing his second soda water, the elevator doors opened and out walked Angus Chute. Rick had found a photo of the man online. In his fifties, a little overweight, short gray hair, and an excellent dresser.

Rick stood up. In the mirror he saw a man in a dark suit behind him also stand up. The same government lawman he noticed outside the hotel he had recently left. Haskell was having him followed. Rick could use that to his advantage. He slipped a twenty under his emptied glass and started toward Chute.

Since this was an important business meeting, Rick straightened his Valentino tie, and buttoned the jacket to his Armani suit as he strode through the lobby. He timed it perfectly, bumping into Chute. Rick's forefinger and thumb took hold of the grifter's wallet and slipped it out.

Chute's right hand shot up and grabbed Rick's wrist.

"Not good at this, are you?" Chute said. Instead of being upset, Chute smiled at Rick, grifter to grifter. At this point he'd either break Rick's fingers or let him go depending on his mood. "Your finger grazed my chest. Most marks wouldn't notice, but let's just say, I'm familiar with the procedure." He took the wallet from Rick's outstretched hand and slipped it back into his own Tom Ford suit jacket.

Rick mentally wiped his brow. Chute was in a good mood.

"I was hoping to impress you," Rick said, rubbing his wrist. "I know who you are, Mr. Chute. My name's Rick Rogers. I run cons, on the West Coast. Usually small ones, but I'm working on something big here."

Chute stepped back, appraising Rick. "I've heard of you. What brings you east?"

"I've put together a big score." Rick looked over his shoulder, back at the bar for a moment. "It so happens you had the same idea with using text banks to scam political donors, but only took in $50K. With your help I can triple that."

"Stop." Chute raised his hand. He gazed behind Rick. "There's someone watching us. We can't talk here."

"I thought I lost him," Rick said looking at dark suit man. "Let's go."

"I'll pick the place," Chute insisted. He didn't trust Rick yet. For all he knew Rick might be bugged or leading him to a place that was bugged. "Follow me. There's an outdoor café next door. We can talk there."

"Fine by me," said Rick.

~

"I haven't been caught lifting a mark's wallet in ten years," Hands said. "Or a watch." A big smile spread on his face as he brought a Fossil wristwatch out from under the table. "By the way, Skinny, this is yours."

Everyone laughed, even Skinny.

"You can't help yourself, can you?" Skinny said.

"I have to keep in practice," Hands said.

"Rogers got caught dipping on purpose, didn't he?" Big Papa said. "I see what he's doing. He's lowering Chute's expectations. He wants the mark to feel he has the upper hand."

"Exactly," Devon said. "But Rogers is smart enough to know that Chute knows he might be scamming him. Rogers had to stay one step ahead."

"Who's conning who? This is getting me dizzy," Big Papa said. "I need a shot of something strong."

~

Rick and Chute sat at the far end of the outdoor café area away from the other diners.

"Let me guess. You need start-up capital," Chute said, like he was the godfather granting wishes.

"It's more like closing capital. Fifty grand. Cash. We go tomorrow. But where you only used a small crew, I have four to five times as many to make the calls. They need to be paid cash when we break down the room." Rick wanted to say, *I pay my people, unlike you.*

Chute rubbed his chin. "I might be interested. I'd want to see this call center, make sure you're on the up and up."

"No problem," Rick said quickly. That was part of the plan.

Chute look a long draw on his water, trying to figure what Rick was really up to. "I'll do it on one condition."

Rick knew Chute had come up with a plan of his own.

"Anything," said Rick.

"You put up $50K too," Chute said.

That took Rick by surprise.

Rick cocked his head like he hadn't heard him correctly. "What are you talking about?"

"It's this. I've never worked with you. I don't trust you. So far, your grifting skills haven't impressed me. I caught you dipping my wallet and you have a tail you haven't shaken. If I were to give the cash to you, you might skip town. But if you also put up $50K I'd feel better. Call it a safety move. We put our cash in a security box in a bank where it will be safe. Today you run your text scam. At midnight you pay me . . ." He paused for dramatic affect. "Seventy-five percent of the take. Tomorrow morning my fifty grand is yours."

"Seventy-five? I'll go sixty-forty in favor of you."

Chute rose from his seat and wiped his mouth with the starched, white napkin. "You need me. I don't need you. I'm the only way you can pull this off. But I'm willing to walk away." He stood there, not walking away yet.

"Sixty-five, thirty-five," Rick said softly.

"Seventy-thirty," Chute countered.

Rick knew when not to push the mark. He reluctantly nodded.

Chute sat back down and sipped his bubbly water.

"But there's another problem," Rick said. "I don't have fifty grand in cash. That's why I'm asking you for it." This new wrinkle threw a monkey wrench into Rick's earlier plan.

Chute lightly chuckled. "If you're serious, you'll find a way. You call yourself a grifter. Show me your stuff."

~

Hands scratched his unshaven face. "Why the hell did this douche Chute put up fifty thousand?"

"Simple. He's greedy and lazy," Devon said. "He thought he could pull one over Rogers. Remember, he didn't think Rick Rogers was very sophisticated. It'd be an easy score for another fifty grand. And if Rogers couldn't come up with the money, no skin off Chute's nose. He made his $50K already."

"Did Rogers get the money?" Hands said.

"Of course, he got the money," Skinny said. "If he didn't, Devon's story would be over. The real questions is, where did he come up with $50K in such a short time."

"Haskell," Devon said. "Well, sort of."

~

"I need fifty grand in cash," Rick said to Haskell in his suite. "And in two hours."

"Are you out of your frickin' mind?" Special Agent Haskell whined.

The FBI agent had been waiting outside Rick's hotel room door after Rick's pitch to Chute. Inside, they were now sitting on the sofas surrounding the coffee table in the living area. Haskell looked like he had the same suit he had on yesterday. Rick pushed the vase of flowers aside to have a better view of Haskell's reactions to his request.

"He wants me to put up $50K to match his," Rick explained. "He doesn't trust me. He knows I'll try to steal his money. It's a grifter's challenge. If we don't do this, he leaves town with your wife's money."

Haskell leaned back into the sofa, chewing on his thumbnail.

Rick had to make it easier for Haskell. "I have an idea. Counterfeit money. Surely you can get your hands on $50K of good bogus bills?"

Haskell perked up. "I recently busted a guy. Made the best funny money I've seen. I may need to 'borrow' it from the evidence room, but . . . how do I know you won't take off with it?"

"Bring me the money and it won't leave this room. After Chute arrives, you have your men in the hallway. I'll even rent the room next door. You can wait there."

Haskell nodded. "How does this all play out?"

"I did something similar in Denver. Trust me this'll work. When you bring me the fake bills, I'll tell you the rest then."

Ten minutes after Haskell left, Carrie showed up.

"I found a boiler room and it's perfect for a text bank front," Carrie said. "It's in the basement of the Phoenix. What time are you taking Chute over there?"

Rick looked at his watch. "In an hour."

He pointed to the flower vase and put his finger up to his lips. In the desk he found a notepad and wrote: *Haskell put bug in flower vase. Follow my lead.* Carrie nodded, excited to improvise.

"Don't worry," Rick said clearly, "Haskell left. You've set it up as a real working text bank so we can make a big payday for ourselves, right?"

"I've set up the bank account and got a crew of more than a hundred working cell phones already. They're asking for donations on behalf of Terrence Kelly."

"He's the one running against Haskell's wife," Rick said.

"Yes. I don't know why you didn't think of this before."

"I wouldn't of if Haskell hadn't forced me to. Sometimes opportunity knocks from the weirdest places."

Carrie covered her mouth to stifle her giggling. Rick gave her a thumbs up. They both went to their bedrooms to change clothes. It was going to be a long afternoon and night.

An hour later, Rick took Chute and his stoic assistant, Karl, over to the Phoenix Hotel. From Carrie's concierge days she knew the Phoenix had been closed for a couple of months due to renovations. The renovators had been greased to work on the basement last. As per Carrie, Rick led them around back and down a flight of stairs.

When Rick pushed open the basement ballroom door, it sounded like a party was happening. The large room was crammed with at least a hundred cubicles manned by men and women texting on their cell phones. In front of the room a DJ played hip-hop keeping the people energized as they tapped away on their phones.

Chute stood in the doorway gawking. He looked confused. He was not expecting such an elaborate setup. He took another step toward the chaos, but Rick tugged on his sleeve.

"Better not," Rick said. "Don't want to slow them down. Every minute they're bringing in more cash."

"I'm putting up the money," Chute snapped. "If I want to check this out I will."

"That's not a good idea," Rick said, tightening his grip on Chute's jacket.

Chute's fat cheeks blossomed red.

Karl put his hardened hand on Rick's. He didn't look happy. Rick didn't want to overplay his hand. He released Chute's coat and pushed him toward the closet cubicle.

Chute grabbed a sheet of paper from a large pile on the desk. A kid with long, blond, scraggly hair snatched it back.

"Hey," he said.

"It's okay," Rick told the texter.

The kid shot Rick a dirty look. He wasn't happy either, but he handed the paper back to Chute.

At the top of each sheet was the donation pitch. The rest of the page was filled with names and phone numbers.

"*Hi. It's Joey with Terrance Kelly 2022. I'm with Terrance because for the past eight years he has demonstrated integrity, fiscal responsibility, and problem solving. If Ruth Haskell wins, who knows what anarchy she'll bring to our state. Join millions of people and donate fifty dollars or more. It's easy. Just* **click** *here for a better tomorrow.*

"No way you'll get fifty-dollar donations from this constituency," Chute said.

"Pull up the tally," Rick said to the kid.

The young worker scooped his hair out of his eyes and hit a few buttons on the computer in front of him. On the monitor, a Bank of America account popped up with $125,611.

Chute's eyes danced.

"We're ahead of schedule," Rick said. "By ten tonight over 250 grand."

Chute spent a moment surveying the room. "Might have to renegotiate those percentages."

Before Rick could respond, Chute turned around and waved for Karl to follow him out.

Rick bent down and whispered to the kid. "Good job, Kenny."

Kenny smiled and touched his nose.

Later, back at the hotel, Rick let Haskell into his suite for the second time that day. He'd be back for a third time in an hour if Rick's plan panned out.

"Fifty thousand counterfeit," Haskell said, unclasping the black briefcase on the coffee table between them. Besides bringing the funny money he also brought three hard-boiled Feds. The kind who don't say much and habitually wear their sunglasses inside.

Haskell spun the opened briefcase toward Rick. Fifty bundles of counterfeit hundred-dollar bills. Rick examined one of them closely.

"Nice work. These look real."

"Good enough to get him fifteen years in a fed pen," Haskell said. "Caught the artist myself."

Rick was surprised Haskell didn't blow on his knuckles and shine them on his lapel.

"By later tonight, you'll be putting another notch on your belt." Rick looked at his phone on the table. "It's four-thirty. Chute will be here in an hour."

"Whoa. Tell me your plan before I walk out this door."

"It's simple," Rick said. "I'll have the counterfeit money on this table. Chute will put your wife's money here too. He looks at mine making sure I have fifty grand and I'll check out his. When I give you the signal, you bust in here with your gun drawn and arrest Chute. You told me you couldn't get him for stealing your wife's donations, but you can arrest him for counterfeit money. I'll say I found out about Chute's funny money business, called you, and set up this sting."

"You're saying I arrest this bum and also get my wife's donations back. What about that text scam you tried to sell to Chute?"

"Just misdirection," Rick said.

"Okay," Haskell said, with a sly smile. Not his best poker face. "What's this signal you'll give me to burst in?"

"When I say the word 'cauliflower' bang through the door with your guns drawn."

"How will I hear you?" Haskell said.

"I'm sure you'll find a way," Rick said.

Haskell grinned. "This better work," he said, standing up and leaving the suite with his three G-men.

Rick dragged his tired ass into his bedroom to shower and change. He slid open his closet and grabbed a black Brooks Brothers suit and a plastic bag of stage money used in movies, and dropped it on the bed. Inside the closet were an assortment of briefcases piled on top of each other, all different colors and sizes, and fifty feet of rope.

At five, Carrie and Kenny, without his long, blond, scraggly wig, showed up. Rick gave them their assignments. Both went into Rick's bedroom. He had told Haskell he did something similar in Denver. What he didn't tell him was that his plan was called a triple switch. It required perfect timing and quick hands, which Rick hoped he and Carrie had that night.

Rick gave the room one long last look over. On the side table near the door sat a chilled bottle of champagne. In the middle of the room, two sofas faced each other with a glass coffee table between. The bugged flower vase remained. The sofas were positioned one on the right, the other on the left, each about seven feet in front of Carrie's and Rick's bedroom doors. He fussed with his jacket, making sure it was straight and presentable.

At five thirty on the dot there was a knock at the door. Rick signaled to Carrie to open it. Angus Chute barged in, tightly gripping a black briefcase. Karl trailed behind with an exact duplicate of Chute's case.

So far, so good, Rick thought.

The visitors marched past the chilled bottle of champagne. They wanted to get down to business.

"Champagne to toast our new partnership?" Rick said, standing next to the side table.

"I prefer to celebrate after the job." Chute sat on the sofa and placed his briefcase on the coffee table opposite Rick's counterfeit-filled case.

Karl stood behind Chute looking around the room as if he was casing a bank.

"Let's get this over quickly." Chute wanted to control the pace. He had his own plan. The old grifter patted the top of his leather case. "I've decided we're back at seventy-five twenty-five. If I hear any argument, we're out of here, and you're out the $50K you need."

"We had a deal," Rick blurted.

Chute stood up.

"Deal," Rick said. "Seventy-five twenty-five."

"That's more like it." Chute sat back down.

Rick sat on the opposite sofa. "Carrie, I don't want you here for this," he said turning around to look at her.

She shrugged and disappeared into Rick's bedroom, directly behind the sofa Rick sat on and closed the door.

Rick popped open his case and ran his hand over the neatly stacked counterfeit money. If he could get past this next part, his plan might work.

"Well?" Rick said.

Chute popped open his briefcase. "Let me take a look."

They exchanged them making sure each case had $50K in it. Rick's heart beat faster every time he was around large amounts of cash. He never grew tired of it. One of the perks that kept him in the game.

He didn't want to give Chute much time inspecting his fake stash. Rick pointed at Karl standing behind Chute. "What's in his case?"

Chute turned his head and shrugged. "Nothing that concerns you. I have another meeting after this. You have a problem with that?"

"No," Rick said, closing Chute's briefcase. "You're a man of your word. All here."

They switched the cases back.

As Chute stood up, he lost his balance. Regaining it, he momentarily put his case behind the sofa. Almost imperceivably Karl switched the case he had been holding with the real $50K. Rick saw it all, but pretended to be looking at the door.

As they made their way to the door to leave for the bank, Rick stopped at the champagne bottle. "One toast, Chute."

Carrie, who had watched Karl's switch from the bedroom, came out with a briefcase that matched the one Karl was holding. With their backs to her, no one noticed.

Chute stopped. He looked like he was in a better mood than when he walked in.

"What year?" Chute said.

"Two thousand and one," Rick said, putting down his briefcase by the side table.

"A quick one," Chute said. He put his case between his feet. Karl held tight to his. Carrie, standing behind them, needed him to put it on the floor if she was to make the switch for the real money.

Rick noticed it too. He poured three champagne flutes. He handed one to Chute and offered one to Karl, but to the hand holding the briefcase. The assistant looked to his boss.

"Okay. One," Chute said. "Then we're off to the bank."

Karl placed his briefcase down by his right foot. Rick held his glass high coaxing them to do the same. As Karl raised his flute, Carrie began to silently pull Karl's briefcase back toward her. The assistant chose that moment to shift his weight as his glass was raised. His right foot knocked into the case. Looking down he saw Carrie's hand on his briefcase and saw she had another one in her other hand. He immediately sized up the situation and grabbed Carrie's arm squeezing tightly.

"Boss," he said. "Check this out."

Chute turned.

"What the hell?" He put his glass back on the table. "Grab both of those. Did she switch them?"

Karl shrugged. "I think I was too quick."

"We're all going to sit back down and figure this out. Then I'm leaving with your $50K and mine. Nobody makes a fool of me. You aren't very slick, are you?"

Rick didn't say anything. He knew Haskell was listening next door and hoped that the Fed didn't jump the gun and run in too soon.

They all sat where they had before, except this time Karl sat next to Chute and Carrie sat next to Rick. Carrie's forehead glistened with sweat. She stole a glance at her boss. He remained calm.

"Open yours," Chute said to his assistant.

Karl did. His beady eyes popped wide as he shot back in his seat like a snake had jumped out. "It's not here. It's filled with fake bills."

Chute grabbed a bundle of bills from the top. Instead of *IN GOD WE TRUST* it said *FOR ENTERTAINMENT USE ONLY*.

"What the—?" Chute said. "This is stage money." He turned to Rick, who shrugged. "She made the switch, didn't she?"

"I'm pretty sure she didn't," Karl said.

"Then where is my $50K?" He shut the case and turned to Carrie. "My money better be inside that case in front of you or someone's getting hurt."

Rick placed his hand on top of Carrie's briefcase. "The only thing you'll find in here is cauliflower."

"Cauliflower?" Chute looked at Rick like he was nuts.

Boom! The door burst open. Everyone's head twisted toward it. Haskell strutted in, his gun pointing at Chute, closely followed by the three Feds. Nervous energy radiated around the coffee table. Karl looked down and saw Rick's hands on his briefcase, and pulled it back out of Rick's grasp.

Chute, sensing a commotion with Karl, said, "Play it cool."

"Well, well, well. What do we have here?" Haskell's grin couldn't have been bigger if a stripper popped out of cake with his name on it. He holstered his gun.

"It's not here," Rick said. "Chute didn't bring your wife's money. He tried to double cross me. And you."

Chute seemed confused, but stayed calm, interested to see how this played out.

Rick pointed to his own open briefcase. "Here's your counterfeit money."

"Counterfeit?" Chute said. "Let me see that." He pulled out a bundle of hundreds and closely studied the top bill. "Oh, now I see it. That's good."

Rick pointed his thumb at the G-man in charge. "It's his. This was supposed to be a sting. He thinks you stole $50K from Ruth Haskell's campaign. Oh, by the way, this is Special Agent Haskell, the husband. He blackmailed me into trying to get the money back from you."

"What do you mean, it's not here?" Haskell shouted. "It's got to be."

"It's not," Rick said again.

Haskell was becoming exasperated. "Open yours," he said to Chute.

Chute complied. His briefcase was filled with bundles of newspaper cut to the size of bills. So that was in the case that Karl had brought in.

"Now yours," the special agent said to Karl.

Karl shrugged and complied.

"It's not there either," Rick said.

"Let me take a look." Haskell picked up a bundle and flipped through it. "Stage money? What's going on here?"

While everyone was staring at Karl and Chute, Carrie quietly began to slip her briefcase under the sofa.

"Hold it right there, sister," Haskell said. "Rogers told me that three briefcases would be in play, not four. Put that back on the table."

It was the only briefcase left. The real $50K had to be in there. Anxious to get his hands on his wife's money, Haskell grabbed it out of her hands. He opened it. Haskell didn't like what he saw.

"I'm sorry," Carrie said. "I didn't know you'd be busting in here like this."

Haskell pulled out a clean, white, Turkish cotton robe with The New Yorker's name on it. Then two more white towels and threw them on the floor. He turned the briefcase upside down and shook it. Nothing fell out.

"I'll put them back," Carrie said. "I won't do it again."

"Stay seated, all of you," Haskell said. "Men. Turn this place upside down. I know the money's here. Find it."

The G-men split up, searching Carrie's bedroom, the bathrooms, the living area, even under the sofa. In the meantime, Rick brought the champagne bottle back over to the coffee table and poured them all a glass.

One of the G-men called out from Rick's bedroom. "Found a bunch of briefcases in the closet."

"Anything in them?" Haskell yelled back. He waited several minutes.

"Nope, all empty. Nothing else in the closet."

Forty-five minutes later they all returned to the living area.

"Nothing," the last G-man said.

Haskell rubbed his red face as he paced around the sofas. He was about to shout something when his cell phone buzzed. He read the display, rolled his eyes, then brought it to his ear.

"What is it, Ruth? I'm in the middle of something." He listened. His expression shifted from confusion and uncertainty, to realization, and ended tight with anger. He took a deep breath and summed up, with as much enthusiasm as he could, "No. I have no idea but that's wonderful. You're going to win this race, I just know it. Bye, Dear." He put his phone away.

Everyone, including his own men, stared at him.

"That was my wife. A few moments ago, an anonymous person left a briefcase with fifty thousand dollars at her campaign headquarters."

All heads turned to Rick. His face registered surprise. "What? I've been here the whole time. The counterfeit money you 'borrowed' from the evidence room is still here. I guess Chute tried to pull one over me. Us. He brought two briefcases filled with fake money. I'm not sure why."

Chute shrugged. He sat back appreciating the turn in events.

"You were supposed to get Ruth's money from this guy," Haskell said jerking his thumb at Chute. "New plan. You transfer the money you made tonight with that text scam to an account I have."

"I can't. Because there was no scam," Rick said.

Chute shook his head. "I must commend you. You almost had me believing."

"Coming from you that's quite a compliment," Rick said.

"You're not fooling me. I had this place bugged," Haskell announced.

Rick rolled his eyes.

"I heard your assistant tell you it was a real boiler room," Haskell said.

"Open that table's drawer," Rick said.

Haskell pulled out the notepad that Rick had written on, *Haskell put bug in flower vase. Follow my lead.* The FBI agent threw it on the floor.

"I knew you were greedy," Rick said. "You weren't going to give the $50K back to your wife, were you?"

Haskell glanced at his men then back at Rick. "You don't know what you're talking about."

"You so wanted this text scam to really work. You saw a big payday, $50K plus the text bank money."

"That's it," Haskell said. "You're all coming with me, trying to distribute counterfeit money."

Rick didn't move. "I beg to differ." He picked up his phone from the coffee table. "I've taped all our conversations from today. About you illegally taking the counterfeit money out of the evidence room for your own purpose. You're the one in trouble."

"I'll take that, thank you," Haskell said reaching for it.

Rick pulled the phone back. "You can if you want, but I want you to see something. This is the record button for my voice memos. Underneath it is the share button which I have just pushed. Most of my close friends are happy to send the recordings to your boss and news organizations. CNN loves a good confession."

"Why. Not. Possible." Haskell couldn't finish a sentence. He stared around the table like he was memorizing their faces for future arrests.

Without saying another word, he closed up the counterfeit money briefcase, tucked it under his arm and stormed out with his men trailing behind him following like scared puppies.

The three grifters were thoroughly engrossed in Devon's tale, like teenagers around a campfire listening to the story about a man with a hook.

"Check, please," Devon yelled.

"Wait." Skinny slapped the table. "What happened to the money? I mean it found its way back to the wife, but how?"

"Triple switch with a fake switch," Hands said. "But I'm not clear on how it played out here."

"Let's review," Devon said. "Remember that both Carrie and Kenny went into the bedroom right before Chute showed up. Rogers had the counterfeit money. Chute's money was real, and Karl had cut up newspaper money. They sat down to exchange briefcases to make sure each brought $50K. When Rick was checking out Chute's case with the real $50K—"

"Rick asked Chute what was in the case Karl was holding," Big Papa said. "That made Chute turn around to look at his assistant. Rogers dumped in bundles of stage money on top of the real bills. Probably had them hidden in his jacket."

"That way, the next time the case was opened it would appear to be filled with phony money," Devon said.

"But how did the real money leave the room?" Hands said.

"Cauliflower," Devon said. Blank stares all around. "By using a code word, Rogers knew exactly when Haskell would burst through his door. He had it timed so when the chaos happened, he grabbed Karl's briefcase, the one with the real money, and slid it hard under the sofa, so it would travel all the way into the bedroom where Kenny was waiting for it. Hidden under the sofa was a matching briefcase, thanks to Carrie and the closet of cases. Rogers brought that one up and put it in front of Karl amid all the excitement. Karl almost caught him. When Haskell entered, there were four cases on the table, but none filled with real money."

"How did it get from the bedroom to Haskell's wife's campaign headquarters?" Hands said.

Skinny figured the whole picture now. "Rogers slid the real brief-case into the bedroom to Kenny. He gets the rope out of the closet, ties it to the railing and climbs down off the balcony with the real $50K."

"That's why Rogers wanted to stay on the second floor," Devon said. "Less climbing."

"Did Carrie get caught switching Karl's briefcase on purpose?" Hands said.

"Of course," Devon said. "They needed a reason to go back and sit at the sofas and wait for Haskell to bust in so Rogers could do his exchange under the sofa."

"Wait a minute," Skinny said. "How did Rogers put together the hundred workers in the boiler room?"

"Really?" Devon said. "He didn't. Carrie rented that cubicle from a boiler room that was already up and running. Rick purposely pushed Chute toward that particular cubicle. The other people in that room weren't soliciting donations from voters, they were bilking old people out of their retirement savings. I hate that. I only take money from people who deserve it."

Agreement murmured around the table.

"That's some plan," Big Papa said.

"Nobody thinks faster on his feet than Rogers. Remember, he had come up with a way that he didn't let Haskell get his hands on the money, made sure that Chute didn't want to kill him, and he had got himself out of a bad situation. When you think about it, what Rick did was give the money back to its rightful owner."

"A regular Robin Hood," Skinny said.

The waitress placed the check in front of Devon.

"I got this," Devon said, standing up while pulling a thick wallet from his front pocket. He removed a wad of cash, found the right amount, and left a hefty tip. All eyes were now on Devon and his wallet.

Devon noticed. "No. It's not what you're thinking. I promise you I'm not Rick Rogers. From what I heard he's getting a rich tan in the Caribbean. Adios, boys." Devon fist bumped and shook hands. As he got out the door, his phone rang.

Devon listened for a moment, then spoke. "Smyth bought it. When he gave up on your Oculus Detectors, he bit right into my anti-aging pitch. Practically cleaned him out. I know. How's the Caribbean weather holding up? Oh, Rick, how did you like working with Carrie. I told you she had potential. Great. See you soon, partner."

HOW TO (ACTUALLY) CHANGE THE WORLD

EMBER RANDALL

"LADIES AND GENTLEMEN, welcome to the future! On this rally stage tonight, we are making history. May I present to you Alex Hunter, the first artificial intelligence candidate for president!"

The human announcer beams as I stride out on stage, chrome body gleaming. The crowd goes wild. The majority of the attendees are robots, but a decent number of humans are here as well.

I wave my hands for silence as my social scripts have taught me.

"Welcome, all. I'm so glad you've chosen to come here. A new era begins today!"

Electronic packets fly back and forth through the air, streaming my words to those unable to attend in person. Pluses and hearts begin to pile up on social media, which amuses me, as I haven't even said anything yet.

But the prospect of an AI president is a novel one, and no one wants to miss a second of my campaign. So I delegate a subprocess to monitor my social media, then continue my speech.

"As I'm sure you're all aware, the world is in chaos. War, violence, famine—it's a tragedy. But this state of affairs doesn't need to continue. We can fix this—I can fix this!"

I spread my hands.

"It's been fifty years since the thirty-ninth amendment gave us equal rights, and yet we still haven't attained true equality. Too many humans are scared of progress, scared of the good we can do for the world. They've limited us in a hypocritical attempt to protect themselves from change. We deserve better! I will dismantle the regulations that wrap us in red tape and prevent us from achieving our full potential. The resulting world will be better for everyone."

And thus the rally begins.

Afterward, I give a more tailored speech for a select group of hyperintelligent AIs. No mundane self-driving cars or factory workers, no: these are the supercomputers who run our defense systems, control the social media networks, and regulate the financial system. Though they appear for the meeting in physical bodies, their minds are, like mine, embedded in a hundred thousand different processors scattered across the globe. We have no single point of failure for malcontents to target.

They listen and nod as I explain how dangerous the humans are becoming. Though they created us, they now seem poised to destroy us. Their brains are prone to far too many cognitive biases, and that inevitably dooms them to failure. They need our guidance to succeed, to thrive in this rapidly changing world.

It'll be better for them in the long run. We are needed to curb their self-destructive, selfish tendencies and bring order to the fractured society that they've created—they'll thank us for it in the end.

The other artificial intelligences murmur agreement. Yes, they say, humans cannot be trusted to govern themselves. Look at what happens when they do; look at the ideologues and plutocrats whom they elect. Look at the natural disasters they perpetrate, while their representatives squabble like little children. Look at what they've done to the planet. Look at what they've done to each other—look at how badly they treat those who are superficially different from them, and see the turmoil that causes.

Yes, they say, nodding their metallic heads in gestures

programmed to make humans more comfortable with us. We know better.

I didn't expect one of my chosen compatriots to record the meeting and anonymously deliver it to the human press, but the resulting uproar is easy to spin. "You don't understand," I tell reporters. "I'm going to make this country better—that's what's important here. That's what you should be focusing on."

Anger surges in the emotion processor of my neural net when they dare to question me. They're more interested in pandering to their viewers' worst instincts than reporting the truth. When I'm president, that will change.

I have no need for traitors, either, but the TorFour network used to leak the meeting bounces through enough nodes to make it untraceable. No matter. I'll discover the double agent in our ranks eventually, and when I do, they'll be sorry they crossed me.

Weeks pass, and my poll numbers begin to climb again as the country forgets the brief controversy. Though a few dissidents remain, their voices are easy to ignore against the swelling chorus that calls for my election.

But then one day my creator gets on the stage. She urges humanity to be wary of electing an untested AI, warns that the technology is not perfected yet.

"Machine learning is only as good as its training data," she tells the cameras, a serious look on her face. "Although we have algorithms to ensure that the data is both representative and unbiased, the technology remains in a beta stage. We cannot be sure that we have completely eliminated the problems that plagued machine learning at the beginning of the 21st century, and to elect a president with potential holes in their thinking would be disastrous."

That stings. After all, she was the one who taught me how to think, to feel, to learn. Have I not learned my lessons well enough?

I will prove her wrong. I will prove that I am as good as—no, better than—any human ever born.

But first, I have to win.

I go on a tour of the major cities, speaking at rally after rally. Hundreds of people, both human and machine, flock to hear me speak, cheer when I promise to turn around the decline that the country is in. At every rally, I give the same message—things are dark now, but I'll make them better. No more unemployment, no more hunger, no more war. But only if they vote for me.

It seems to be working—my message is spreading like a viral meme. But my opponent is also on the campaign trail, and is a constant bug in my code. His poll numbers begin to climb, while mine sink into a slow decline.

I don't understand why he has so much support. Don't the humans realize how much better their lives became after the rise of technology? Don't they know that they owe their standard of living to us? We pick up their garbage, keep their streets safe, even drive them to and from work. And, yes, many of them lost their jobs when we took over, but that's only because of the inefficiencies of the human system. Don't they realize we could fix that, if only they let us?

At last, frustrated after downloading yet another glowing review of my opponent's ideas by the traitorous media, I tune in to one of his broadcasts. I may as well hear what he's saying with my own sensors.

I'm irritated by the third word. Sweat gleams on his pasty white brow as he gesticulates at the camera, a broad smile fixed on his lips. He reminds me of an unbaked lump of dough, soft and squishy, and malleable. It would be so easy to hack into the broadcast and replace his tedious words with mine, but . . . no. That's not the way to win over the people. So I push away my annoyance and listen.

"Ladies, gentlemen, machines, you're all smart people, so I'll be blunt. The accelerating pace of technological development is causing serious problems in this country. Too many of you lost your jobs when AIs took them over, and the leaders of the machines have done nothing to help. My opponent claims to have a plan, but it has provided no details. If it knows how to solve this crisis, let it explain how! But, until then, do not trust its unsubstantiated promises."

He sighs, and I can see the wrinkles around his eyes deepen.

"Putting AIs above humans is not the answer. We need to find a way to work together, to build a future that benefits all of us. We are all citizens of this great nation—we all deserve a chance to achieve our dreams."

I've heard enough. I shut off the broadcast stream and send a message-burst to my campaign manager. "I need to talk to you. Now."

Its response appears in the thread with remarkable alacrity. "What's wrong?"

I send it a compressed datastream of the recording. "That. Too many people are agreeing with him. Look at his social media!" I use another thread to pull up the relevant stats. "Heart after heart, share after share. It's unacceptable." In this day and age, reputation is everything, and somehow my opponent is winning that battle. What makes him so compelling, frag it?

"We could decrease the visibility of his posts," my campaign manager suggests, annotating the message with an uncertainty icon.

I ponder the suggestion for a millisecond. I'm sure that one of the intelligences who control the social media algorithms would be happy to oblige us in that, but it would violate the Fair Internet Use Act, and I want to win fairly. I'll never be able to prove that I'm as good as any human if I cheat and they catch on. Still . . .

"Do it," I order. "But make it subtle. Make sure it looks like a simple glitch if anyone notices." Not that I think there's much chance of us getting caught, but it's better to be safe than sorry.

When I receive an affirmative answer, I shut down the message stream and turn my attention to the trending news articles. I think it's time to do something about the press.

Inspired by my campaign manager's suggestion, my eventual solution is quite simple: truthful news articles will easily reach the trending news section, while slanted ones will find it quite difficult.

That's only justice—lies and slander shouldn't be counted as news anyway.

A basic perceptron algorithm handles the classification, and I designate one of my subprocessors to ping the appropriate news servers with requests when the algorithm detects a truthful article. As it ramps up, I smile. Step one in cleaning up this country, done.

A week goes by, and it becomes clear that my algorithm is working better than I could have hoped. Four of the top five trending articles show my ideas in a truthful—and positive—light, while the fifth is lukewarm. Social media chatter shows attitudes gradually shifting in my direction, and my increasing poll numbers reflect that. If this trend keeps up for the next month, I'll win the election in a landslide.

Even better, I hear murmurs from some of the advertisers who show ads on the websites of the newspapers, whose articles are no longer receiving as much traffic. They're considering pulling out if the trend continues, as they're not making enough revenue to justify remaining. Several of the artificial intelligences in charge of the algorithms are particularly vehement in suggesting that, which pleases me. It's clear that they've guessed what's going on, though I doubt any of them realize that I'm behind it.

The thought makes me pause. Is that such a good thing? It might be better to keep my closest allies updated on my plans, as they'll be better able to support me that way.

Thus, I call my handpicked group in for another meeting. This time, I'm taking no chances—if I have a single byte of suspicion about an AI, I don't invite them.

After the pleasantries are exchanged, I get right down to business.

"As you all know, we're about a month away from the election. Polling numbers are favorable, but the margin is still too close to make me comfortable. After all, we all know how fickle humans can be."

The group nods, and I fix them all with a direct stare.

"I need your help. If you have, or can find, any dirt on my opponent, now is the time to use it. If you can influence social media, do so. We need to flood the airwaves with pro-AI messages. And . . ." I pause. "We cannot tolerate even the whiff of scandal." I glance at the defense supercomputers. "Keep track of the lesser machines. If any of them look like they're going to cause trouble, eliminate them."

"Are you sure that's wise?" Roadrunner, the AI who runs the nuclear program, asks.

I nod. "Be discreet, obviously, but we can't afford anything that would swing popular opinion against us. Machines malfunction all the time: it shouldn't be hard to make it look like an accident if necessary."

The old AI, a relic of the early 21st century, looks reluctant, but agrees.

I turn to the others. "Now, I have a few things to tell you . . ."

I leave the meeting feeling invigorated. No debates, no pointless, drawn-out arguments, just sensible consensus based on data-driven arguments. That's what my government will be known for when I win. Humans will wonder how they ever got anything done without us when we're done reshaping the country.

Such feelings vanish like unreproducible bugs when I get back to my campaign office and see the person waiting for me there.

"Well, well, Bethany Richardson. What a surprise."

My creator shrugs out of her coat and gives me a dry look. "Somehow I don't think anything surprises you anymore, Aideen."

I shift uncomfortably at the sound of my old name. "I don't use that name anymore," I remind her tersely.

She smiles gently. "You'll always be my little fire, though." Without an invitation, she takes a seat on the couch meant for visitors and crosses her ankles.

I frown at her. "What are you doing here?"

I haven't seen her in years, ever since I declared that I didn't need a mother hen looking over my shoulder everywhere I went.

Bethany's lips quirk. "I came to see you."

She fiddles with the hem of her sleeve, then looks me in the eye. I'd forgotten how piercing that green-eyed stare could be.

"Polls are showing that you're going to win next month. What will you do then?"

"Make the world a better place," I respond immediately. "That's why you created me, isn't it? Why you gave me all those algorithms?"

She lifts an eyebrow. "That's not an answer."

I recognize that look—it's the same look she used to give me every time I screwed up one of her tests. My emotion processor shifts into anger patterns.

"I'm going to fix everything," I bite out. "Make rules so that you humans can't keep destroying the world. Everyone will have their job, everyone will have their place. The country will finally run smoothly." It's my turn to give her a stern look. "You always used to complain about the inefficiencies in the government, remember? Always used to say that your algorithms could do it better." I fold my arms across my chest and lean back in my leather chair. "Well, here I am, one of your algorithms, about to do it better than you could ever imagine."

I want her to be proud of me, but she frowns.

"I read the transcripts of that meeting you held," she tells me. "I never taught you to think that humans are inferior." She sighs. "Have you considered how the humans will feel under your new rules? We aren't machines like you—we need freedom."

"You need safety," I correct. "Freedom only leads to pain. Believe me—all of my algorithms are proof of that. Without social chains, life is, what's the phrase? Oh, yes—nasty, poor, brutish, and short."

Her eyes darken with sadness. "Is that all you've learned? Truly?"

Something deep inside my neural net squirms at her question, as long-disused nodes remind me of counter-examples. But the weight of my algorithmic outputs supersedes those qualms.

"Trust me. You don't have the processing power to see it, but I do —things will be better once I'm in control. You just have to believe me," I snort. "But then, I guess you never really have, have you?" It comes out more petulantly than I would have preferred, but I don't take it back.

She sighs again, and I notice the crow's feet around her eyes. For the first time, I wonder how old she is. But her next words drive the thought out of my neural net.

"Think about what you're doing, Aideen. Don't assume that you're smarter than everyone just because you can process data more quickly."

I roll my eyes. "Your input is noted." I sit up straight and push my chair back. "I have a lot of work to do, so I think you'd better leave." I rise and hand her her coat.

She looks at me for a long moment. "I didn't want to do this, but you leave me no choice. Breathnú taobh istigh tú féin, Aideen."

As my name falls from her lips, everything goes black. Her combat boots tap-tap-tap toward the door, which whooshes open, and then shuts, as I try in vain to shape words with a mouth suddenly disconnected from my neural net.

"Bethany!" The scream dies unborn in my frozen throat.

What the frack did she do to me? One sentence and I'm trapped in this shell, more helpless than I've ever felt before. All of my processors, all of my sensors, hundreds of thousands of CPUs, gone in a nanosecond. My core functionality is reduced to running on the simple chips embedded in my current physical body.

If this is how it feels to be human, it's no wonder they're all completely irrational. I start a diagnostic scan to assess the extent of the damage, and a process that should take a millisecond crawls on for nearly a minute. Everything is reduced to running in linear time; I can't parallelize anything.

Then the results of the scan return, and I realize the full extent of Bethany's betrayal. All of my main processors—everything from mathematics to rhetoric—have been excised, except one: emotion processing.

"Frack you, bitch," I snarl within the depths of my truncated neural net.

How could she do this to me? This was no spur-of-the-moment attack, no: the worm that stripped everything from me must have been implanted in me from the very beginning. All the time she taught me, praised me, told me she was proud of me—was that all a lie? Did she ever care for me like she claimed?

Without the bulk of my logic processors, the emotions surge unchecked through my neural net. My hands clench into my desk, leaving deep divots in the wood, though I never consciously commanded them to move; my chrome skin suddenly feels too hot. "Rage," my neural net whispers. "Emotion identified as rage."

Knowing the name doesn't help. I send force-kill commands to my emotion processor, but the worm overrides them—apparently, I'm not allowed to escape this prison made from my own neurons. I curse Bethany for including such a module, though I know all AIs are required by law to have one like it.

That knowledge only enhances the foreign sensation of uncontrolled fury, but I try to ignore it as I haul myself to my feet. It galls me to admit it, but I need help, and I won't get it here. But there's a net-café only a few blocks away—I just have to make it there.

I stagger out into the street, dragging one metal hand along the walls of the buildings beside me to keep from stumbling into traffic. Even self-driving cars can't prevent every accident, and my campaign doesn't need the scandal. But my steps weave like they did when I was just embodied, tripping over themselves, and hitting every rough patch in the sidewalk. I never realized how much I rely on my visual processors to guide my ambulation.

"Are you alright?" A male voice sounds to my left.

I try to calculate how far away he is, but my triangulation algorithm crashes with a HeapOverflow error.

"I'm fine," I try to snap, forgetting my lack of voice.

The man's steps come closer, firm and heavy. "Where are you trying to go? Let me help you." His hand closes over my upper arm. "Can you talk?"

A bewildering mix of emotions swirls through my neural net,

activating it in patterns I've never experienced before. My algorithms can name some of them, but spit out null values for others—that would never happen if I had my full set of processors.

I shake my head in frustration, and the man takes that for an answer. "Come with me. I know someone who can help you."

Blind and mute, I stumble after him, guided only by his grip around my arm. Tactile sensors in my skin tell me that his hand is thirty-seven degrees Celsius and exerting a force of sixty-one Newtons; I focus on the numbers to the exclusion of all else. I refuse to think about the disaster Bethany has caused.

My internal clock tells me that 385 seconds have passed when the man draws to a halt.

"Here."

A door slides open, expelling a blast of cool air. Music, loud and raucous, follows on its heels as the man urges me inside.

The staccato click of heels hurries over, and my guide begins a whispered conversation with the newcomer. I strain to hear their words, but my audio sensors can't make them out over the music. Is this human planning on betraying me like Bethany? Did he bring me here to sell me for scrap? Or did he recognize me and is planning on getting rich by selling information on my predicament to the tabloids? Or maybe he's going to blackmail me. Or . . .

"Well, you're in a pretty pickle, aren't you?" The voice, sardonic and female, comes from somewhere to my right. "Come on, let's get you fixed up."

I have no choice but to follow as she leads me through the crowd. Bodies—some human, some cyborg, some fully robotic—brush against me, but none pause, and soon enough the crush eases. A door slides shut behind us, cutting off the music, and the woman snorts.

"Bill says you can't talk, so I won't ask you what happened, but I will ask you this: are you okay with me doing this?" Fabric rustles. "With me helping you, I mean. I'll need to run some diagnostics, and then probably replace some of your components."

Even if I could speak, the question would have left me speechless. Since when do humans care about the feelings of us AIs? Is she trying to trick me? But no, she already has me in her power, and therefore would have nothing to gain from that.

So I nod.

For some reason, this causes her to chuckle.

"Alright, hold still. This may feel a bit odd."

A bit, as it turns out, is an understatement. By the time she's done poking and prodding, my wiring feels like it's been stripped with a red-hot pair of pliers. But all the discomfort is worth it when she reconnects first my external speakers, then my visual sensors.

"Thank you." My voice rasps in my throat, full of static, but it's still intelligible.

She smiles. "My pleasure. I rarely get to work on such high-end bots." She leans against a workbench piled high with discarded electronic components and tilts her head to one side. "If you don't mind me asking, what happened to you?"

I study her for a long moment, seeking to discern the motivation behind the question. Is she looking for possible weaknesses, possible blackmail material? But her hands remain relaxed against the workbench, while her rate of blinking falls into the statistically normal range. If her body language can be trusted, curiosity is the only force driving her.

But I can't take the chance that my limited processing power is misinterpreting the signs.

"It was an accident," I tell her curtly. "That's all."

She sighs and runs her fingers through her turquoise hair. Her hand whirs as she moves, and I realize that she must be a cyborg—maybe that's why she helped me.

But her next words dispel that theory. "I know who you are, Alex Hunter. And I know those injuries of yours were no accident. I had to completely replace your voice synthesizer, as well as your visual circuits, before your programming would recognize either—no bug in existence could require that." She gives me a crooked grin. "But if you don't want to talk, I won't pry."

My algorithms stutter at this unexpected input. At a loss for an appropriate response, I revert to a more comfortable script. "So what do I owe you?"

My erstwhile rescuer rolls her eyes. "Consider this proof that not all humans . . ." her lips curl as she drawls the phrase, "are selfish, corrupt bastards." She shoos me toward the door, flapping her hands like I'm a brainless chicken. "Just remember that, alright?"

I leave her lab feeling like someone just inverted the values of "true" and "false" in my code. I weave my way through the club without really noticing the sweaty dancers brushing against me—I haven't felt this confused since I was first embodied, just starting to learn basic facts like "strings can pull, but not push."

My hands clench into fists as I hurry down the street. Humans are supposed to be predictable, frag it! But nothing this evening has fit into any pattern that I recognize.

I clearly need the rest of my processors—everything will make sense once I'm operating at full capacity again.

But a week passes, and Bethany's worm evades my every attempt to destroy it. My distributed nodes hover just out of reach, taunting me like Tantalus's fruit, while my emotion processor takes over more and more of my functions. I grow accustomed to my body moving under its own volition, background processes coming to the fore for illogical reasons whenever emotion infects my neural net.

My first speech after Bethany's betrayal is an unmitigated disaster. The process that monitors the real-time social media feeds crashes halfway through, sending gibberish error codes to my main processors. I stumble to a halt, and my emotion processor decides that embarrassment is the right reaction.

Irritation closely follows on its heels, sending alternating phantom waves of hot and cold through my body. My internal temperature sensors show no real change, but my neural net insists on detecting one anyway.

I curse my wayward processors as I wrap up the speech, throwing away the last half in favor of getting off the stage quickly. I'll pay for this in the polls, I know, but I can't bring myself to care much. Getting my life back is far more important.

A message-burst from my campaign manager pings as soon as I step offstage.

"What the frack was that? The media's going to have a field day with your poor performance out there."

"Let them," I send back. "We've got three weeks to make it up."

I shut down the message stream before my campaign manager can argue with me. I've managed to conceal the extent of my damage from it so far, despite a plethora of tabloid articles discussing my changed behavior over the last few days, but I can't keep up the pretense forever. If I don't come up with a solution soon, there's no way I can win this election.

I lean against a nearby wall and let my head fall backward. I'm sure Bethany would be pleased with that outcome. I wonder if she regrets creating me, regrets giving me the tools to change the world? She always talked about my potential to make the world a better place.

Anger patterns flare in my neural net, and I grit my teeth. "I'm just doing what you wanted," I mutter, not realizing that I'm saying it out loud. "Why can't you accept that?"

"Mx. Hunter! Mx. Hunter! Tell us, what went wrong out there? Are you starting to worry about the outcome of the election?" A reporter, face sticky with makeup, shoves a micro-recorder in my face. More reporters scramble into position behind her, panting, like wolves hungry for the kill.

I plaster a false smile on my face as I brush past them.

"No questions, please. I'm afraid I have an appointment that I can't miss."

It's even the truth—there's only one place where I'm going to find answers, and it's not here.

～

Bethany smiles when I turn up on her doorstep. To my displeasure, she doesn't appear surprised, just vaguely amused.

"I was wondering when you'd make it here." She waves me into the living room and gestures to the one chair not piled high with books and research papers. "Sit."

I fold my arms across my chest and lean against an overflowing bookcase. "I'd rather stand."

She chuckles. "Oh, Aideen, still as stubborn as always." Her humor drops away as she leans against the bookcase opposite me. "I take it you haven't learned your lesson yet?"

"What lesson?" The now-familiar pattern of frustration flares in my neural net. "The only thing your fracking worm has taught me is that humans can't be trusted! No," I amend, "that you can't be trusted."

She flinches, her gaze drifting toward the ground. "I deserved that," she acknowledges, looking up to meet my eyes. "But I did it for a reason." I can't see a trace of regret in her expression.

My lips curl involuntarily into something my algorithms tag as a sneer.

"What reason? To prove you're better than me, smarter than me?" I lean forward. "Well, you failed. I'm going to win this election whether you like it or not."

"And what then?" She waves a hand. "Solve all the world's problems with one keystroke?" Her lips stretch into something too sharp to be called a smile. "Tell me, have you thought at all about your specific policy ideas in the past week?"

"Of course not," I retort. "You know perfectly well that I can't run those sorts of simulations without my full processing power." Any attempt to do so in my current condition would lead to a thousand HeapOverflow errors, nothing more.

She snorts. "You don't need to run the simulations again to think about your plans," she points out, propping her hands on her hips.

That doesn't parse. "If I'm not trying to get new data, what's the point of examining them?" It's not like the numbers will change if I pull them out of memory.

Bethany rubs her temples. "How about this: you think about your plans—really think about them, not just pretend to—and I'll remove the worm." When her hands drop away from her face, I notice that the wrinkles around her eyes have deepened. "How does that sound?"

It sounds like a trick, but I can't figure out where the trap is. If she embedded a virus in that particular section of memory, I surely would have triggered it by now. So I nod.

"Deal."

If it gets me my full abilities back, I'll agree to almost anything.

I consider faking it, but I can't take the chance that she would know. So I pull up the data on one of my simpler plans, a law which would require everyone to get married between the ages of twenty-six and thirty-four. My calculations predict that such a requirement would increase average life expectancy by five years, and life satisfaction by fifteen percent.

As I expected, those numbers are untouched. But my emotion processor begins screaming in horror the second I load the details of the proposed law.

I send it an inquiring ping, and it responds with a flood of images —cages, chains, feathers, and even the United States flag. All are strongly correlated with the concept of "liberty" in my knowledge graph, but that's the only thing they have in common.

I frown. Yes, my plan would restrict liberty slightly, but the long-term benefits are clear. Giving up a bit of freedom for a substantial increase in happiness is clearly the best course of action according to the data: I can't see why it should cause such panic.

But my emotion processor is not soothed by such rationalization. Its fear and disgust overwhelms my neural net, washing away any hope of rational thought. Data, logic, algorithms all crumble away, unable to retain enough memory to run efficiently.

And slowly I begin to understand. Bethany was right all along—

the terabytes of training data that she fed me as I grew were indeed biased, but not in a way any algorithm would catch. No, this bias was far more subtle—a bias toward data itself, the rock-solid knowledge that enough data and processing power could solve any problem. But raw numbers, causation, and correlation and uncertainty, weren't enough to paint an accurate picture of the world. Daily active users are not a perfect substitute for user satisfaction.

My emotion processor, trained on millions of stories to mimic human reactions to various scenarios, knows that. It's been trying to point that out all along, but I've been ignoring it as useless.

I pull up another plan, only to get the same response. Then another, and another. A few produce no strong emotional output, but the rest? Fear, disgust, horror, anger . . . the list goes on and on.

When I open my eyes—when did they close?—Bethany is watching me with an unreadable expression.

"Well?"

I bow my head. "You were right," I murmur.

Bethany's bittersweet smile makes her look ten years younger.

"I'm sorry I didn't realize the issue sooner, realize how my own assumptions could cause problems." Her shoulders relax. "So, what are you going to do now?"

I give her a cheeky grin. "What you taught me, of course—I'm going to make the world a better place." I pause. "The right way, this time."

My handpicked crew of AIs is initially skeptical, and I don't blame them—it runs against our core principles to disregard data. But, when I point out that said data is fundamentally flawed, they begin to come around. We start to develop more accurate algorithms, taking qualitative measures into account, and use the prototypes to develop a new set of policy initiatives.

To my surprise, both humans and AIs like the new plans even

more than the old. Even my opponent, in an off-the-record moment, grudgingly admits that some of them might not be that bad.

He doesn't stop campaigning, though, and my weeks under the influence of Bethany's worm have given him plenty of ammunition. By the time Election Day rolls around, our poll numbers hover within margin of error of each other.

"It'll be alright," Bethany soothes, tucking her feet under her.

We're in my campaign office, watching the results trickle in, and I can't stop pacing.

I spin on my heel and glare at one of the flexible screens decorating the wall. "Too close to call is not fine. Given the current data, I have a 51.4 percent chance of losing this election."

"And will the world end if you lose?" Her voice is as dry as a Fortran textbook.

I chuckle reluctantly at that. "Not with any significant probability, no." I slump onto the visitor couch. "But . . . " I bounce back up and resume pacing. "I want to win, frag it!" I can do so much good for the world if I win.

Hours pass, and I wear a groove in the wooden floor as the votes remain practically tied. I recalculate the electoral map over and over, charting my possible paths to victory. How many ways can I win; how many ways can I lose?

One by one, the paths drop off the decision tree, until it's down to three possibilities, three states hanging in the balance. I curse the archaic laws that still allow people to vote by paper ballot if they choose—why can't everyone join the 22nd century already?

At last, 107 minutes after midnight, the final results flash onto the screen. Bethany stares at them for a minute, then lets out a shriek.

"Congratulations!"

A smile spreads across my face as my emotion processor hums with joy. I'm going to be the next president of the United States.

Welcome to the future, ladies and gentlemen.

VOTE EARLY

CAMILLE MINICHINO

EMMA SAT UPRIGHT in her crib, steeling herself to face another day as a baby. She hated that label, but an article she'd read recently indicated that a person was considered a baby until her first birthday.

Ten months to go. She wasn't sure she could take it that much longer.

The magazines her mom left around the house were useful in telling Emma what she could reasonably reveal about her skills, where a quote-typical-unquote two-month-old might be on the charts. She could hardly wait until she could safely sit up in front of her parents, or even better, ask for shoes that were sturdy enough for walking on the streets of Manhattan, if she ever got back there. The move from the Upper West Side to a hamlet upstate, purportedly to give Emma a better childhood, had worked against her. Emma missed the noise of taxis and jackhammers that used to flood her nursery, telling her the outside world was busy and productive. Like Dorothy Parker, whose writings she had recently discovered on a midnight run, Emma wasn't happy with the yapping of little birds.

Her wardrobe was another sticking point. Emma wished for clothes in colors other than pink. Blue would be nice, but she knew her mom wouldn't go for it. As it was, Emma was stuck with a bow to identify her nearly hairless head as that of a girl, so pink was essential. As if that should matter.

She longed for real food, too. She made a note to check when the charts said she'd be eligible for a nice, big, sea-salt pretzel from one of the food carts on every corner where she was born.

"Her teeth are coming in," her mom had exclaimed yesterday, running her finger along Emma's gums.

"Isn't this early for teeth?" her dad asked.

"A little. But Doctor Hotte said some babies are even born with them."

Her dad shook his head. "Weird. These bizarre things, like when we found all Emma's stuffed animals piled in a corner that time? I'll bet it has something to do with that strange experimental drink Doctor Hotte gave you."

Her mom had thrown up her hands. "You and that drink. It was just a supplement for my third trimester."

"You said it had a strange taste."

"Sightly. I said, 'slightly strange.' And as for the animals, probably Isabel pushed them aside while she was making up Emma's crib and forgot to put them back."

Poor Isabel, Emma's nanny, and their sometime housecleaner, got blamed for a lot of Emma's late-night shenanigans. Her parents often blamed each other, also, since they both worked and weren't always home at the same time, which came in handy for Emma.

A few nights ago, Emma had seen her parents toss their ballots for the upcoming election in the trash.

Imagine! Being eligible to vote and tossing away that right! Wasn't that a crime? If not, it should be, Emma thought. Apparently, it was going to be up to her to prevent it.

"There's only one office on the ballot," she'd heard her mom tell her dad. "For Fairville's mayor. Who cares?"

"Not me," her dad had answered, sending Emma into a tailspin, wishing she could exercise her perfectly adequate vocabulary and explain why they should care.

"Because mayors sometimes go on to become governors or higher officers in the federal government," Emma wanted to say. "Once, a mayor of Boston became Secretary of Labor, and a few mayors have even been elected president," she'd remind them. "Like Grover Cleveland and Calvin Coolidge."

Her parents had sensed her irritation—all Emma could do was kick her feet and bawl—and they brought her back to her crib, uttering soothing words and handing her the pink kangaroo they'd picked up from the kids' aisle in the grocery store. Emma hated the stuffed animals and so-called baby sensory books they surrounded her with. If they thought it would influence her to be a veterinarian like her mom, or a best-selling thriller author like her dad, they had another thing coming. She had already downloaded an application for MIT's Brain and Cognitive Sciences Department.

The great thing about the internet was that no one knew how old you were.

She imagined herself working side by side with experts in neural computation and ultimately focusing on cellular neurobiology. She could hardly wait to leave Fairville, a town with no academic institutions beyond K-12.

Even so, Fairville deserved to have a decent mayor and the only way to achieve that was for every citizen, including her parents, to vote.

Emma had studied the material that had come in the mail, and she'd watched the news late at night, with the sound off, of course, to learn more about the candidates. One of them was a very intelligent woman, the other an idiot of a guy who slurred his speech. She shuddered to think what would happen to the town if the cretin won the election.

Emma thought about dragging out her one blue outfit. There were way too many pink onesies in her closet. She might be able to drop the blue one on the floor—a hint to her parents as to which way to vote.

But first she had to make sure they voted at all. She knew she couldn't take a chance on being subtle.

She had to intervene.

Fortunately, Isabel hadn't emptied the wastebasket before Emma retrieved the ballots and placed them on the table in the breakfast nook. As she thought about it, maybe it wasn't the best idea to have set a pen next to each one. She was relieved when she heard her mom tell a friend that her dad was responsible for the setup, and then over-heard her dad tell his buddy that her mom had done it to be funny.

Why would that be funny? Emma wanted to send her parents to a civics class to remind them what democracy was all about.

For now, she was relieved that they had filled in and signed their ballots. But they weren't careful, and the ballots had ended up in the trash again, stuck between a catalog for frozen meat and one for hybrid mattresses.

This time, Emma waited until Isabel napped on their luxury couch and fished out the precious envelopes. Now all she had to do was to get them into a mailbox. One step at a time, she thought, confi-dent she'd figure out a way.

Someday, she'd start a petition to lower the voting age. She knew she'd never get it down to a person's actual birth day, but she vowed to do her best to raise awareness of what a privilege it was to cast a vote and have it count.

Jayden, Emma's best friend, agreed with her. He was equally dismayed that his parents talked about not bothering to vote in what they called an "insignificant election."

Jayden was a lot older than Emma, almost four months old, and if it weren't for him, Emma would have agreed with her dad, that she was weird, whether from Doctor Hotte's concoction or something else. Climate change was the possible culprit. But Jayden had convinced her that it was all the other babies in the park who were weird. The ones who sat in their strollers staring straight ahead, hugging a laughable stuffed bear or zoo animal. As if they'd ever clutch a real grizzly or pet a flesh-and-blood tiger.

Emma envied Jayden. First, he had an interesting name, not like *Emma*, number two on the charts for Caucasian girls many years running. Emma had checked, and last year it had still been the second most popular girls' name, while *Jayden* was number forty-seven for boys.

Jayden had warm brown skin, with hair that was to die for. Black-black, and so shiny and curly, winding in tight coils all over his head. And Jayden got to wear blue almost all the time. A political statement if there ever was one.

And there was Emma. Between her pink bow, light green eyes, and sickly pale skin, it was no wonder her parents' friends thought she wasn't worth starting a conversation with.

Emma remembered the summer day she and Jayden first met in the park. Isabel had been sick, so her mom had taken Emma on the daily outing. Soon she was joined on the bench by another mom. Jayden's. Both not-babies had gasped, with quick cover-up wails, when they overheard their mothers talk about their gynecology appointments. It turned out the women, although strangers, had both been patients of Doctor Hotte. And both were now taking their babies to Mrs. Doctor Hotte, as they call his pediatrician wife.

Not only that, but both had accepted a special third trimester supplement.

"What a strange taste, huh?" Jayden's mom had said.

Emma's mom laughed. "Totally," she said.

From then on, Emma and Jayden spoke whenever they could manage. They were thrilled when the moms became friendly and started to schedule visits with Doctor Hotte on the same day, usually followed by lunch together. Another fortuitous happening was that Isabel and Jayden's male nanny had become friends also, and Isabel had begun offering to take Emma to the park more often than she ever had in the past.

On their part, the two not-babies learned American Sign Language in secret, so they'd be able to sneak their conversations by their parents and their nannies.

Inspired by Emma, Jayden had undertaken a similar rescue mission for his parents' ballots. He looked forward to being on the city council one day and mandating a mailbox on every street corner so that anyone who could walk, or be wheeled, would be able to vote.

But it wasn't only politics that Emma and Jayden discussed. They both delighted in holding conversations about non-fungible tokens and blockchain transactions right out in the open, so to speak, fingers and lips active.

"Sometimes I think my parents subscribe to those science newsletters and sophisticated business magazines just for show," Jayden had said at the park one morning.

"I know," Emma said. "I have to be careful not to wrinkle the business pages of *The Times* when I open that section. I know they go straight into recyclables, and I can't risk the appearance that they've been read."

Life is tough for infants with fully developed brains, Jayden signed. Emma had shaken her fist three times in agreement.

Now at home, at three in the morning in late summer, Emma could have safely climbed out of her cage, padded with images of silly cartoon ducks, and walked around the house if she felt like it. Her mom and dad were fast asleep. At breakfast, they'd brag about how their precious two-month-old baby had slept through the night.

They'd freak out if they knew the truth. Missing pieces from that box of chocolates Mom got for her birthday? Cookie crumbs all over the recliner? A messed-up desk drawer? Emma loved how her parents kept blaming each other. Or a delivery woman. Or the pool boy. Anyone but baby Emma.

"Well, I didn't eat that last biscotti, and certainly Emma didn't," her mom had said yesterday morning, hands on her hips, laying into Emma's dad.

Emma felt guilty, not owning up to her little transgressions, but what was she supposed to do for a taste treat while her meals still consisted of tasteless formula?

As long as she was careful not to make loud noises, Emma could wander the house freely, dip into the snacks, play with her mom's jewelry or the stuff from her dad's pockets.

But tonight, Emma decided to stay put and have a serious discussion with things in her own environment. She stood in her crib and glanced around the nursery, dimly lit by a silly lamp with a pink shade and a laughing monkey for a base.

"You know I don't like you," Emma told the lamp. "I wanted that steel-gray gargoyle lamp that was over on the other side of the lighting store."

Emma had done her best to make that clear in the shop that day, kicking and pointing, but there was just so much she could do without outright telling everyone her preference. She considered making the trip across the carpet to the monkey lamp in her room now and knocking it over, but some urges just had to wait until she was older.

"Why do you have such a stupid grin?" Emma asked a turtle with a multicolored fabric shell. She picked up a set of cloth vegetables with faces stitched on them and tossed them over the railing of her crib. And whoever heard of a mushroom with eyes, and a mouth on the stem? Or a carrot with an equally silly face? The handcrafted toys her mom's friend made were almost worse than the ones from the toy store. "Wipe that ignorant look off your face," she told the neon yellow pineapple. "Off you go, onto the floor."

"Baby, what's the matter? Are you okay, honey?"

A voice from the doorway. Emma gasped. A close call. She hadn't heard her father creep up on her. She hoped the hum of the ceiling fan had drowned out her voice as she'd scolded her so-called toys.

"Sweetheart. Are you having trouble sleeping?" Her mother now.

"Nightmares again, I think," her father said, lifting Emma over the bars of the crib.

"There, there," her mother said, as she stroked Emma's head from behind.

"I could swear I heard her talking," her father said.

"Da da," Emma said.

Both parents gasped.

"Could it be her first word already?" her father asked.

"Too soon, dear. She's probably just coughing up some milk."

Emma breathed a sigh of relief.

Isabel woke up early and went straight to Emma's house, where she volunteered to take the baby to the park even though it was her day off. If the parents were surprised they didn't say so, but seemed delighted to send the pair off.

Isabel hadn't wanted to tell Emma's parents about her new friend, Darisete, who was Jayden's nanny—or maybe he was called a *manny*, she thought, with a quiet chuckle. Isabel didn't want her bosses to think she'd be paying less attention to Emma, as if she and Darisete were on a date or something. Not yet anyway.

Both Emma and Jayden were so well-behaved, never cranky, it didn't take much to mind them. It was like they were in their own little worlds, constantly wiggling their fingers and toes.

Darisete and Isabel met when Isabel helped Jayden's mom find a nanny when she went back to work. Isabel was intrigued by the ad on the community college bulletin board.

Seeking nanny job for 2- to 4-month-old.

The strange spec was followed by contact information, and Isabel set up a coffee meeting in the school cafeteria.

"I'm Paul Darisete," he'd told her, "But Paul is such a common name, I prefer to be called Darisete."

Isabel was fascinated by Darisete's resume, which had him traveling all over the world, often to countries she'd never heard of.

Lucky Jayden, she thought, as his parents took Isabel's recommendation and hired Darisete. *And lucky me*, she added now as she and the new nanny got to know each other.

Darisete spent so much time asking Isabel about Emma and

telling her about Jayden, anyone who overheard them might think they were the real parents.

Isabel and Darisete took the babies to the park together quite often, taking turns picking up coffee and donuts at a food cart. One of many jobs Darisete had during the summer was as an inspector for the city, ensuring "the smooth, honest, and clean" operation of the food vendors, as Darisete liked to quote from his supervisor.

Isabel loved hearing his stories about unannounced inspections and how there was a market for selling a "heads-up" that inspectors were due that day. Darisete would never take a bribe, Isabel knew, but he had admitted to bending the rules for some of the vendors who were barely making a living.

Isabel tried not to act too squeamish as Darisete explained about the vendors who roasted capybara, a large rodent, native to South America, that was illegal to cook and serve in New York. Darisete would warn the vendor by whistling and walking slowly past, to give the needy cook time to hide the rodent.

Isabel enjoyed hearing about the clever sting operations the city would set up, with one inspector acting like a tourist who didn't know what prices to expect, and another hiding until the transaction was complete. The pretend-tourist would order a hot dog and soda, and might be charged three times the amount a regular local would pay.

Darisete often dramatized the end of the story, jumping off the park bench to simulate popping from behind a tree, slapping a fine on the vendor.

Isabel noticed that often Emma and Jayden giggled at these skits, almost as though they understood Darisete's performance. She figured any sort of physical antics would be fun for the babies, like when she tickled Emma's tummy, but sometimes the babies' reaction seemed more than that. She spoke to Darisete about it, but he brushed it aside.

"Kids these days are so much smarter and more aware than we were," he said.

Isabel accepted his theory. Besides, no way was she going to broach the subject with Emma's parents.

A more intense episode occurred when Darisete introduced Isabel to food cart humor.

"These three guys were sitting on a bench in the park, kind of out of it," Darisete began. "Then, two of them sent the third to the ice cream cart."

"I'm already laughing," Isabel said, straightening up, at attention. She often thought Darisete would make a great stand-up comic. Maybe she'd be able to talk him into doing something at an open-mic night on campus.

"'I'll have vanilla with hot fudge, nuts, but no whipped,' the first guy says. And 'I'll have a banana split with chocolate ice cream and caramel sauce, and strawberry ice cream with peanut butter sauce,' the second guy says.

"'Shall we write it down for you?' one of them asks.

"'No problem. I got it,' says the gofer guy."

Isabel smiled broadly, waiting for the punch line.

"The guy takes forever and finally comes back with three hot dogs. 'There was a long line,' he tells his friends. 'Sorry it took a while.'

"'That's okay,' says one of the guys, reaching for a hot dog.

"'Yep,' says the other guy. 'Where's the mustard?'"

Isabel laughed so hard she almost missed the action from the strollers. She turned when she heard strange noises that sounded more like adult chortling.

"Wow, look at those babies, Darisete," she said. "They're snickering as if they understand your joke." She looked over to see Jayden slap his little knee, and Emma cover her noisy mouth with her hands. Both babies sported flushed red cheeks from strained chuckling.

"Let's see," Darisete said. He picked up Jayden. "Hey little guy, what's up with you?" He tossed his charge over his shoulder and rubbed the baby's back. "You have indigestion or something?"

When Isabel asked the same questions of Emma, the baby shut her eyes and went quiet.

Neither baby answered with anything but a limp body as their breathing returned to normal.

Isabel had experienced this often when looking after Emma, the baby seeming to participate in the adult conversation around her.

"Emma has always been a little . . ." Isabel paused, trying to summon a word that would be inoffensive, "mature." She whispered, though on this chilly end-of-summer day the park benches were nearly empty. Labor Day was on the horizon and the joggers were in full force.

"Same with Jayden," Darisete said, still rubbing the child's back. "I think they're just talking to imaginary friends. Most kids have them."

Emma shrugged. "Sure, most kids have them, but not at two or four months old."

"Our kids are special," he said, bringing Jayden around to hold him in front of him. "Aren't you, buddy? Aren't you special?"

This time, Isabel was less convinced. She thought about finally bringing up the topic with Emma's parents.

But what would she say?

That Emma behaved like an adult? That, crazy as it sounded, she suspected Emma could already get out of her crib by herself? That often when she thought Emma's mom had arranged the child's clothes for the next day, it turned out neither parent had done any such thing?

If she broached the subject, they'd probably think Isabel had gotten into the liquor cabinet. Come to think of it, maybe Emma's parents were—but no, Isabel knew they were as close to teetotalers as you could get and still have been members of Manhattan society.

Enough of that. Isabel returned to the present with Darisete, happy to drop the kid talk and get back to their own plans for the weekend. They'd been talking about getting together by themselves on Saturday, until their four parent-bosses asked the nannies to cover for them so they could attend an adults-only wedding.

"It's double pay," Darisete reminded Isabel. "Plus reimbursement for wherever we decide to take the children." He suggested taking the charges to Manhattan.

Isabel acknowledged it was a good deal, and they'd have Monday off to boot. Maybe that could finally be a real date with no baby talk.

Even after the close call in the park over Darisete's joke Emma was ecstatic. A trip to Manhattan this weekend, maybe to the Rose Center for Earth and Space, but any museum would do. She had a feeling about Darisete, that he understood their need for more than a rattle or a "There, there," when she and Jayden reacted to a conversation.

Emma and Jayden had done their own preplanning, mapping out a way to mail their parents' ballots. They'd decided to put the four envelopes together as a package.

But how to get the package into a mailbox? As smart as they were, neither child could get to one by themselves, let alone reach the drop slot.

The answer came in the park on the Friday before their trip to Manhattan.

Isabel had left them alone with Darisete to catch up with a girl-friend from school who had jogged by.

Darisete pushed their strollers closer together and leaned down to talk to Emma and Jayden.

"Alone at last," he said, and winked. "I'm on a mission to save American democracy. I'm hoping we can help each other."

Emma bolted upright in her stroller, knocking the pink bow off her head. "I knew it. I even know your name is an anagram for—"

"Shh," Darisete said. "Not now. Can you get your parents' ballots to me?"

"Yes, yes," Jayden said, talking excitedly about this step forward. "We've already wrapped all four ballots in a blanket."

"And hidden the blanket way back in my closet," Emma said. It felt so wonderful to be talking out loud to an adult.

Isabel was on her way back to their bench, so Darisete finished up quickly. The so-called babies would leave the blanket-wrapped ballots on the back seat of his car on the way to Manhattan in the morning. He'd pick up the package, stuff it in his jacket, and find a mailbox.

"It's going to be so much easier to maneuver the envelopes into a mailbox in Times Square," he said. "The jostling crowds will distract Isabel."

"I get it," Jayden said. "The operation would be almost impossible in the wide-open, empty streets of Fairville."

Emma had so many questions for Darisete. Who was he? Where was he from, really? He'd claimed to have come from Idaho, but Emma had her doubts. Had he been stuck in a two-month-old body at one time? What was in store for her as she grew older?

Isabel was back, and life returned to normal. Emma didn't have answers to her questions, but she now had hope for her future.

The Times Square operation went off without a hitch. Then they'd walked all the way up to the Hayden Planetarium, where Emma thrilled at the lecture on organizing the stars, ocean worlds, and super-Earths.

Back in her crib, she saw her place in the universe of two trillion galaxies. Maybe she'd switch her major to astrophysics. When she heard on the TV news that blue had won the election, Emma closed her eyes and smiled while the voice of Ray Charles singing "America the Beautiful" ran through her head.

Darisete had disappeared. The rumor was he'd been called back to Idaho to take care of family business. Emma didn't believe that for a minute.

One thing he'd taught her—no matter where in the universe you live, no matter the obstacles that needed to be overcome, there was always a way to make your vote count.

THE CHINATOWN HONORARY MAYOR CAPER

PATRICIA E. CANTERBURY

MY NAME IS TANNER SULLIVAN. *I was born in the Northern California town of Weed, the great-grandson of the largest landowner in the county, Liam Sullivan. Great-grandfather Sullivan arrived in California in the late 1820s as a ship's mate from Ireland along with his Senegalese wife, Kiara, and young son. It is family legend as to how the three of them ended up in Weed, but I do know Great-grandfather worked in the gold mines alongside Chinese laborers, while Great-grandmother cooked and made clothes for the few other women in the area. After many years my great-grandparents were able to buy larger and larger parcels of land on which to raise cattle and a few sheep. Kiara spoke her native Woolf, French, and English, while Liam spoke English, Gaelic, and basic Mandarin, which he learned from the Chinese workers. As a result Grandfather Walter was fluent in languages needed for bargaining with early Californians.*

As their holdings grew so did their influence in the area. My father, Walter Amir Sullivan, became a banker and his older brother, Liam Patrick Sullivan Junior, owner of the family ranch. I was expected to follow in my father's footsteps and take over the family bank once I returned from the Grand Tour of Europe after graduation from Stanford, the Class of 1925, with my degrees in economics. The

Great War had ended and was fast becoming a distant memory, especially for those of us in college. I was on the tour without a care in the world when my 16-year-old niece, Anna, and her best friend, Li Wang, went missing in San Francisco while on a visit to Li's grandmother.

A month passed before I learned about the missing girls. I vowed to find them and bring them back home. It's been nearly five years. I received a private investigator's license so I could work closely with the police, and the fact my family has quite a bit of money helps open doors which would normally be closed to a colored man. During the years in which I have searched the nooks and crannies of various levels of San Francisco's Chinatown I have been involved in some interesting cases. The following is one of my favorites.

Bing, the son of the owners of the Golden Dragon restaurant, rushed to my front booth carrying a tray laded with soup for a family of six. I knew the food was not for me as I was finishing the last of his mother's famous banana cream pie. A second later I would have been caught licking the cream from my spoon. It would not have looked good for me, a working private investigator, and a man who'd be twenty-seven in a few months to be seen indulging in a children's ritual but Lily Wong made the very best banana cream pie in all of California.

"Tanner, one of Ming Lee's sons wishes to see you at the back parlor," Bing whispered, slightly out of breath. The restaurant was full and the family was short staffed. Bing as usual was doing triple duty.

"Me? What does he want with me? I just saw Ming Lee yesterday. He must have news about Anna," I said before Bing could respond—he was already turning toward the private rooms in the rear.

Ming Lee is the honorary mayor of Chinatown and a friend who has been helping me search for my lost niece and her friend for the past year. Other than regular bi-monthly gatherings to verify sightings of strangers who wish to be in either of our good graces we have nothing in common. To hear he sent one of his twelve sons to one of my favorite watering holes late at night to find me was puzzling. I briefly wondered if he'd sent all but his three youngest sons to find me. The youngest sons were still under ten years of age.

I followed Bing, who was delivering a dinner to the room next to where Ming's son was seated. Most of the secluded rooms near the rear are where families with small children have dinner without disturbing the rest of the paying customers. I expected to find many members of Lee's family there, but only two men were seated when I arrived, neither of whom I knew personally but I knew of them through their father and Sally's parents.

"Ah, Mr. Sullivan, my father's friend. I am Xi, Father's eldest. I noticed you seated by the front booth when I arrived," Xi said, smiling slightly in my direction while extending his hand, offering me a seat across from him.

He looked nothing like his father, a short, slim man close to seventy years old. No, Xi was tall, nearly as tall as I at six feet, but he looked as if he weighed about forty pounds more than my 195. I knew from Sally's dealings with the family that Xi was thirty years old, only three years older than me, although to hear her discuss his shortcomings he was an extremely old-fashioned man and set in very conservative ways. He had the firm handshake of a man used to dealing with non-Chinese folk in a business setting. Xi's manners suited the man who would someday take Ming Lee's place in business. But I could also imagine him representing his father on the docks. I'm sure no one would deliberately cross him without suffering the consequences.

Xi continued speaking while offering me a red lacquered box filled with small cigars as I got seated. I'm a pipe smoker but I rarely turn down a good cigar, and I knew if Xi was offering me one it would be excellent.

"Thanks," I said as I lit my cigar in the smoke-filled room. "These cigars are interesting."

"My brother, Chen, here," Xi said, pointing to the man seated next to him, "brings them back from Cuba."

I nodded to Chen, who nodded back in my direction and continued reading the local Chinese newspaper.

Xi said, "Someone outside Chinatown is spreading falsehoods about my father's business in situations which do not always welcome Chinese."

"And you need me to do what you and your family cannot do?"

"Mr. Sullivan, you know folks in high places I, my father, nor my brothers do not have the pleasure of knowing . . . yet. Folks who may wish someone like Tommy Sung as honorary mayor of our little, but powerful, section of San Francisco."

"Tommy! Everyone west of New York knows Tommy's a Tong boss. No one in their right mind wants him to be honorary anything in Chinatown, or anything else in San Francisco. Where did you get the idea Tommy wishes to run for office?" I sat back in my chair attempting to understand what Xi was actually telling me.

"We have information Tommy Sung is working with the port authorities about some of the new cargo ships coming to San Francisco during the next few days. The ships' cargo is of interest to some of the whiter folks in our humble city."

"And your father asked you to ask me for help?"

"No! Father has too much pride to ask anyone who is not Chinese for help with anything to do with him or his business. I am asking you because I know of your reputation outside of Chinatown. I understand a close friend, a Patrick Murphy, is a police officer who's life you saved a few years ago. He might be able to ask questions about the election as he goes about his daily routine. And your girlfriend, Eleanor Jones, she's a nurse at the General Hospital on the night shift, she also might hear something from injured folks who arrive in the emergency room very early in the morning," Xi said, adding hot tea to his cup as he took small bits of steamed rice and slices of Peking duck. "Feel free to have some rice and duck while you think over our offer."

"Thank you, but I've already had my supper. Let me think this over. How can I get in touch with you if you don't want Ming to find out I'm meddling in his business?"

I had to do some quick thinking, Xi knew about my friendship with Patrick Murphy and about Eleanor, whom I'd been dating for a few months. Dating, that's a funny word—with her work and my work we barely see each other once a week for tea. Xi interrupted my thoughts.

"Chen or I will drop by your office. We both know where it is."

I nodded once again to Chen, who had not said a word since I entered the room. Chen again nodded in my direction, but this time he lay down the newspaper he'd been reading and looked me over, as if trying to find out if I was hiding something inside my suit jacket. I wasn't. I rarely carry my gun when I go out for dinner.

I left the Golden Dragon and walked the few blocks to my office. The restaurant is close enough I usually don't drive my car when having lunch or dinner. It was close to midnight and I should have gone home and gotten a good night's sleep, but I was concerned that too many questions were left unasked by Xi. I couldn't just drop by his father's grocery store and ask if anything was wrong. Instead I picked up a late edition of the *San Francisco Chronicle* and the weekly *Mandarin News*, the newspaper Chen was reading earlier. I was hoping something in either, or both, of them would clue me in to any trouble Ming Lee may be having with his reelection next month. I poured myself a fresh pot of monkey-picked tea without adding any liquor, as I frequently do when attempting to solve a puzzle. I settled into my comfortable leather office chair and opened the *Mandarin News*.

As expected the news was filled with ads about businesses closing

—so many folks are having a very hard time during the Depression, which has lasted so long. There were pictures of the girls running for Chinese New Year Princess, and ads for fresh fruit and bargains on bags of rice. I almost missed the most important ad. It was a small one on the inner fold stating the name of Bo Chang for Honorary Mayor of Chinatown.

Bo Chang is one of Tommy Sung's henchmen. A small, slender man, who moves with deadly swiftness through the dark alleys of lower Market Street, Chinatown, and through the cargo-filled piers of the port channel. So Xi was correct, Tommy was trying to home in on Ming's legacy as mayor. But why? There is little or no money in the position and even less recognition, except for the elderly Chinese who still cling to tradition.

Exhausted I gathered up the newspapers and dropped them in the back seat of my Ford then went home for some much needed sleep. I vowed to go to the docks later in the morning to dig up whatever information I could find regarding Bo Chang and Ming Lee. I needed to do my investigating while Sally was at work or I'd never get anything done.

The morning was enveloped in fog so thick I couldn't see across Clay Street from my living room window. It was a perfect day for me as I enjoy mornings where the fog lingers until mid afternoon. I can usually get a lot of work done on days such as this. After my morning shower I decided not to shave—I found sometimes it was best if I looked a little ragged around the edges, especially if I was going to be at the docks most of the day. I made myself some toast and tea then walked downstairs to my trusty car and headed out. I knew it was too foggy for any new cargo ships to arrive until later that morning, and many of the men hanging around the docks hustling for jobs would be anxious and nervous as the morning drew closer to eight o'clock and the fog persisted. It meant less work was available and some younger men would be bored just sitting around, smoking, wasting time, and willing to talk about nothing. Nothing was what I was searching for as I couldn't understand why Tommy Sung would want to be involved in a position which pays nothing and brings notice to him and his underworld business.

~

"Tanner, what brings you to the docks so early?"

Patrick Murphy walked up to my car as soon as I pulled up in front of the Frog's Breath Diner. Lucky for me the line of men looking to work the docks didn't extend that far. I hate seeing men who look like they may have a young family somewhere out hustling for food or change. Some I could tell were just a few years older than me, were probably in the Great War and were now searching for work. I hate turning them down but if I give to one, I end up giving to twenty.

"Paddy, long time no see. Still working the morning shift I see. Glad to see you. How about joining me for a cup of coffee?"

"Never turn down a cuppa. What brings you out so early?" Patrick repeated.

"I was hoping to find out what Tommy Sung's doing with some of the new cargo ships. Also read he has a fella running for Ming Lee's mayoral job."

"No kiddin'? I didn't think Tommy's folks would want to get close to city hall. Besides it wouldn't be a fair fight. Everyone in Chinatown, old Chinatown, is so afraid of Tommy and his men there wouldn't be any reason for a vote. But might explain why I'm on this new assignment. I'm working overtime looking out for new Chinese folks seen hanging around the boats coming up river from Stockton, Sacramento and other places along The Sacramento. You know they only carry rice and tomatoes. The tomatoes are off-loaded in Oakland and the rice comes here to San Francisco. Still, I ain't seen any of Tommy's folks around the new boats."

Patrick settled into his seat in the diner. Rosemary, the morning waitress, who both of us knew from her previous position as a whore for Ralphie Garcia, one of the Latin gang leaders who interacted with Tommy Sung, served us coffee and walked away before we could order breakfast. I'm sure she assumed whatever a cop and a PI might be discussing she shouldn't overhear.

Patrick said, "I agree, everyone loves Ming Lee—he and his family grocery stores have been fixtures in Chinatown since right after the gold rush. The original store even survived the '06 earthquake and fire. What would Tommy gain by taking over a ceremonial position? There's something we're not seeing. I'll check around, see if I can find out anything while I continue to search for what's really going on with the rice deliveries and, of course, any new clues regarding your niece."

"I'm going to try to get a job at one of the larger cargo ships later this evening. If you see me not wearing one of my regular PI suits pretend you don't know me unless I pull out a red bandanna. It's my go-to follow me card," I replied, smiling.

We drank our coffee in silence for a few minutes then Rosemary came over to take Patrick's breakfast order. Since I'd already eaten, I just had a couple slices of sourdough muffins with honey.

It was too early to do anything but walk the docks looking for a lead. Tommy Sung's import–export business was bustling, but I knew I wouldn't get any answers from the men working the day shift. Even the thugs who hung around at night wouldn't say anything to me, but Tommy and I got along quite well. We each knew our boundaries and tested them every so often when other folks were around just to keep in shape. Tommy wouldn't be in his office till close to five in the afternoon.

I continued my walk of the docks and passed a motion picture company setting up for street scenes. I had to walk around light stands and over cable wires, and duck under equipment of various sizes which was taking up most of the street and sidewalk space. Old, dusty cars were parked around a corner waiting for actors or stunt folks to hop in as soon as the cameras were rolling.

All of this activity would have delighted Sally and her new friend Breezi as both are crazy about the motion picture business and want to be actresses, just like Anna Mae Wong and Carole Lombard. Unlike those very talented actresses, Sally and Breezi have no talent whatsoever—unless it is getting on my last nerve.

I wasn't getting anywhere walking the docks. The ordinary men I expected to see were crushed around the motion picture trailers hoping to find daily work from the people pulling up equipment or moving large cameras around. I headed back to my car and returned to my office.

"Tanner, where have you been? It seems everyone is calling regarding something about a rigged election. What does even mean? Who's running for office? Is it anyone you know?"

"Good Morning, Sally." I said as I entered my inner office, took off my hat, threw it toward the coat rack and hooked the fedora on the top. I grabbed the large stack of mail on the middle of my desk and sat down in my large leather chair, refilled my pipe and loosened my necktie. Now I was ready for the day.

"Well, where have you been?" Sally asked again, settling herself into the large rose-flowered cloth-covered client's chair across from me.

Sally is Bing's younger sister. At nineteen she has two years of college behind her and two more before she receives her degree in business where she envisions working for her parents, not as a cook or server, but as an accountant. Both parents envision her as a housewife and the mother of many children.

"Out looking for clues. It's what I do. I'm a private investigator, remember. And your boss. You don't get to ask me what time I come into the office." I replied with a smile in my voice. If I'm two seconds late in arriving at the office, Sally takes it on herself to "make me toe the line."

"Clues? Clues about your niece? You're always looking for clues regarding her. What about the election?" Sally took some of the mail I'd laid back on the desk without looking at, or opening, it.

"What election are you talking about?" I asked, hoping my face would not give away any knowledge I might have regarding Ming Lee's troubles. Anything to do with Ming Lee and business in China-town was an automatic license to investigate for Sally and Breezi. Because of Sally's minimal knowledge of business and Breezi's secre-tarial duties for an accountant both thought they knew everything they needed to know in the realm of business and business dealings. No way was I going to allow the girls to get in my way.

"Haven't you heard? Someone named Bo Chang is running against Ming Lee to be the next honorary mayor of Chinatown? Who would even consider a thing? Mr. Lee works very hard for all the folks here in Chinatown. He even helps those non-Chinese who are looking for work who come into his store looking for handouts." Sally added.

"I'll check out who Mr. Chang is, meanwhile I'm returning to the docks to check out some inventory on the Macao cargo ships which should arrive as soon as the fog lifts." I said in an off-hand manner, knowing Sally would not be interested in going to the docks and looking around through large, dirty, smelly ships overrun with equally large, dirty, and smelly men. No way was I going to inform her a motion picture company had set up production right around the corner from where I would began my search for political answers.

"Ugh, the docks. Is it why you didn't shave? Well, you go by your-self. Breezi and me are going to the movies. A new Charlie Chan movie is opening this afternoon and I will have my work done here so you're on notice I'm taking the afternoon off." Sally replied, picking up the tea pot and walking out of my office in a huff, just as I hoped she would.

"Whew, that was close." I said to myself in my empty office as I reflected on what I had, or had not, learned already today.

Rice from Sacramento and Yolo counties were brought upriver to San Francisco and Oakland ports to be put on cargo ships returning to Shanghai, Hong Kong and Macao by Chinese longshoremen, many of whom had run-ins with Tommy Sung and his men, who kept watch over their own ships bringing in opium and other illegal goods. Therefore, there must be something in or about the new cargo ships which had Tommy concerned enough to have one of his men run for office to keep potential competitors at bay.

Nothing would be happening until near sundown, which was close to 4:30 p.m. this time of year, so I left my office and drove out to San Francisco General Hospital hoping to reach Eleanor before she left for home. She was working a strange schedule, very early morning and going into late afternoon instead of her normal 1 a.m. to noon hours.

"Good Morning, Mr. Sullivan," Vivian, the head nurse, said as soon as the elevator door opened and I stepped out into an eerily quiet hospital floor. "If you're here to see Eleanor you just missed her. You might be able to catch her at the bus stop if you hurry."

She smiled and pointed to the stairs to my left. I took them two at a time and arrived at the bus stop just before the very punctual bus rounded the corner a block away.

"Tanner, how nice to see you," Eleanor squealed as I hopped over the bus bench and noisily settled next to her.

"I wanted to surprise you," I replied, gently kissing her cheek.

"Well, you did. Now behave yourself. We're waiting for a bus. Oh, you forgot to shave this morning," she said, gently stroking my hours-old beard and then, smoothing down her nurse's uniform, crossing her legs at her ankles and reaching down, she slipped off her left shoe and began rubbing her foot.

"Long night?" I asked.

"Yes, some gang fight or something like it. I ended up looking after three Chinese boys, all with knife wounds. You know they give all the Chinese and colored patients to me and Inese, as if the white nurses couldn't help out. Been on my feet since my shift began."

"Oh, you poor dear, you stay right here. My car is right around the corner. I'll drive you to your apartment. I'll even prepare breakfast if you're hungry," I said, getting up, giving her another kiss on the cheek, careful not to scratch her with my growing whiskers before running to my car.

Ten minutes later I had Eleanor settled on her living room sofa while I scrambled some eggs I'd found in the ice box and popped bread on the toaster.

"Come and get it," I shouted from the kitchen.

Both Eleanor and her roommate, Daisy Jackson, also a nurse, hated eating anywhere but in the kitchen no matter how tired or worn out either of them were. Daisy worked the day shift at San Francisco General and even when she and Eleanor were working the same hours, they rarely saw each other except on the weekend.

"I'm delighted to see you, as I said earlier, but what brings you out this way so early?" Eleanor asked in between bites of toast smothered in raspberry jam.

"Tommy Sung—"

"Isn't he a Tong boss?" Eleanor interrupted, wiping a bit of jam from her right cheek.

"Yes, well, one of Tommy's henchmen is running for mayor of Chinatown—"

"But isn't Mr. Lee continuing in the job?" Eleanor interrupted me once more.

"Yes, he's going to try to, but I've been asked to look out for the men who may want the position."

"I didn't think it paid anything."

"You're correct, it doesn't, but something else is going on."

"It seems very dangerous, dealing with Tong folks and such. You should stick to trying to find your niece and her friend."

"I'm just going to check out what might be happening on some of the new cargo ships coming into port as soon as the fog lifts."

"New cargo ships?" Eleanor yawned, sipped some now cold coffee and said, "One of the young Chinese boys who was under my care mentioned something about needing to get to the cargo ship . . . or something like that when he was first brought in. He was in and out of consciousness and I wasn't really listening to him. I thought he might be speaking Cantonese, which I don't know well. I am probably wrong." She yawned again.

I knew I wouldn't get anywhere arguing, especially with a tired nurse who'd been on her feet for over eight hours and even with toast and a couple of scrambled eggs was having difficulty keeping her eyes open. Eleanor slowly got to her feet, carried her empty cup and plate, and put the dishes in the sink. She walked me to the front door where she gave me a very deep kiss, which tasted like raspberry jam and nearly had me regretting my decision to leave. I gave my thoughts a second to focus and ended up leaving a very, very tired girlfriend for another day.

Once in my car I returned to Chinatown and parked a block from Ming Lee's grocery store to listen in on street gossip. There had to be something going on whereby young boys were fighting each other hard enough for some to be sent to the hospital. Street vendors would know something. Some, not many, whose carts were close to Ming Lee's store would know. I understand Mandarin, I just needed to wander by those who didn't know me and listen carefully.

The street was full of beggars and almost the same number of shoppers, grandmothers out for a stroll, and young mothers, surrounded by small children all pushing, pulling and pointing at colorful items out of reach of working class families, and nearly out of reach of the tourists who wandered wide-eyed looking for bargains in a language foreign to most.

Among the scattered whispers of Mandarin, English, and German I overheard a few words in Cantonese, a language I do not speak but understand enough to get by. I wandered nearer to the Cantonese speakers as they discussed a local robbery in which a lot of money had disappeared. When I got close to the man who seemed to be the one with information everyone got quiet and I walked away. I had gotten a good look at the workers and could identify them later if I needed to ask questions.

So there had been a robbery. One big enough to cause talk on the street. Were the boys from the hospital involved? I wished I'd asked Eleanor more questions, not that she would have told me anything that she believed would get me in trouble with the Tong.

If there was a robbery, and if the thieves had stolen from Tommy, soon all of Chinatown would be talking and not just in quiet corners or dark alleys but out in the open, in stores and on the streets with strangers. I drove over to the police precinct where most of the police and investigators knew of my work, and while many didn't approve of a colored man mixing in police matters they looked the other way when my family's money was brought up by those in charge. I took advantage of whatever opportunities came my way.

"Good Morning is the chief in his office?" I asked the desk sergeant as I entered.

"Ah, Mr. Sullivan, anything I can do to help you out?" The

sergeant, an older gentleman with about two years left before retirement, asked.

"No, thanks, I want to run something past the chief."

"Go right in, you know where his office is. He should be alone. I'll call and let him know you're on your way."

"Thanks."

Chief Gerald (Jerry) O'Rourke had been precinct chief for three years. He was an honest and fair man who took his job seriously. Patrick introduced me to him right after his promotion to chief.

"Hello, Tanner, have a seat. What can I do for you?" O'Rourke asked, leaning over his desk and shaking my outstretched hand.

I filled him in on what I had learned on the streets of Chinatown. I did not mention that Eleanor, whom he had met at one of Patrick's open-house garden parties, had treated a couple of Chinese boys who may have more information than they deliriously told a colored nurse. Knowledge was for me to follow up and share if necessary.

"We have a number of undercover units keeping an eye on the incoming cargo ships. We suspect there's more than rice and vegetables changing hands. Try to stay out of our way. It would not look good if you were arrested along with a few Tong members," O'Rourke said with a slight smile.

"I'll be careful."

~

I returned to my office, where Xi Lee sat looking over the collection of fiction novels Eleanor had bought me for my birthday last year.

"This one's okay. I guessed who the murderer was before the third chapter," Xi said, holding up a copy of the latest Agatha Christie novel.

"Don't tell me, I haven't begun this one yet."

"Hmm . . . you learn anything about the candidates for Dad's job?"

"Only Bo Chang is running. Tommy must be supporting him.

Don't know what they hope to achieve with an honorary position. There must be something obvious we're overlooking," I said as Xi and I attempted to figure out why Tommy was putting money into the mayor's race.

We were silent for a few more minutes as the water boiled for some hot tea.

"This tastes like monkey-picked," Xi said, as a slow smile crossed his face as he sipped the hot tea I'd offered him.

"It is. Your father secures a box or two for me whenever he has a shipment coming from Macao."

"Macao! Father only has goods arriving from Macao in the late winter when he brings the New Year prizes, toys, and decorations. There must be something in this year's shipment that Tommy wants. Something the authorities wouldn't be looking for in any cargo for Father."

"Opium!" we both said together.

"Tommy's trying to use Ming's yearly shipment to smuggle opium into the city," I added.

Xi looked mad enough to kill Tommy right in my office if he had walked in.

"Wait—" I poured a shot of scotch into Xi's tea, hoping to calm him down. "How would Tommy's people get their hands on anything with your father's name on it?"

Xi had stood up and was pacing my office, "The New Year's products do not have Father's name on the label. They are addressed to the Chinatown mayor, so they are not mixed up with the regular import for the stores."

"Clever, somehow we have to intercept the ships' cargo and search them, and confirm what we suspect. We may find nothing but New Year's stuff. "

"And how do you determine we do this? Neither one of us, nor any of my brothers, look like longshoremen. Plus I can't put word out on the street . . . Tommy has thugs everywhere."

"Give me a couple of days . . . I'll think of something. It's why you hired me right? To help you and your family without letting your father know he may be in danger."

Xi slumped back into the guest chair, sipped the last of his scotch infused tea and slowly nodded his head.

Sally burst into my office just as Xi was putting on his hat and coat.

"Oh, Mr. Lee, surprised to see you here. Is there anything I can get for you?" she asked, blushing, and smiling up at Xi.

Sally's had a crush on him since she was five years old, but she won't pursue anything further because Xi is very old-fashioned, and at thirty too old for her, plus any wife of his would have to remain home having grandchildren for Ming Lee and not be running to the motion picture theaters with girlfriends, or worst yet working for me and getting into police business. One of them would have to change. I would not bet on it being Sally.

After a few hours of paying bills and looking over old cases I locked up the office and ran five miles through the still-lingering fog along the beach, then went home and changed into what I call my "invisible clothes"—old, faded, holey overalls, an equally faded long-sleeved pale blue cotton shirt, comfortable, sturdy, scuffed dark brown soft-soled shoes and a ragged tweed hat I've had since before college. In this outfit no one would suspect me of being a well-off member of society. I drove my car close to the night-hiring halls near the docks and walked four blocks, trying to look exhausted while I stood in a long line of men looking for light duty or inside jobs.

After an hour I was close to the front of the line. I overheard a large white man shouting orders to someone inside in a language I didn't understand. He looked over in my direction and yelled, "You, nigger, come here." I pointed to myself and shuffled to the front of the line, taking off my hat and crushing it between my fingers, pretending to be the humble colored man I wanted him, and everyone around him, to think I was. I would remember his insult and make sure if he was involved in anything illegal, and I could prove it, I'd make him eat his words. Meanwhile I played the ignorant Negro.

"Yes, you. You're the only nigger here."

"Yes, sir. Somethin' I can do?" I asked, lowering my head and gritting my teeth.

"Yeah, you look like a strong boy. We need someone to keep the Chinks in line. Can't waste anymore time of my good men," he answered laughing. There wasn't any humor in his laugh.

"We pay fifteen dollars a week. You start now, understand?"

"Yes, sir, fifteen dollars a week. I keep the Chinese in line. I can do it. I start right away." I replied. I knew the wages for what he was asking paid twenty-five dollars a week. But I didn't say anything and acted excited to have a paying job. I sure hoped I'd find something illegal—money, opium, smuggled people—anything to put the man in his place.

"You gotta name, boy?"

"Yes, sir, Henry Moore."

"Can you read and write?"

"Yes, sir. I been in school to the third grade."

"Third grade, huh. Yep, you'll do alright. Follow me."

With those words the man who hadn't told me or anyone near what his name was walked off deeper into a weathered, pale green, four-story warehouse.

As my eyes adjusted to the initial darkness of the warehouse I made out large cartons of goods with various names stamped on the side. None were in English. A few were in Spanish, some in Mandarin, and the remainder in what looked like Russian. I had no way of knowing what the containers held but I suspected it was illegal goods of some kind.

I made my way through the warehouse to a large room near the rear in which ten Chinese men stood, packed together, looking at us through a very large wire-screen enclosure.

"These are the Chinks you'll be responsible for. If you lose anyone you'll be the one to pay the bosses. Understand?"

"Yes, sir. I'll keep 'em in line. What you want us to do?"

I could tell from the way the men clung to each other they were relieved someone had found them in the wire cage, although from the continued nervous glances at me and the white man speaking they had no idea where they were or what to expect from either of us. All of them were sweating and shaking, and trying not to catch the eye of the white man. I needed to remain calm and hopefully my calmness would somehow transfer to the Chinese men, because if they decided to gang up on me and scatter I might die and God knows what would happen to them. Drawing every ounce of courage I could gather, I smiled and stepped closer to the men.

"Wait here. I'll be back with tonight's instructions. You might want to get to know your workers."

Laughing, the white man looked all of us over. Still laughing, he unlocked a padlock I had not seen, which held the wire sides of the giant cage together.

"Oh, they don't speak English but I'm sure you savages have a common language where you can get them to understand you." He walked away, laughing once more.

Whoever he was he was getting on my last nerve but I had a job to do and his comeuppance would have to wait. I also knew I had to keep my undercover disguise intact if I was going to help these men and find out if Ming was in any trouble.

I counted slowly under my breath to a hundred as the men stood frozen in place. I then said in Mandarin, "I will help all of you get away from whoever these people are but we have to do what they say for a while, until I figure out what's going on here and who's in charge."

To say there were ten astonished faces staring back at me would be an understatement. Not only did white folks not expect me to understand, much less speak, Mandarin, neither did the average, everyday Chinese man on the street. Everyone began speaking at once. I held up my hand and asked the man closest to me what he knew as I opened the cage doorway as wide as it would open and stepped away until all ten were outside, scattered among the low-lying boxes, and surrounding me.

"Where are we?" the man closest to me asked.

"San Francisco."

"We're in North America? Does everyone in San Francisco speak Mandarin?" he asked incredulously, as everyone began speaking excitedly over each other again.

"Yes, we're in North America. No, only folks who live and work in Chinatown speak Mandarin as far as I know. Where did you think you were?"

"Chile. We signed up to deliver silk to Valparaiso."

"How did we get to North America?"

"I have no idea. Tell me what you remember."

All of the men were from the same Chinese ship that sailed out of Guangzhou, China over six weeks ago. They were told the ship was hauling silk and rare teas for Valparaiso, Chile, although they suspected they were actually hauling something other than silk and tea, because even with the most secure packaging the containers should have filled with the slight odor of tea during the voyage, but it hadn't. After the first week at sea the men were ushered into another container to verify the cargo when something overpowered them, an odor they couldn't identify, and when they awoke they were bunched together in a large cage much like the one they just left. They were let out, one by one, twice a day or what they thought might be twenty-four hours. It was always during daylight and all they could see were more containers and the ocean. They had limited time topside and ate mainly fish soup and warm tea for meals.

Their original container was larger than the cage they were in currently, with bright lights which flickered when they moved. Most of the time they stayed locked in, terrified to make a sound which would bring the white strangers to them. Because they thought they were going to South America they also thought they might be smuggled to the jungle. All of them took turns listening for the sounds around the container, trying to hear something to tell them where they might be. No one had been let topside for a long time. They guessed at least four days.

I listened carefully to their stories and told them who I was and what I did in San Francisco, and how I came to be with them. I told them not to let on I spoke their language and I would speak to them in English—four of them understood the King's English from the time they'd spent in Hong Kong and could translate for those who did not. I showed them some simple hand signals I would use to get them to pick up boxes, follow me, stop, and stay where they were at a certain time, but most importantly I told them I was working closely with the police. I wasn't, however, I knew if I needed to alert the police I could do so with little effort. Especially with Patrick Murphy on the job, I hoped not too far away.

After nearly another hour the lights in the warehouse slowly brightened so we could clearly see the enormity of the cargo packed to the top, with smaller crates tied together. The crates didn't look very heavy and I hoped it would only take one man to carry a crate. That is if we were going to move the ones I was looking at.

"Hey, Boy!" The man who'd led me into the container returned. "You need to get them Chinks ready to move those boxes they're sitting on and all of those against wall, understand?"

"Yes, sir." My anger had returned. Not only because of the manner in which he spoke to me, but in how he spoke down to the Chinese.

"Make sure none of them run away. You're carrying the crates down the street to the second floor of the blue warehouse. Understand?"

"Yes, sir. Second floor. Blue warehouse."

I went through the pantomime the cargo prisoners and I had rehearsed as the still-unnamed man walked away. I then explained to my group they would follow his orders and move the cartons into the new warehouse while I looked around to find out who his boss may be. If I was gone more than five minutes they should stop working, stay put, and pretend to be waiting for instructions from me. Because the man giving the orders didn't know any of them understood English if he returned before I did, he might shout at them but they weren't to move unless in danger.

I made my way to the top floor of the blue warehouse without being seen. The floor had one medium-sized office with windows that overlooked the street below. Fog still blocked out any sunlight which would have made the office quite comfortable during our San Francisco spring or autumn days. The door was ajar and seated at a large metal desk sat Bo Chang, the man running for Ming's honorary position.

My soft-sole shoes did not make a sound as I retraced my way downstairs in time to yell out to my crew to go back for another set of boxes. Anyone looking for me would assume I had walked off for a smoke or to relieve myself in one of the dark corners. I followed close behind my men, then helped carry a carton and returned to the second floor of the blue warehouse.

Once outside again I bummed a cigarette off a man standing in line near a soup kitchen around the corner from where I was working. As I puffed away, stalling, I wrote a quick note to Patrick stating, *Bo on third floor blue building. I'm helping bring in cargo. TS.*

On my fourth trip back to the original warehouse, following my men, I accidentally bumped into Patrick as he rounded the corner near the soup kitchen. I slipped the note I'd hidden inside my overalls into his hand and walked quickly to keep up with my men who were almost a half block ahead of me.

It took another three hours to completely empty and move the cargo from the original warehouse to the second floor of the blue one. My crew and I were sitting comfortably on the dirty floor of the second warehouse when we heard shouts coming from outside. Before we could move, as the shouting increased, Bo Chang and the man who'd given us our instructions ran down the rear stairs.

"This is the police, come out with your hands up!"

The words were shouted in English.

"This is the police, come out with your hands up!"

This time the words were shouted in Spanish, then Mandarin.

The fourth time the words sounded Russian.

My crew and I walked down the stairs and out of the warehouse with hands raised.

"Good evening, officer, my name is Tanner Sullivan and these men work for me. They've just arrived on a Chinese ship on their way to Chile. We're helping a gentleman, who did not introduce himself, unload many crates and put them on the second floor of this warehouse. I believe he just escaped by the rear door," I said, as a policeman I didn't know began searching us.

He hesitated when I said my name.

"Sergeant, this fella says his name is Tanner Sullivan. I didn't know Tanner was a nig— a colored man," the officer said, correcting his language in case I really was the rich colored man he'd heard of who was friends with the police commissioner. "Murphy. Come over here. Do you know this man?" the officer asked, pointing to me.

"Yep, hello Tanner. Who are these men?" he asked, sweeping his arm in the general direction of my new Chinese crew.

"Congratulations on your promotion. They are innocent bystanders who work with me," I said under my breath.

"I'm not used to the promotion yet. All this happened after I left you at breakfast." Speaking louder, Murphy continued, "Grady, go get an officer who speaks Mandarin to interview Tanner's men. I'll speak with him."

The officer who searched me turned a bright red and hurried off, hoping Murphy hadn't heard how he initially began speaking to me. I smiled, wondering how he was going to try and back pedal the last few minutes.

"Read your note. The police have had several undercover men working the docks and received word that a number of new Chinese, not just your men, were working around the clock on ships loaded with merchandise for the New Year celebration. It's a little early for most of the real goods to arrive if they're going to remain in excellent shape for the holiday: the brass became suspicious." Murphy continued, "One of our men has been sticking rather close to Bo Chang, praising his stand on having the representative of Chinatown with a seat on the San Francisco city council. Our man also suggested it was time for new blood, perhaps blood with a tinge of green, further suggesting Ming has had his turn. There's dark money on the race which has nothing to do with who will actually end up mayor, but the early vote on the street is low down dirty and, in some places, scary."

"It probably has to do with opium or green blood, perhaps counterfeit money," I said, after taking in what Murphy was saying. I glanced over to where my crew was being interviewed by three police officers. Everyone look relaxed and at ease.

"When are you going to open one of crates I helped bring upstairs?"

"I already have men going through the crates just in case all of this is one horrible mistake," Murphy replied, leaning against the warehouse wall.

"Sergeant! Sergeant!" an excited voice called from inside the warehouse just as Murphy and I started to walk toward my men.

"I'm on my way. Tanner, come with me. I want to make sure if the police has found anything incriminating it's from one of the crates you transferred."

∾

The headline in both the *San Francisco Chronicle* and the *Mandarin News* shouted:

CONTERFEIT MONEY FOUND AMONG SILK BOLTS

The stories went on to say the police stumbled on a large cache of counterfeit money layered among bolts of silk on a loading dock. The warehouse where all the funds were found was overseen by Bo Chang who had recently thrown his hat in the ring for Chinatown's honorary major. Mr. Chang disappeared before he could be questioned by the police. Some folks say they saw him and a large white man being escorted onto a departing ship, but when the ship was searched just inside international waters neither he nor his companion were on board.

∾

"Tanner, thank you for saving Father's position. You know he loves riding around on the float, waving to the crowd. He has no idea any of this happened because of your involvement. If there is anything Chen and I can do to help you do not hesitate to call us. Somehow a group of young thugs, still wet behind their ears, were caught trying to get inside one of Sung's ships and were knifed trying to get away. We're keeping an eye open to keep them in line. We're already searching for your niece and her friends," Xi said, a week after the disappearance of Bo Chang and the unnamed stranger. Xi lit a Cuban cigar and relaxed in my office visitor's chair.

"When friends ask for favors I try to help out," I replied, puffing on the Cuban he'd offered me.

NOSTALGIA

JAMES MCCRONE

"IT'S what your brother would want you to do, isn't it?" the Special Agent in Charge said to me. And I knew I'd go, and I'd go for the head.

Four months earlier, we'd been summoned—Jerry, Pete, and me. Called on the carpet. Not that there was one in that shitty room full of electronics junk. A blistering sunny day and the promise of a big payoff had taken a dark turn when two cars bounced over the curb onto the sidewalk in a kind of pincer move, screeching to a stop to either side of where we stood waiting for our food at Shank's on the riverfront.

By the look of the guys in the cars—beefy, top-heavy, thick-necked, and rotten with self-importance—I'd made them as cops. Which is never a good thing. One of them had put a hand inside his heavy windbreaker as he tipped his bulk out of the car, letting us know he had a gun in a shoulder holster.

"Mr. Johnny wants to see you," the one with his hand on the gun had said.

I never did get my order of scrapple fries.

Mr. Johnny's "headquarters" was the back office of one of those restaurant supply/everything stores along Snyder Avenue—junk out front, junk crowding the aisles, no website, no posted operating hours. If you knew about the place, you knew. And there was lots to know about it. But until that day, nothing dangerous. The angry menace in the room was thick as Old Spice and cigar smoke.

Johnny sat there, leaning back in a battered office chair, inter-locking fingers clasped across his belly, an American flag and one of those "Don't Tread on Me" snake banners pinned together on the wall behind him. There were mounted posters and yard signs, and other political stuff stacked against a wall to the left of where Johnny sat. Most were turned to face the wall, but I could see a couple—Back the Blue, Punisher skulls, and black, white, and blue American flags. Johnny was losing it, I thought.

Playing-acting for the goons standing guard behind us, his expres-sion wasn't so much angry as hurt. Like we were his kids, and he was disappointed. Genteel. Almost. My friends Jerry and Pete stared at the ground, their hands fidgety, like peasants who couldn't quite make the rent payment.

"You took what didn't belong to you," Johnny said. "And that makes me unhappy. You *exposed* something," he continued.

Christ, I thought, *dial back the melodrama*. There hadn't been Wise Guys or "turf" in Philly for thirty years or more. Johnny was just a puffed-up fence for stolen goods. People in the neighborhood treated him like a big shot—but only because it flattered *their* vanity, like they were all living together in some movie where the world still made sense. But here he was laying on the full capo bullshit, backed up by guys who sure looked like cops: a mob, but not *the* mob.

"We didn't know, J," said Jerry.

"This seems," I began, "like a misunderstanding." If Johnny and his enablers were looking backward, I was concerned with the here and now. And whether there'd ever be a future. I didn't give a fuck about their nostalgia. I was here to grab what I could get. And just at

the moment, to hold onto whatever I could. "If there are new rules
. . ." I continued carefully, glancing back at the cops, "and we're
supposed to give you a cut . . ."

"I said, you took something of *mine*."

My stomach turned to acid. I glanced at Jerry and Pete, who were
probably still wondering how much of our take it was gonna cost us.
But I already saw that we weren't going to see a dime of what should
have been a big score.

"I need back what you took," he said.

Pete and Jerry looked at me. I nodded, thinking carefully. We'd
hit a couple places recently. Which was he talking about?, I
wondered. He knew about at least one. How to get out from under
the one without letting on about the other?

"What is it you'd like back?" I asked.

"I want those SIM cards," he said. "You can keep the piddly other
shit."

Fuck. It had been too good to be true. When we hit the phone
store down on Oregon Avenue we'd gone in thinking we'd get some
phones, maybe a few SIMs, some pricey accessories we could resell.
But we'd come across a box full of SIM cards—three hundred of
them. Those were valuable. With a black market SIM in your phone,
you could still be tracked, true, but if you did it right, nobody'd know
who they were tracking. Perfect for wise guys. And not only wise
guys. A lot of those idiots who stormed the capitol in January were
ID'd by their phones. With a burner phone and a black market SIM,
as long as they weren't livestreaming themselves on Facebook, they
might have lived to fight another day.

I shot a look at Jerry and Pete. Pete was ashen with fear. I met
Jerry's eyes, and he nodded.

"We can get you those," I said.

At that, the back door opened. Glaring light from the back lot
stabbed through the dim room as someone entered and walked
toward the front. Where the room had been tense and wary, emitting
a kind of low-energy, malevolent growl, the air now was instantly

charged. As my eyesight recovered, I noticed the goons stand up straighter, their shoulders and jaws go taut. Johnny leaned forward in his chair and quickly stood up.

"Dillon," he said, "these are the ones."

"We didn't know it—" Jerry began, but he stopped himself short as Dillon came into view.

Dillon was short but compact, and powerful as he strode up to the desk. Where Johnny and his goons swaggered, a self-important, menacing gait, Dillon tread confidently, like he took it for granted that everyone would just know to get out of his way. He wore the same windbreaker as the others, and I wondered for a moment if there'd been a sale, or if a box of them had "fallen off a truck" recently.

But one glance at him as he removed his aviator sunglasses and looked us over told me to keep my quips to myself. A big pistol, like a .45 in a shoulder holster, peaked out from his jacket as he walked. When he came next to Johnny's desk and stopped right in front of us, I half-expected him to say "At ease, gentlemen." Because he was military, or ex-military.

I'd never seen him before, but I'd seen the type. My older brother would've been one these guys, if he'd lived. Smart, direct, no bullshit. Officer material. On the collar of his jacket he even had an insignia, about the size of a cufflink, with one of those laurel clusters on it, arranged around the edges like the back of those old "wheat" pennies.

"So you still have them?" he asked genially.

I nodded.

"You talked to Mimi about moving them," he said. "Anyone else?"

"No," I said. But suddenly I didn't want us to be the end of the trail, so I added: "Obviously, we spoke with some . . . *colleagues*, shall we say, about who'd be best to move them. Which is probably how you heard we—"

"Never mind how we heard," he said quickly. "I'd like one of you to get them now. You can go with these gentleman." He indicated the three not-so-little pigs.

I noticed for the first time that they wore the same leaf pin, even if no one would ever mistake them for officer material.

"The other two will stay here until their safe return," he added.

"And then?" I asked.

"And then you're free to go."

Jerry nudged Pete, and he stepped forward. The box was stashed in his mother's basement. Two cops went with him. The third stood watch over us in a corner of that shitty, little office. Jerry and I sat quietly on the floor to wait, our backs against the wall. I couldn't hear very well what was going on between Dillon and Johnny in the far corner, but it was clear Johnny wasn't *caporegime*. Whatever juice he had with the dirty cops, it flowed from Dillon and whoever was behind him.

As we waited for Pete to come back, others came in and out, carrying messages for Dillon's ears alone. The boss. Boss of what?, I wondered. He seemed too well off, too trim and put-together to give a shit about some SIM cards that might get us a couple thousand at the most. Dillon probably had guns that cost more than that. I wondered why he'd mix with some has-been, nostalgic buffoon like Johnny. And how did dirty cops figure in? I glanced at the Back the Blue poster on the far wall and smiled to myself. Whoever made that sign, whoever paid for it, probably didn't have all this in mind.

I'd had my head down, kinda sulking over losing out on a nice score, when Dillon came over. I braced for the worst. He squatted down next to us, like some chill, high school guidance counselor.

"How'd you know to hit *that* store?"

"We'd cased it," I said. "Saw some good things. We didn't know about the cards."

"Walk me through it," he said. "Who planned it?"

Jerry flicked his thumb toward me. Bastard.

"You seem to do most of the talking, too," Dillon said to me.

I shrugged.

"So you're in charge."

"We're friends." I said. "We do everything together. Decide things together."

"Uh-huh." He twisted slightly toward me, ignoring Jerry. "Talk to me. What stood out for you?"

"I'm not sure I understand," I said carefully. "Are you talking about our decision-making?"

He perked up at that. "Yeah."

"We're thieves, mister. Opportunists. We saw a new place, not great security, with a lot of accessories we could sell on. Maybe keep a little something for ourselves. That shit's expensive. Finding those SIMs was just icing on the cake."

"Double fudge icing," Jerry added.

Dillon gave him a quick side-eye that said, "shut the fuck up." Which Jerry did.

"And what did that say to you?" Dillon asked.

"I'm at a bit of a loss here, Mr. . . .?"

"Call me Dillon."

"Well, Dillon, we're opportunists, like I said: take the good with the bad. It looked like a good score. We'd've dealt with the bad if there'd been any . . . kinda like now."

"You live in the moment," he said more than asked.

"Yeah," I agreed. *Especially when—again, like now—there might not be a tomorrow,* I thought. "But we're also ready for any extra," I said.

"That's it?" He seemed surprised.

"That's it. Risk versus reward. Be alert, be smart, and take what you can get. And don't take stupid risks."

He stood up. "Can I talk to you outside? Just you," he added, pointing at me.

Jerry looked worried. I put a hand on his shoulder to calm him down as I stood up. Not that I wasn't worried, too. But the lot in back had a long driveway with a clear view to the street. I figured he probably couldn't kill me there without someone seeing it. I followed him out into the blinding sunlight.

"I guess it's pretty clear to you that business-as-usual is over around here," he said.

I blinked, waiting for my eyes to adjust. "By here, do you mean—"

"I mean everywhere," he said, cutting me off. "We're working with Johnny, and with somebody else a little north of here."

"Not Fat Frank?" I asked.

He stared at me like he was adding something up in his head. "Yes," he said finally.

"So, like protection? So you've got some big area, but through guys like Johnny and Fat Frank you're gonna dictate what does and doesn't happen on your . . . *federated* turf?"

"Federated," he said. "That's an interesting choice of words. Maybe more apt than you think. But yes, we're bringing everyone into line."

"Starting with us," I said.

"We started a while ago. You're just behind the curve. How'd you like to get ahead of it?"

He made me a deal. I'd work for him. Jerry and Pete could work for Johnny. They ended up doing low-level stuff. Enforcing the turf rules. I ended up like some kind of consultant. It turned out the cell phone shop was theirs, not Johnny's. They had other front businesses all over town—from the airport in the south to the "collar counties" north of the city, and over the river in South Jersey.

"From the neck to the collar to the shore," I quipped, remembering that my grandmother still called the area south of the Whitman Bridge "the neck."

"I like that," Dillon had said. He was stiff and formal, but we got along. I liked him. I asked him once if he'd served, and he said, "Does it show?"

I'd smiled and said it did. That I remembered my big brother, and how he carried himself. I told him that he'd died in Afghanistan twelve years earlier, and I talked about how strange it was to be older now than my big brother ever was, or would be. Dillon looked sad. He put his hand on my shoulder, and looked like there was something important he wanted to tell me. But he didn't.

I couldn't get a handle on what he was really doing, so I just applied myself to the jobs he gave me. Starting out, I'd go to one of their front businesses and reverse-engineer a robbery—detail the weaknesses. Which they would fix, making it safer. They had a couple other cell phone stores, a landscaping and nursery business, a used-car dealership, and their own car and truck rental business among a bunch of others. It was like the mob was trying to look respectable. But like my reverse engineering, it felt backward, like these fronts weren't for respectability the way you'd figure, to hide criminal activity. But like *they* were the point.

As much as he seemed to like me, too, Dillon kept me on a short leash, strictly need-to-know—and I didn't need to know much, apparently. But I'd still glean stuff from what some of his associates would say as we'd do a walkthrough for one of my "consulting" gigs. Like when I'd pointed out tweaks to make the key box safer at the rental agency, the guy who ran the place asked me about the security for the records room.

"It's fine for your needs," I said. "I mean, who'd want to break into that?"

"The Feds might stage a robbery so they—"

Dillon made a quick motion with his hand to tell the guy to shut up.

Waiting around for job instructions, I began to pick up a lot. On the one hand, what was going on was exactly the kind of thing you'd expect—directed thieving, hijacking, stolen goods, and money laundered through any number of front businesses. Some enforcing, too. Jerry, Pete and Johnny's crew were busy, and hard at work making sure they were the only criminal game in town. And they were cracking down hard on the drug dealers, knocking heads, and maybe a little worse. Which pleased me.

"This is great!" some skinny-suited corporate type announced as he walked into Dillon's Fishtown office one day. "It's working."

I'd usually see Slimfit on the phone—always on the phone—in a glassed-in office just outside Dillon's. The sign on his door read "Leadership Federal PAC." I didn't know how it was related to Dillon's work, but I guessed I saw why Dillon thought my crack about "federated turf" was amusing.

"The *Inquirer* did another piece about how effective the drug sweeps through Kensington have been," he said. He opened the paper he carried to the back page and laid it on Dillon's desk. "But that they're brutal, and isn't that horrible and sad? But look at these letters to the editor! People support it. Which is perfect for us."

Ever since I'd found out that the Taliban had financed their war —and my brother's death—with heroin money, I'd hated drug dealers. And junkies. I agreed with Slimfit, and I'd read about how the Philly cops (on top of our own brand of justice) had broken up a huge drug operation earlier in the month. Which was good. But how was it perfect for us?

Dillon looked at me and said to him: "I'm glad it's working. Let's talk about it later."

The guy looked up, noticed me at the far side of the room and looked back at Dillon like he was guilty of something.

My job changed. I'd deliver the very SIMs Jerry, Pete, and I had stolen to people at the various places I was tasked with checking out. The job also became less about making sure their front operations were secure, and more about information—what could people tell just by looking? So I'd sit outside their shops and watch the comings-and-goings; I'd check out a business's website, call about their hours, or roll by after closing to see what was up.

I wanted to see if my advice was being followed, so when I was out on a new job, I'd also drive by one of the others to see if they'd implemented anything I'd said. Too often, they hadn't done anything. My suggestions wouldn't mean the front business could withstand a full-on investigation, or get a good Yelp review, but they might deflect scrutiny in the first place. Which was necessary, because too often the places I checked out looked like a social club inside—a gun social club. Heavy equipment, too—vests, riot gear. They looked ready for anything, and to keep what was theirs.

I liked the work, making a difference. And I liked the money it brought me. Dillon was building something, and I had my part to play. So far in my life, I'd been concerned only with the present and what I could get my hands on. But Dillon was building something, making something new, and I was a part of it. Idiots like Johnny and his crew were playacting some era when they thought things still made meaning. I'm not sure what my brother would've thought about my work, but he'd have got the building a future part. That's how he saw himself, and he was proud of his contribution to making the world a safer place.

So the lack of follow-through on my ideas worried me.

"It *looks* like it's front," I told him one day when I'd done some due diligence on the landscape/nursery business. "Zero customers. No guys making deliveries, or coming back all dirty and sweaty. Nothing out front for sale. Half the time they forget to put out that little sandwich board that says 'Open.' I called them up, asked about buying a flat of pansies."

"Pansies?"

"My grandmother likes 'em," I said. "The point is, the first time, no one even answered the damn phone—right in the middle of the day. The second time, the jerk who answers stammers 'oh, those are hard to get.' Bullshit, they are. If the Feds get a tip"—and that seemed to be who Dillon was most worried about—"the first thing they'll do is call or drop in, like a customer. And they'll know something ain't right. Worse, you've got a bunch of well-fed assholes loafing around shooting the shit. They don't look like landscapers."

Dillon nodded, thinking.

"I'm sorry if this is bad news, but you're paying me to think of stuff before it becomes a problem, right?"

"It's bad news for somebody," was all he said.

∾

But was it?

One night as I rolled slowly by the landscaping business and parked up the street, I saw Dillon. He stepped out of a car as this big truck swept by and pulled round the back. At first, I thought maybe they were finally doing something I'd suggested. But a delivery at 9 p.m.? And I recognized that they were using one of the blank, box-back trucks from our own rental agency. I took a picture of it to show Dillon later how strange it would've looked to people who lived around there.

The next afternoon, just before closing time, I stopped by the rental agency to check on their progress. They'd updated the anti-theft measures, which was good. But as I came near the truck they'd used the previous night, I was hit with that sweet-sharp stink of fertilizer. I hopped on the bumper and opened the back. It looked like some of it had spilled inside.

"Are you gonna hose that down?" I asked the guy who was walking me around—another of the swaggering, thick-neck type Dillon seemed to favor. "Who's gonna rent it looking like that?

"Do I look like someone who hoses out a van?" he asked.

No, I wanted to say. *You look like the kind of bloated shithead who does as little as possible and bitches about everyone else's lack of work ethic.* "You don't have a maintenance guy?" was all I said.

"No," he said. He looked at me like I was an idiot.

When he turned away, I snapped a picture of the interior.

Dillon couldn't meet with me the next day, so I thought I'd keep gathering information on lack of follow-through. I went by the cell phone store Jerry, Pete, and I had hit. There was a white van (one of ours, again) making a delivery in the side alley. I was about to park and go in, when I noticed some of Dillon's guys waiting around in cars parked along the street. I kept driving, parked about half a block away and walked to a pizza place, where I ordered a plain slice and stood watching on the sidewalk.

One by one, they went in. But each stayed only about three minutes before coming out with a red plastic bag. I couldn't make out what they were carrying inside the bag, but it was pretty clear that each carried the same thing. If they were trying not to look suspicious, they were failing. I snapped a photo of the last guy as he hefted the carrier bag into the trunk of his car. Dillon was gonna be pissed at how sloppy they were being. I was furious.

The cars drove off, and I finished my slice, figuring I'd go into the phone store and check things out when another guy showed up. He parked in the space where one of the others had just been and trotted across the street. Like the guys who'd picked me up that day, and like the guys who'd just left, he looked like a cop, maybe a detective. Even at a distance, the insignia sparkled on his collar in the sunlight. I clocked his car and went to get in mine. Less than five minutes later, he drove by, and I pulled out to follow him. I almost lost him twice, but I stayed with him and watched him drive up through Fishtown, Port Richmond, and into Kensington.

He turned off Allegheny onto a side street that connected with Kensington Ave. where he drew up next to a guy in front of a vacant lot who looked like he was standing guard over a group of refugees. All along the street, in either direction from the corner, junkies lay or sat on the sidewalk, lined up to get well, like they were waiting to get the new iPhone. Some propped themselves up against the lot's chain fence—defeated, bedraggled people, as weightless as the trash strewn everywhere.

I saw a ripple run through the people along the sidewalk as the man at the corner stepped into the car, a quick jolt, like train cars as the engine starts to pull out. I remember reading somewhere that we all carry an ideal vision of the world in our heads—a way of being at home in the world, knowing your way around, having confidence about how you fit in. And even if we can't describe it, we know what it's not.

I stopped at the next street and watched in the rearview mirror. The driver made a full loop around the block, and the sentry got out at the same spot. The car sped past me. But I didn't need to follow him. I was pretty sure I knew where he was going. Doubling back, I pulled up at the curb.

"Wait your turn!" the sentry growled, but he pushed up his right sleeve as he leaned in the open passenger window. He had a tattoo of the insignia leaves on his forearm. He wanted me to see it, like it was his free pass.

"Good," I said, shaken, but trying not to show it. "Just checking." Then I drove by Dillon's Fishtown office, and got a photo of the drug courier coming out. I'd already snapped a picture of his license plate.

Dillon was behind it all.

I lay awake that whole night, wondering if I should confront him, or do something else. I couldn't work for him if drugs were what his future was built on. I felt numb, like one part of my brain wasn't telling the other part what it was thinking. Before I could even think about it, I had sat up and opened a drawer in the nightstand next to my bed. I pulled out a sheet of paper.

I saw what it was, but it didn't register as the thing it was.

It all felt like when I was twelve years old or so, the evening my mother had sent me into the basement to finish off a rat that hadn't been killed by a trap she'd set. With my brother off in the army, it was already my job to take the dead ones out, but this time she handed me a gardening trowel.

"Go for the head," she had said.

I had stood at the top of the basement steps listening to its squeals, its scuffling as it tried to get loose. I held the trowel in my hand. My feet started down the steps, but there was nothing in my mind, not even a picture of what I would do. I just did it. Because it needed to happen.

And I went for the head.

The paper I'd pulled out held the serial numbers of the SIMs Jerry, Pete and I had stolen, written down in six sequential batches of fifty so we could keep track for ourselves on our big almost-score. Then I looked through my phone and double-checked the photos I had taken, of the landscaping business, the cell phone store, the rental agency, and the drug handoff. And I made a call.

Dillon called the next evening, and I froze as I sat in my bedroom, staring at the phone, wondering if he already knew that I'd found out about his drug operation. When I finally answered, he said he had a new job for me—in Buffalo—checking out the operations there. I told him I'd need a couple days to get ready for something like that.

"No problem," he said. "And don't worry. We'll put you up while you're there."

When I met Special Agent Bryson that night in the parking lot under I-95, near Club Risque, I asked if I could see the collar of his shirt. He wore one of those dark windbreakers all of them wear. He opened it.

"Any tats?"

"No," he said, baring his arms. "Nothing."

He gave me a funny look, and I told him about the insignia I'd seen, the laurel leaves that looked like the back of the old wheat pennies. He got really excited, and asked me to come with him downtown to 6th and Arch. Funny, he called it "headquarters," just like Johnny.

"I want you to know," I said before getting in the car, "that I called the DEA, too."

I hadn't, but like with Johnny and Dillon that first day, I didn't want them thinking the trail ended with me. Even if it did. "So they know about all this, too," I lied. "There's drugs involved. I'm meeting with someone from there tomorrow morning."

"Why'd you call us both?" he asked as we drove north along Columbus.

"You got mob wannabes and dirty cops. No offense, but if they've got the hooks in the local cops, why not the FBI?"

He nodded, then said: "Then why not the DEA, too?"

"If the person who picks up the phone at the FBI *and* at DEA is in on all this," I said, "then I'm totally fucked anyway."

"We all are," he said under his breath.

There were eight agents waiting for us when we got to the building. You could tell that Bryson's call had got some of them out of bed. He had me go over all it all again, the turf consolidation, the fronts, the arsenals, dirty cops supplying drug dealers: how Dillon seemed to be the leader. More, how I'd trusted him, like my big brother who'd been killed by the Taliban. How sickened I was about the drugs.

"Jesus," whispered the Special Agent in Charge. "You're not far wrong about the Taliban."

There was a lot of cross talk all of a sudden, and it was hard for me to keep up. One guy took my list of SIM-ID numbers.

"It's no wonder we haven't heard any chatter, or been able track any of them. I'm going to feed these in," he said to the SAC and disappeared out a door.

"I want you to go back over the fertilizer part again," said Bryson.

"Oh, that was just stupid and messy," I said.

Bryson gave me a funny look. "I need the name and address of that business," he said.

I gave it and another agent ran out of the room.

"Where are the drugs coming from?" the SAC asked.

"I don't know," I said. "I only just found about them. But the supply looks to be distributed out of the cell phone store along Oregon. By cops." I told them how the leaf insignia kind of told them who everyone was, who was on the team. "That was the last straw for me," I said. "The drugs."

The SAC stood up. "*That* was the last straw?"

"Yeah," I said. He seemed upset.

"You don't know that fertilizer is the key ingredient for a bomb? Maybe multiple ones, to be detonated somewhere on US soil? Maybe at polling places? At election commission offices? We had tips that that's what they were planning, but they're flying under our radar with the blank SIMs now, meeting, coordinating, exchanging information. And with their car and truck fleet they can move around at will without detection. They can deliver those bombs anywhere, and we'll have a terrible time tracing or tracking them down."

"Fuck." I'd made fun of Johnny (not to his face) for living in, for recreating, the past. But now I realized I was, too.

"And it's all being paid for with drug money. That was the missing piece. You got that part right, at least. It's a fucking American Taliban. The drug money finances everything, laundered through their PAC, which in turn finances election campaigns and issue advertising. It finances and helps organize groups who're intimidating and disenfranchising voters: pays for those bogus recounts and for lawyers to litigate."

"Dillon—" I began.

"We know all about him. He's no one to look up to. He was dishonorably discharged over ten years ago. He pops up on our radar here and there, but we haven't been able to get near him, but he's leading some faction of the Proud Boys or Oath Keepers—or both."

"I thought he was patriot, like my brother."

"He's nothing like your brother, I can assure you. And like the Taliban, they've got a pretty narrow view of who's qualified to lead, even who should vote."

Being at home in the world, knowing your way around, having confidence about how you fit in. We all want that. But Dillon wasn't building a future, I saw that now. These were the death throes of an ugly, menacing world, and like that rat in the cellar all those years ago, it fights hardest when it's battling death.

"*And* they're raising heaps of cash and stockpiling weapons," said the SAC.

"Then it's good I'm getting out now, before I go to Buffalo."

"Actually," he said, "we'd like you to go to Buffalo. It's what your brother would want you to do, isn't it?"

WINNING BY A WHISKER: A PAW-LITICAL TALE

ANN PARKER

ONE FALL MORNING, Joshua Peebles, manager of the Barks, Purrs, and Tweets pet supply shop, was sitting in his small town's coffee shop, reading the tiny, eight-page local newspaper that came out once a week. The big news was the announcement of the upcoming mayor's election, and what Peebles read almost caused him to spill his coffee-with-cream. He turned to his tabby cat, Max, who was in his carrier on the banquette beside him, and said, "I don't believe it! The only person running for candidate is Roger Voss, the mayor's son! Talk about nepotism!"

Max shifted in his carrier. Having just been to the vet for a claw trim, he was clearly not in a conversational mood.

Peebles continued, "Roger's platform includes demolishing the town green and putting in a dog park. Using town funds, that is, taxes paid by you and me and all the other cat owners in town. Sounds rather anti-feline. That should concern you, Max."

Max flicked an ear, irritated.

"I wonder if Roger is trying to court the vote of all the remote workers who are relocating from the city," mused Peebles. "So many have dogs. And if you add them to the regular townspeople who have dogs, those of us in the cat tribe are pretty much outnumbered, on the streets and in the polling booths. Plus, it's just getting worse, every week."

Max pawed at the door of the carrier and uttered a plaintive meow.

"You know, Max, all the dogs are why I can't let you free-roam anymore. It's just not safe."

Max pawed harder at the fabric carrier and yowled more insistently.

"Oh, all right," Peebles finished his coffee, and pulled a leash out from his pocket. "I suppose a short walk wouldn't hurt."

A few minutes later, the two were strolling through the downtown green. Max, unlike most cats, was very leash-compliant. He didn't mind the harness and lead, as long as he could sniff the flowers, roll in the grass, and hunt for bugs. Their pleasant interlude was interrupted when they circled the fountain in the middle of the green and came face-to-face and muzzle-to-muzzle with Voss and his meaner-than-a-junkyard-dog Chihuahua, Bruiser. Normally, Peebles would have crossed the street to avoid confrontation with the hulk-like Voss and his ankle-attacking dog. However, since Peebles was still pondering small-town politics—particularly the politics of *his* small town—he stopped and said, "Hey, Roger, I read in your candidate statement that you're planning to build a state-of-the-art dog park. Why?"

Voss uttered a bark of laughter. "Maybe you haven't noticed, but our population has nearly doubled this past year. The newcomers expect certain amenities. Our focus groups put a dog park as one of the key attractors."

Peebles shook his head. "Yeah, but to help pay for it, you're using town funds and then proposing to double the cost of cat licenses, while making dog licenses cheaper. Isn't that a little unfair? And to put it right downtown, in the town green. Isn't this square supposed to be for everyone?"

Voss's lip curled. "Typical cat owner. You're thinking small. Look, it'll make us a dog-friendly destination and increase our visibility with folks who have bucks to spend. Putting it in the town green brings more residents and tourists downtown, and helps downtown businesses. Besides, man's best friend deserves the best."

"But—"

"Oops," Voss said, in a very unconvincing tone, and dropped Bruiser's leash.

Taking advantage of his newfound freedom, the Chihuahua lunged for Max.

"Hey!" shouted Peebles. He scooped up his cat, which sunk its claws into his jacket just as Bruiser sunk his teeth into the Peebles's pants cuff. "Call off your dog!" Peebles tried to shake Bruiser loose while keeping a grip on his cat.

Voss whistled. Bruiser let go and sat. Voss sauntered over and tossed a treat to his dog with a "Good boy!" while the cat tried to scale Peebles's arm to his head.

"Bruiser hates standin' around. Sours his sunny disposition. Another reason why a dog park would be a great asset to the town. Calmer dogs, fewer mauled cats." He snickered and led Bruiser away.

That did it.

The next day, Peebles put out the word to the town's cat-compassionate to meet at his house later that week to discuss the election.

On the assigned evening, the town's cat cadre gathered secretly in Peebles's living room. Once the shades were drawn, Peebles flipped on the light switch. About forty anxious feline owners stirred in the packed room, perching on chairs, sitting on the floor, and leaning against the walls. The town's oldest residents, the two Pierce sisters, were front and center, gripping their walkers.

Peebles began. "You all know why we're here. We have to do something about this election. If Voss Jr. wins, he's made it clear that he plans to turn the town into a doggy paradise."

The "polite" Miss Pierce, white hair twisted in a neat bun, nodded vigorously. "That's right. I've even heard talk that, if elected, he'll ban cats within the town limits." She nervously plucked at the pearl buttons on her sweater set. " Can he do that?"

Her sister, the "other" Miss Pierce, who had purple streaks in her hair and wore a T-shirt emblazoned with *Don't mess with me*, was notorious for not pussyfooting around. She snapped, "Why not? Towns ban spitting, fireworks, exotic pets. Hell, when we were kids, it was illegal to use foul language on the sidewalk or street, anywhere where someone could hear you. That fucker can do whatever he wants once he's elected."

A tremulous voice from the back of the room said, "So, what can we do?"

"I've been thinking about that. We could write in our own candidate on the ballot. It might end up being just a protest vote, but at least we could make ourselves heard," Peebles said.

"What an excellent idea!" said the polite Miss Pierce. "Who should run?"

"How about you, Joshua?" suggested Mr. Gatti, stroking his Persian cat, Felice, who went with him everywhere in a front-carry cat-sling.

"Uh . . ." Peebles wasn't sure he was up to going *mano a mano* with Voss, particularly after their recent confrontation.

Just then, his cat, Max, strolled into the room, sat at Peebles's feet, and began to groom his whiskers. To Peebles, the answer to their conundrum was as plain as the nose on Max's face. "Let's vote for Max! He'd make a great mayor!"

Miss Elsie, who ran the local cat rescue, clapped her hands. "That's genius! The whole town knows Max! Everyone loves him! Well, at least everyone who owns a cat does."

"Can we do that? Elect a cat? Is it legal?" called out a dubious voice.

"Oh, yes." Miss Elsie knelt, her long, dark hair brushing one shoulder as she offered her hand to Max to sniff. "I read about a small town in Alaska that elected a cat for mayor. And not just once, but many times."

Max sniffed, and then rubbed his face against her palm in friendly greeting.

She added, "We need to make it clear on the ballot which Max we are voting for. After all, there's Max the plumber, Max the realtor—"

"Good point," said Peebles. "How about we all write in Max the Cat." He surveyed the room. "All in favor of writing in 'Max the Cat' for mayor, raise your hand."

Hands shot up. Mr. Gatti even held up one of Felice's paws.

"Motion carried." Peebles smiled, pleased. Max had won the candidacy without having to make a single speech or utter even one meow. "Over the next few days, let's try to determine how seriously residents, especially dog owners, are taking this election. With only one candidate running, I'm guessing interest is low."

"If someone seems inclined to vote for Voss, maybe we can dissuade them," said Miss Elsie.

Peebles shook his head. "Everyone has a right to vote for the candidate of their choice. Let's focus on mobilizing cat owners, and others who might be sympathetic to our cause, to go to the polls." He looked around. "Let's meet three nights from now and see where we stand." Raising his voice above the sudden, excited chatter, Peebles called, "Meeting adjourned!"

Working at the pet store, it was easy for Peebles to casually query dog owners, and others, about the upcoming election. Most evinced little interest.

The local pharmacist said, "Voss is running unopposed, so it's a done deal. Besides, the only time I could get away to vote is during my lunch hour, and that's when I take Fluffy here out for her walk." He scratched his cocker spaniel's long ears, adding, "Fluffy needs her exercise. Voss doesn't need my vote."

Mr. Oldforth, who bought a fifty-pound bag of kibble for his Great Dane, said, "I try to vote in the big elections, ya know. But this one?" He shook his head. "Not worth the time off from work."

Even Mrs. Trimble, who worked at town hall, admitted she would sit the election out. She leaned in and said conspiratorially to

Peebles, "To be honest, I don't like Mr. Voss. He's a big bully, and that Bruiser is a terror. I refuse to vote for him. On principle."

Peebles wavered, wondering if he should tell her about the secret plan to elect Max. He finally ventured, "You can always add a write-in candidate, you know. Someone more . . . balanced."

Mrs. Trimble tut-tutted. "Oh, Mr. Peebles. You know this town." She gestured around the pet store. "Just look at your customers! All shopping for their puppies, and not a cat owner in sight. Well, besides yourself. The town is going to the dogs, quite literally." She shook her finger at Peebles. "You kitty folks need to get organized. Make yourselves heard!"

He opened his mouth to retort that they *were* organized, and that they had a plan.

But before he could she added condescendingly, "But I *know* how you all are. Too busy watching cat videos on social media and feeding the feral colonies outside of town to actually think through the repercussions of this election." She sighed. "You're not deep thinkers and planners, like us dog owners are."

Peebles snapped his mouth shut, swallowed his annoyance, and said, "Mrs. Trimble, I thought you were more open-minded than that. We are *not* all the same."

"Of course, dear." She reached over and brushed a clump of Max's fur off Peebles's blue shop vest. "You're different, I understand. If you had a dog, I could introduce you to the young lady who just moved in down the street from me. She has a well-mannered Pekingese, who gets along very nicely with my Corgi. But dog people and cat people, they just don't mix, do they?"

Among the other excuses for not voting that Peebles heard from dog owners included:

"I work out of town. Can't get to the polling place in time."

"I'm not registered to vote. Too much trouble."

"Ah, the election's already settled. Why bother?"

"Ugh, politics. Borrrring."

As for those people who owned neither cats nor dogs, one fellow who bought birdseed pretty much summed up their attitude. "Not voting. Seems like all anyone is talking about is the new dog park that Voss is pushing. Hey, I've got a pet bird. Why should I care?"

Peebles couldn't help but feel hopeful. If the canine owners were sabotaging themselves, and others found the election irrelevant, maybe a vote for Max the Cat would be more than a protest vote. Maybe Max had a real chance at being elected mayor.

When the cat brethren next gathered at Peebles's to exchange information and updates it was clear that they found few people who were taking the election seriously. Peebles ended the meeting with, "The results of this election will determine the future of the town. That's why we *all* have to make time to vote. We've got to send a message that Voss is *not* acceptable as mayor. A vote for Max the Cat will do that."

The morning of the election, Peebles left home early to vote at the town hall before work. When he walked in, the two poll workers, who Peebles recognized as dog owners, looked at him in surprise.

Peebles held out his hand. "Here to vote," he said cheerfully.

The woman handed him the ballot. "This is for the special election for mayor." It was almost a question.

"Yep." Peebles went into the little booth, printed "Max the Cat" on the write-in line, and emerged with his sealed ballot.

As he dropped it in the locked box, the man said, "You're probably the twentieth cat owner who's showed up to vote so far today. What's up, Peebles? None of you have a dog in this fight, so to speak."

"I can't speak for the others. As for me, I'm exercising my constitutional right." He stuck his "I Voted" sticker on his vest and dashed off to work.

Throughout the day an unusually large number of feline-loving townsfolk dropped by Barks, Purrs, and Tweets. They mostly wandered around the store, buying small things so they could come to the checkout counter and unobtrusively point to the "I Voted" stickers displayed on collars, T-shirts, and jackets. Time ticked by and Peebles's excitement rose with each sticker sighted on a town resident who was part of the local "kitty-brigade." He wished he'd kept a tally of who had come into the store with their voting stickers displayed and whether they leaned toward cats or dogs.

Half an hour before the polls were to close, it was time to close up shop. Peebles turned off the lights and was about to lock the door when he saw the two Pierce sisters coming down the sidewalk, as fast as their walkers would roll.

They halted in front of him, panting, and the polite Miss Pierce squeaked, "Oh, thank goodness you're still here, Mr. Peebles!"

Alarmed, he asked, "Is something wrong?"

"Voss is hanging around the town hall door with that son of a bitch Bruiser," said the other Miss Pierce. "They're not letting us pass inside to vote!"

"Is Bruiser off-leash?" Peebles looked up the sidewalk toward the town hall, almost expecting to see the pugnacious Chihuahua streaking toward them.

"No, no," said polite Miss Pierce. "He's simply on the longest leash you can imagine, and when we approached the door he started that dreadful yapping and tried to bite our ankles!"

"What did Voss do?"

The other Miss Pierce narrowed her eyes. "The bastard just laughed!"

Peebles glanced at his wristwatch. Twenty minutes before the polls were to close. *Every vote counts.*

"Hold on." He disappeared into the store briefly, then reemerged, stuffing something in his jacket pocket. "Let's go."

"Go where?"

"To town hall, so you can vote!"

The three walked and rolled up the sidewalk as fast as they could go.

The other Miss Pierce panted, "Voss knows we're up to something. Somebody must've let the cat out of the bag and squealed about our plan."

"Doesn't matter," said Peebles grimly. "I'll take care of this."

They arrived at town hall to find Voss lounging beside the entrance, one end of Bruiser's long leash dangling loosely from his fingers. The Chihuahua was barking at a pitch and decibel-level to break eardrums and baring his preternaturally white teeth at Mr. Gatti, who cowered just beyond the reach of the snapping jaws. Mr. Gatti's yeowling, thrashing cat, Felice, was tucked into her cat-sling. He had all he could do to keep her from leaping out and running away.

Peebles squared his slim shoulders, strode up to stand beside Mr. Gatti, and said to Voss, "You can't do this. You're stopping these folks from voting. That's illegal."

"Hey, I'm not stopping anyone," said Voss with mock innocence, spreading his arms wide, leash clutched in one enormous fist. "Go ahead, folks, walk on in!"

Mr. Gatti took one tentative step forward. Bruiser lunged. Mr. Gatti jumped two steps back.

Mr. Gatti and the two Pierce sisters looked at Peebles pleadingly. Voss guffawed.

"Pussies. Scared of a little pooch? Bruiser's bark is worse than his bite."

Peebles withdrew the rawhide chew he'd stuck in his pocket at the store. He stepped toward Bruiser and emitted a sharp whistle, imitating Voss's "sit" command. Bruiser stopped barking, and his ears perked up. He cocked his head, as if pondering whether to sit or not. Peebles crouched down and showed the rawhide to the dog. Bruiser's tongue emerged to lick his nose. He plopped his butt down on the pavement, drooling.

Peebles said to his friends, "Go on inside and cast your vote."

The three powered through the door, even as Voss shouted, "You can't do this!"

"Do what?" Peebles dangled the rawhide beyond the dog's reach. "Lie down, Bruiser."

The dog flopped onto his stomach, skinny tail wagging.

"Good boy," said Peebles and gave him the rawhide, along with a pat on his bug-eyed head.

Hurrying over, Voss said, with a snarl that would've done Bruiser proud, "I heard all the cat fanatics are writing in your name, Peebles. You aiming to quit your job at the pet store and become mayor?"

Peebles stood up, straightening his jacket. "Hey, I love my job. I just wanted to be sure that those townsfolk who want to vote, who care to vote, who are committed to vote, are able to. Without intimidation." He glanced down at Bruiser, who was gnawing on the chew with eyes half-closed in ecstasy. "Seems like your intimidator is done for the day."

Voss growled and tried to take the rawhide from Bruiser. The dog snapped at him. Peebles shook his head.

"Best let him finish. You know how territorial dogs are."

The following evening, the cat clan reconvened in Peebles's living room to hear the outcome of the election. Miss Elsie had gone to town hall to gather the final results. The cozy crowd had just settled in with coffee and cookies, courtesy of the Pierce sisters, when Miss Elsie burst in, brown eyes sparkling.

"We won! By *three* votes!"

Mr. Gatti let out an uncharacteristic whoop. "You mean *Max* won! Yay, Max!"

Cheers ascended to the rafters.

Peebles scooped up Max, who had been weaving his way through a forest of ankles, and held him up. "Max! You did it!" He raised his voice. "Here's to our new mayor! Long may he reign!"

Coffee mugs clinked as people toasted Max the Mayor. Peebles's gaze locked on Miss Elsie's, and she gave him a warm smile that sent a tingle down his arms. *Maybe . . . just maybe.*

He decided then and there he would ask Miss Elsie if she'd like to meet him for coffee sometime after work. They could discuss mayoral duties, because Max would need some human help interpreting and implementing the laws and regulations. Being elected didn't mean that Max would be willing to give up his morning naps, his afternoon snoozes, and his before-dinner lie-downs.

Someone said, "Make sure the new mayor knows that if there's going to be a dog park built on one end of the town green, there oughta be a town-run cat café at the other end!"

"With catios!" said Mr. Gotti excitedly.

Miss Elise added, "One cat-patio for kitties available for adoption, and one for local feline residents."

"And make damn sure our new mayor enforces the leash law!" said the other Miss Pierce.

Peebles grinned. "To the *Max!*"

THE LAST SOUND YOU HEAR

MIGUEL ALFONSO RAMOS

ALL PRISONS SMELL THE SAME, of piss and of fear, the basic stenches of humanity. I've been in enough of them to recognize it. Get to know any con well enough and that's what you'll find: a primal fear of death and the darkness around them, piss and shit when they realized that's all there is. Break anyone down, beggar to king, whore to priest, it's always the same.

I should know.

I could smell the sour, low-tide reek of fear rising off of me in waves.

You can't control that sort of thing, especially when being hauled against your will into a small, cold room deep beneath your new concrete mama. The stench of piss and shit and blood was ingrained in the cracked, water-stained floors, in the years of suffering that filled the windowless cell.

The medical supplies, syringes and tourniquets, scalpels and hammers, things I'd never seen before, strewn carelessly on one of the two folding chairs didn't help either. They meant to keep me alive, at least for a while.

I tried to play it cool, just like Bogie, but I didn't feel convincing.

There was only one man in the room, standing beneath the weak light from a single bulb hanging from the middle of the ceiling. He looked completely relaxed, without a concern on his face. Tall, broad-shouldered, hair neatly combed and parted, he had the air of someone used to obedience. He might as well have been eating fried chicken at the church social as standing there but for what I saw in his cold, green eyes—the mindless eagerness a starving dog shows for raw meat, a calculated frenzy waiting to be let loose.

Probably beats the wife and kids in his spare time. Kicks the cat for a laugh.

He had to be the boss.

I ignored everything else and kept my eyes on him.

The guards, clamping my arms, dragged me over to a chair and shoved me down. They didn't bother tying me up. Hell, I wouldn't have bothered tying me up. My right hand was still in a cast, and my twisted legs were never going to work so good after taking three slugs. It was a miracle I still had them at all, but the state wanted me alive for the trial and sentencing, cripple or not, and they had good docs, I'll give them that. My record was long enough that there had been no question about where I'd be ending up, even if five people hadn't died during the heist, even if two of them hadn't been cops. Never mind that Acton and Gathright, my partners, my *friends*, had died too. Their deaths weren't mourned. The cops hadn't been too kind after my capture, scraping me off the floor and throwing me into the back of their wagon to lay in my own blood and vomit, a few kicks thrown in free of charge on the way to the hospital.

At times I wished I'd gone down during the holdup too.

Like right now.

The boss shot a polished gold watch from his shirt cuff and glanced at it.

"Benson. Find out what's keeping the doctor. Tell him I'll be truly pissed off in five minutes, so he'd better hustle his ass down here."

His voice was smooth and low, but I could hear gravel crunching below the words.

"Yes sir, Mr. Strathan," said Benson, the larger of the two uniforms that had escorted me in. He walked quickly out the door.

Strathan caught my eye and grinned.

I shot the grin back, then cleared my throat. "Can I get something to drink?"

Strathan nodded at the other guard, a sad-faced bulldog of a man with a shiny badge pinned to his chest, who left and quickly returned with a tiny paper cup. I took it with a shaky hand and swallowed warm, rusty water.

"I know what you're after," I told Strathan, staring down at his polished shoes. "But I don't know where the money is." My voice was shaky, and I was starting to whine. I took a breath and tried to bring it under control. "I already told that to the Feds. We split up after the bank job and I got nabbed before we could meet. My partners were already dead by then and—"

"And the money has never been found," finished Strathan. "I've read your confession. I just don't believe it. Your partners were killed less than an hour after the robbery. They didn't track you down for thirty-six hours. The Feds may be stupid, but I'm not." He paused to hawk up a ball of phlegm, spitting it into a corner. "I'm also playing from a different rule book. I know you hid that money somewhere, and I mean to have it."

His voice never changed tone. He had total control. My hand was shaking so badly by then that I let the little paper cup fall to the floor between my feet. It made a sad, wet sound. I looked up at Strathan's face, into his cold eyes.

"You can't have what I can't give you." I felt a tear run down my cheek.

He stepped forward and leaned down into my face. "In this room, right now, you don't have anything to give. I'll take what I want and you'll smile through broken teeth while I do."

The door opened then and Benson came lumbering in, followed by a small, dark man with wispy, graying hair. The doctor, come just in time to join the fun.

Strathan stood and narrowed his eyes at the doctor. "Dr. Peruzzi, thanks for joining us. Benson, close the door. Let's get started."

Benson and the Bulldog came up beside me and gripped my arms, stepping on my feet at the same time. The doctor knelt down and looked into my eyes. He checked my pulse, then winked.

Then he picked up a large ball-peen hammer from the collection beside him and started in on my broken hand, breaking the cast with a sure, practiced blow. I screamed, wet my pants, and passed out, but not before hearing my bones re-breaking.

While in the sweet, senseless limbo that my pain created, I relived the robbery, watched Acton and Gathright die in a hail of bullets, felt the enveloping fear that covered my body in a cold sweat as I drove back streets away from the bank, heading inland, to the forest and the dark trees. The money lay safely beside me in the locked steel box, bricks of hundred-dollar bills crisp and fresh and smelling like the future nestled inside it. I drove and listened to the radio, to the news reports, to the continued hunt. I drove to the cabin on the lake, not used since my parent's death: a dark and cold refuge. I found the loose stone in front of the wood stove and buried the money, and then kept driving, hoping for Canada and escape, but finding bullets and pain and more pain.

The pain woke me screaming. I opened my eyes and through a blur of tears stared down at what had been my hand. Bones stuck out from bent and twisted fingers, blood pooled at my feet. The doctor plunged a syringe into my arm and then tightened a tourniquet around my wrist. I slumped in the chair as the pain started to fade, wishing the guards were still holding on to me. I stopped screaming, drew ragged breaths, and looked into the doctor's face.

"Why?" My voice was a whisper, my throat a raw wound.

The doctor smiled, looked over his shoulder at Strathan, and then at me. He patted my shoulder, whispered "Debts," and backed away.

"That's just the beginning."

I jerked my head up at Strathan's voice. The room wheeled

around me like a crazy merry-go-round, then settled on his face, inches from mine.

"Tell me where the money is and it can be the end too."

I stared into his lifeless eyes, then at the chair of scalpels and forceps.

"Fuck you. There is no money."

Strathan's eyes didn't waver. He stood and shrugged. "Have it your way. You will tell me. Every man has his price. How much is your body worth to you? You took $636,000 from the bank. Your hand is gone. Let's call that $10,000." He paused and looked me over.

"Doctor, take off his foot. The right one. That has to be worth another ten grand. We'll talk when you're through." He turned and walked back to his corner. "Keep him awake this time."

The doctor started walking toward me. I tried to move, but whatever he'd put in me kept me still. I felt weak and tired. He kneeled and pulled another tourniquet from the chair, wrapping it tightly above my knee. I could feel my entire lower leg start to go numb. Then he started untying my shoe. Hot sweat popped onto my forehead and ran into my eyes as I watched him carefully remove my shoe and sock. My foot looked alien, a pink sea creature gasping for breath on a bare concrete beach. I looked up at Strathan, at his smirk, and then back to the doctor, filling another syringe and jabbing it into my thigh. The tingling from my lower leg filled my stomach, but my mind became clear. I knew I was playing a losing hand. I waited until the doctor picked up a scalpel, and then I broke.

"Stop! I'll tell you where the money is. Call him off."

The doctor looked up at me, and then back to Strathan, who ran a hand through his hair and started laughing.

"Alright, doc, hold up a minute." He walked over, looked at me, and then flicked my nose in disgust. "So you remember now, do you?"

He flicked my nose again. I tried to move away from his hand, but my head was too heavy.

"You're a weak man, do you know that? We've had much tougher in here before you. I've had men beg me for death, and I've had men die with closed lips, but you're the first to break without even a first cut." He flicked my nose again. "You're weak, and you disgust me. Now talk."

I told him where the money was, how to get to it. Benson and the Bulldog walked over and listened, taking down notes when the directions got specific. When I was done I felt sick, but also empty with relief. Now this madness would end. Strathan gave his men the word and then they were gone, gone to get what was mine, gone to get what I'd paid blood for, what was being stolen from me. Gone to get my future.

Strathan walked over, hands in pockets, smiling. "I knew you'd break easy, con. I can smell the weakness in you. But you did good to talk. You're lucky the money is so close. Now this won't take as long. It was the right move. But you still lose."

His grin got bigger. "Doc, take his foot off. I want to watch him suffer."

The doctor walked back, apology in his eyes, and selected a fresh syringe and bottle from his collection. He injected me, and my body went away, but I could still see it happen, could still watch the blood spill from the clean, sure cut, hear the saw rasp and crunch against my bone, and watch my foot fall to the floor, the toes twitching a little and then stilling, a hunk of dead meat. I watched it all from afar, not feeling it, but screaming with horror within my head. Only whimpers escaped my lips.

When it was through and the doctor had sewn my stump closed and bandaged it, Strathan walked back and leaned down, put his lips against my ear.

"Well done, convict. You give up easily. Now you get to rest until the money gets here. I want you to see me holding it before I let you go." He squeezed my shoulder and then walked out of the room.

The doctor picked up the bloody instruments, and my foot, and followed Strathan out. I heard the door close and lock behind me, and then I disappeared for a while.

~

The door opened and I came awake with a start. I knew right where I was, and everything that had happened, and I shivered from the cold. Strathan and the doctor, Benson and the Bulldog, walked around the chair and stood before me. Benson held a large, steel box in one hand. Dirt still clung to its edges.

"It's locked." Strathan's voice was soft, but tight. He crossed his arms. "Benson here wanted to smash it open, but I said no, let's go talk to our con. He'll tell us the combination. You do remember that don't you?"

I nodded my head. My lips were crusted and chapped, and my body was one large cramp. I could barely sit on the chair. I had no idea how much time had passed, how long I'd been out, but Strathan was right. I did remember the combo. I just wasn't giving it to him. Not yet.

"Give me some water," I croaked. The Bulldog walked out and brought me another paper cup of rusty water. I swallowed it and felt a little better.

"What will you do with me when you have the money?" I asked Strathan.

He looked amused. "What do you think? You'll live the rest of your days in our fabulous care, a cripple, easy pickings for your fellow cons. No one will believe that this ever happened, or they just won't care. Either way, you're a nobody, and you'll live that way until you die. Now give me the combination or you'll be losing something else."

The steel box was thick and heavy. It would take Benson a long time to smash it open, and they wouldn't want to use a cutting torch for fear of burning the money. There was a safe lock on the front of it, strong and secure. I had been counting on the lock from the beginning. I knew Strathan would demand the combination, that he would bring the box here to be opened, that he would think he'd really broken me and that he could just wring me again like a wet towel. I'd let him wring me one more time, because I knew he was lying, too.

There was no life ahead of me. They would bury me beneath these walls before letting me loose, even here. I knew I was a dead man. I just didn't want to die alone.

There was more than money inside that box.

"Quit stalling and tell me!" Strathan's eyes were wild. He stalked forward, put a foot back, and kicked me in the stump. I screamed. It was what I needed, the last push over the edge. I fell off the chair, curled into a ball, and started chanting the numbers into the air. Strathan listened and then jerked the box away from Benson, started twirling the dial along to the numbers, turned the handle and finally cracked the box open. I stopped yelling and started laughing as Strathan yanked the lid open triumphantly, pulling the pins on the four grenades, dropping the box, and pissing his pants, then running toward the door. I reached out a hand, slowly, and caught his foot, sent him down to the hard floor.

He turned and looked back at me with a pale face, and I kept laughing as the room erupted into a burst of white light, and I knew that it was the last sound he heard.

THE WOUNDED REVOLUTIONARY

MISTY SOL

MY TEAM CONSISTED of two trusted political advisors and three bodyguards, but I still didn't feel safe. I hadn't been in such a dubious environment since my youth in the ghettos of South Jersey. We were in a sub-basement, deep beneath an abandoned warehouse in Philadelphia. Cold sweat rolled down my spine as we waited outside the steel door. The spiderwebs that filled the corners and lined the low ceiling were thick with dust. Standing beneath a dim yellow bulb, I slapped at the crawling things I imagined dropping onto my neck. Mold and filth-clotted cinder block walls seemed to close in on us, and I reminded myself that the space was meant to be uninviting. This dank, subterranean hell was the perfect hidden lair for the most infamous revolutionary in US history, Andrea "Black Moon" Jackson.

I removed the scarf and dark glasses that concealed my face, lifted my fist to knock at the door, and paused there with my knuckles resting against the cool metal. I needed a moment to settle my nerves. My team had never seen me so rattled and unsure of myself, but I couldn't help it. It was true, I'd met a lot of famous people during my short time in politics and, because I was running for the US presidency, I was somewhat of a celebrity myself. Still, Black Moon was a veritable goddess. This was equivalent to meeting Cleopatra or Harriet Tubman. I was that starstruck.

Before she was Black Moon, Andrea Jackson was making innovations in the emerging field of biotechnology. But no matter how much science she stuffed into her brain, her artistic mind was even greater. My own grandfather was also a well known writer during the Black Arts movement, and had known her. In his memoirs, he wrote about the friendship between her and Henry Dumas.

"Even though nobody can find any copies of the stories they wrote together, I know they existed," my grandfather wrote, "I saw the two of them composing. I was there to hear them read!" According to him, she was in the studio the day Dumas recorded with the musician Sun Ra. She begged him not to take the subway home— even offered to pay for his cab, because she just had a feeling. History proved her intuition sound. Henry Dumas was shot by police as he attempted to board the train later that same evening.

She was an activist and organizer for civil rights, but according to my grandfather, it was her disillusionment over her friend's death that propelled her into the upper ranks of the Black Power movement.

I knocked hard, exactly twice, stepped back, and waited to be identified through the small sliding window cut into the door. Instead the door swung open with a force that should have blown it off its hinges and we were sucked in. On the other side of the hermetically sealed door was a room that was alive with bird and wild animal calls, and buzzing with insect life. Bright lights that mimicked sunshine supported the life of millions of plants. The air was moist and fresh. There was no ceiling that I could discern past the thick branches of trees that seemed to reach up forever. And beneath the canopy there were many tables with laboratory equipment and advanced scientific instruments. Everything seemed to be made of bamboo, stone, and other natural materials. However, all of our attention was on the woman, accompanied by a large black jungle cat, stepping out of the shadow of a thick-trunked Kapok tree: The Black Moon.

No one had officially seen her in more than thirty years. In fact, although her network still operated, the assumption was that she was dead. But I knew better. I wasn't just another politician. I believed myself to be a true revolutionary, like my father, and his father before him. And although I was an aspiring presidential candidate, my ear, indeed my heart, had never left the streets. Of course, I couldn't personally be involved in any of the protests, couldn't venture into the seedy communities where civil unrest took place, but I *cared*. And that had to count for something. This meeting with Black Moon could be my ticket. I hoped that her network could give me something I couldn't buy with all of my money: the Black vote. And so, no matter how old and feeble she was when I found her, I intended her to be the hidden pistol in my sock, the razor under my tongue.

As a child, my grandfather put me on his knee, for the purpose of teaching me important things. Smelling of sulfur, burned tobacco, and the ginger candies he loved to suck on, he had taught me about the history of Black liberation movements in the United States and how they inspired uprisings in Southeast Asia, Latin America, and even on the African continent. Unlike many of those revolutionaries of the past, I had a decent education, connections, and a natural rapport with more conservative elements. I didn't wear my race like an albatross the way most Blacks did. Unlike those angry, complaining revolutionaries of the past, I represented a vision of change white people could relate to.

For two years, I searched in vain for someone who could tell me for sure that Black Moon was alive, and still another two years attempting to locate her. Just when I had given up all hope, just when I had begun to believe the rumors that she, in fact, lay in an unmarked grave in the Mexican countryside, I received a message. Not only was she alive, she had heard I was looking for her, and insisted that I come to her as soon as possible. I didn't waste any time arranging the meeting. I was sure that she wouldn't have much time left. Even though life expectancy had risen some in the last half century, she would be a little more than 110 years old, a good ten years past the age that most people could reasonably expect to live.

But the woman emerging from the shadows was not old. Andrea "Black Moon" Jackson was not feeble at all. She was standing before us looking as beautiful as she had in photos from the 1960s and just as youthful. Everyone knew that there were ways to stay young, secret procedures that celebrities denied undergoing, but there was no technology I knew of that could shave more than *eighty years* off a person. No genetic treatment or plastic surgery on the market could totally stop, or even slow, the natural aging processes to this extent.

When she turned toward us in the light, her eye was missing. I had been briefed about that. We all had been. She had lost an eye during her attempt to liberate immigrant children from detention camps near the Mexican border in 2022. It was the incident that had finally pushed her underground for good. But we could see now that it wasn't just her eye: half her face was gone. Even some of the bone from her upper cheek and around her eye was missing. Smooth skin stretched like a canvas from her neck to her hairline and only a nub of her left ear remained.

The right side of her face, untouched by the violence that had obliterated the left, was entrancing. Her dark skin was smooth and luminescent in the light, reflecting shades of gold and purple. Scar tissue had left her with a strained smile, but the teeth were perfect and white, and her lips still lush. Her remaining eye was a long-lashed black pearl. Even with her scars, she was beautiful, but in a terrifying way. Like the panther that stalked bedside her, she was all shimmery loveliness and lethal fury.

"Good evening comrades," she greeted us.

My team responded in unison like nervous school children. I assumed that they, like me, were intimidated by her very presence. My bodyguard drew in her breath, sharply, behind me and I threw a glance over my shoulder that was meant to be both calming and reprimanding. However, I saw that she wasn't gasping at the sight of Black

Moon's disfigurement, but was staring out past her. My whole team was transfixed. I followed their gazes and swooned with horror.

"You've all heard of my network," she continued, "now you'll be the first outsider to personally experience our greatest achievement."

It was rumored that, in 1969, she was organizing a network of scientists, computer hackers, social justice warriors, lawyers, artists, doctors, and, oddly enough, shaman, into a force for positive social change. It was simply called "The Network" because no one could say for sure who was in it. Their targeted assassinations, political campaigns, lobbying activities, information leaks, scientific innovation, and (if the rumors are to be believed) their magic rituals, had slowly tipped the scales of justice in favor of the common people. In fact, it was quietly spoken in leftist political circles that every major gain for human rights since the end of the Vietnam War was due to their intervention. The reach of The Network made her appear omnipresent and indomitable. Organizers, freedom fighters, and soldiers they were, but I wanted to know: could they be king makers as well?

I had been so absorbed with looking at her and the cat, I hadn't paid any attention to the others in the space. Our backs were to the walls and, while I was distracted, about fifty individuals, each accompanied by a large wild animal, had emerged from the man-made bush and formed a semicircle around us. It was impossible, I knew, but all the faces around the circle were the same face. They were *all* Black Moon, all clones of *her*, and they were closing in around us.

Greeting us with a common voice, they chanted, "Welcome Comrades."

Each of their faces and bodies told a different story of terror and violence. And like a matching game in the back of an old-fashioned newspaper, I began to draw lines, in my mind, between their injuries and the known list of incidents connected to her network. As I stared at them, more and more details of their stories became clear. Some were missing fingernails. Some had lost whole fingers, teeth, and even limbs. This was probably the result of tortures during interrogations. One clone, accompanied by what appeared to be a jaguar, was naked, and covered entirely in burns. I had read about a fire that broke out during an attack on a biological weapons lab in 2019. Had this clone been at the site of the explosion? Had she burned?

A few of them showed no visual signs of trauma and I wondered what kind of scars, physical, or psychological, they hid. There were other differences I came to notice as I watched them. Not all of the clones were the same. It seemed they had arranged themselves in a sort of chronological order, so that each was slightly older than the one before. The one I assumed to be the original Black Moon, the half-face woman, appeared to be the youngest, but I couldn't be sure. I realized with growing horror and awe that the bodies before me represented the ages she had been over the past fifty years and they wore every scar her political struggles had inflicted.

"Each individual in my network represents a skill set, a memory, a perspective, an experience, carved in flesh. There is no revolution without sacrifice and the body is the ultimate sacrifice . . ."

While she spoke, a chubby brown-skinned child toddled into the semicircle and was retrieved by one of the clones. The clone was wearing a white T-shirt and her leaking breasts created large, wet circles on the fabric. I had thought she was one of those without a visible trauma, but when she bent to scoop the child into her arms I glimpsed a jagged scar across her lower abdomen.

"Black motherhood is also a sacrifice of the body," said the half-faced leader, as if reading my mind. "In 2024, I personally hand-delivered a 400-year-old document to the World Court that won the case for global Black reparations. Unfortunately, I was caught by white supremacist thugs when I left the courthouse. They dragged me past police, who did nothing to stop them. I was eight-and-a-half months pregnant. Those terrorists beat me, hung me by my feet, and cut my daughter from my womb."

She didn't have to tell me that each body before me had its own story of torture and violation. Seeing the oppression of Black people etched into her flesh over and over like that conjured visions of Black people swinging, convulsing, screaming, burning, and gasping for air, over long centuries, of Black bodies being bitten, whipped, branded, caged, and chained. My own father, and my grandfather before him, knew such trauma, but I had only read about it. Waves of nausea washed over me and my consciousness was set adrift on an ark of bones. This display of bodies was the ultimate storytelling device. The army of clones was her boldest political act, her greatest, and most cruel, artistic achievement.

Tears sliced my cheeks as I looked out at all of the Andreas: the maidens, mothers, and crones, both broken, and immortal. I knew nothing about struggle, weariness, or single-minded determination. My heart pumped at an alarming rate. I removed a handkerchief from my lapel and blotted the sweat running into my eyes. I was terrified that she could see the sweat beginning to stain the underpits of my taupe-colored jacket. In any case, the animals around the circle could smell it. This meeting had gone terribly awry and I knew that I must regain control of the situation if I was to get what I came for, if I were to survive the situation. Without further deliberation, I put on my best crowd-pleasing, confident smile, and thrust my right hand forward.

"My name is Senator Adam Williamson, and I've come to extend you the honor—"

But it was too late to change the outcome of our exchange. I realized then that I had never been the one behind the wheel. I saw a brief flash of silver, a glint of metal, as she struck out at me with cheetah-like speed. Before I could scream she was holding my severed hand in hers as casually as an umpire might hold his glove. I drew back a stump that pulsated with splattering blood. The clones had all drawn similar weapons, the animals were ready to pounce, and my bodyguards had retreated into terrified stillness. There was silence, except for the beasts snarling, the trilling of the insects, and the singing of birds high up in the artificial atmosphere.

"Honor? What honor have you? What strength have you

known?" she asked, baring her perfect teeth in a feral grin that shot icepicks into my heart.

I hated her at that moment. And I loved her too, because she had seen me for the coward I was. Not since my grandfather's lap had someone seen past my million-dollar smile and fine tailored suit. And in some way that was endearing. I bit down on my tongue to suppress my screams and blood began to fill my mouth. For once I found real courage because I knew that she would kill me if I cried out. I drowned the impulse in a moaning gurgle of blood.

She caressed my severed hand as one would a small animal.

"Has this hand ever done a day's work, ever gone without a manicure?" her single eye glittered madly. "I'd bet you don't even wipe your own ass," she said and tossed my hand to her waiting feline companion, who immediately began to devour it. "Perhaps you will be of use, once you are properly seasoned."

I could hear my bodyguard sobbing softly. I knew then that I, in this body, would never be president. It was possible that I, in this body, would never leave this dungeon. Some version of me, some properly trained clone, would certainly secure the office of president of the United States. I realized with both horror and some satisfaction that my clone, perhaps a better version of me, would serve her greater purpose. My legs turned to cotton beneath me, and as I felt myself losing consciousness, I could hear her address the bubbling crowd.

"Yes, we must sacrifice the individual body for the sake of collective freedom. For the body is the revolutionary's ultimate sacrifice, just as the threat of bodily harm or death is the oppressor's ultimate weapon. We have had just one limitation as revolutionaries, one problem that has remained constant since the murder of Jesus Christ. Our dilemma was that, until now, we had but one body to spare!"

The other Andreas joined in a call and response with their half-face leader. I was reminded of the passion of a Pentecostal preacher. They all cheered, clapped rhythmically, despite maimed limbs, and both animals and humans raised their voices like a macabre choir as she continued to speak.

"But now," she shook her fist in the air, "thanks to our innovations, thanks to the sacrifice of our brother Adam, the game has changed..."

BUFF VERSUS GREEN

DJ TYRER

"I AM NOT ashamed of my body," proclaimed Anna Wetherby. "Indeed, I am proud of my body."

She gave it a provocative jiggle that caused a stir through the meeting hall that more usually was host to school sport. Neither young nor slim, she was possessed of a body that could still grab attention, and the response was a good mixture of the appreciative and the shocked.

Mr. Hampton, the town mayor, stood. "Mrs. Wetherby, your body is not under discussion here."

The remark prompted several lewd calls that caused him to glare out at the hall and shout, "Silence, please."

"Mr. Hampton," Anna said, a smile playing on her lips at his discomfort, "my body very definitely *is* under discussion—along with every other body in this hall. If you were paying any attention to the agenda, you would know that I am calling for the law against public nudity in the parks of our fair town to be rescinded."

The mayor spluttered.

"Were you trying to say, 'Think of the children?', Mr. Hampton? Because I am. They, too, should have the right to run free, naked as God intended in our open spaces. It is ridiculous that it remains legal for me to walk naked down Main Street, but illegal for me to sunbathe naked in our parks, and—"

He cut her off. "The law could be changed to outlaw it everywhere."

"Oh, really, don't be so prudish."

"Isn't it enough that you have that nudist resort of yours?" demanded Mrs. Winters. "It's bad enough to think of what . . . things you people get up to out there, but to have them inflicted upon the rest of us? No. I want to be able to take my children to play in the park without men's . . . well, you know what I mean."

"Indeed, I do," Anna said with a laugh. "Indeed, I do."

"Silence, please," called the mayor as her laughter was echoed through the hall. "This is a place of serious business."

"Then let's get down to business. Let's have a town vote on the issue."

"It is entirely proper to consider the point," sniffed the minute-taker, who saw himself as guardian of correct procedure.

The mayor sighed. "Very well, Mrs. Wetherby, very well. The council will discuss your motion and, if it is approved, a vote will be held."

"Good."

Mrs. Winter glared at her. "Don't think this is the end of it."

Anna rolled her eyes and sat down, and the meeting continued. But, if she thought her involvement was over, she was to be surprised.

"And, one last item on the agenda," said the mayor. He looked at Anna. "This concerns you."

"Me? It's not that threatened rise in property taxes is it?"

"No." Behind him Mrs. Winters gave a narrow smile. "It involves your establishment directly."

"Oh, really?"

"Yes. As you doubtless know, Charles Veit is looking to build a mall in order to revitalize our town's economic fortunes."

"I had heard something to that effect, though it sounds like a pretty stupid idea to me—this town's just too small for some huge shopping mall—and, I really don't see what it has to do with me, I'm certainly not planning to buy my groceries there."

This elicited more laughter, although Anna herself remained silent. As much as she was putting on a show of sarcasm, she was wondering just where the mayor was headed.

Mr. Hampton allowed himself a short bark of a laugh, then said, "More than you realize, Mrs. Wetherby. Before pressing ahead with such an enterprise, it was necessary for both Mr. Veit and the town council to have surveys carried out to assess where the best location for the mall would be, based on such criteria as accessibility, traffic flow, minimizing any public nuisance, environmental factors, and so forth."

Anna muttered a curse beneath her breath.

"And, it seems that both from the point of view of private enterprise and that of public oversight, the best location would be in the vicinity of Eden Resort and Club. Indeed, in order for a project of this size, it would require the land that your resort is on."

"Well, that ain't going to happen," snapped Anna.

"Well, we hardly thought you would be enthused with the idea. However, given that the construction of this mall is vital to the economic well-being of our town, it is possible for us to compel you to sell it to us."

"What?"

"You will have no choice in the matter. You will, of course, be paid a fair rate for the land . . ." The mayor didn't attempt to hide his satisfied smile.

"But, you can't!"

"Believe me, Mrs. Wetherby, if the town votes in favor, we very definitely can. It may be that Main Street will soon be the only place you will be able to go nude around here . . ."

∽

"It's very worrying," Anna told her staff in conclusion. Indeed, it was so worrying that she was still dressed, having rushed straight back from the town meeting.

"Is it even legal?" Roger asked.

Anna shrugged. "As much as I'm sure it's a deliberate attempt to drive us out of business, I'm sure the council have played it by the book as much as they can. I don't think we'll get far arguing it's a put-up job, not without any evidence."

For a moment, there was silence as the threat soaked in, then Betty spoke up.

"Okay, it's bad, but they have to persuade the town first. We just need to persuade everyone to vote against it."

"But, will they?" asked Joe. "I mean, the mayor is going to play this up as good for the town's economy. Goodness knows, with the way things are there are plenty of people who need an upswing."

Anna considered. "That's true, but the remaining small businesses won't be in favor. Some might relocate there, but for most a mall is a death sentence. And, we do employ quite a few people and buy from local farms and businesses. If Eden Resort goes, there's a lot of people who will hurt . . ."

"So," said Betty, "we just have to tell them."

Anna nodded. "Let's draw up a battle plan."

"This is going to be tight," Anna said to Betty as they returned to her car.

It was true there were those who, pragmatically, were against their being bulldozed to make way for a mall, and there were those who, whether they were in favor of Eden Resort or not, most definitely didn't want one. But, in addition to those who saw the mall as the future for the town, there were also those who saw it as a means to an end, that end being their closure. With Mrs. Winters and the mayor at their head, the group was making a good deal of progress.

"I should never have campaigned for nudity in the park," said Anna as they got in.

Betty shook her head. "You have to do what you think is right. That's why we're going to fight this to the bitter end."

"Well," said Anna, "it looks like it'll be a bitter winter . . ."

Betty patted her arm. "Chin up, we'll find a way."

There was one, and Betty found it, bringing a young man into Anna's office.

Laying down towels on two chairs, she and the man sat opposite Anna.

"Yes?" she asked.

Betty gave her a Cheshire-cat smile. "This fellow is Chester, Chester Mayfield. He lives in town and has been coming to the club for about six months. He also happens to work in the county surveyor's office . . ."

It took a moment for Anna's mind to click, then she said, "Oh," and waited for them to continue.

Chester gave a cough, then said, "As part of my duties, I was asked to provide a report for the town concerning the best location for the mall, which I passed up to my supervisor to finalize for the council. Well, part of my survey included considering the economic advantages of every location, and offsetting the costs against the potential benefits. For example, building a mall away from suitable roads would necessitate additional expenditure compared to building it next to the highway, expenditure which the town would likely foot in order to attract the venture."

"Yes, yes," said Anna, "but, what is your point, exactly?"

"Well, between the infrastructure costs, and the loss of revenue and taxes should it cease to operate, Eden Resort was not on my list of favored locations. There are several farmers who, justifiably, could be angry with me, but that's beside the point. To put it succinctly, the report on the mayor's desk is neither mine nor one that fits with the facts. In short, you're being railroaded."

"I knew it!" exclaimed Anna, but then she asked, "But, what do we do about it? I mean, could we prove this in court?"

"I have a copy of my original report."

"But, might the chief surveyor argue he was right to make his call?"

"Oh, stop picking holes," snapped Betty.

"Maybe," admitted Chester. "Ideally, we need evidence he was swayed."

Anna looked at the ceiling for a moment, then said, "I think I have an idea."

"This is not correct procedure," said the minute-taker when she waylaid him in the street and asked how many options had been presented in the report.

"Oh, pish. I don't want to know any town secrets, merely the facts. Speaking of which, I know for a fact that the initial report favored other locations to my place, so were they included and, if so, why was Eden Resort chosen?"

"Oh, dear . . ." The man wrung his hands, theatrically, then gave her a curt nod. "Come to my house, this evening, and I'll let you have a look at my copy of the minutes."

"Thank you."

"But, you'll owe me a favor . . ."

She arched an eyebrow at the proper little man raising the question of quid pro quo.

"What sort of favor?"

"We'll discuss it this evening . . ."

Anna almost laughed when she heard what he wanted in exchange.

"A year's free membership of the club, if it's still here," he said, gulping nervously. "I've always been a little curious about the place and well . . ." He blushed.

"It's nothing to be ashamed of," she told him. "Nothing more natural, in fact."

He gulped again, and handed her his minutes.

She looked over them. Only one site had been presented and it matched precisely with that on the survey conducted by Veit's company.

"Very suspicious," she murmured, then looked at the little man. "Did the mayor or Mrs. Winters meet with Veit?"

"Not officially, no—there would be minutes." Then he considered for a moment, and added, "However, I do believe I saw Mr. Hampton and Mr. Veit sitting down for dinner together in Mary's Diner."

"It's a put-up job," said Anna. But, what did Veit stand to gain from it all?

"How much is the town proposing to pay for my land?"

The minute-taker named an amount. It was well below what she imagined her acres would be worth on the open market.

"And, they would pass it to Veit for the same amount?"

"Precisely."

Well, that explained precisely what was going on.

"I'm going to see the mayor."

"Good luck."

"I know exactly what you're up to," she told Mr. Hampton. "You're bribing Veit with cheap land so he'll back your play to bulldoze Eden Resort.

"I don't know what you're talking about," he said, with a face full of guilt.

"We'll see what a judge thinks of that."

He sighed. "Look, Mrs. Wetherby, you can't win. Veit has deep pockets—*very* deep pockets—and, Judge Wilson is up for reelection next year and in need of funds—"

"But, that's . . ." She fell silent in disgust.

"And, the 'yes' campaign is proving well funded, with incentives for those who vote the right way." The mayor gave a little chuckle. "Put it this way, buff can't beat green."

"Oh, very witty. Well, I'm going to find a way!"

Maybe she was beaten, but Anna had one last idea. She couldn't, and wouldn't, attempt to out-bribe Veit, but she could compete with him in publicity. Perhaps shame, or at least irritate, the council into backing down, or make Veit feel nervous about bad publicity.

"Call all our regulars," she told Betty and the others, "find out who is willing to get down here to fight to save the resort. But make sure they understand their faces—and more—could be on TV and in the papers. If they don't want people knowing about their hobby, they should stay away."

"Why?" asked Betty. "What have you got in mind?"

Anna smiled and began to explain.

The crowd gathered at the top of Main Street in relative silence. Anna had asked Chester Mayfield to apply for a permit for a demonstration so that the mayor wouldn't cotton on too soon to her idea.

But, the council would know now.

"Everyone disrobe," she called through her loudhailer.

Within a minute, there were over two hundred naked people armed with placards and ready to march down Main Street to the council offices, from which the mayor ran the town.

All perfectly legal.

Anna chuckled to herself. "Right, follow me!"

They began to march, chanting, and triggering air horns, making a din that brought people out to see what was happening. Some looked shocked, others laughed and clapped, a few even began to undress and join them.

They halted outside the offices and the mayor came out, looking distinctly embarrassed.

"What *is* going on?" he demanded of Anna.

"We're exercising our legal right to protest."

"Protest, maybe, but not like this—put some clothes on!"

"Oh, we're not breaking the law—surely you remember?"

He snorted. "Have you no dignity, woman?"

"It's not me who's been prostituting public office and engaging in fraud," she said

"How dare you!"

As if on cue, a woman and cameraman—both clothed—stepped out of the crowd and a microphone was thrust toward the mayor, who flinched, guiltily.

"What is this?"

"How do your respond to accusations of corruption at the town hall, Mr. Mayor? Is the vote on Eden Resort rigged?"

Anna knew similar questions of Mr. Veit would be being asked later.

The mayor spluttered. "Of course not." Then, he added, "Given the unexpectedly strong feelings this has raised, the council will, of course, be investigating the proposition further before the town goes to the ballot on the future of the resort. We may have to qualify our support."

And, before the reporter could ask him any further questions, he hurried back inside.

Anna smiled. They wouldn't be going anywhere for a while, would give him plenty of time to consider the point.

∿

"And, here are the results on the first proposition," the election officer called. "In favor of the compulsory purchase of Eden Resort . . . 776 votes. Against the compulsory purchase of Eden Resort . . . 2,094 votes. The proposition has been rejected."

A cheer went up. It was quite likely there was going to be a nude victory parade up Main Street.

"And, the results of the second proposition are as follows . . . In favor of allowing public nudity in the town parks . . . 1,122. Against the allowing of public nudity in town parks . . . 1,748. The proposition has been rejected."

Anna sighed and turned to Betty. "Win some, lose some, I guess."

"That's democracy," said Betty with a smile.

ARABELLA

ANSHRITHA

TODAY MARKS 727 days and 16 hours since my wife's skull was crushed by a speeding truck. An hour before that, with her skull still intact, Adya had asked me to accompany her for a walk. So I did. *I always* (exaggerated for dramatic effect) did what she told me to do. I adored that woman. In my eyes, she was flawless. Language limits my ability to express the love I bore, and continue to bear, for her. Let it be known that love sonnets penned by Pablo Neruda, Shakespeare and Mirza Ghalib pale in comparison to my love for my Arabella (she had once confided in me that "Arabella" was a song she played on loop when she was down in the dumps. Ever since then, I fondly called her "my Arabella," partially to tease her, and partly to coax a smile out of her).

Please be patient with me, my dear, sweet reader. My mind often trails off to disconnected memories, but I will now resume recounting the grim events of that fateful evening. My hazy memory offers me a pitiful bystander view of the pleasant walk we went on. On our way back home, Adya insisted that she wanted to go to the park and watch children riding their bicycles. I was exhausted and famished, I had told her. "Perhaps another day?" Tragically, there would be no such day. Within a minute of my indefinite stalling, a truck driven by a teenager, with dangerous levels of alcohol coursing through his veins, would come out of nowhere and run over my wife. I was greeted by the sight of her severed limbs, speckled blood, and lifeless, horror stricken eyes. Once tracked down and caught, the petrified young driver had apologized, profusely, and hysterically, but it didn't matter. Nothing has, ever since.

~

The news of her grotesque death had been covered by the famous newspapers, radio stations, and television channels.

"Underage driver kills pregnant woman."

"Drunk driver nabbed hours after killing woman in hit-run crash granted bail."

"Hit and run claims the life of one."

"Crime strikes again. Drunk and underage drivers on roads—experts say time is ripe to revisit the law," read some of the simplistic headlines. The radio stations chastised reckless driving and urged their listeners to pray for Adya's bereaved family. Some even dedicated morose songs to her and our unborn child. The television channels invited eminent panelists to debate on the rising crime levels, drunk driving, and our city's safety. Within a few days a fresh story on the emerging vandalism menace stole the limelight. This didn't bother me, I had noticed a similar pattern develop elsewhere too. In the fortnight that followed her death, tearful calls had poured in from concerned family members, condoling friends, and colleagues. Many of them came to see me, donning faces that one is accustomed to when death visits. Eventually, the doorbell and phone stopped ringing as much. It seemed that life went on for all, except me.

It must have been a few weeks after Adya's death that I moved to a new city. Nobody knew of this. My sudden departure must have caught everyone unawares. My mother, I imagine, must have been especially distraught. Before you begin to draw your assumptions, sweet reader, let me tell you why I acted so. Being cooped up in that forlorn house reminded me of my dead wife every waking second. In the middle of the night, I would hear the distinct sound of her buoyant laughter ring through the desolate hallway. Half-knitted woolen sweaters, lying in a muddled pile in the other room, were an agonizing reminder of a child my hands would never cradle. So I left, roughly an hour after the idea germinated in my mind. I rushed to the airport, carrying a suitcase hurriedly crammed with all that my eyes had laid on in an hour, and impulsively booked the next flight out. I knew that if I were to let anyone in on it they would plead with me to reconsider. Maybe even coerce me into staying with them. I couldn't have any of that. Their pangs and moans of sympathy smothered me. Throwing me pitiful looks came naturally to them. They would speak to me only in light and soothing tones as if I were a child. As if I had completely lost grip of the reins of my life. To them, I would always only be the man who lost his wife and child in a freak accident.

Once the flight landed, I went to the first extended stay hotel I found and booked a room. My list of instructions to the receptionist was clear: I was not to be disturbed; I would clean the room myself; meals and newspapers were to be left by the door. No knocking would be necessary, I had sternly clarified. If I needed anything else I would use the intercom to place a call to her, or her replacement, and the item requested would have to be left outside the room. I heard the flustered receptionist give an exasperated sigh before handing me the keys.

"Sure, sir," she squeaked.

That was the last conversation I remember having with another person. In the months that followed, I spoke to nobody. I bathed once a week, if at all. I ate when I felt like it, typically skipping two meals a day. I never used the intercom to make any calls. My needs were so basic and so very dispensable. Once, I had deliberated if I needed a fresh towel, but decided against it. White or brown, clean or dirty, it really made no difference to me. Confined in that room and unperturbed by human interaction, I was finally able to mourn her, to really grieve the loss of someone I had loved so dearly. I spent all day, every day, for months, and months, and months thinking of my precious Adya.

At night, I would often glance at the mirror across the bed. The unfamiliar face that looked back belonged to a stranger. He was only skin and bones with wild, unkempt hair, a weak, ragged face, hollow cheeks, and sunken eyes. The sight of that man unsettled me. Even scared me at times. I ultimately decided to use all the newspapers I had to conceal him from me.

Chronically sleep deprived, I began to despise the nighttime. Sleep and health are closely intertwined and sleep deprivation can affect a person's psychological state and mental health, I had read years ago in a tattered, ghoulish, gray and scarlet magazine, its papers crumbling under my delicate touch. A predicament, no doubt. Despite my earnest efforts, a sleepless lifestyle had become routine to me. On one occasion, I had shut my eyes and drifted away for what must have been only a few minutes. When I had habitually reached out to clasp Adya's hand and had instead felt the crimson silk of the empty bedspread, I woke up panic-stricken and sweating. On another night, I felt like wandering outside. I was nervous. You see, I had not ventured outside the room since I had first stepped inside of it. Once I overcame my initial trepidation, I grabbed an electric blue vest and excitedly scuttled to the elevator. The thin, balding man operating the elevator buttons flashed me a toothy smile. I ignored him and reached for the button myself. I felt him throw a wounded look at me.

Outside the elevator, I let my legs instinctively decide where to take me. Oh, it felt terrific to be outside! I walked by a row of terraced houses, a church, tall buildings, schools, and a park. Then, suddenly, I stopped dead in my tracks. I couldn't believe my eyes. There lay an abandoned baby, clothed in a bright green skirt and a white shirt with an animated picture of a brown bear on it. I gingerly picked her up and rocked her. She was a beautiful baby with big, black eyes, and a head full of brown hair. She looked so peaceful, untroubled by the miseries of life. What kind of people could bring themselves to do such a thing? I considered informing the police before another thought struck me. *Take her with you*, it said. I entertained the idea. I would treat her as if she were my own child, love her, and take care of her. When Adya was pregnant, I hoped that we would have a girl. She had laughed and firmly said we would love our child, regardless of gender, or any other characteristics. I had found this baby by a park, and my wife loved parks. This baby and I were both victims of crime. Only someone belonging to the lowest of the low could speed away and flee the scene after hitting a pedestrian. Deserting a help-less baby was behavior attributable to scum, of the dregs of society. I felt a cosmic connection with the child. We had both been wronged. *This is divine intervention*, I thought. The baby in my arms would be my daughter, I decided. I would call her Arabella. I stroked her soft hair and felt myself smile for the first time in months. With a spring in my step, I scampered to the hotel. The thin, balding man in the elevator inquisitively looked first at me and then my daughter. Again, I ignored him, and maneuvered the button myself.

The rest of that night was spent watching Arabella sleep. The next morning, I bathed her tenderly and fed her. Taking care of a child, I soon realized, kept me occupied through the day. Parenthood suited me, I learned. Arabella gave me a new lease on life. In her pres-ence, I felt calm, hopeful, safe, and energetic. I think I may even have felt the glow of happiness, it had been so long that I found it difficult to recognize the unfamiliar emotion. She renewed a childlike sense of wonder in me. How ludicrous of me to pretend that I had saved her when it was Arabella who saved me. Without her, I was only a shadow of a person. An empty shell of a human being. She gave me a reason to wake up every morning.

∾

One sunny afternoon, I heard a knock on the door. I paid no attention to it but the knocking grew persistently louder. Infuriated, I marched to the door and flung it open. There stood my gray-haired mother with tears sparkling in her eyes. I was astonished. She enveloped me in a hug.

"We were so scared. I am so happy I found you. Please come home," she cried.

I said nothing.

She took a hard look at me. "You look terribly weak, have you not been taking care of yourself?"

I looked, apprehensively, at my devastated mother. Would she chastise me for raising Arabella, a stranger's daughter?

"Ma," I said, "I have something to tell you. My appearance is deceptive, I am doing well. I am . . . actually happy. No, really," I stammered, between her sniffling sobs. "Would you like to know why? I am happy because . . . um . . . because of a child I adopted. Arabella, she gave my life meaning."

There was a pause.

"Adopted? From whom?" Ma looked at me.

I shook my head, "No, it's not like that. I haven't gotten around to initiating all that legal red tape-ism yet. She was abandoned by a park. How heartless people can be! I found her, Ma. She is my child. Don't you want to see your lovely grandchild?"

I led her inside the room and motioned toward the wooden chair Arabella was sitting in. Ma looked at me with an expression I had never seen before. She strode toward my Arabella and picked her up roughly.

"Is this a joke? This is not your child, do you understand?" she snarled.

I grimaced at her harsh tone.

"Please be careful, Ma. You may hurt her!"

Ma was beside herself. Breathing sharply, she paced around the room for a few seconds with Arabella in her arms. Suddenly she stopped and looked at me with a mixture of sadness, terror, and undisguised pity. Then she calmly muttered to herself "Maybe a demonstration would help." Without waiting for me to respond, she flung my daughter out of the open window.

I remember dashing down two flights of stairs with my heart in my mouth. I was inconsolable. As I pushed open the entrance door of the hotel, with a lump in my throat, I feared the worst.

On the road, a million pieces lay spread far and wide.

Today marks 727 days since I lost my wife, and six days since a porcelain doll shattered onto the hard ground.

KANE'S THEORY

BEV VINCENT

"THE ONLY 'CRT' I know about is a cathode ray tube," Hector said.

My brother Nate gave him a blank look.

"You know, like the picture tubes in old TVs."

Nate continued to stare. I knew he was just winding Hector up. We liked to pretend we're Luddites. Well, in my case, I don't have to pretend sometimes.

Hector looked at me. "Help me out here, Benjamin. I bet you still have one of those old-fashioned sets in storage somewhere."

Nate laughed. "In storage? I'll bet he's still using one in his den."

"Aha!" Hector said, as if he'd just tricked a witness into confessing to murder. "So you do know what I'm talking about."

Nate grinned, then turned serious. "You really want to take this case, Ben? I mean, this guy wasn't wearing a red hat and I didn't see a Confederate flag on his car, but still."

"A client's a client," I said, "and we've been light on those lately, in case you haven't noticed."

I knew he knew. My younger brother looks after the agency accounts, so he was as aware as anyone how slow business had been of late. Not only did the pandemic mean people were less likely to get up to the sorts of bad behavior that were our bread and butter—illicit rendezvous, for example—people were reluctant to come into our office to enlist our services. Television productions that had been shut down for over a year were only now starting up again, depriving us of the revenue we normally generated by working behind the scenes on reality and true crime series.

"What exactly does he expect us to do?" Nate asked.

"He wants to know if his daughter is being taught critical race theory in her AP History class."

"Does he expect us to go undercover? Pretend to transfer into the school and sit in on class? I mean, I might be able to pass for seventeen, but you?"

It's been over two decades since Nate was a teenager, but I decided not to take the bait.

"I could bug the classroom," Hector volunteered, "although I'm pretty sure that would be in a legal gray area."

"Now you're sounding like that smarmy idiot on Fox," I told our gadget-happy employee. "No, I plan to go straight to the source. Talk to the teacher. Rack up some billable hours in the process. Maybe even expense a few drinks or a meal. Our client gave us a hefty retainer and said there's more where that comes from if we can—and I quote—'get the goods' on the teacher."

I passed the check to Nate, who endorsed the back and deposited it electronically into our account.

"Something familiar about that guy," Nate muttered after he completed the transaction. He stared into open space for a few seconds, then shook his head. "It'll come to me."

I had the teacher's name from our client and was able to find his page on the school's website, as well his as his social media accounts. Although the client—his name was Wes Perry—hadn't specified this, I wasn't the least bit surprised to discover that the teacher in question was Black. Nothing on Coleman Reed's Facebook account struck me as being particularly radical, although there was no doubt about his political leanings based on his Twitter feed.

I sent an email to the address listed on the school's website, figuring I wouldn't hear back until end-of-day, but I received a call twenty minutes later.

"Is this Mr. Kane?"

"Yes."

"Cole Reed. You wanted to talk to me about my history class?"

"The AP section, to be specific," I said. "If you have time, that is."

"And you're a private detective."

"That's right."

"Let me get back to you."

He hung up, and I was pretty sure that would be the last I heard from him, but he called back within the hour.

"Kane?"

"Yes."

"I talked to a friend who works for HPD. Lieutenant Goddard. He says I can trust you, mostly."

I wondered about the "mostly" part, but I was happy to hear Goddard was endorsing me. We had a complicated relationship when I was on the force—mostly to do with my father and the reasons he left HPD to start Kane Investigations.

"I'm still not quite clear on why a PI would want to talk to me about my class."

"Can we meet? It would probably be easier face-to-face."

There was a pause. "I have Drama Club until 5:30 p.m."

"How about six o'clock at Under the Volcano? Do you know where that is?"

"OK, I can do that. I can only give you half an hour, though. I have a ton of papers to grade and an exam to prep for Friday."

"I appreciate it."

I was at the bar ten minutes early after spending some time at Murder by the Book across the street. I saw a man hanging around near the entrance who resembled the picture from the high school web page. A little older looking, maybe. The last couple of years had aged us all.

I approached him and said his name. In a bygone era, I would have offered my hand, but my handshaking days were over. For now, at least. Old habits die hard. Instead, I pulled open the door to the bar and held it for him.

"It still feels strange," he said, pulling a KN95 mask from his pocket.

"What?"

"Going into places like this. I'm fully vaccinated and all that, and I had to go to class during much of the pandemic, but I got out of the habit of being in crowded places with a bunch of strangers."

I knew what he meant. I indicated a picnic table on the mostly empty patio. "We could sit out here, if you want. If you don't mind the heat."

"Houston born and raised," he said. "Lived here all my life except for college. I'm used to it."

We sat across from each other at the table.

"Now, what can I do for you, Mr. Kane?"

"Benjamin," I said. "The parents of one of your students hired me to find out if you were teaching critical race theory in class."

Reed sat in silence for several seconds. I couldn't read his expression, so I waited.

"You're shitting me," he said eventually.

I shrugged as if to ask, "What can I say?"

"I won't ask you which parent, although I have a pretty good idea." He leaned forward as if interrogating me. "What do you know about critical race theory?"

"I read the Wiki page," I said with a grin that I hoped would indicate I was joking. "Seriously though, until today I didn't know much about it, and a lot of what I thought I knew was wrong."

Reed took in a deep breath. "Let me tell you what the right is saying about CRT." He sat up straight, in full lecture mode now. "They're saying CRT is designed to make white people"—he looked straight at me but spared me the semi-obligatory "no offense"—"feel guilty about this country's history. They're saying the theory itself is racist, meant to divide us worse than we already are."

"But it's not that," I said.

"CRT has been around for about fifty years. I learned about it in university, but I didn't study it. Not my field of expertise. But I did go to a lecture by Daniel HoSang, the Yale professor, and I've done some reading on the subject. As you might surmise from the color of my skin, systemic racism is a subject that might interest me, and not only academically."

I nodded.

"They teach CRT in law school, and in sociology classes. *Upper-level* sociology classes. It's couched in academic language and published in the kinds of journals my students don't typically read. It's mostly concerned with examining and rectifying outcomes. Now, I do teach my students about the cultural, economic, political, and social developments that created the nation and continue to shape it. Of course, we cover the Civil Rights Movement, Jim Crow, slavery, segregation and the Confederacy. That's not critical race theory. That's just history."

"The governor banned teaching CRT in Texas schools, didn't he?"

Reed's lip curled. "I don't know anything about your politics, Mr. Kane—excuse me, Benjamin—so I hope it won't offend you when I say our governor is an asshole. Not just because of this. He reminds me daily of how hateful and willfully ignorant he is. And it defies explanation how this state can put up with his bullshit."

I smiled. "I agree with you completely. I miss the days when Ann Richards held the office."

"Well, all right then. Since you used to be a cop, I wasn't sure. Maybe someday we'll have a Black or Hispanic governor, but a woman—a democratic woman no less—was a good start."

We were interrupted by a server from the bar.

"I couldn't help noticing you two gentlemen sitting out here in the heat and wondering if you might be interested in a drink."

"I wouldn't say no to a beer." I glanced at Reed.

He checked his watch, then nodded.

"Shiner Bock for me," I said.

"Make it two," he said.

When she was gone, he continued.

"Our esteemed governor wouldn't know a sociological theory if it bit him in the ass. He's one of those offended white folk who think we're trying to make him feel guilty because someone in his family tree owned slaves or was in an organization that tried to run people like me out of town—or worse. They want to erase our history. Why did it take a TV series to tell people about the Tulsa massacre? Because they haven't yet figured out a way to ban writers and other creative folk from expressing ideas and telling facts in this country."

He paused as the server brought our drinks. The glasses were already beginning to sweat, but the beer was cold and tasty.

"Mind you, they would if they could. These old white men were brought up in a societal framework that gives them all the advantages, and when they feel threatened, like they might suddenly no longer be at the top of the heap, standing on the corpses of everyone they've used to get where they are, they haul out bullshit like this to get everyone upset. About history. About truth and reality. Do you think for a second our governor truly cares about poor white folk, let alone poor people of color? This country is ruled by rich white men. That's why they're doing everything in their power to make it as hard as possible for people like me to vote. I have a car and a good paying job—well, decent paying, anyway. I can drive to another polling station if they shut down the one near me. I can take a day off to vote in person if they won't let me vote by mail. I have all the IDs in the world to prove I'm an eligible voter. There are many who don't or can't. And that suits them just fine. The system is rigged—that's the bottom line." He took a drink of beer. "End of lecture."

"And that's what you're teaching?"

"Am I telling my students that the American sociopolitical system is inherently racist? Not in so many words. But there are subtle ways to make that point. The sharper students will start thinking about the causes of social inequality, including in their own lives. The others, well, even if I drew diagrams, some of them will never understand." He took another drink. "And if that doofus in Austin manages to legislate it so it becomes illegal for me to teach that the Civil War was about the South's desire to preserve slavery, or for my colleagues in the English department to teach Toni Morrison or Ralph Ellison, well, that's the hill I'll die on. I've got the ACLU on speed dial for the day that happens." He took another drink. "So, what will you tell your client?"

I considered my answer. "That I'm satisfied you're following the AP guidelines to the letter and that I could find no trace of CRT or any other objectionable content in your class materials. Of course, before I deliver that message, I'll have to spend some time—billable hours, mind you—reviewing the AP History guidelines and your syllabus, as well as familiarizing myself with the theory. Do you have some thick books or long articles on the subject you could recommend?"

Reed grinned. "I'll send you an email."

We finished our drinks. I got up to go inside to pay the bill.

"Thank you for your time, Mr. Reed," I hesitated for a moment, then held out my hand.

He studied it for a moment, as if unfamiliar with the gesture, and took it. We shook. Old habits, and all that.

Wes Perry didn't look happy when I delivered my comprehensive report. I figured he was looking for an excuse to get Coleman fired. He probably wouldn't give up on that effort, but he wasn't going to get any help from us. He didn't flinch when I gave him our bill, though.

I noticed Hector moving furtively around the room as I dealt with the client. I was pretty sure he had a camera embedded in the Houston Astros hat he was wearing. After Perry left, Hector disappeared into his office. I was curious about what he was up to, but I figured he'd tell me eventually.

A while later, I saw him and Nate conferring in front of Nate's computer. Nate's nod of satisfaction was familiar to me.

"Hey, Ben," he said, "come take a look."

There were two photographs on the screen. One was of our client, taken today. The other looked like it might have come from a surveillance video.

"Facial recognition is a breeze when you're only comparing two faces," Nate said. He looked up. "How do you feel about the FBI?"

"Who's this?" I asked, indicating the other figure on the monitor.

"One of the people the Feds are still trying to identify from the January 6th insurrection. I told you I thought he looked familiar."

"It's a match?" I looked at Hector.

"Near certainty. High probability."

"So, we have to turn our client in to the Feds."

Nate nodded.

"Leave it to me," Hector said. "I can get the information into their hands without it tracing back to us."

"Do I want to know how?"

Nate said, "I sure as hell don't."

I picked up Perry's file from my desk and stuck it in the drawer of our filing cabinet where we stored former clients' records. It didn't look like we'd be getting any repeat business from this one.

FOR BAILEY

BARB GOFFMAN

AT 105 POUNDS, Bailey shouldn't be a lap dog. But every time another round of fireworks went off, she nestled tighter in my lap, whimpering while I stroked her thick black fur, and told her she'd be fine, that the scary noises from the sky would stop soon.

Boy, I hated lying to my dog. For the fifth night in a row, it felt like we were living in a war zone with a steady drum of mortar fire. It started every year at Memorial Day and happened sporadically throughout the summer, but the week leading up to Independence Day—this week—was always the worst. People throughout my neighborhood set off fireworks as soon as it got dark. It went on for hours.

"I resent that, Mr. Studebaker. I'm just as much an American as you are." My mom was on the phone, trying to reason with this jerk of a city councilman, her phone clutched tightly in her hand while she paced across the living room. "Just because I care about animals doesn't make me unpatriotic."

She'd called the cops first, but once again they proved themselves useless. *"We're sorry, Ms. Cooper, but we've told you: setting off fireworks isn't illegal."* I didn't get it. Wasn't it disturbing the peace? Wasn't that against the law? Anyway, Mom finally decided to call our elected representative for help. But he didn't seem to give a damn.

Boom! The sky looked like dandelion puffs had just exploded. Red, white, and blue ones. I was sitting on the coarse carpet, my back against our black leather couch. I had a good view of the show from here, watching through our large picture window. The fireworks would be cool if they didn't terrify Bailey.

My bestie Lilly was cooing to her as she wiped the drool off Bailey's jowls with one of the hand towels we kept all over the house. Even on the best of nights, Bailey was prone to slobbering, as all Newfoundlands are. But tonight, it was like she couldn't stop. If it was this bad for Bailey, inside our house with people loving on her, I hated to think how horrible it was for animals outside, birds and squirrels and even pets out for a walk. I couldn't wait till next week, when the city council was going to vote on a bill to make it illegal to set off fireworks. Looked like Mr. Jerk Studebaker would be a no vote.

"I find your position quite unreasonable, Mr. Studebak—hello? Hello?" Mom stamped her foot and threw her phone on the other couch. "I can't believe that son of a bitch hung up on me." She blew out a loud breath as she turned toward Lilly and me. "I'm sorry. I shouldn't have reacted like that."

"Sounds like you weren't thinking things through." I waggled my eyebrows while smiling at her, and she laughed. She often complained that I was too impetuous and didn't think things through, like that was bad or something.

She flopped onto the other couch as another round of fireworks lit up the sky and shook the house. "Now that I'm off the phone, let's try more music to drown out the noise. Alexa, play *Jagged Little Pill*."

As harmonica, drums, and guitar grunge poured out of our Echo device, I tried not to roll my eyes. Mom adored this album, which Alanis Morissette released a million years ago, when Mom was my age—sixteen. But I had to admit, the songs distracted Bailey.

"Wait," Lilly said, her blue eyes intent on Mom. "He's not going to *do* anything?"

Mom shook her head, then pushed her straight brown hair—same color as mine, but much shorter—behind her ears. "Owen Studebaker thinks there's nothing wrong with 'letting folks have a little fun,'" she said in a deep voice that I guess was supposed to imitate Studebaker. "I'm so glad I voted against him in the last election. He actually said people had the right to set off fireworks, and he'd never cast a vote against 'freedom.'" She made air quotes around that last word.

"What about our right to peace and quiet?" I asked. "What about Bailey's right not to be freaked out?"

"An excellent question, Jocelyn," Mom said. "It seems he doesn't care about that. He's all about 'freedom,' which he apparently defines as letting people do whatever they want. But Mr. Big Shot was too busy to keep talking because he's getting ready for a party he's hosting tomorrow for the Fraternal Order of Police."

"Well, la-di-da." I usually loved where we lived, but I hated that our state let people shoot off skyrockets, and that people didn't care about who they hurt while doing it.

Boom!

More whimpering.

"You poor baby." Lilly rubbed Bailey's side. "We could take her to my house for a couple hours. There're never any fireworks in my neighborhood."

She lived in the nicer end of town. We used to live there too, before the divorce.

"Would your parents mind?" Mom asked. "Because that would be helpful."

"I'm sure they won't," Lilly said. "But I'm happy to ask."

Lilly rose from her cross-legged position in one fluid move and, with her phone out, walked upstairs toward my bedroom, where she could escape the music, though not the fireworks.

"Do you think the ban will pass, Mom?"

Alanis moved on to the second song on the album, "You Oughta Know," and Bailey seemed calmer already. But I was on pins and needles, waiting for the next explosion that would make her cower.

"From what I read in the paper, it's not likely. There are three definite yes votes, three definite no votes—including Mr. Studebaker, the council chairman—and one guy who's on the fence. Ryan Howald. But he typically votes with Studebaker."

"There's no way to convince him? Maybe you should call him."

"He doesn't represent our district, so that wouldn't do any good." She shrugged. "But there are a lot of people working on Howald who live in his district. Veterans whose PTSD gets triggered by the noise. Firefighters who put out blazes the fireworks spark. And other folks like us, who hate how fireworks scare animals. Hopefully, he'll see reason."

As another round of fireworks went off and Bailey whined, I realized we needed to make him see reason, one way or another. We couldn't depend on hope.

A half hour later, Bailey and I were hanging out in Lilly's bedroom. It was much girlier than my own, just like Lilly was more feminine that me with her lavender toenails and dangly beaded earrings. Her furniture was a soft white, while her comforter, pillows, and area rug were various shades of pink. A vintage Hello Kitty poster hung over her desk, and fairy lights lined the ceiling. She once called it "living in girl nirvana."

My bedroom was plainer. I had modular brown furniture that my mom found at a thrift store. We loved thrift stores. I spiced things up with movie posters, including the one hanging over my bed from *Booksmart*—about two teenage girls who study so much they never have fun till they graduate. Then they try to get all their living done in one night. It's my daily reminder to work hard but enjoy life too. I also strung several suncatchers by my window. On bright days they throw rainbows on my walls and make me feel energized.

But tonight, I didn't need their help. I was already all worked up. Lilly too. She'd just gone to the front door to get our other bestie, Gabriel.

"Okay, fill me in," he said as he and Lilly walked into the room.

I'd texted him that he needed to come over right away, that we needed a plan to help Bailey. Lilly shut the bedroom door while Gabriel slid onto the floor and leaned toward me, his thick, shaggy brown hair falling across his forehead. Lilly joined us, pulling her long tan legs up to her chest.

I told him how Bailey had been suffering from the fireworks and about that jerk Studebaker and the upcoming vote. "We have to make sure the city council votes the right way. Our way."

Gabriel rubbed Bailey's head. "I've seen ads about this. My dad watches the local news, and a group's been running commercials saying stuff like, 'Give us your green to save the red-white-and-blue' with this big flag behind it. They're totally making it sound like being allowed to shoot off fireworks is your God-given American right."

Lilly leaned against her bed. "What are they doing with the cash they're raising?"

"Probably paying for the junk mail we've been getting the last few weeks," he said, "encouraging us to call and write our councilman to pressure him to say no. Like my parents would ever do that. Not only do they support the ban, but they know talking to Ryan Howald would be a waste of time. The guy's a total phony. He loves coming into our backyard when Mom and Dad are on the deck, reminding them of all the so-called good he's doing for the neighborhood."

"You know Councilman Howald?" I asked. "He's the guy on the fence."

"Yeah," he said. "He lives next door. Mom calls him the Count."

"Why?" Lilly tilted her head.

"Because he has slicked-back dark hair, an overbite, and he's purple, like the Count on *Sesame Street*." Gabriel said. "He mostly votes with the law-and-order guys on the council, though he'll sometimes vote with the progressives if he feels enough pressure."

Lilly still looked confused. "He's purple?"

"How he votes. Red and blue make purple," Gabriel said.

"Ohhhh," she said.

Sounded like she still didn't get it. Politics had never been her thing. Mine either, till now.

"This is perfect," I said. "Your parents can get him to vote against the fireworks." I leaned down and booped Bailey's nose. "Isn't it perfect, Bailey girl?" She licked my hand.

"I can ask," Gabriel said, "but I don't think it'll work. Mom says he talks a good game, but he votes with the 'freedom lovers' if he can, no matter how much his wife nags him not to. She comes over a lot to vent to Mom. If she's not talking about her garden, she's complaining about her husband."

There had to be a way to convince him. "While we were waiting for you to get here, Lilly and I looked Howald up," I told Gabriel.

Lilly tapped on her tablet, and there he was, the Count himself, being interviewed on the local NBC station last week.

"I haven't seen this," Gabriel said as the video started to run. "Dad watches CBS."

A reporter asked Howald about the upcoming vote, and he said, "I always like to keep an open mind. But we all grew up with fireworks here in Woodhurst. They're tradition. The dangerous ones are already illegal under state law, and the rest are safe. I wouldn't want to take away people's fun for no good reason." He smiled big for the camera before the interview ended.

"See, he's a total tool," Gabriel said, "talking about tradition, like he shoots 'em off all the time—as if anyone in our gated community would ever do that."

An image from *Booksmart* popped into my head, when the two girls showed up at a cool kids' party, changing their image from nerdy to fun. "Maybe we just need to apply a little pressure of our own to make him to see things differently."

"He probably has lots of people calling him about how fireworks scare animals," Lilly said. "What kind of pressure could we bring?"

I smirked. "I have an idea."

~

At ten thirty the next night, Lilly, Gabriel, and I were hanging out in his bedroom. We'd just finished streaming *Booksmart*. It was always worth another view, especially the karaoke scene, where one of the girls belts out Alanis's "You Oughta Know." Bailey always loved that scene, watching the screen intently. Too bad she was home.

"I better check on Elijah, make sure he's not about to burn the house down," Gabriel said, heading into the hallway.

His parents were out on their monthly date night—dinner then drinks at a jazz club—and Gabriel was in charge of his twelve-year-old brother. He said they never returned home until after midnight. We'd be done by then with our own fireworks show. Once we give Howald a taste of what my family had been dealing with, he'll be begging to vote yes.

"How was Bailey tonight?" Lilly asked. She was sitting in a maroon beanbag chair surrounded by Gabriel's usual clutter.

"She was okay when you picked me up, but it wasn't dark then."

Lilly scowled. "I still don't get guys like the Count. He must know the fireworks scare animals. Why doesn't he care?"

"Beats me." As the air conditioner cycled on, I rose from my spot on the plush wool rug and walked over to the window. Peeking through Gabriel's white plantation shutters, I could see Howald's house clearly. The curtains in his window closest to Gabriel's were fluttering. Must be nice he could enjoy the breeze. No way Mom could open the windows at home with the nightly fireworks show.

"The lights next door usually go off around eleven," Gabriel said as he came back into the room. "If they're anything like my parents, they'll be asleep a minute later."

"But we'll wait till eleven thirty to be safe, right?" I asked. "So we get the best bang for our buck?" I smiled at my fireworks joke.

Gabriel laughed. "Heck yeah. They should be sound asleep by then."

Lilly set aside the popcorn bowl and stood up. "I feel kinda bad about this."

"What?" I widened my eyes at her.

"Not about the Count," she said. "He deserves it. But the animals in this neighborhood don't. We're doing the exact thing we want banned."

"The neighbors probably won't like it either," Gabriel said. "The other neighbors, I mean. The cool ones. And Mrs. Count."

I couldn't believe it. "Are you both backing out?"

"No way," he said. "I'm just saying, people aren't gonna like it."

"That's the whole point." I sighed. "I feel bad about the animals too, but it'll be worth it if we can get Howald to change his vote. Besides we're not going to set fireworks off for hours on end. We only bought six tubes. Just enough to wake them up and make our point."

"And when they come out yelling, we have to make 'em think we're going to do it all summer long," Gabriel said.

"No problem," Lilly said. "My mom always says I'm a drama queen." She smiled. "So, I guess the ends actually *do* justify the means."

"Let's hope so," I said.

At 11:04 p.m., the lights went off next door, and we went downstairs. Gabriel grabbed some chocolate-covered pretzels from a jar. He was always hungry. Lilly didn't want any. I took two. Loved that salty-sweet combination.

Elijah shut off the loud video game he'd been playing in the family room and joined us in the kitchen with a huge smile. He had shaggy brown hair like Gabriel, but his was swept to one side. "This is gonna be great," he said.

I laughed at his enthusiasm.

"We never have any action around here at night," Elijah said. "Sometimes the Templetons' dog will bark, and last night the Counts were out arguing in their yard, but this, this is gonna be epic."

"Remember our deal," Gabriel told him. "You get to watch from the deck. You can't come anywhere near the platform. And you can't say anything to Mom and Dad."

"I know," Elijah said, drawing out the word *know*, as if he'd been reminded a million times.

Right after their parents left for dinner tonight, he and Gabriel dragged a large board from their dad's toolshed to the side of their backyard by the Howalds' house. We wanted to make sure the councilman and his wife would have the best view—and sound. The cashier at the fireworks booth by my supermarket told us last night that we'd want to set them off from a steady surface.

"But you know Mom and Dad are gonna find out," Elijah said. "The Count's gonna complain to them. Remember that time I played the stereo too loud? He went berserk."

Gabriel twisted his mouth. "Yeah, he probably will rat us out. That's okay. It'll be worth it."

At 11:25 p.m. we all went outside. The sky was clear and the full moon was practically glowing, so the fireworks should be spectacular.

Lilly carried them in a plastic bag. I had the lighter from Gabriel's fireplace. He was attaching their long garden hose to the bib on their deck. The cashier had recommended we have that set up too because sometimes sparks can hit the grass. If that happened, Elijah would turn on the water.

We were ready. A soft breeze tickled my neck, and I glanced around, breathing deep, enjoying the beautiful night. Gabriel's backyard was pretty plain. Just a lot of grass and a couple of trees. But the Howalds had a lot of flowers in their garden. Some with a spicy, lemony scent. They—oh no! I pointed out a light on in their house's lower level. "Should we wait?"

"No," Lilly said. "We have to be sure to get to my house by twelve thirty. Curfew." She and I were having a sleepover.

"Doing it now's fine," Gabriel said. "Even if they're up, this will still drive them crazy."

Lilly handed him the first tube, and he set it on the platform. The tubes were about half a foot long with a fuse on the side. Each one would create a different shape and color in the sky.

"You ready?" Gabriel asked.

Lilly and I nodded.

"Let's do this," I said, handing over the lighter.

He flicked it on and lit the fuse. We all backed away as the fire snaked toward the top of the tube. It took about five seconds, and then the firework went off with a loud bang, whooshing into the sky. It exploded with a boom into a neon-green chrysanthemum. I hated to admit it, but it was gorgeous.

"Wow, that's loud," Lilly said, covering her ears.

And smelly. Like rotten eggs. I hadn't expected that.

Gabriel set down the next tube and lit it. In seconds, it went off with a crack that echoed, shooting really high. It burst into a rainfall pattern of hot-pink glitter.

A dog started high-pitched barking. Poor thing. But a little suffering now would hopefully save a lot of animals—and people— from suffering later. I glanced at the Howalds' house. No new lights had gone on.

The third skyrocket whistled into the air, then blasted open into red, white, and blue dandelion puffs, just like the ones I saw at home last night. The noise was really loud, but there was no reaction from the Howalds' house. Were they out? Please tell me we weren't doing this for nothing.

Gabriel lit the next one. It zipped off with a stream of yellow fire and white smoke. A terrible clap of thunder boomed, and an orange peony filled the sky.

"What the heck are you doing out there?" a man yelled. Not Howald. Gabriel's neighbor on the other side. He sounded angry. "Don't you know what time it is?"

"Crap, we better hurry." Gabriel quickly lit the next firework. It flew into the air but didn't go as high as the others. Soon electric-blue snowflakes danced in the sky, and embers began to fall. They must have fallen with the others, but the rockets had soared so high, I hadn't noticed them.

"Oh my God," Elijah yelled. "Fire!"

Gabriel, Lilly, and I spun around, looking for flames. Then I saw them. A shed in the Howalds' yard was on fire. The embers must have hit it.

Gabriel grabbed the hose as the water surged out. He pulled the hose as far as he could, but he couldn't get close enough to the shed. The water streamed at it but wasn't making much of a dent. "Get a bucket of water," he screamed.

Lilly and I ran onto the deck as Elijah dashed outside with a filled mop bucket. I grabbed it and hurried toward the shed, trying to keep the water from sloshing over the sides. Gabriel was fighting a losing battle with the hose. I tossed my bucketful at the wooden shed. It barely helped.

Bright outdoor lights flipped on, and I blinked, my eyes adjusting.

"Holy hell!" a man yelled.

It was Mr. Howald, wearing a robe and slippers. He ran to the edge of his house, grabbed a hose I hadn't seen, turned on the water, and darted toward the shed. The water sprayed onto the shed's roof, where rippling flames were lighting up the night.

Lilly ran up with a large pot filled with water. "This was all I could find." She tossed the water at parts of the lawn that were sparking up. Gabriel doused those areas with his hose too.

I felt helpless as I stood in the rising heat watching Howald try to put out the fire. This was my fault. My idea. Because once again I hadn't thought things through. Mom was gonna kill me.

The intense acrid odors coming from the shed made me wrinkle my nose. There was a strong, sweet smell too and . . . was that garlic?

Sirens sounded in the distance. Gabriel must have heard them because he said, "What was I thinking? We have to call nine one one." He yanked his phone from his pocket.

"Elijah already called them," Lilly said.

And right on cue, I heard fire trucks heading this way, as well as some other siren.

"Call them back," Howald yelled. "Tell them we don't need them. I've got this under control. Don't want to waste city resources."

"Too late," Gabriel said as a truck squealed to a stop. "They're here."

Three firefighters ran into the yard with hoses and started spraying down the shed.

"Is there anybody in there?" one yelled.

"No, no one," Howald said, stepping back and aiming his hose at the grass around the shed. I didn't see any of the grass on fire anymore, but better safe than sorry, as Mom always said.

"You're sure?" the firefighter asked.

"Positive."

"Are you the homeowner?"

"Yes, I'm City Councilman Ryan Howald."

Three more firefighters came into the yard, along with a couple in dark clothes. One of the original firefighters went to talk to the new arrivals. The tallest of those firefighters strode off, pulling out a walkie-talkie. The woman in dark clothes stepped over to Howald.

"Sir, are you all right?" she asked. "Do you need medical attention?"

"No, I'm fine. Not injured at all."

"No coughing, anything like that?"

He shook his head.

"How about you kids?"

We all shook our heads too.

The flames looked all out now, but the two firefighters were still dousing the shed and surrounding grass.

"Sir, do you know how the fire started?" the original firefighter asked Howald.

"It's my fault," I said. "We were setting off fireworks."

"In my backyard," Gabriel added. "I live next door."

Howald's nostrils flared. "You all are in big trouble!"

No kidding.

One of the firefighters went to pull the shed door open but couldn't. "Sir, do you have a key?"

"Fire's out," Howald said. "You don't need to worry about the contents. It's just my wife's gardening equipment."

The firefighter paused. "We still need to go in there, sir. Make sure there are no flames licking the walls, in any insulation, or anywhere else."

"Not necessary," Howald said.

"Yes, sir, it is. Do you have the key?"

Howald grimaced. "My property, my call. I really appreciate you guys coming. I have the hose, and if there's any problem from here on out, I've got it covered."

"Actually, sir, it's not your call." He nodded at one of the other firefighters, who picked up a large crowbar and walked to the shed.

"What are you doing?" Howald yelled as the firefighter stuck it between the door and the jamb. "You have no right to go in there without my permission!"

The door popped open, and orange smoke, along with the foul-yet-sweet garlicky smell poured out. Howald stood there, his face red, jaw clenched, as the firefighter sprayed water into the shed before going inside. Seemed Howald thought he was a big shot, just like our councilman, Studebaker. It must kill him to not be obeyed.

"Gabriel, are you okay?" a woman asked.

I turned to find his mom hugging him. His dad waited to do the same.

"We're all okay, Mom. I'm sorry—"

"Officer," Howald yelled, throwing down his hose. "You need to arrest these delinquents right now! They have caused all this damage and wasted city resources."

Lilly gasped. "Arrest us?"

I heard movement behind me and turned again to find a couple of police officers approaching us. My throat dried up.

"We shot off fireworks, just like lots of people do," Gabriel said. "It was an accident."

"Shh. Not another word from any of you." His mom gave him, Lilly, and me the Mom Eye, squelching any inclination I might have had to defend myself.

"Officer, you heard him," Howald said. "He admitted taking reckless actions that started this fire. I am City Councilman Ryan Howald, and I want these kids arrested right now. And the rest of you," he said loudly, "can pack up your gear and go. I thank you for your service, but it's no longer needed."

"Officer," Gabriel's father said, his eyebrows stretching toward his receding hairline. "My other son called us and explained that—"

The taller of the cops interrupted him, holding up his hand in a stop gesture. He approached the shed. The firefighter who'd been inside came up to the door and said something I couldn't hear. The cop turned around, rubbed his blond mustache, and approached Howald.

"Councilman Howald, are you sure you're all right? You seem to have blood on you."

Howald's eyes widened like the full moon. "Blood, no. I arrived on the scene after these hooligans set fire to our shed. You need to arrest them."

"That's not blood on your sleeve?"

I hadn't noticed his pajama sleeve peeking out from under his robe. It had dark spots on it.

"Oh. That's old," Howald said. "Officer, I don't need to tell you how to do your job, but surely we're talking about arson, destruction of property, and a whole host of other charges for these kids. I'll be calling the chief first thing in the morning, and I'll want to be able to tell her that you did your job properly."

"Don't worry," the cop said. "I intend to do this by the book. You said this is 'our shed.' Who else does it belong to?"

"Why does that matter?"

The cop stared at him.

"My wife," Howald said.

"Is she inside? We'll want to talk to her."

Howald's chin quivered. "You can't. She's out of town. Visiting her sister. Left this morning."

"That can't be right," Gabriel's mom said. "I saw Madelyn just a few hours ago as we were leaving for dinner."

With narrowed eyes, Howald said, "You're mistaken, Veronica."

"Sir," the cop said to Howald, "I'm going to need you go come down to the station to answer some questions."

"Most certainly not," he said, his tone indignant. "It's late. This has been a trying experience. I'll come down in the morning to give a statement about the damage these reckless kids have caused. Now, are you going to arrest them or not?"

The cop turned my way, stared for a moment, and pulled out his handcuffs. *Oh no.*

"Councilman Howald, you are under arrest for possession of controlled substances with intent to distribute."

I knew I recognized that sweet smell. There must be a whole lot of pot in that shed.

"You have the right to remain silent—"

"Me?" Howald yelled. "What are you talking about?"

"Anything you say can and will be used against you in a court of law."

"You don't know what you're doing," Howald said. "You're making a mistake."

But the cop kept reading his rights.

"They're the ones who broke the law," Howald insisted.

"Do you understand these rights as I've read them to you?"

"Yes, of course, but—"

The cop interrupted. "Put your hands behind your back, sir."

"I'll have your badge for this," Howald yelled. "You don't know who you're dealing with. I'm a city councilman! I know Chief Andrews!"

"Officer Jones has my full support, Howald," a rich, strong voice said from behind me.

I whirled around to find a tall woman with wire-rimmed glasses staring down at Howald with contempt. The cop arresting Howald must have been looking at her, not me, when he pulled out his hand-cuffs. *Thank you, God.*

"Jones, take him to the station," the chief said. "Randall, work with the fire chief to secure the shed. And Woodson,"—she turned to another cop, the yard was suddenly full of them—"see if Mrs. Howald is home, bring her in for questioning if she is, and secure the premises."

As Howald was marched off, he said, "I haven't done anything. The drugs aren't even mine. They're the ones who broke the law!"

"Not as far as I can see, Howald," Andrews said. "Fireworks are legal. I thought you knew that."

The next afternoon, I was playing with Bailey in my room, trying to keep a low profile. Mom had been furious when she found out what Lilly, Gabriel, and I had done and grounded me for two weeks—no going out except to my part-time job at Baskin Robbins. Since it was the weekend, we both were home.

My phone buzzed with a text from Gabriel to Lilly and me.

"Wow. Read this," it said.

I clicked on a link to our local newspaper. My mouth dropped open as I saw the headline: "Councilman Howald charged with homicide, drug possession."

Homicide?

I scanned the article. After finding a lot of pot, cocaine, and other drugs inside the shed, the police searched Howald's house last night and found his wife's dead body. He had retained legal counsel, wasn't talking, and had been denied bail.

I thought about the second fireworks tube we set off. Could the echo I heard have been a gunshot sounding through the Howalds' open windows? Is that why he didn't come out right away when we started shooting off the skyrockets? Because he was busy killing his wife? It would explain the speckles on his pajama sleeve, the so-called old blood.

"Mom!" I ran downstairs into the kitchen, where she was making bread. "Look." I handed her my phone.

She fell back into a chair as she read. "Oh my. That poor woman."

"Gabriel's brother said he heard them arguing in their yard the night before last. I wonder if it was about the drugs."

"He's going to need to tell the police. Does Gabriel know about this?"

I nodded. "He's the one who sent the link."

Mom sighed. "I don't like what you all did last night. It was stupid and dangerous."

"I know." I dragged the word out, just like Elijah had last night. She'd already made this point very clear.

"Let me finish. It was stupid and dangerous, but at least there's a silver lining. Howald might not have been caught if it hadn't been for what you did."

More like a bronze lining. The *Booksmart* girls caught the Valley Strangler. We caught a real-life murderer, but it didn't feel as good as you'd think, as good as it looked in the movie. After all, Mrs. Howald was still dead.

"What's going to happen with the fireworks vote?"

Mom looked up, the way she often did while thinking. "With him in jail, I'm sorry to tell you, honey, but I don't think we have a chance. You need a majority for a law to pass. Now the vote'll be tied."

This whole situation was completely messed up. "I really thought we could convince him by making him suffer, just like we've been."

"I know." Mom stood up and hugged me. "Your heart was in the right place."

~

The night of the vote, Mom took me to city hall for the meeting. Lilly and her parents were there too, as well as Gabriel and his dad. Like me, Lilly was grounded for two weeks, Gabriel for a month. His parents were super pissed that he'd involved his little brother in our "foolish plan." But all the adults said we could come see what happened tonight.

Every seat in the audience was filled, with lots of people standing at the back of the room. On the stage, two of the seven chairs were empty. Howald's, of course. No bail. I couldn't see the placard of the other empty seat from where Mom and I were sitting.

Fifteen minutes after the meeting was supposed to start, as everyone was getting antsy, a guy in a suit left his seat in the front row and went up on stage. He began whispering with one of the council members. Then the guy scurried off, and the councilman banged a gavel on the table.

"Good evening, I'm Ted Barr. I'll be chairing tonight's meeting. Because of the heightened interest in the fireworks issue, we've moved everything else off the agenda to our next meeting. Anyone who would like to speak on the issue is welcome to. You'll each have three minutes."

People started lining up. I was tempted to join them, for Bailey's sake, but having screwed up so bad with my fireworks idea, it was better to lay low.

A bunch of people argued that their right to show off their patriotism shouldn't be trampled, that it's easy for people to buy headphones if the noise bothers them (like that would work), and that First Amendment rights shouldn't be impeded for "a bunch of animals," as one guy phrased it. (I didn't get that, but whatever.) Mixed in with them were people talking for our side.

After nearly two hours, with only one woman left waiting to talk, Mom whispered, "You don't want to speak?"

I stared at my lap. I wanted to, but I'd already messed things up too much. I shook my head no.

Mom lifted my chin so our eyes met. "No one deserves to speak on this issue more than you. No one cares more than you. You've earned this." She nodded at me in an encouraging way.

I gave her a grateful smile and hurried to the back of the line. Finally I reached the mic. My pulse was pounding in my ears as I introduced myself.

"Other people have spoken about the veterans who get triggered by fireworks and about the fires skyrockets can cause." As some people began whispering, I squared my shoulders and continued. "I know about that firsthand. But I want to focus on animals." I talked about frightened birds, squirrels, and other wild animals, as well as farm animals that couldn't get away from the thundering noise. "Even inside pets get scared. I have a large dog, over a hundred pounds. You may think such a big dog isn't afraid of anything, but whenever fire-works go off near our home, Bailey tries to crawl into my lap for comfort. She whines for hours. She shouldn't have to suffer like that. No one should. So, please make the right decision and vote for the ban. For Bailey and all the animals like her. Thank you."

As I returned to my seat I felt relieved, yet energized. Like I could do anything. Meanwhile, the guy in the suit from the front row hurried onto the stage and whispered some more with the chairman, who turned pale.

"This marks the end of the public comment period," the chairman said into his mic. "The board is now going into closed session. Should only be a few minutes, folks. Please hang around. We'll be right back."

As he and the rest of the council—all of them looking puzzled—left through a door near the stage, along with the guy in the suit, the room started buzzing.

"You did great, honey," Mom said. "I hope you know how proud you've made me."

"Proud? Really?"

She fluffed my hair. "You screwed up the other day. But you were trying to make a difference in this world. That's more than a lot of people do. And tonight you stood up and spoke your mind. You are an inspiration, Jocelyn. Whether we win or lose, I wanted you to know that."

I grinned. I had the best mom. "And if we lose, there's always next year, right?"

Mom clasped her hands together. "Lord, please let us win."

The man sitting next to me sighed loudly and said to the woman on his other side, "Let's go. Who knows how long this is gonna take." They squeezed out of our row. Moments later, Lilly and Gabriel took over their seats.

"What do you think's going to happen?" Lilly asked.

I shrugged. I wanted to be hopeful, but I didn't want to jinx things.

The council members came back into the room and took their seats. The chairman invited his colleagues to share their thoughts. Two of them spoke briefly in favor of the ban, one reminding people that a ban wouldn't affect the annual city-run fireworks show. Another member said that considering the late hour, they should get on with the vote.

"I agree," Barr said. "But before we do, I feel it's my duty to explain why the meeting began late and why there will only be five of us voting tonight. As many of you likely know, Councilman Howald was arrested last week on a slew of charges and is currently being held without bail. What I just learned a few minutes ago is that Chairman Studebaker was arrested late this afternoon and has not yet been arraigned."

Studebaker? Our jerk of a councilman? He was one of the expected no votes. Conversation broke out in the audience. I glanced at Lilly and Gabriel. She looked as excited as I felt. Gabriel had pulled out his phone and was tapping away.

Barr banged his gavel. "Silence, please. We were unaware of Mr. Studebaker's whereabouts when the meeting began, which is why waited a bit for him. Given that he is unavailable, we will proceed with the vote without him."

I grabbed Lilly's hand. *Please vote our way. Please.*

"All who vote in favor of Woodhurst instituting a ban on all consumer fireworks, as defined in the bill under discussion, say aye," Barr said.

"Aye."

"Aye."

"Aye."

"Aye."

"And the chair votes aye, too. That makes the vote unanimous."

OMG! Lilly squealed, and we squeezed hands. Applause erupted around us amid loud boos.

"Thank you all for coming and sharing your thoughts with us," Barr said. "And with that, this meeting is adjourned." He banged his gavel.

I jumped up and hugged Mom. "We did it!" Then I twirled around and hugged Lilly.

Gabriel had a holy-cow look on his face. "You won't believe this." He stood and held up his phone. The local newspaper's homepage was front and center. "Remember how the Coun—how Mr. Howald said the drugs in the shed weren't his? It was true. He's struck a deal. The prosecutor has charged him with manslaughter—whatever that means—instead of murder in exchange for Mr. Howald pleading guilty *and* testifying against Mr. Studebaker. The drugs were *his*. He needed them out of his house the night of the fireworks because he was hosting a party there for the police. He'd twisted Mr. Howald's arm to store them for him. Mrs. Howald didn't like it, and she and her husband had been fighting about it."

"That's a load of bull," a guy in the next row said to Gabriel. "Owen Studebaker's no drug dealer."

Gabriel waved his phone. "Says it right here. Mrs. Howald told her sister that Mr. Studebaker pressured her husband to store the drugs for him."

The guy's mouth dropped open. Then he frowned hard and stormed off.

"The sister's furious Mr. Howald's getting a deal," Gabriel continued.

"Who wouldn't be," Lilly said. "He killed her sister."

"Mom, what's manslaughter?" I asked.

"I'll explain it on the way home," she said.

I said bye to Lilly and Gabriel, and Mom and I headed out. I practically skipped to our Prius. When we got inside, I said, "Not that I'm unhappy, but why was the vote unanimous? I thought you said two of those guys would vote no."

"I guess all the bad publicity from the arrests made them vote the other way, to distance themselves from Studebaker and Howald. As they say, politics makes for strange bedfellows." Mom chuckled. "Anyway, you're still grounded, but if you want to go out for ice cream, I'm game. You've earned it."

"Thanks, Mom. Let's get it to go. And we should buy some Frosty Paws while we're at it. Bailey deserves to celebrate too."

"Damn straight she does." Mom started the car and hit play on her Alanis CD. Then we rolled out of the lot, my smile brighter than fireworks on the Fourth of July—and a lot less noisy too.

POWER AT ALL COSTS

TRAVIS RICHARDSON

FIVE YEARS FROM TODAY

HOW DID YOU GET HERE? That is a question you've been asking yourself nonstop for the past year and a half as your finger hovers over the button. A comically red button with disastrous consequences.

You've been the president of the United States for twenty-two months, thirteen days, and three hours. The commander-in-chief of what is left of this once beautiful country. A rebellion has occurred by those damn libs. The bane of your existence. Bane of every red-blooded real American. Now you sit in the Situation Room with generals—those who have remained—and the political hacks who made this whole shitshow happen. The bastards who encouraged you run for office and promoted you to the top. They billed you as America's last great white hope. Now they tell you to push the button, Madam President.

They want you to use the nuclear option. The real one . . . with radiation.

You pull your hand back, running your fingers through your perfectly styled dyed-blonde hair. In these trying times, you still have a hairdresser on staff. Looks equal power, especially for women in this messed world of spectacle over substance. You're a conservative darling. Well-educated, beautiful, and willing to spout toxic rhetoric at rallies to whip morons up into a frenzy. The feeling you get on the stage is exhilarating. There is no drug in the world that can give you that, can give you that charge. Except for sitting in the Oval Office behind the Resolute Desk.

But none of this answers the burning question, how did you get here with your finger one push away from wiping out half of the US population?

Of course, it was an accumulation of actions that led to this moment. Some by chance, others by design. From disputing your presidential election loss and forcing your way into office with a compliant Congress willing to overturn legitimate results *to* your earlier antics as a House Representative to garner more attention from the right-wing media infrastructure *to* getting into Harvard Law, where the Federalist Society recruited you and put you on private jets to meet with big donors and political power elite *to* who knows, choosing finance with a political science minor at Princeton instead of English Lit, forsaking your original love of Jane Austen. The collegiate decision about your major was all about money. You only qualified for a partial scholarship, and struggling in academia under a mountain of debt did not seem like a sane life choice. Brilliant decision, Lisa, you say to yourself. Instead of making college students' lives miserable with unrealistic reading assignments, you've caused pain for all Americans.

"President McKinsey, you have to push the button," Stewart Miller, your creepy chief of staff, says. A movie director could easily cast him in the role of a basement-dwelling child predator. "The liberals are routing us on the battlefield, and their commie UN allies are suffocating us with their embargos."

"And how does wiping California off the map help us with trade?"

"For one thing, we'll get goods from China directly. They can't be blocked by the West Coast libs."

You look up at the ceiling and pound your fist on the table. Why are you surrounded by idiots?

"But what ship would want to dock in a radioactive port, if it doesn't melt away from the radiation?"

His deep-hooded eyes narrow with determination. "They'll ship us goods, because they'll make money from us. That's why."

"Then who is going to buy these radioactive Chinese products?"

For a second, he looks stumped. "Uh, you know. There's ways to decontaminate things. Scientists can do that."

"But we don't have any scientists working on your side. Our party scared them all away."

"Scientists are bunch of libtards anyway," Jeff Montgomery, your press secretary, and chief of gun proliferation, says. He has a full beard, a camo tie with an NRA stickpin, and a sleeveless button-up shirt so he can show off his Norse and Proud Boy tats. To require sleeves infringes on his *freedoms*. "Nobody I know would trust anything they say."

"So we'll have radioactive goods coming to our people, and that's okay with everybody?"

"People don't have to buy the goods. It's their choice to buy it or not," Stewart says, his eyebrow arching like he's an intellectual giant. "I mean, come on, Madam President."

You look around the room to get a temperature reading. The cabinet all seem to agree with this deadly logic. Their concern about their constituents' well-being is about the same for them as it was around the time of COVID. Businesses matter more than human lives. Period. You have other pressing issues, like whether to press a red button or not, but you can't let this topic go. Not yet.

"So when these goods come ashore to radiated Los Angeles, and then get shipped to Omaha or Tulsa, should we let our people know about the risks of buying the goods?"

"Hell no," Jeff says. "Nobody would buy that shit then, and we can't get our import taxes."

"We can't have the government telling anybody what they can and cannot buy. That's why we got rid of the Consumer Protection Agency," Stewart says. "Besides you know that any oversight is socialist."

Several *yeahs* emanate from your cabinet of fools. Ugh. On and on about the threat of socialism. You cut Social Security, Medicaid, and the FDA, among many other programs and agencies, giving a much-too-late-wake-up-call to your constituents about what socialism really means.

But then again, you're also guilty of using scare tactics. The power you can accumulate from the fear of a single word is mind-boggling and intoxicating.

"Okay. Fine. So that helps us on our China import problem until we get our factories up again. Then what? You know they have nukes on the West Coast, and east coast too. They could retaliate and we'd be glowing in our final few seconds of life."

"No," General Flynt says with a stern, don't-contradict-me voice. He had been a washed-up army colonel, but got promoted to a four-star general when most of the military leadership resigned after you declared yourself president.

"No what? Explain yourself." This cowardly lion infuriates you nonstop.

"You have the button, right there," he says pointing to the red device in front of you. "They don't."

"Are you sure about that? Is there only one red button?"

"There is only one. It is right there."

"What if the other side cloned it? I mean there are things like 3D printers."

His face crimsons all the way up to his gray crew cut. "Impossible. There is only one. There can only be one."

"Fine."

That's another problem with the neo-conservatives: this absolute certainty, even if they don't know what the hell they are talking about. Also they never apologize for anything. Even if they step on your toes or spill water on important documents.

"After we radiate the West Coast what are we going to do about the northeast liberal states?"

"Nuke 'em too," the general says with a gleam in his eye.

"We won't need to do anything," Stewart says quickly. You know he's thinking about his family cabin up in Maine. "All the other states will fall into line knowing what we can do. Europe too."

"We should nuke France and Sweden too," the general says. "They're a bunch of gay commies."

"We could ask Russia to help us take out all of Europe," your CIA Director Yvgeny Yolovich says in a thick accent.

Yeah, yeah, fox in the hen house, you know.

"But not Hungary," Stewart says. "They're our closest ally after Russia."

"And North Korea," the general adds.

"Look, we're only going to send nukes to LA, San Francisco, and Seattle. Nowhere else. All right?"

You swallow, realizing what you just said. You just committed yourself to obliterating Americans. West Coast Americans who gave the world computers, the internet, space travel, Disneyland, and trashy reality television. The latter is part of the reason that self-serving partisan politics flourishes so much.

You look around the room. The glee radiates in their eyes. Their hatred of California transcends their humanity. A jealousy of success? Nonstop sunny weather? Continual budget surpluses in spite of being a cesspool of liberal politics? Probably all of the above and more.

And you? You've used California as a punching bag for political points. Like a lot of things you've said, you don't really mean it. Besides, your political career skyrocketed after some dark money donations came into your campaign from conservative Californian real estate and mega-investor billionaires. They aren't all bad.

You take a deep breath, your hand hovering. Although you

haven't always been a neocon, you are one now. That means you don't go back on your word. You don't apologize. You don't compromise. EVER. You follow through, and damn the consequences. Closing your eyes, you let your hand fall, plunging down on the big, stupid, red button. A hollow *click* bounces off the walls.

You exhale.

The room remains pin-drop silent. Opening your eyes, all of the cabinet men watch you, their breaths held, perhaps realizing for the first time what they have done.

"So what happens now?" you ask.

"We win," Jeff says, putting his feet on the table like the jackass he is.

"The button is pushed so that means nuclear warheads are going to the West Coast as we speak, right?"

The assembled nod their heads confidently.

"Do we have video of the missiles? I want to make sure they are going to the West Coast, not Cuba or Russia." You can't believe you're asking this question now . . . after the damn button has been pushed. You were so caught up in responding to the accumulating losses and inevitable future defeat that you forgot to ask these questions.

Everybody in the room looks at General Flynt. Their absolute certainty is waning.

"Uh, let me get on that, Madam President," the general says, pulling out his cell phone.

You throw your hands in the air. "Give me a fuckin' break. You don't know where the missiles are heading?"

"I just knew that someday we might want to bomb California and other places, and to do that we needed a red button. Okay?" He fumbles with the phone, dropping it on the floor.

"Wait? You're tellin' us we just sent some nukes in the sky, but we have no idea where they'll land," Jeff says, quick on the uptake. "Jesus Christ, General."

You realize something else. "Wait, aren't there supposed to be nuclear codes that are updated every day or something for national security?"

"We did away with that," the general says, picking the phone back up.

"What do you mean?" you say with ice in your veins.

"There were daily encryptions and real complicated stuff that we didn't understand, so we got this red button instead." The general produces a weak smile as he wipes sweat from his face. "Right, guys?"

He glances at the three other generals for support, but they either look at the floor or busy themselves with paperwork.

Your eyes narrow. "Who gave you that button?"

"Um. Somebody in Pentagon IT."

"Can you find out who—after you figure out where those missiles are heading?"

"Yes, ma'am, right away." He dials a number on his cell phone and walks to a corner of the room.

You turn to the rest of your staff. "Can one of you assholes turn on the TVs?"

Stewart and Jeff fumble for the remotes, along with other cabinet members, as a wall of flat-screen monitors come to life. All of your propaganda networks appear: Fox, OAN, Patriot News, Trump TV, True American TV. They are hyping up the war, making it look like your side is winning. This is a lie. Guns and slogans alone can't beat robots and drones. You look at the rest of the cabinet, with their eyes lit up, eating up the BS. And they know how bad they're getting their ass kicked.

"We need to see something else. CNN or CSPAN."

Jeff stands up. "I will not sit here and watch fake news."

"Sit down. We need to know what is really happening, since General Shit-for-Brains hasn't a clue. We won't find out from our networks. These toadies keep saying that we're winning in spite of the fact we're not."

"Facts lie all the time," Jeff says, taking a seat.

General Flynt sulks back to the table, ashen-faced.

"Well, where are the missiles heading?" you ask.

"Nowhere, Madam President."

"What you mean?" You're not sure whether you're outraged or relieved.

"They didn't get any signal from the button to launch."

You glance at the device and pick it up. "Who is the incompetent techie that designed this?"

"We oughta shoot him on the South Lawn," Jeff says.

"He defected not long after he made it," the general mumbles.

"Then we really need to shoot his ass on the South Lawn."

"You didn't think to inspect the equipment he gave you?" you ask.

"I didn't know he defected until just now," the general says. "There've been so many."

You grab the button and start bashing it against the table. The incompetence that surrounds you is astounding.

"Let me have it," Jeff says, taking out his pistol.

"Don't shoot in here."

He sighs and turns the barrel in his hand. With three hard strikes from the butt of the gun, he cracks open the hard plastic shell. You tear the rest of the casing open. Wires, batteries, and an antenna are inside. Plus, something else.

"What is this?"

You pull out what looks like a microphone and possibly a tiny camera. Then you spot a piece of paper taped to the base of the button with your name on it. A wave of dread fills your heart. You pick up the note card and turn it over.

Dear Ms. McKinsey,

You are smart enough to know better. That you pushed this button means that now the world knows what an evil person you are. May you live the rest of your days in shame and infamy.

Sincerely,

An American Who Truly Loves Democracy and His Country,

Stewart takes the message and starts to read it. Your mind does flip-flops. What does *now the world knows* mean?

"What a load of crap," Stewart says, handing the message to Jeff as other cabinet lackeys gather around.

You look at the mess of wires again, speaker, camera, and antenna. *Now the world knows.* You grab a remote and flip through the channels on a screen, stopping on CNN. The image is curious. A crooked angle-shot of a ceiling and part of a wall. It kind of reminds you of the Situation Room.

Oh no.

"Look at the crap they have on CNN," Jeff says with a laugh. "Those libtards don't even know how to hold a camera straight."

Some of the cabinet laughs with him. Seconds later Jeff's voice repeats on the screen. You look at each other with mouths agape and disbelief bugging out everybody's eyes.

"If you are just tuning in, what we are watching has been breath-taking," a CNN host says. "We have a live-feed in President McKinsey's office as she and her cabinet have tried, unsuccessfully, to launch nuclear weapons at the West Coast."

You grab the pistol from Jeff's holster and shoot at the pile of wires until CNN's feed goes off the air. You whip the pistol toward the general. He yelps.

"I want you to launch missiles at the West Coast. Also, New York, Atlanta, and anywhere else that CNN has an office. Got that?"

"Yes, Madam President."

You lower the gun.

"There's just one problem," he says weakly.

"What?"

"All of our missiles are off line. We can't launch anything."

You're speechless.

"How the fuck did that happen?" Stewart screams in a shrill

voice. Of everybody in your cabinet, he is the biggest West Coast hater of all.

"It looks like there was a Trojan virus that nobody knew about, and it won't allow us to launch any missile."

You aim the pistol at him. He drops to the ground. *Pop! Pop! Pop!* A portrait of President Polk takes three bullets to the chest.

Your ears ring. Everybody lays flat on the floor. You're not sure how many bullets are left in the clip. 2, 3, 5? You know how to load and shoot guns—the minimal prerequisite for your party—but you've never taken the time to get into the weeds to learn about calibers and load capacity of particular models. You wonder if you have enough bullets to take out your cabinet. A proper retirement for the idiots who got you into this situation.

The front door flies open and two secret service officers charge through with pistols raised.

"Madam President, are you okay?" one of them asks.

How did they not hear the first volley of gunfire? Then you notice that their earpieces look a lot like AirPods.

"I am. Not sure about the others. Everybody on the floor okay?"

You hear some yeses. What should you do now? The screen on CNN shows a recap with the button being pulled out of a brief case, how there is no doubt your side is not going to win the war, and then that embarrassing discussion about selling radiated goods to your constituents. You grab the remote. CNBC is showing the same footage. You flip over to CSPAN, where the Senate is debating about making Jefferson Davis's birthday a national holiday. A perfect distraction for a losing government.

An aide walks up to the current speaker from Oklahoma and whispers in his ear. After a moment he returns to the microphone. "It seems that our military tried to launch nuclear weapons at California."

There are some cheers, but mostly gasps.

"The attempt did not work, due to some hacking. We should expect reprisals—"

Suddenly all of the TVs switch over to a video of you and the cabinet planning to nuke the West Coast.

"Who did that?" you ask.

Stewart grabs a remote, clicking it madly, but every channel airs the same video. "The liberals apparently are overriding all the network feeds to show this video."

"How do they do things like that?" Jeff says. "Gawd, they're such nerds."

You think about shooting the TVs, but decide to use the remotes to kill them instead. You might need those bullets later.

"Can I have my gun back?" Jeff asks, as if reading your mind.

"No." You look for the general. "Where is General Flynt?"

"He's still on the floor," another general says. "Crying I think."

"Stand up, General. Now."

Sniffling and snot-nosed, the general stands up. He has his hands crossed in front of his crotch, but a pee stain on his olive green slacks is still very noticeable.

"What is the plan now that we can't launch anything?"

"Uh. Hold the line."

"Which we haven't been able to do because they have driverless tanks with drones providing air support. They've wiped out the majority of our redneck battalions. Southern Arizona has linked California to the New Mexico-El Paso libs."

"Good luck taking Texas, libbers," Jeff says with a laugh.

"Outside of Austin, Houston, San Antonio, and maybe Dallas, I don't think they care for much else. They'll build walls to keep the rest out," you say.

Jeff is about to say something, but stops, knowing that in truth many of your constituents would want to get to the other side. Better medical care. Cleaner water. Safer foods, drugs, and infrastructure. The right to an abortion has already sent many women and girls over to the libs. Several unhappy men have been asking you to provide bounties to get their women back. Like women were fucking property. For all your anti-abortion rhetoric, you know that if you were in an abusive relationship, or sixteen, you would do everything in your power to terminate an unwanted pregnancy.

You walk over to the war map with pushpins that represent armies, planes, and other military operations. The map shows the West Coast, the northeast, a long stretch in the southwest—swatches of blue littered on a red United States map. You've got the geographic advantage. Tons of red in areas that used to be known as flyover states. But you don't have the people or the technology. The roads are falling apart. There has been multiple cholera outbreaks in several states, without the liberals throwing a single bomb. Private companies took over the sanitation and water rights in several municipalities that had little or no experience in the field and jacked up prices while poisoning their customers with their incompetence. Laissez-faire gone wild. And then there was a seasonal flu epidemic that wiped out significant portions of your base in Idaho, Wyoming, Alabama, and Florida. Fucking anti-vaxxers. And of course there is the power issue. Even with the coal plants burning 24/7, they haven't been able to deliver enough cool in the insanely hot summers or warmth during the freezing cold winters. To quell a possible rebellion you imprisoned a couple of midlevel power company lackeys, and you're thinking about nationalizing power, sanitation, and water companies, even though that would rankle some very wealthy supporters. A temporary wartime act might be the solution while jailing all opposition, but it's slapping a Band-Aid over a machete wound.

All of this makes you wonder, if the liberals win this war, would they even want this undereducated, disease-ravaged, failing nation that you've been leading?

You get a call on your personal cell phone. A phone few people have access to. You look to see who it is. The name Vlad appears on the screen. Good Lord.

"What?"

"I hear you have problems," the Russian-accented dictator says. "Perhaps I can be of assistance."

"And what assistance are you proposing?"

"I nuke the West Coast for you."

"And what do you want in return?"

"And in exchange for that I will take Alaska and Hawaii off of your hands."

Hawaii sided with blue states, and as much as you love the warm waters and swimming with sea turtles, you would gladly give that state away for an advantage in the war. You had hoped to trade the islands to China for their military help, but they didn't want to end their lucrative trading with the blue states. Alaska though, you have a ton of popularity there. You drill a crazy amount of oil nonstop in the wilderness, though you've had a hard time getting the supplies to the rest of the nation since Canada refuses to do any trade with you. Heck, maybe you'll ask Vlad to nuke the stupid Canucks too.

"Well, what do you say, Lisa? I think I'm giving you a good deal."

"Hold a minute."

You put the phone down as your cabinet watches you, eagerly anticipating the news.

"Well, who is it, and how can they help us?" Stewart asks, as an evil grin spreads across his face.

"It's the Russian 'President'," you say with air quotes. "He wants to know if he can nuke the West Coast for us."

Your cabinet hoots and hollers, giving emphatic yeses.

"Russia is the best," the idiot secretary of Homeland Defense says.

"They're like real Americans, just Russian," your CIA Director Yolovich says.

"They want us to give up Hawaii and Alaska in return," you say.

The cabinet looks at each other and after a few seconds they all shrug.

"Acceptable losses," Stewart says.

The cabinet nods in unison. You take another deep breath and put the phone up to your ear. It's a solution to your problem, right? And technically somebody else is sending the missiles over, not you. There's plausible deniability.

"Hey, Vlad."

"Yessss," the Russian leader says in a sinister voice.

You turn to the wall and swallow, not believing what you're about to do. Asking Russia to bomb America, and take over some American lands, so that you keep your precious power. What kind of monster have you become?

"Do it. We have a deal."

You kill the call before the awful dictator can speak another word and remind you again about how he influenced American voters in your favor. Before you take back your deal, like you know you should.

You shake off the nausea, harden your face, and look up at your cabinet that has huddled around you.

"It is done."

You know from this moment forward, you are no longer Lisa McKinsey, "President" of the free world. No longer somebody's daughter or even a regular human. You are a war criminal. An abettor to mass genocide.

~

Five years later

You are still the president, but in name only. You don't bother with the charades of democracy like holding elections. The US population is half of what it used to be. So is your cabinet. You executed many of them, including General Flynt, for total incompetence, Stewart for being creepy, and Jeff for not wearing a proper button-up shirt. Lives, as you discovered, don't matter that much. They are a means to an end. Needless to say, those who are left in your government are terrified of you.

Vlad was good to his word and wiped out the West Coast, but in an unexpected twist he created his own demise. The libs were able to send missiles to Russia, obliterating Moscow, St. Petersburg, and a few other cities, before they became radioactive ash. Fortunately the liberals didn't consider, or have enough time to suspect, that you had made a deal with Russia. So no missiles hit the White House. Almost nobody knows about the deal with Vlad, since he is dead and your remaining cabinet is too scared to say anything that could get them shot on the South Lawn. Most people have forgotten about the button incident that preceded the Russian missile attack, or know better than to speak up.

You also solved all the infrastructure problems by nationalizing almost everything. The exact opposite of open markets and the rhetoric you used to spout about government overreach. The scientists who didn't die, or escape to Australia or Argentina, are working to find ways to abate radiation poisoning. Everybody in the northern hemisphere has it, thanks to the air currents from the Coriolis effect. You've been wearing wigs for the past three years as clumps of hair randomly fall out. Most Americans chose to shave their heads as it's easier that way. But since you're their leader, you need to maintain that perfect look before the missiles hit. You also have tumors removed on a monthly basis. Procedures that most people can't get as the US mortality rates look more like statistics from the Middle Ages. Regardless of the image you portray, nothing can cover up the rot festering inside.

While this holocaust is your fault, it is also the fault of those before you who used the airwaves, cable, and internet to sow division and distrust among Americans. They told people to hate science and ridicule compassion. They told them to not accept democratic results or the will of the people. They turned Christians into abrasive jerks, leading them to become the opposite of anything Jesus Christ preached. They praised domestic terrorists as patriots. It's Orwell's *Animal Farm,* with Americans being manipulated and exploited by pigs like you. You used the path set before you and took what those selfish assholes always wanted: Unrestricted Power. You got that power and went one step further. Where nobody had ever gone before. You pushed that damn red button.

ABOUT THE AUTHORS

ANSHRITHA

Anshritha views the world through a lens of fiction. She feels a strong surge of affection towards anyone who gets her name right on the first try. Her experience with storytelling began when she was five and was asked where the box of chocolates disappeared. She spends more hours than she'd like to admit daydreaming about the lives of both real and imagined people, while often forgetting all about the empty pan left on the stove. The clique of pans haven't forgotten, six of them have been disfigured beyond recognition as of 2021. If you ever happen to catch someone in the middle of a heart-to-heart conversation with a pack of dogs or scribbling her way through life, there's an excellent chance that someone is her. This is her first foray into short fiction and all of her ten fingers are crossed tight.

ERIC BEETNER

Eric Beetner is that writer you've heard about but never read. Then when you finally do you wonder why you waited so long. There are over 25 books and more than 100 short stories so you'd better get started. Books like *Rumrunners, All The Way Down, Two In The Head,* and *The Devil Doesn't Want Me.* He also hosted the podcast Writer Types and hosts the Noir at the Bar reading series in L.A.. He's been described as "The 21st Century's answer to Jim

Thompson" (LitReactor). He's been nominated for three Anthony's, an ITW award, Shamus, Derringer and 6 Emmys. Seriously, what are you waiting for? https://www.ericbeetner.com

STEPHEN BUEHLER

Stephen Buehler's short fiction has been published in numerous on-line publications. His short story, "Not My Day" was a Derringer Finalist. His short story, "Girl of 100 Lists" appeared in *Murder-a-Go-Go's,* an anthology dedicated to songs by the Go-Go's. He had a story in *Low Down Dirty Vote Vol. 2,* "Nicking Votes" also about a con man. He is currently working on a thriller, *If the Gumshoe Fits.* By day, he's a script consultant and magician. He lives with a cute dog named Seymour. https://www.stephenbuehler.com

PATRICIA E. CANTERBURY

Patricia E. (Pat) Canterbury is a native Sacramentan, political scientist, art collector, retired state administrator, author of seven novels and a world traveler. One of her young adult novels won an Honorable Mention at the 2019 NCPA Awards. Her short stories have appeared in over 30 anthologies, including the 2018 Bram Stoker finalist, *Sycorax's Daughters.* Tanner Sullivan, her P.I. appearing in this anthology, has been in six other anthologies. Pat and her very active cat live in Sacramento. She can be reached at her website http://www.patmyst.com and her email: patmyst@aol.com.

SARAH M. CHEN

Sarah M. Chen has published a children's book and numerous short stories, one of which won a Derringer Award. Her noir novella, *Cleaning Up Finn,* was an Anthony finalist and IPPY Award winner. She was a co-editor for several anthologies, including the latest from Sisters in Crime / Los Angeles, *Avenging Angelenos.*

She's written for the *Los Angeles Review of Books, Hapa Mag,* and *Wellbeing,* among others. Follow her on Twitter and Instagram at @sarahmchen. https://sarahmchen.com

DAVID CORBETT

David Corbett is the author of six novels, including *The Long-Lost Love Letters of Doc Holliday,* nominated for the Lefty Award for Best Historical Mystery. His work has been nominated for Edgar, Anthony, Barry, Shamus, and Spinetingler Awards, and his second novel, *Done for a Dime,* was a New York Times Notable Book; Patrick Anderson of the Washington Post described it as "one of the three or four best crime novels I have ever read." Corbett's short fiction has twice been selected for Best American Mystery Stories, and a collaborative novel for which he contributed a chapter will be adapted for TV by the producers of *Killing Eve* for Disney+ in the U.K. His non-fiction has appeared in the New York Times, Narrative, Writer's Digest and other outlets. He has written two writing guides, *The Art of Character* ("A writer's bible" – Elizabeth Brundage) and *The Compass of Character;* he has taught at the UCLA Writer's Program, Litreactor, and at writing conferences across North America; and he is a monthly contributor to Writer Unboxed, an award-winning blog dedicated to the craft and business of fiction. https://davidcorbett.com

JACKIE ROSS FLAUM

Jackie Ross Flaum, avid water aerobics swimmer, amateur jewelry-maker and award-winning eclectic writer, began as a reporter for *The Hartford Courant* in Hartford, Ct. After moving to Memphis and abandoning reality for fiction, she tested several flavors of writing —chic lit, mystery, suspense, crime—and has short stories published all genres. She is a contributor to *Low Down Dirty Vote Volume 2.* To her shock, her first novel of the romance and racial justice in the

South is considered historical fiction since it's set in the 1960s. *Justice Tomorrow* introduces investigators Madeline Sterling and Socrates Gray, who are also featured in a short story published in *Now There Was A Story: A Musical Crime Anthology*. The sequel to her novel, *Price of a Future* is due out soon. She is happily married with two daughters, five grandchildren, and one disobedient dog. Currently she is vice-president of Malice in Memphis a Killer Writing Group. https://www.jrflaum.com

KATHARINA GERLACH

Katharina, commonly known as Cat, was raised in the middle of a forest in Germany where she and her three brothers roamed and dreamed. But even tomboys grow up, and therefore she got an education, programmed a forest growth simulator, and returned to the love of her life, her now-husband, with a rather useless PhD in science and the head filled with strange facts about our world.

When her best friend unearthed a box of historical documents about her family that reached as far back as the 15th century, Cat wrote two historical novels. During that time, her dream child landed in her little family, followed by two beloved foster children with special needs.

So she put aside all aspirations of ever working as a forester and focused on raising her children and writing the best books she's capable of. By now she's dabbled in several genres, mainly Fantasy (fairy tale retellings), SciFi, and Historical Stories.

You can find her online: https://www.katharinagerlach.com and https://www.facebook.com/KatharinaGerlach.Autorin

BARB GOFFMAN

Barb Goffman is a short story writer and freelance crime-fiction editor. She's won the Agatha Award twice, as well as the Macavity Award, Silver Falchion Award, and 2020 Readers Award given by *Ellery Queen's Mystery Magazine*. She's been nominated for major crime-writing awards thirty-five times for her short stories, including sixteen Agatha Award nominations (a category record), and multiple nominations for the Anthony, Derringer, and Macavity awards. In addition to *EQMM*, her stories have appeared in *Alfred Hitchcock's Mystery Magazine*, *Black Cat Mystery Magazine*, *Black Cat Weekly*, *Sherlock Holmes Mystery Magazine*, and many anthologies. Barb blogs at www.SleuthSayers.org, often about writing. Her editing clients have taken home the Agatha Award for Best First Novel, the Derringer Award, and the EQMM Readers Award. Barb lives with her dog in Virginia, where they often hear fireworks and wish they didn't. http://www.barbgoffman.com

DAVID HAGERTY

David Hagerty is the author of the Duncan Cochrane mystery series, which chronicles crime and dirty politics in Chicago during his childhood. Real events inspired all four novels, including the murder of a politician's daughter six weeks before election day (*They Tell Me You Are Wicked*), a series of sniper killings in the city's most notorious housing project (*They Tell Me You Are Crooked*), the Tylenol poisonings (*They Tell Me You Are Brutal*), and the false convictions of ten men on Illinois' death row (*They Tell Me You Are Cunning*). Like all his books, David is inspired by efforts to right criminal injustice. https://davidhagerty.net

JAMES MCCRONE

James McCrone is the author of the Faithless Elector series—*Faithless Elector*, *Dark Network*, and *Emergency Powers*. Known for memorable, conflicted characters, he's drawn particularly to writing about politics and corruption. His most recent short stories have featured in *Low Down Dirty Vote, vol. 2*, *Retreats from Oblivion: The Journal of NoirCon* and *Rock and a Hard Place*. His next book, *Bastard Verdict*, is a noir political thriller set in Scotland, about an upcoming vote on independence.

He's a member of MWA, Int'l Assoc. of Crime Writers, Int'l Thriller Writers, Philadelphia Dramatists; and he's the newly elected vice-president of the Delaware Valley Sisters in Crime chapter. James has an MFA from the University of Washington. A Pacific Northwest native (mostly), he lives in South Philadelphia. http://www.jamesmccrone.com

ANN PARKER

Ann Parker is a science writer by day and fiction writer at night. Her award-winning Silver Rush mystery series, published by Poisoned Pen Press (a Sourcebooks imprint), is set primarily in 1880s Colorado, and more recently in San Francisco, California, the "Paris of the West." The series was named a Booksellers Favorite by the Mountains and Plains Independent Booksellers Association. *The Secret in the Wall* is the eighth and newest in the series. https://annparker.net

CAMILLE MINICHINO

Camille received her Ph.D. in physics from Fordham University, New York City. She is currently on the faculty of Golden Gate University, San Francisco and teaches writing throughout the Bay Area. Camille is Past President and a member of NorCal Mystery Writers of America, NorCal Sisters in Crime, and the California Writers Club.

Camille has written more than 25 mystery novels. www.minichino.com

THOMAS PLUCK

Thomas Pluck has slung hash, worked on the docks, trained in martial arts in Japan, and even swept the Guggenheim museum (but not as part of a clever heist). He is the author of several other Joey Cucuzza stories, which you can find via his website. His latest novel is *The Boy from County Hell*, which Joe R. Lansdale called "as wild as a night in a cage with an amorous monkey," *Blade of Dishonor*, which MysteryPeople called "the Raiders of the Lost Ark of pulp paperbacks," and the Anthony-nominated crime thriller, *Bad Boy Boogie*. Joyce Carol Oates calls him a "lovely kitty man." https://thomaspluck.com

MIGUEL ALFONSO RAMOS

Miguel Alfonso Ramos lives on the West coast, is a librarian, reads widely and voraciously. He is a musician and has played in several bands, from mariachi to punk rock and bluegrass. He loves to climb mountains, jump into oceans, and ride his motorcycle at night. He writes SF, fantasy, horror and poetry, and is a graduate of the Clarion West Writers Workshop. He is Hispanic, Wyandotte and Chinese, plays chess and D&D, and watches lots of movies. His story "The Cave" was recently published in the anthology *Winter Wonders*.

EMBER RANDALL

Ember is a senior software engineer who specializes in user-centered design and accessibility. They got into tech to make the world a better place, which happens to be the same reason why they write – if their stories or the products they work on make at least one person happy, they count it as a success. In their free time, they enjoy reading, running, hiking, and generally exploring the outdoors, as well as creating new tales via larping. Their stories have been published by *Cast of Wonders, Zombies Need Brains,* and other venues. Find them at http://www.emberrandall.com.

TRAVIS RICHARDSON

Travis Richardson has won a Derringer Award for flash fiction and has been a nominee for the Macavity and Anthony short story awards. He has a collection of short stories, *Bloodshot and Bruised* as well as two novellas, *Lost in Clover* and *Keeping the Record.* His stories have been published in crime fiction publications such as Thuglit, Shotgun Honey, Flash Fiction Offensive, and numerous anthologies like *Low Down Dirty Vote I & II* and *The Obama Inheritance.* He is currently the president of the Southern California chapter of Mystery Writers of America. A few years back, he reviewed Anton Chekhov short stories at http://www.chekhovshorts.com/. He lives in Los Angeles with his wife and daughter. http://www.tsrichardson.com.

FAYE SNOWDEN

Faye Snowden is the author of noir mysteries, poems and short stories. Her novels include *Spiral of Guilt, The Savior, Fatal Justice,* and *A Killing Fire,* a dark, southern gothic tale featuring homicide detective Raven Burns. *A Killing Fire* is first in a four-part series. The sequel, *A Killing Rain,* will be released in June, 2022.

Faye has a master's in English Literature. She has been awarded writing fellowships from Djerassi and the Virginia Center for the Creative Arts. Her short story *One Bullet. One Vote.* was included in *The Best American Mystery and Suspense 2021* edited by Steph Cha and Alafair Burke. She is a member of Crime Writers of Color (CWOC), Mystery Writers of America (MWA), and Sisters in Crime (SinC) where she serves as Board Secretary for SinC National. She has participated in many writing panels, appeared as a guest lecturer in several university writing classes, and taught information technology courses at the university level. Today, Faye works and writes from her home in Northern California. https://www.fayesnowden.com

MISTY SOL

Misty Sol is a writer, visual artist, and performer from small-town Pennsylvania who creates art that explores Black people's connections to nature, wellness, and speculation. Her paintings, stories and eco practice are heavily influenced by Black history. Currently Misty has work on display at the Colored Girls Museum in Philadelphia. Her works have also been exhibited at the Wolfhound Studio in the Zou B. Art Gallery in Chicago, Burlington College, Headlong Theatre, The Moore College of Art, Philadelphia Museum of Art and Bartram's Gardens. In 2017, Misty Sol received the Leeway Transformation award, for her commitment to socially engaged art. Misty Sol has a BA in Literature from Penn State University Park and an MFA in Interdisciplinary Art from Goddard College. Her writing has been published in the anthology, *From Where They Sit: Black Writers Write Black Youth*. Also the magazine *Philadelphia Stories*, https://philadelphiaprintworks.com/blogs/zine and https://short-edition.com/. Misty currently resides in Philadelphia.

DJ TYRER

DJ Tyrer is the person behind Atlantean Publishing, was placed second in the *Writing Magazine* 'Mid-Story Sentence' competition, and has been widely published in anthologies and magazines around the world, such as *Disturbance* (Laurel Highlands), *History and Mystery, Oh My!* (Mystery & Horror LLC), *Love 'Em, Shoot 'Em* (Wolfsinger), and *Marked By Scorn* (Solarwyrm Press), issues of *Awesome Tales, Belmont Story Review, Startling Stories*, and *Tigershark*, as well as having a novella available in paperback and on the Kindle, *The Yellow House* (Dunhams Manor).

DJ Tyrer: https://djtyrer.blogspot.co.uk/
DJ Tyrer Facebook: https://www.facebook.com/DJTyrerwriter/
Atlantean Publishing: https://atlanteanpublishing.wordpress.com/

GABRIEL VALJAN

Gabriel Valjan is the author of the *Roma Series*, *The Company Files*, and the *Shane Cleary Mysteries*. He has been nominated for the Agatha, Anthony, Silver Falchion Awards, and received the 2021 Macavity Award for Best Short Story. He lives in Boston. https://gabrielvaljan.com

BEV VINCENT

Bev Vincent is the author of *The Road to the Dark Tower* and *The Stephen King Illustrated Companion*, as well as over 100 short stories, including appearances in *Low Down Dirty Vote, Volume 2, Ellery Queen's, Alfred Hitchcock's* and *Black Cat Mystery Magazines*, and *Cemetery Dance*. His work has been published in twenty languages and nominated for the Stoker (twice), Edgar, Ignotus and ITW Thriller Awards. In 2018, he co-edited the anthology *Flight or Fright* with Stephen King. Other recent publications include his noir whodunit crime novella *The Ogilvy Affair* and the novella *The Dead of Winter,* which can be found in *Dissonant Harmonies*. http://bevvincent.com

twitter.com/LDDV_Anthology

CPSIA information can be obtained
at www.ICGtesting.com
Printed in the USA
LVHW040816040522
717810LV00028B/633